WHAT A MOTHER'S LOVE DON'T TEACH YOU

WHAT A MOTHER'S LOVE DON'T TEACH YOU

Sharma Taylor

virago

VIRAGO

First published in Great Britain in 2022 by Virago Press

1 3 5 7 9 10 8 6 4 2

A CIP catalogue record for this book
is available from the British Library.

Hardback ISBN 978-0-349-01551-4
Trade Paperback ISBN 978-0-349-01552-1

Typeset in Bembo by M Rules
Printed and bound in Great Britain by
Clays Ltd, Elcograf S.p.A.

Papers used by Virago are from well-managed forests
and other responsible sources.

Virago Press
An imprint of
Little, Brown Book Group
Carmelite House
50 Victoria Embankment
London EC4Y 0DZ

An Hachette UK Company
www.hachette.co.uk

www.virago.co.uk

To the Creator
who makes all things possible.

A Wise Ruling from King Solomon

Now two prostitutes came to the king and stood before him. One of them said, 'Pardon me, my lord. This woman and I live in the same house, and I had a baby while she was there with me. The third day after my child was born, this woman also had a baby. We were alone; there was no one in the house but the two of us.

'During the night this woman's son died because she lay on him. So she got up in the middle of the night and took my son from my side while I your servant slept. She put him by her breast and put her dead son by my breast. The next morning, I got up to nurse my son — and he was dead! But when I looked at him closely in the morning light, I saw that it wasn't the son I had borne.'

The other woman said, 'No! The living one is my son; the dead one is yours.'

But the first one insisted, 'No! The dead one is yours; the living one is mine.' And so they argued before the king.

The king said, 'This one says, "My son is alive and your son is dead," while that one says, "No! Your son is dead and mine is alive."'

Then the king said, 'Bring me a sword.' So they brought a

sword for the king. He then gave an order: 'Cut the living child in two and give half to one and half to the other.'

The woman whose son was alive was deeply moved out of love for her son and said to the king, 'Please, my lord, give her the living baby! Don't kill him!'

But the other said, 'Neither I nor you shall have him. Cut him in two!'

Then the king gave his ruling: 'Give the living baby to the first woman. Do not kill him; she is his mother.'

I KINGS CHAPTER 3 VERSES 16–27
(New International Version)

Historical Note

The mid–1980s represent a turbulent period in Jamaica's political and social landscape, which began in the 1970s.

The two major political parties (the Jamaica Labour Party and the People's National Party) are locked in conflict, caught up in the Cold War ideological struggle between capitalist America and communist Cuba and Cuba's ally, the Soviet Union. The People's National Party's growing closeness with Fidel Castro's Cuba fuels America's support of the Jamaica Labour Party and its capitalist beliefs.

Both parties establish garrison communities – fortified enclaves of party supporters – and arm thugs with weapons. These Area Dons are installed to wield power over these communities to ensure votes. Politicians turn a blind eye to their criminal activities.

The result is that loyalties are divided. Crime skyrockets.

PART ONE

Son-Son's Birthday

Dinah

Mi wake up this morning like mi moving under water that too green. Something mi can't see sitting on top of mi weighing mi down. Mi nearly knock over the enamel cup on the side table next to the mattress. The same mattress that sag in the middle like a ole donkey wid a bruk back. The likkle room weh mi live in for the past twenty years all of a sudden seem strange. Like mi turn duppy – lost inna smaddy else nightmare. Is like the Lord God Almighty Himself take Him giant hand and lift mi up inna the night and rest mi down on a different woman bed.

Mama snores like dem coming from a distance, though her breath hot on mi neck-back. Mi roll out of bed on the left side. The mattress jerk and wake Mama. Mi watch her watching mi and looking 'round de room trying to figure out who mi is and where she is. I don't say nothing but a soft-soft 'mawnin' and squeeze her shoulder before mi get up and leave the room.

Mi barely notice the brown and green floral wallpaper in the hallway peeling off where the pickney dem who come to the yard grab it. I buck mi toe on a old hammerhead that push against the wall. A roach creep inna de corner of the green rug that smell like rat piss when it wet. Termites feed on the carcass of the cabinet. Mi open it and take out mi tea cup. It feel like it take more than a hour to make the cup of Milo tea in the kitchen we share with the rest of the tenement yard. Mi head is on low fire.

'Lemelemelem-ho,' Mama chanting now. Her brain work like a mash-up bicycle – sometimes the chain break off and spin her backwards to her days as a Pocomania member. When she and the others sing around the coloured flagpole in the Pocoyard. Is the only picture mi have of her: a Polaroid she get from one American student studying weh him call Afro-Caribbean religion. In it, she have her long hair pack up tight under a white scarf with a pencil sticking out from the tie-head beside her ear and this red woman look regal. Her bauxite-dirt skin make we think she descend from Maroons who breed with Tainos in the hills; or she could be the pickney of a drunk German immigrant who rut with a Black woman in the bush. She tell me mi father was midnight-black, which is why mi look like tar. She never talk about him.

Sometimes at night she tell mi about the days in St Mary, when she was young and pretty and life had promise. She cry sometimes when she see the picture of herself on the night-stand, asking mi who that was and when she did dead. Her long fingers search the hills and valleys of mi face in the dim light, as if mi hiding truth from the cobwebbed veins under her skin. She never ask mi about the empty picture frame right beside it – that suppose to hold Son-Son's photograph.

After making the Milo tea, I tell Mr McKenzie – him room next door to we – don't forget to lock the gate with the padlock when him come home on lunch break from the garage. Most days, the gate wide open. Last week, Mama walk straight through, all the way to Three Miles and then Kingston Harbour. If a postman never see her standing there swinging her arms like a fast bowler she woulda leap in and drown. Him bring her back home on him bike. But Mr Mack don't hear mi or he don't care to. Him suspect him wutliss eighteen-year-old girlfriend, Regina, sleeping with the plumber downstairs, who live beside Mrs Sinclair and her boys. Mrs Sinclair is a squeaky-voice dressmaker who mainly keep to herself. Her boys spend more time outside the yard than inside it.

Mr Mack's eyes already move from me to the clothesline, where Regina in her shorts – batty-cheeks on display for all to see – pinning up him once-white merinos she destroy doing the washing. Most days, Mr Mack's face set like a cloud passing over it.

In her room, although she can't see mi, Mama yelling: 'Dinah, Dinah, Dinah, don't look so gal, fix yuh face!' I bathe her with water from the pan near the bed, empty her chimmy in the pit latrine and go to the standpipe to catch water to wash mi private parts. Although the house have pipes, dem real old and sometimes the plumbing give problem. Is like everyday, the water have to decide if it want to come inside. And if it come, sometime it run real clear, other times it brown and rusty-looking, so you have to boil it good before you drink it.

I greet Damian; him outside singing, stark-naked, bathing with water from the standpipe. Mi know him from him was five and him is eighteen now. I watch him soapy, dark muscles and the suds he scrubbing between him legs and mi feel like someone tickling mi between mi thighs. *Merciful Saviour! Heavenly Father!* mi say under my breath. I stumble with the pan.

'Mawnin', Miss Dinah,' him say, singing my name, showing teeth as white as milk. Damian mother use to live in the tenement yard too, until she go America and never come back. For a time, Damian was like my son. I make sure him get breakfast and go to school and wash him clothes and see that him do him homework, until Damian feel him turn into him own big man and want to make him own way inna the world. Him stop needing mi. Sometimes pickney can be so ungrateful.

A sharp pain in my chest come and mi eyes tear up for no reason other than I thinking of Son-Son. I imagine Son-Son is Damian height and complexion and he would be mannersly too, saying *pleases* and *thank-yous* because no son of mine could be without manners. *Manners take yuh through the world*, Mama say.

After I wash, I put Mama in front the TV, turn the knob so she can watch JBC when the station sign on and ask Regina to check on her every two hours to see that she eat the callaloo and bully beef I leave. I tell Mama goodbye out of habit. She not going notice mi not there. I put on the blue and white plaid uniform the Browns gimme.

I walk down the road leading out of Lazarus Gardens, past the signs on the wall with the giant painting of the Party leader in a green shirt, and posters of our Member of Parliament, Wendell Simms, from the last election in 1980 still on the light poles. I pass three bus stop with bullet holes in the zinc that the buses don't come to any more. A old *Gleaner* newspaper page blowing in the street and catch mi foot. The headline say: *1985 Bloody Year: 12 More Dead in Kingston Massacre.*

I go all the way to the bus depot a mile away. I board the bus, giving the fifty cent fare to the conductor. The other women onboard greet mi with a glance or a nod. They also on their way to the big houses where we all work as helpers. They in all kinda uniform: green and white stripe, grey, plaid, black and white, and dem sitting so stiff. Like me.

'Mavis, yuh mean to tell mi say Mrs Palmer *still* nuh pay yuh fi the days work yuh do pon the public holiday las' month?' Maude turn to the passenger beside her – a woman with folds of flesh that make her look like a melting candle.

'Humph,' Mavis grunt: 'Nuh worry. Mi find some US dolla under the dresser when mi clean it last week that mi aggo keep. But mi have something fi har though, man. Di wretch nuh know say is her toothbrush mi use clean the toilet.'

After the laughing die down, we sit in silence as the bus creak up the hill, puffing black smoke. Mi look out the window at the people on the street, men on dem motorbike and bicycle, heads bobbing. Pickney with dem dusty bare-foot walking and playing in the street, chasing one another and screaming. Women with basket on dem head carrying produce to or from the market, hands akimbo, chatting and laughing wid dem friend. Mongrel dogs barking as the bus pass, dashing in and out like dem want to run under the bus wheel. When mi belly start growl, I realise mi never touch the cup of Milo on the kitchen counter.

◆

Mr Brown in him study when I reach. I only dust in there on weekdays when him at work because him don't like to be disturbed on weekends. I hear him on the phone now:

'Yes, Raymond. Brilliant idea.'

Through the crack in the door, I see him nodding, as if the person on the phone can see him.

'We'll give him great exposure at the firm. The partners and I would be happy to have him. Yes, he can start on Monday.' He listen a moment and pick him teeth. 'No trouble at all. Since he's your son, I know he has the brains for it.'

After giving directions to the house and hanging up

the phone, him nearly knock mi over when him burst out of the room.

'What's wrong with you, Dinah? Why are you loitering around here?' Him walk off before I could say 'sorry sah'.

'Cindy!' his voice boom from the kitchen. 'You remember my old college roommate, Raymond?'

Mrs Brown don't answer.

'You met him when we were in DC last year. And their son kept talking like he was some kind of rapper? Woman, don't you remember anything?'

Him sigh. 'Anyway, he and his family will be in Jamaica for the next five months . . . we've arranged for his son to do an internship at the firm before he starts at Princeton.'

I hear her 'uh-uhs'. Unless is spa dates or shopping trips, it hard for her to pretend interest in most things, especially when they relate to Mr B. She live to go beach, play tennis and swim in the pool. Mr B always trying to get Mrs B to pay him attention. That's why him always restless in him own house. Him don't have no peace. But Mrs B not a bad woman. When I dust and break a figurine, she don't take money out of mi pay. When Mama sick and I had to stay home two days, she don't short mi money. When I come back though, the place did messy with plenty dirty plate in the sink. Rich people just too nasty.

As for Mr B, the one good thing mi can say is that him never once put man-and-woman argument to mi and try get inna mi panty. That is more than mi can say for some bosses mi did have. And at least Mr and Mrs B don't have no likkle pickney mi need to run behind and clean up after.

One time I hear Mr B tell Mrs B is time dem have pickney. Mrs B say she have nuff thing she want to do and him must try understand. Him seh him been trying to understand for five years now and ask if she don't love him. She suck in har breath and say yes, so dem can try. But I know she still taking her birth control pills. She hide dem in the bathroom, behind her tampon box.

One time when Mr B bring up the baby argument again, I hear Mrs B say: 'Christ! I'm just twenty-six!' I don't like when people take the Lord's name in vain.

Mr B is two times her age. I understand why Mr B want a child before him turn a old man. But Mrs B go on like a pickney herself, with the vex-up silence, shouting, slamming doors and fighting 'gainst Mr B's rules. But is not a bad job; once mi do mi work good, dem OK.

'Ray left Jamaica nearly twenty years ago,' Mr B saying now. 'The son is in college. They've rented a car and will be here in a few hours. Make yourself presentable.'

Mi picture Mrs Brown rolling her eyes and drumming her long blue fingernails on the granite countertop.

'What do you think they'll want to eat?' she ask.

'Ackee and saltfish, bammy, oxtail and rice and peas. None of your hors d'oeuvres foolishness. Make sure Dinah finishes it by the time they get here.'

As usual, Mr Brown talking as if mi not there. *Cho.* Again, mi feel like a ghost – a uptown duppy – fading into the wall. I look at the titles as I dust the books in the study. *Commentaries* by Sir William Blackstone. *Modern Equity* by Harold Granville Hansbury. *Chitty on Contracts.*

'Dinah! It's Saturday! What you doing in the study?' Mi never hear him footsteps coming back. He sound vexer than usual.

Is a big kitchen the Browns have. Black and white check-ered tiles and a giant kitchen island. Pretty wooden cabinets. Dem have a big white fridge and a stove weh dem get from America that mi wipe down every morning and evening. Mr Brown like things 'spotless'. Him want to see him reflection, him say, on every surface. If him see likkle grease is a problem.

I take out the saltfish from the pantry and put it to boil. Mi sweep the whole kitchen first then take out the mop and bucket of warm water and wipe the floor. Mi wondering who is this family coming here today.

I picking out the bones from the saltfish when I prick myself. A long black car climb up the driveway.

Out of nowhere, I hear in mi head a saying Mama chant plenty time:

> Ole time don't keep,
> Ole life will leak,
> What was lock will open up
> wid the right key.

Is like mi memory closet creak open.

Mi remember that today is Son-Son's eighteenth birthday.

Dinah

When I was eighteen, Leroy, mi wutliss boyfriend from All Age school, wrestle with mi one evening in the canefield. I still had on mi shorts and panty, so it was pure shock when mi period stop. Nine months later here comes a cotton-hair boy-pickney. Hair picky-picky like mine. Skin smooth like Leroy, head just as big. Face wide and beautiful. Mi never see eyelashes long so yet. Lips so fine and full and him likkle fingernails so pink and perfect. Long, long fingers like Mama. A strong, firm nose, like him know him going to be one important man.

Mama nearly get epileptic fits when mi tell her mi pregnant. Is just two years I in the job with the Steeles, a expat couple who work for the US Embassy in Kingston. Mi neva know what work Mr Steele do at the Embassy but because of how everybody talk to him, I figure he must be a big shot. Dem say him work for the CIA, but mi don't know if is true. People even say Steele wasn't dem real name. That is a false identity and dem in Jamaica to spy on we 'cause Uncle Sam suspect we going get friendly with Fidel Castro in Cuba and Americans never want any more communism in dem backyard.

'Let him get yuh a US visa!' Mama used to say; but mi never ask and the Steeles never offer.

Mr Steele white, pale like a full moon. Mrs Steele was a

Black woman, but she much more light skinned than Mama. Her scarves dem did smell like lavender and she did wear plenty bangle that look like dem about to drop off har hand. She used to dye her hair red. When it was growing out, the roots used to black. The red hair usually drop across her eyes, so it not easy to see her small face.

She let mi borrow her books and I read dem when I finish work early.

'That's poetry from Shelley,' she did say. 'Or Lord Byron.' Mi study poetry I never understand and talk it out loud. The recitals did please her. Mi learn Keats' 'To Autumn':

> Season of mists and mellow fruitfulness
> Close bosom-friend of the maturing sun
> Conspiring with him how to load and bless
> With fruit the vines that round the thatch–
>   eves run . . .

'Dat ooman filling up yuh head wid words,' Mama say and suck her teeth. 'Yuh can eat dem, fool-fool gal?'

Mi picture Mrs Steele in a white apron serving some plump and juicy words on a plate, and mi laugh.

Some evenings Mrs Steele tell mi about the years dem did live in Africa, their postings in places I never hear about yet but she show mi on a map. She teach literature at universities there, she said, and I watch her eyes turn glass, like she was in a trance.

'Such beautiful people,' she said. 'Sweet little babies . . .' And then she would get quiet.

The Steeles never have any children, although mi used to hear Mrs Steele telling her friends whenever dem come over to the house with dem pickney, how much she did want a baby of her own.

Mi surprise when they say they having what Mrs Steele call a 'baby shower' for mi. The party did dead: between mi acting like mi want to be there, the too-sweet drinks Mrs Steele make, the balloons losing air, the stale biscuits and the crush-up 'Happy Delivery!' sign across the hallway. It was just the four of we – dem, Mama and me. Mama did wear her only good dress – a stiff, white-collared black shift that make her look like all the blood suck out of her face. The Steeles did wear some loose trousers and floral tops Mrs Steele say dem buy in Ethiopia.

I was in distress since Leroy take up with a browning named Shelly and move to Montego Bay. Mama say she not surprise: Leroy wouldn't want a black girl like mi.

During the baby shower, I still reeling with shock, sick from the baby or the break-up, or the two of dem together. Mi couldn't stop wriggle in the chair.

'So you have no support?' Mrs Steele say. I never know how to answer so mi look over at Mama drinking her Darjeeling tea.

'We could solve your problem.' Mrs Steele voice shaky bad. She look on her husband who did stand up beside the glass window. Mr Steele all of a sudden looking hard-hard on something outside.

She rub her throat with her fingers and cock her head to one side. Then she say: 'You've worked for us a long time, so I know *you* know I'd be a good mother . . . I always wanted my own child.'

I wondering what that have to do with me. Same time, she come out and spell it out plain: 'How about we adopt the baby when it's born? After all, you can't possibly look after it. I promise I'll take good care of it . . . I mean, the child. Think what it would be like for them, growing up in a big house like this.' She move her arms around the

13

room, like she swimming in the middle of the ocean doing a backstroke.

Mama cup bang in the saucer. She pinch and push out her lips 'til dem look grey.

'Think about it, Dinah. What mother doesn't want the best for her child?' Mrs Steele float to the window and hold on to her husband hand. 'What can you give a baby that we can't?'

Her words sting mi. I just was thinking mi could give my child myself. Before I get to ask why that not good enough, Mama blurt out: 'What unnu want wid her baby? Unnu tink is puss pickney that people give out inna cardboard box?'

'Now, now—' Mr Steele trying to calm down Mama while Mrs Steele bury her face in his chest.

'I not going allow it. Unno think that 'cause unno rich, is OK to do as you like?' Mama eyes is fire.

'You're taking this the wrong way, we want to help.' Mr Steele say.

'Yuh mean "help yuhself to her pickney"!'

I don't remember all what happen next except Mama storm out, with me behind her. That night while mi rubbing mi swollen belly all I thinking 'pon is Leroy. Mi back ache, the shadows from the *Home Sweet Home* kerosene lamp dance like somebody with the devil inside dem and Mama snoring sound like a hoarse cat clearing it throat beside mi. Then I thinking 'bout my son – somehow mi know it was a boy – and picturing him here next to mi in the bed. I could see him wiggling him arms and legs and looking 'round this tiny room, and for the first time mi feel like we in prison and mi know I had to get him out before the walls fall down on all of we.

Dinah

I didn't tell Mama what mi decide. We couldn't support a pickney. The chemical spill at the garment factory where Mama used to work did nearly blind her. That and her weak back mean nobody going hire her as a helper, which was the only job she had schooling for.

When mi son born, the Steeles say they had a couple weeks left in Jamaica. They come to the hospital and Mr Steele face shining like a proud father. Mi trying to remember everything about the baby. To cement everything in mi memory. How him wrinkle him nose when him yawn, how him smell, how him move him fingers and the feel of him soft hands in mine. Him skin on mi chest, him eyes digging into mi own, swelling mi heart. How him mouth latch on mi nipple; mi even remember the pain. Mi look at him, thinking him was worth the pain of the delivery, which mi honestly never did ready for and think was going kill mi. 'Stop the noise and behave yuhself,' the nurse did say. 'Just push.'

'Take mi wid yuh,' mi beg the Steeles, desperate to keep him. 'Mi can take care of him as him nanny.'

Mrs Steele say: 'No, it's better for the baby that there's a clean break, you understand? He's got to think I'm his mother.'

'Yuh will write mi?'

Mrs Steele say: 'Of course, Dinah. We have your address and we'll write you to let you know how he's doing once we settle into our new house.'

'Yuh promise?'

'Yes, of course.'

I remind myself Mrs Steele just trying to help mi and my child.

They take him five minutes after that. Before mi get to give him the protection necklace Mama make for him in mi bag. Before mi get to give him a proper name, so I decide to call him Son-Son.

◆

The Steeles leave a box of books, a old settee, fridge and rug for mi. Mi sell what I could to get money while mi look for work. Nobody wanted to buy the books. Mi was glad to keep dem anyway, so that mi would have something to make mi forget. Dem first few months I would wake up wailing, pillow wet from dreams mi couldn't remember in the daylight. For a while, me and Mama did sing sankeys, hoping Son-Son would catch my voice like a cord so I could pull him back. We dance like the flame on the wick in the kerosene lamp – dance around the room anti-clockwise, bending we bodies forward in every step. We turn into a frenzy of arms, shoulders, hips, rib cages ... spinning and dipping. The spirits would come then. Like currents in a river dragging mi into a deeper place weh mi feel everything and nothing same time.

And after, we collapse on the bed, out of breath and sweating.

Mama used to beat the drum or shake tambourine; now dem things gathering dust in the corner of we room. Back then, the drum was we heartbeat. Mama tell mi Son-Son's spirit is strong but I never feel him, not even after Mama and I do a baptism ceremony for him.

In the beginning, I used to write Son-Son a letter every morning and tear it up every night until the words and tear up paper blur in mi head. The Steeles never give mi no address. They never write mi one time. But I never move from the tenement yard in Lazarus Gardens, just in case.

◆

'Dinah, you're making a mess!' Mrs Brown's voice bring mi back to right now and the black car parking. 'What's gotten into you today?' Mi hear the people coming in. But mi not paying dem no mind since mi nowhere near finish all the things the Browns want mi to cook. Is where the time gone?

Mrs Brown leave the kitchen carrying the jug of otaheite apple juice mi did make. She tell mi to follow her into the living room with the tray of glasses.

'Ray! Great to see you again!' I see Mr Brown hugging a fat white man with brown hair like bird feathers. 'Celeste will be right inside. She left her glasses in the car.'

'This must be Apollo!' Mr Brown in him element now, vigorously pumping an outstretched black hand. A tall, nutmeg-coloured young man in grey jeans, blue T-shirt and black and white sneakers walk in. Him have thin, neat locs, light brown at the ends, tie up in a ponytail.

Mi see the long eyelashes, the nose that take up almost half his face, the full mouth, the neck. I look at his wide shoulders.

I let go the tray. Right there on the terrazzo tiles.

Time fall away and gone. I don't care about the shock on the Browns' faces or about anyone else in the room.

I say to the boy: 'Son-Son a yuh! Is really yuh!'

'I'm sorry?' him say. Him is a boy in the body of a man: broad face, knobby-head like Leroy-own.

17

'Mr Steele!' I say to Mr Steele who looking at mi now like him don't know mi.

'Dad.' The boy look at Mr Steele, too. Mr Steele is the colour of uncooked shrimp. 'What's she talking about?'

Mr Steele, the same Mr Steele with the floral shirts and crisp white pants, talking now: 'Sorry, lady, but you're confusing me with someone else. We don't know you.'

'Is *me*, Mr Steele. Dinah.'

'Dinah, shut up!' Mr Brown say. Shame fill up his face. I don't care what him think.

'Mr Steele, yuh don't remember mi?'

'She hasn't been herself today,' says Mrs Brown.

In my head I scream: *Don't offer nuh excuse for mi, yuh son-of-a-bitch! Mi not aiding and abetting yuh to have criminal thief mi pickney again!*

'I know mi child! That's Son-Son!' My voice sound strange but I not under water any more. The drum exploding in mi ears now.

I grab Apollo's hands, stepping on glass that look like points of light glistening on the floor. His fingers like Mama's; fingers that use sticks on drums to release spirits in the dark.

Mr Steele is barking now at Mr Brown: 'Christopher, *who is this woman?*'

'If you don't stop this madness right now, Dinah, I'm calling the police!' Mrs Brown scream.

But I pull my son to mi and rub him head – his hair still coarse but no longer picky-picky like when him was a baby. I like the sweet smell of his fuzzy hair. I kiss his mouth. The mouth that is like my mouth. He is the part of mi that is outside myself.

'That's it!' Mr Brown shout. He and Mr Steele's hands are on mi now, fingers digging into the flesh of my shoulder trying to pry mi off Son-Son, but mi too strong fi dem.

The pandemonium bring Mrs Steele from the car outside. She run in, her nostrils flaring like a bull about to buck.

'Take your hands off my son!' she yell and slam her body into mine, knocking over the coffee table.

Mi on the ground before mi realise what happening. She pin mi to the floor, then her husband drag her off mi, kicking and screaming.

'Dinah! Dinah! Get out!' Mrs Brown is in hysterics and I hear Mr Brown, pitiful sounding, saying: 'Sorry about this, Ray.' He warn mi now: 'Dinah, if you put one foot inside this yard again, I'll have you locked up for assault!'

Mr Steele's white face blood-red. Son-Son still standing there, body quiet like him feet in cement.

'I'm sorry,' he says again. 'What's going on?'

'No more sorrys, yuh here now, my *son*. Mi can't believe is yuh,' I say.

We eye lock. I see me in him. Him embarrassed I trying to take him back in the open. 'Alright. I'll be patient, my son,' I say under my breath, but I know him hear mi. Only he can hear. The phone in the hall start to ring, adding to the madness. Mi sure that neighbours hear the screams.

Mr Brown still throwing expletives like stones when mi gather my bag and leave. I don't care what him say: not about Mr Steele's fake amnesia or about Mrs Steele acting like she not Mrs Steele, now that her skin look some shades darker.

I need my child. I need my Son-Son and mi can't wait to get home to tell Mama mi find him.

Apollo

On the drive to the Browns' house, Apollo sits in the back-seat, thinking about how he's been in Jamaica for over a week and is no way closer to a beach. Even worse, he's stuck inside an air-conditioned car on the way to his dad's friends who also don't live near a beach; driving over potholes that make the car creak.

His mother tells Pops, 'Be careful, Ray,' in that soft tone she has that's packed full of steel underneath. His stepfather presses the gas pedal hard, driving in that purposeful, self-assured way he does everything. Celeste eyes a map, carefully tracing the veins of streets with a red-painted nail. The map reminds Apollo of the ridges on the underside of a leaf.

They make a turn that takes them on to the same street for the third time.

'Pops,' says Apollo. 'You sure you know where you're going?'

'Hush your mouth, boy,' Celeste answers but he can tell she's wondering the same thing.

Ain't no way this is the Jamaica I pictured, he thinks. Beggars hover at the traffic lights when they stop, pressing sweaty, dirt-streaked faces to the car window, splashing water on the windscreen, wiping it off with dirtier sponges on sticks, leaving smears. Many of them are barefooted children, begging them 'a money'. They stick out their tongues, bellies or bottoms in defiance when Celeste shakes her head no.

Raymond makes a left turn.

'This street isn't even on the map,' Celeste murmurs. 'Jamaica has all these undocumented sideroads. How can people find anywhere?'

Apollo bites back a curt remark.

Raymond says: 'It's not like I remember it, but that's alright, I just need to get reacquainted with the streets ... don't get me started on them driving on the wrong side of the road.' He pulls his right earlobe, the way he does when he's confused, reverses, turns right and speeds on.

Apollo sees buildings, more and more of them passing the car; he narrows his eyes and they become a haze of browns, oranges, blues and whites. He opens his eyes wide again.

The people are all Black. Like him. No pale faces on the street; just Black people, carrying their groceries, talking to friends, moving about their everyday lives, never thinking that their singular Blackness might strike anyone as remarkable.

A motorcyclist veers in front of the Benz and Ray swerves into a pothole full of water, splashing a man on a bicycle in a torn grey shirt and jeans. The man jumps off his bicycle. Raymond rolls down the window to apologise and the man says: 'Move yuh bumboclaat, yuh dutty whitey!' Raymond is bathed in unfamiliar curse words. He rubs his jaw as if the insults are running down his cheek.

Celeste's mouth falls open. Apollo doesn't believe what he's hearing. He's appalled but oddly proud that a Black man can speak to a white man like that and face no retribution.

Ray makes a hasty retreat.

All the cops are Black. Apollo sees one officer in a neat

uniform – red-seamed black pants with a blue and white striped shirt – directing cars at a traffic light that has stopped working. The hollow of the lights look like eye sockets. The lanky officer waves Ray to come across and he obeys. Ray finds a familiar street and his smile returns.

'We're nearly there. You're gonna love this guy, Celeste, so long as Brown doesn't tell too many stories about the drunken antics we got up to at Princeton . . . things that would disqualify us from running for public office!' He laughs. Celeste smiles politely, stiff in her seat.

'How far's the beach from here?' Apollo rolls down the window to get some fresh air. His mother swivels in her seat and tells him to bring it back up again. He wishes his parents would turn on the radio so he could hear some reggae.

'Moms, I'm gonna borrow the car later and try to find—'

'This is Jamaica, Apollo. What did they tell you at the hotel about going out at night? And by yourself?'

'Yo, this ain't Jamaica, it's a goddamn prison! And y'all actin like you the *po-po*,' he blurts.

'Apollo, why do you insist on talking like that?' Celeste asks, a frown creasing her lips.

'Like how?'

'Like you don't know how to speak English. We taught you better than that. You're not . . . like that.'

'Like what?'

She doesn't answer. He knows Celeste means like the Black rappers and athletes on TV, who she calls 'a certain *type* of Black people'.

'I don't like the people you're hanging out with. That Kevin boy—'

'Why don't you say what you really mean, which is: "why am I talking to the gardener's son?"'

'He's got you talking like nobody raised you right!'

22

Apollo shakes his head and falls silent again. No amount of ebonics or urban slang made Apollo feel at home with his Blackness. No matter how he tried, he just couldn't fully connect.

Before now, he'd only seen Jamaica through the Jamaica Tourist Board commercials run on TV: children frolicking on white sand beaches, couples holding hands in twin hammocks, drinking coconut water from straws, tourists with dimpled, cottage-cheese thighs running along the shore and lying on sand frothy with waves ... a mocha-coloured girl in a yellow and green bikini leaping from a large rock into the river below while a toothless Rastaman mouthed Bob Marley's 'One Love'.

He'd asked his parents every year about going to Jamaica, instead of Disney World, Aspen or Martha's Vineyard. He had no Black friends at his small private school. The few he did meet thought he wasn't 'Black enough'. He once told his mother: 'The other Black kids call me Oreo. Can't we go somewhere where I won't be the only Black person in the room?' His mainly white friends came from homes that had been pre-approved by his parents. These guys wore sweaters with their jeans, played tennis and read the *Wall Street Journal*.

His stepfather came from an old money family, who'd lived in Washington DC for generations. Politically, they were Republican, of course, and their acceptance of his Black son showed they were 'progressive and socially inclusive'. His mother, who was his stepfather's second wife, came from a family of Black entrepreneurs – with enough respectability to make her agreeable to her in-laws. Apollo was dutifully trotted out by Raymond's family at fundraisers, the opera or the golf club as an example of how *accepting* they all were of minorities. It annoyed Apollo that the more he asserted his Blackness in his dress and manner, the stronger his white family's desire to embrace him, as a sign of their magnanimity. 'Have you met our grandson/nephew/cousin Apollo,' they'd say. 'He speaks French, plays the violin and the saxophone and he *just* signed a petition for a Black rights course to be on his school curriculum!'

Once he'd learnt Raymond wasn't his biological father, he pestered his mother about his real dad and growing up in the South. As a teen, Apollo decided to rebel, to stand out in this sea of white with his style of dress. Especially after what happened with his former best friend Michael. At sixteen, Apollo grew shoulder-length locs and dyed the ends light brown. He made it a habit, in the middle of polite conversation, to interject: 'Yo, dog, that's some *bull* right there,' making his grandfather, aunt, uncle and cousins sip their drinks nervously.

He had a poster of Nelson Mandela in his room: the loft they'd converted the pool house into. He read Marcus Garvey and Malcom X. Listened to Nina Simone and John Coltrane, Run DMC, Dr Dre and Ice Cube. He wore dashikis with his Nikes to his parents' formal events.

He began to have recurring dreams. A woman's voice singing in a language he didn't know, but it was a song he'd heard before. He has never seen her face in the dreams, but he smells her. Like salty wind, like wet earth. They move towards each other in the dark, feeling their way against a gust of wind or under the weight of water. But just when she nearly reaches him, he wakes up in a sweat. Panting.

In his mind, Jamaica became an escape. He'd imagine how the white sand would feel under his bare feet, how cool the coconut water – straight from the coconut – would be on his tongue. He pictured that girl from the commercial, in her yellow and green bikini, snuggling against him in that hammock, him slipping his fingers between the fabric and her skin, just below her belly button.

His parents always seemed to dodge the idea of going to Jamaica. Too much crime, they'd say. There was always somewhere else they wanted to take him – Rome, Paris, Greece, Spain. He'd been to Europe but never to Central or South America or the Caribbean.

So it was a surprise that just after his seventeenth birthday they announced a family trip to Jamaica the following year. Dad had business meetings planned for his NGO's work in Latin America and the Caribbean. His old Princeton friend, Christopher Brown, was a partner in one of the most reputable commercial law firms on the island where Apollo could do an internship.

He had a whole year of anticipation.

But the place didn't seem the way it did on TV. For one, they were staying in Kingston, so there were no beaches nearby. 'For the really great beaches, you'll have to go to Ocho Rios or Mobay,' said the desk clerk of the New Kingston hotel where they stayed the first week, while they waited for the Jack's Hill house they were renting. The clerk showed Apollo a road map and said it would take hours to get to Mobay. The hotel staff also warned him not to venture out alone at night.

Just outside the hotel, there were the sounds of men yelling at passengers trying to fill already crowded buses, bikes and taxis weaving in and out of traffic, doing illegal turns, while pedestrians stepped indiscriminately into the street. And the heat! The sun and smell of cigarettes, piss, garbage and jerk chicken wafting from oil-drums strewn on the roadside, higglers selling spicy shrimp, peanuts, oranges, bananas and mangoes so juicy he wanted to devour his yellow-stained fingers and suck all the juice before it streamed down his elbows. The Blue Mountains – always visible in the distance when they drove through Kingston – were aloof but scandalously

exposed their beauty – like a prostitute turning her bare but-
tocks to the roadside to advertise her wares.

His parents rented a breezy mansion set back from the
road. A Jack's Hill neighbour had told him about a recent
string of robberies in the neighbourhood and so his dad had
the landlord install burglar bars, which soothed his parents
but made him feel like a caged bird. The same way he was
feeling now, cooped up in the car.

Raymond tightens his grip on the steering wheel. 'Your
mother is only trying to protect you. Trust me, there are lots
of bad people in the world.'

'You better believe it, boy,' Celeste echoes.

'You can't protect me from life!'

'Look,' Celeste says, 'we brought you here like you wanted.
Let's get through the next five months then you're off to start
your freshman year at Princeton. Just do a good job at this
internship. And stop talking back.'

Apollo squeezes his eyes shut and leans his head against the
headrest, listening to the hum of the air conditioning, feeling
the cold blasts chilling his chest through his cotton T-shirt,
and wishes he could fly away.

◆

Apollo is glad when they finally get out of the car. He tells
his parents sorry for his outburst. Not because he means it,
but it's just easier to let them think they've won. That way,
when he eventually sneaks out of the house they won't see it
coming. Raymond throws an arm around his shoulder and
tries to ruffle his hair like he used to when Apollo was a kid
but his fingers get tangled in his dreadlocks. Apollo escapes
his grasp.

They make their way into the living room; Apollo's tongue
feels dry. He gazes at the juice pitcher held by the woman

who he figures is Mrs Brown as his father and friend embrace. Mrs Brown is young and pretty, with a beauty spot on her left cheek. Too skinny for his liking though, all tanned arms and legs, spindly like an overgrown spider. A maid enters with a tray of glasses and he gives her a courteous nod and smile – the way his parents had always taught him to treat the help.

The Browns' ebony-skinned, heavy-set maid has hips that strain against her faded blue and white plaid uniform and she comes at him from out of nowhere, kisses him full on the mouth and calls him 'Son-Son'.

Then everyone goes berserk.

Mr Brown's neighbour, Assistant Commissioner of Police Linford Davis, a tall boulder of a man, responds to the commotion by coming over himself, arriving shortly after Dinah leaves. He takes statements but no one wants to press charges against Dinah. Davis writes down her address, in case anyone changes their mind. Mr Brown says: 'Davis, let's forget the whole sorry business,' and the three men retreat to his library for drinks. They close the door behind them.

His mother helps Mrs Brown clean up the smashed glass. Apollo bends down to pick up the tray and realises that Dinah dropped something from her bag, a piece of paper that he shoves into his jeans pocket when nobody is looking.

◆

Later that evening in bed, Apollo stares at the ceiling, listening to the crickets outside, watching the fireflies blinking through the open wooden louvres. The sound of car horns and traffic sound way off in the distance and the air is fresh. But Apollo can't sleep. His arrival caused the maid, Dinah, to lose her job over an honest mistake. She was just a regular Jamaican who probably needed the money to survive.

He wonders: *what happened to her son?*

What it is about her that makes him lie awake? It wasn't her face. She had large eyes, full of sadness and wisdom, a prominent broad nose, her lower lip naturally red. Her hair was short and mostly covered by a scarf that matched her uniform. Although some individual features may have been striking, on the whole, it was an unremarkable face in its ordinariness. Still, he wasn't able to take his eyes off her face when she grabbed her handbag and gave him a look he couldn't read.

A look he knew he would have to see again to understand its meaning.

Celeste

Today I decided to bake a cake. I'm no good in the kitchen; never was. This used to scandalise my mother. 'What kinda Southern wife are you going to make?' she'd ask, convinced she'd spoilt me since I kept my head in the books instead of over a bubbling pot on the stove. But I'm making a cake now, to clear my mind. To give my hands something to do.

Ray's not home. Off to some meeting or the other and Apollo is brooding in his room. I'll have to interview a couple of maids tomorrow, who both come highly recommended from a neighbour's fiancée. She was jogging past our gate last week in a pink and green tracksuit and stopped to chat – probably because she wasn't used to seeing another Black woman in the neighbourhood, not one who looked like they owned the place, anyway.

As I place the mixing bowl on the counter, I smell the freshly cut grass of our lawn coming through the kitchen window. The mango tree's branches shuffle in the breeze, making a sound like bird's wings. Birds are chirping an unfamiliar song that's strange and wonderful in its beauty, and a neighbour is doing yoga on her front porch. I can see from the look on her face, flat-eyed and as impenetrable as a pebble, she's in her 'quiet place' where silence is drowning out the sound of everything, and I'm jealous of her peace.

It's a chocolate cake. I found the Betty Crocker cake mix in the International Foods aisle in the grocery store. An old lady in a gaudy floral dress bumped into me with her cart. I apologised immediately – automatically – even though she was the one who'd run her trolley straight into my right ankle. It was something Mama always taught me to do. Respect your elders. The woman started talking.

I *loved* the sound of her voice, the smooth richness of it; sonorous and textured as a seashell with the sound of the ocean trapped inside it, so I let her talk without interruption. Her words fell over me in waves as my ankle throbbed.

When she realised I'd just recently arrived from the States, she said I was lucky I wasn't here in the late 1970s. 'Chile, you couldn't even get rice to buy. People pushing and shoving for a bag of detergent. Not to mention the rationing of salt and flour.' She said Prime Minister Manley's brush with socialism spooked our government so much that America imposed trade embargos, and removed foreign aid, worsening a weak economy already on its knees because of the global oil crisis. The result was import shortages. 'Tell me why a country like Jamaica can't grow its own rice?' she said scoffing, 'Or make enough bread, cooking oil, margarine or cornmeal to feed ourselves?' She told me middle-class Jamaicans had to hoard Foska Oats, skimmed powdered milk, soft drinks and toilet paper as prices shot through the roof when supplies dropped. There was rioting outside stores. 'Women like my daughter couldn't find sanitary napkins for their monthly period and you know what the government, a government full of *men*, mark you, came out and said?'

I shook my head.

'Use a piece of cloth! Imagine! *Cloth* like what my grandmother used to use!'

She told me she'd gotten sick back then and was turned away by the hospital. They'd shut down because of a shortage of drugs, bed linen and food for patients.

That's all why, she said, rich white and brown-skinned upper-class Jamaicans took advantage of Manley's famous socialist speech where he told them there were five flights a day out of Jamaica to Miami and they should get on one if they didn't like how he was running the country. The home of the United States Embassy political liaison officer was shot up. So the business class booked their tickets, sold their companies and left the island in droves. People lost their jobs at factories. And the country sunk further into debt, borrowing to repay its creditors, hat in hand, like a beggar, going from one First World country to another asking for handouts.

I felt my neck getting hot. The warmth radiated to my cheeks. Was it guilt, about what she said our government had done? Was it true?

She drew nearer to me and lowered her voice. She said the Jamaica Defence Force aborted a coup to overthrow Manley's government. Elections were called. And as if for spite Hurricane Allen came and blew down all the banana trees, worsening the food shortage. Crops languished because farmers couldn't get fertilisers and insecticides. The JLP campaigned with slogans like 'Deliverance Is Near' and 'Money Will Jingle In Your Pocket' and launched an anti-communist smear campaign on the PNP and they won. The change in political party brought prosperity. President Reagan backed new Prime Minister Seaga's government. Seaga was a shrewd, business-minded Lebanese-Jamaican who was friendly with the US State Department. Jamaica started to attract large foreign investment from US corporations. Farm and industrial production grew and tourism boomed.

The old woman said: 'We're capitalists now. Look on the

streets. BMWs and Mercedes-Benz everywhere but the cars running low on gas and they can't even patch a blasted pot-hole! Meanwhile, prices still going up. People still killing each other. The government better take care or this country going go to the dogs.'

I wondered why I had never heard any of this before. It was baffling. I couldn't see why this woman would want to lie to me, but if true, why was nobody talking about this? I knew from Ray that, at times, America had to intervene in the politics of other countries, but that was to safeguard democracy, to help people, to save them from corrupt and crazy despots. Megalomaniacs. Men who cared nothing for the people they were privileged to lead. But nothing she'd said suggested Manley had been any of those things. Ray says: 'America does what's necessary. It's our job to protect the world.' He admitted that we get it wrong every now and then. Truth was, I was embarrassed as she spoke. And upset too. Outraged that we had destabilised a whole nation out of fear.

I caught her staring at the Betty Crocker box in my hand. She didn't judge me for buying the cake mix, instead of making it from scratch, like a good housewife should. 'I wish we had that in my day,' she said, poking the box with a wrinkled finger.

Then she disappeared down the fresh produce aisle. I wasn't ready for our conversation to end.

Something about how she cocked her grey head reminded me of Mama, but a gentler Mama. Mama who always smelt like sandalwood, roses, oranges and lilies. I wanted to lean in and inhale more of this woman's musk — she smelt like sweat and talcum powder. I wanted to open my mouth and tell her what I was going through, even though it would be ridiculous. Here I was, a privileged American housewife, longing to unload my problems onto a stranger, albeit one with kind eyes.

Instead, I just followed her, until she stopped in front of the oranges, squeezing each one like the cheek of a small child, and I passed on by.

I read the back of the cake mix box which said: 'Just add eggs.' I wished my life was like that. Easy. Not full of turmoil, like Jamaica. Invisible faultlines running through it, running through me, threatening to crack us open any moment.

Sometimes I get these tingling sensations in my stomach. My Mama would have called them premonitions. She was always getting those, and she'd have these 'spells' come on her when she knew things before they happened. And you know what the funny thing was? Mama didn't see Raymond coming. When I asked her how she missed it, she nearly slapped me in the face.

I'm stirring the dark cocoa powder mix into the pale eggs with a large wooden spoon, watching as they marble and melt into each other. I don't regret choosing Ray. I'd do it again. He's a great dad to Apollo. He gives him stability, structure and love. I don't care what Black folks or white folks think about our marriage. And it's OK that Ray and I don't share the same views on everything. We don't spend time debating politics, because Ray knows we're not always on the same page.

Using the spoon, I make giant circles in the batter the way I'd seen Mama do it and I slice a single path straight down the middle of the pan after each circular stir. The mixture is looking good. I pop everything into the oven and wait.

Mama was pissed when John King and I got married. She told me I was young and stupid. John was a beautiful piece of dark chocolate and had nothing but his looks and shrewdness. 'He's common,' Mama said. He was the nephew of Papa's mechanic. He'd come to the house with his uncle, dropping off one of Papa's Cadillacs and he would wink at me and my knees felt like buckling. John made me feel alive in a way I didn't know was possible. He noticed the little things about me, how I held my head when I was curious, how I wiggled my nose when I was scared, how the birthmark on my neck is shaped like a boot.

My Mama had a quilt that her grandmother had made her. It was meant to go to my child, to get passed down through generations. After I got married to John, she told me I'd never get that quilt.

So when John got into a car crash and died, Mama thought she'd gotten a second chance to set me straight. To re-educate me on the importance of marrying well. I needed to strengthen our family's financial position. 'White folks do this all the time, Celeste,' she said and gave me a lesson on preserving intergenerational wealth. She schooled me on why it was important. A prominent Black family like ours had a social responsibility to be an example in the community. Because Black folks had been through too much, struggled too hard and needed to know it was possible to rise. And I knew Mama was right. But maybe I was tired of doing what she and Papa thought I should do.

So I fell into Ray headlong, like leaping into a moving train. A bond fortified by the sudden and devastating deaths of our spouses. Our hearts were raw.

When I married Ray, my family acted like I had just axed the family tree. When, in fact, I was the branch that they had chopped off.

As for Apollo, I grew him carefully, like tending my orchids. But now, my son, the boy I raised since he was small, the baby I held in my arms, is rootless. He doesn't know where he came from. He doesn't ask much about my family and I don't tell him. He'll never have my great-grandmother's quilt. And it's my fault. Sometimes, I think: *Celeste, this is what you get. Don't fool yourself: actions have consequences.*

And after it all, I burnt the damn cake. I took my eye off the clock. It stayed in too long. When I grabbed it from the oven, using a thin towel, forgetting the oven mitt, it was too late to salvage it and I burnt my hand.

It rose like a blackened volcano on the kitchen table. I tossed the whole thing into the trash, pan and all, and went for the butter to soothe my fingers. I was glad for the pain. To feel something.

Apollo

The day after the incident with Dinah, Apollo begged his parents to let him explore a bit of Kingston on his own, to see the Bob Marley Museum or go to Devon House. No, they could keep the car, he told them, assuring them he would use the reliable taximan the hotel staff had recommended. And yes, he would be back by the afternoon, way before dark.

He had memorised the address he'd heard Mr Brown give his police friend. When Davis heard Dinah lived in Lazarus Gardens, he'd raised an eyebrow and paused his pen.

'Do you know how dangerous it is to let somebody from down there into your house?'

Mrs Brown had looked defensive. 'Look, Linford, before today, Dinah never gave us any trouble. I mean, apart from being a little slow and distracted lately, she was the perfect helper. Never stole anything—'

'—that we know of,' Mr Brown interjected.

'And we told her *never* to bring anybody from Lazarus Gardens to our house, whether to help her work or visit her.'

◆

When Apollo told Eddie, the driver, where he was going, Eddie's eyes nearly popped out. He immediately dropped the fake American twang he'd used when he first greeted Apollo. 'My man, why yuh wan' go *deh* so?'

Apollo didn't know. All he could think to say was that something had fallen from her bag. A prescription of some sort. Maybe she needed it.

'Is nuh any and any taximan wi carry yuh deh, ennuh. Dem people in Lazarus Gardens nuh like stranger.' Eddie paused. 'But yuh lucky mi niece come from down deh. She is the Area Don main babymodda. Is a good thing yuh call mi 'cause if yuh drive there on yuh own, yuh dead.' Apollo thought: *Jesus! What kinda place was this?*

They drove through progressively narrow and potholed streets. Eddie stuck his head out the window and shook a fist at the driver of a passing truck who extended his middle finger to Eddie and sucked his teeth.

'Listen mi, man,' Eddie said to Apollo, 'if yuh going be in Jamaica, yuh going need to learn how to chat the bad-word dem. Jah know. Repeat after me: baxide. Rassclaat. Bumboclaat . . . '

Apollo twisted his tongue into sounds that made Eddie chuckle, his huge Adam's apple bobbing. 'OK, yuh almost get it right. Just gwaan practise dem.'

Finally, with a loud screech, Eddie stopped the red Lada in front of a squalid, multi-level structure. As he stepped out, the scene reminded Apollo of what the apartments in the Projects looked like on TV, except worse. He could see rusty zinc fences with faded signs advertising dances, political party posters demanding votes, dogs with their ribs sticking out drinking from the grey water meandering through the lane, dribbling from manholes with missing covers.

It stank.

The sticky humidity almost overwhelmed him. The sun

was high and unrelenting. Tiny clouds the size of a child's fist dotted the sky.

He and Eddie agreed that Eddie would return for him in three hours. No one but Eddie knew where he was. Panicked, he thought about going back to Jack's Hill. But Eddie's car had long disappeared, trailing puffs of black smoke behind it.

'Yow, Rasta! Ah who yuh?' A gravelly-sounding voice came from behind. He spun around to face a dark man with muscles rippling from under his sleeveless Chicago Bulls jersey.

'Man, I'm- I'm looking for somebody ...' Apollo stammered, not wanting the man to think he didn't belong there, and worse, to rob and kill him. The murder statistics in Jamaica suddenly flashed in his mind and he could feel the sweat pooling under his armpits and the clamminess of his palms. Why was he so eager to come here anyway? It occurred to him now that nobody would ever find his body, or what was left of it, after they'd chopped him up with machetes and fed him to hungry mongrels.

'Who yuh looking for, bwoy?' the man asked. Menace hung in his voice. '*Who* yuh?'

Apollo's hands felt damp. His throat was closing up.

The man started coming towards him, reaching behind him for something in his waistband. Apollo's legs froze even as his eyes darted around for a means of escape. He found none. His stomach tightened.

'I'm Dinah's son,' Apollo mumbled weakly.

'Bloodfire!' the man exclaimed. He stopped mid-stride and the unseen object, half-pulled from the back of his pants, went back to its original position. 'Dinah nuh have any pickney,' the man said, clearly sceptical, but his tone had softened.

'Yeah, I'm her kid,' Apollo said again, feeling foolish. 'I'm from overseas.'

'Overseas? Yuh mean farin?'

'Foreign. Yeah. America. Grew up there.'

'So yuh grow wid relatives?'

Apollo nodded. At least the lie didn't come from his mouth. His parents had taught him to always speak the truth. But now his life was on the line.

'Rasta, it nuh right fi yuh deh pon dem ends weh nobody nuh know yuh. Which part of farin yuh come from?' his interrogator asked.

'Washington DC.'

'Mi fren get ketch last year bringing up ten kilo to DC.'

Apollo wasn't sure what the appropriate response was.

'Bloodclaat DEA!' the man said.

'Yes, the bumboclaat dem. Rassclaat! Jah know.' Apollo was thankful for Eddie's lesson.

The man said: 'Relax, man. How yuh sweating so?'

Apollo touched his forehead in disbelief. He hadn't realised he was sweating. He'd felt so cold.

Satisfied that Apollo had shown enough righteous anger at his friend's arrest, the man flashed almost blindingly white teeth. 'Any son of Dinah is mi bredda, yuh see mi? Mi name Damian, aka Congo King.' The man embraced him and they bumped fists.

Putting his arms around Apollo, the man guided him into the yard, ushering him to two rusty metal chairs under a mango tree. Studying him more closely, Apollo realised they were probably the same age.

'So should I call you Congo King?' he asked, feeling awkward.

Damian laughed. 'No, star. Yuh can call mi Damian. Congo King is mi stage name. Mi going be a big deejay. Mi can sing too and write song. The world going hear 'bout mi. Mi working on mi first album now.'

'That's cool, man.'

Damian examined him. 'Dinah deh a church. Mek we reason yahso 'til she reach back. Want a spliff?'

Damian reached into his bag, humming a tune and kneading some marijuana in his palm. Apollo had taken a hit a few times before – even his pre-screened friends had a friend or two who his parents would call 'bad company' who brought drugs, discreetly, to parties. Once he'd even smoked a Cuban cigar. But he'd never had the good stuff from Jamaica. He wasn't sure how he'd react to the high. The thought of losing control out here, in a strange place, unnerved him.

'Nah.'

He saw the expression on Damian's face darken and quickly changed tack. 'Alright. I mean, yeah mon.'

Damian politely looked away as Apollo coughed on the first long draw. His chest felt like it was exploding.

'Is di real stuff dis, my yute!' Damian said proudly, slapping Apollo's back. 'No counterfeit or joke ting.' They sat for a while in what felt to Apollo like an uncomfortable silence. Damian lay back in his chair, his eyes half-closed, fingers laced behind his head, soaking up the sun.

A bowlegged girl bent over the giant, communal standpipe, her back to them, filling a huge bucket of yellow-brown clothing with water. She wore a red and white tube top with no bra and blue jeans shorts.

The boys admired her.

Damian's eyes sparkled.

'Regina,' he responded to Apollo's unasked question. 'McKenzie dawta. The ole man cyaan manage har. She nuh *stop* mad de man dem inna de yard. She half-Indian so she have white liver.'

Apollo suspected this had something to do with sex but

he couldn't figure out what and didn't ask. Just outside the gate, women made their way to and from church, in brilliant red, blue and green hats with feathers and white stockings and he studied them carefully, the way a bird-watcher looks through binoculars, willing his sudden erection to disappear. He blamed it on Regina and the weed mellowing him.

'Yuh want to meet har? Regina!' Damian bellowed before Apollo could reply. 'Come yah gal!'

Apollo's female friends in America would have slapped him in the face if he spoke to them that way. Regina giggled, her arms akimbo, then pursed her lips and turned away, as if she had no intention of coming over. But in the next minute there she was, much too close, the front of her top soaking wet.

'So yuh like har?' Damian asked him.

'Sorry?'

'Mi seh: yuh like har?'

Apollo shuffled his feet.

'Yuh nuh haffi ask,' Regina said, pointedly resting her gaze on his crotch. It was obvious however much he tried to hide it.

Quickly bored of the awkward stranger, Regina flashed a gap-toothed smile at Damian's bag: 'Damian, yuh have anything fi mi?'

'Yeah, but mi know Mr Mack nuh gi yuh money Friday evening since him spend it off a Jackie bar. So wah yuh have can trade?'

'Five minutes to yuh friend,' Regina said. Damian laughed and nodded. Apollo didn't realise what was happening until she grabbed his hand and led him to a small shed at the back of the tenement yard. 'Look, you don't have to do this—' he started to say.

She unzipped his jeans and her pink fingernails felt rough against his skin.

He was uneasy with the idea of being caught with his pants down in a place like this. He told her to stop but his own body disobeyed him. He felt his hardness between her fingers as she began to stroke him, never once making eye contact. It was strangely impersonal, mechanical but efficient and, in about five minutes, he ejaculated into her fingers. She let go. Together, they watched his semen spill on to the dusty ground. The whole time she remained silent.

Damian was grinning when they came back to the front of the tenement yard. Without a word, he handed Regina a small brown paper bag and she promptly disappeared inside. Damian didn't ask about what happened in the shed.

They sat together and downed a few Red Stripe beers Damian produced from his bag. Apollo told Damian about DC in the winter, what the cold felt like, how white skin felt to touch, what white pum-pum felt like (here he embellished, as the extent of his sexual experience was making out, a couple of blowjobs and clumsy sex twice with his high school girlfriend). Damian sang him lines from the latest song he'd written for his first album and explained he was saving up money to go into the studio to record.

'So you got any songs out?' Apollo asked him.

'No man. Mi nuh buss yet. That's why mi working on the album. Then mi going get dem on the radio. Mi going big like Bob Marley!'

Damian asked where he was staying in Jamaica.

'Jack's Hill.'

'Yeah mi yute, mi like dem place deh. Di people have nice stuff inna dem house.'

Apollo didn't want to ask how Damian would know this. He didn't seem like the type to be invited to neighbourhoods like those. He knew if Damian came to his gate, his mother would take one look at him, lock the door and probably call the police too.

Where was Dinah? It seemed like his watch wasn't working. Damian saw him tap the face of his Movado. 'Is almost four o'clock. Dem must be having church convention or something why she taking so long.' Damian wore a gold Rolex watch that was too big for his wrist. If it wasn't a knock-off, it cost more money than some people in Jamaica saw in a year.

'Mi good fren String can fix that watch. When mi get this one it wasn't working, even after the battery change. In two-twos String get it to work. Him can fix radio, TV, you name it.'

'Uh, I see.'

'Yuh can leave yuh watch wid mi and mi can ask him to fix it.'

'I dunno man, it was a birthday gift from my mom.'

'How Dinah afford to give yuh that?'

'I mean, I got it from a relative.'

'String can fix it. Is no problem.'

'Nah. It's alright.'

'What happen? Yuh nuh trust mi? Yuh nuh think yuh woulda get back yuh watch?'

'Relax, man,' Apollo stood up. 'I'm not saying that. But I only just met you and—'

Before Damian could respond, the gate creaked. It was Dinah, in a white and purple hat, holding a huge, weather-beaten Bible.

'Miss Dinah, mi find yuh son!' Damian said proudly, as if he had delivered Apollo to her personally.

Dinah paused at the gate, looking hard at Apollo's reddened eyes; she obviously smelt the ganja. Then she ran over and hugged him tightly. Joy beamed from her upturned face. Her cheekbones were raised from smiling. The top of her head came only as high as his chest.

'Mi know yuh would find mi!' she said, making him unsteady with the force of her body. 'Mi Blessed Saviour bring yuh to mi! Hallelujah! Thank yuh Lawd!' Her eyes were wet.

He allowed her to embrace him but kept his arms at his sides. Though her body felt sturdy and strong against his, she was trembling slightly, with every quiet sob.

'Here, I brought your prescription.' He took the piece of paper from his pocket. 'I figured you'd need it.'

Ignoring his words, she paused from hugging to look up at the sky: 'You who have done great things, O God. Who is like you?' Leading the way into the house, she wiped her face with the back of her hand. 'Mama inside. Come. Come! Come meet yuh grandmodda!'

His role as watchman fulfilled, Damian didn't follow them.

Apollo took it all in. The ceiling was low and he had to bend his head slightly as he came through the doorframe. The window was open and faded blue and yellow curtains barely moved in the stuffy heat. His eyes adjusted to the darkened living room. The naked bulb hanging from the ceiling barely shone, causing the furniture to cast eerie shadows on the peeling brown and green wallpaper ... the scruffy rug ... the rotting cabinet. The place smelt of burnt oil and garlic.

Dinah took him into a small room with a sagging mattress, a tiny table and a caramel-coloured woman wearing a head wrap. The figure stirred and he saw her thick plaits of salt and pepper hair.

'Mama, Son-Son come home! Him finally come home.' Dinah was triumphant. Jubilant.

The older woman blinked slowly, her eyelids heavy with interrupted sleep. As her gaze settled on him, she reached out.

'Come here, boy!' She grabbed his face with her veiny hands, squashing his cheeks. 'Is you? A really yuh?'

Dinah started weeping. 'You are mi son.' She wiped her face again. 'I give yuh up eighteen years ago. To – to dem *people*.' Her face hardened. 'Dem treat yuh good?' she asked.

'You mean my parents? Yeah. They did, I guess, but why do you think I'm your son? We don't look alike or anything.'

'I know. Yuh take after your fada. Yuh look exactly like him.'

'Where's he?'

'Gone. Long time. Before yuh born. A no-good man.'

'You have a picture?'

'Where mi must get that from? The man run gone leave mi long time. I don't even know if him alive or dead and I don't care either. Listen, Son-Son, I was just a pickney miself when I make the decision to give yuh away. What mi know about being a good modda dem time? Not a thing. Yuh know what a terrible choice that was to make? I hope some day yuh will understand and – and more than that, forgive mi.' She paused, 'Yuh handsome, eh? What a good-looking boy yuh is.'

He didn't know what to say, so he just mumbled, 'Thanks.'

'But mi did want yuh, Son-Son. Mi always did want yuh. Mi glad di day yuh come back to mi.'

She pulled out a drawer and gave him the necklace made for him to wear as a baby – a shell on red string that was so small she had to wrap it around his wrist.

'Mi been keeping dis fi eighteen years. Dis will keep yuh safe.' She drew close to him. 'Mi never did want to give yuh up. Mi need yuh to understand that.' Her eyes skewered him. The earnestness pinned him down.

He nodded.

'Mi never know how to find yuh.'

Apollo shifted and squirmed in his chair as Dinah grabbed

both his hands in hers. She was so close he could see the bead of sweat on her upper lip and her chin hairs. The stuffiness of the little room was invading his nostrils, making him dizzy. His ideas that this trip would have been thrilling now made him feel stupid.

Dinah told him about his no-good father, Leroy, who she heard was living in Canada after running away during a temporary farm work programme. She told him all she knew about the Steeles, which was very little. Dinah didn't remember their first names.

'Mi just used to know dem as Mr and Mrs Steele.'

'But Dinah, how can you be sure? Maybe you're confused.'

'Mi nuh confused,' her voice was edged with a hard anger. 'Is dem.'

'Do they look the same?'

'Mr Steele definitely. Mrs Steele a bit different, but is her.'

'Dinah, Ray was married before . . . '

'Don't try to mix up mi brain. Mi know what mi know.'

How could this be true? It was absurd. His parents: baby-stealers. Him, the long-lost Son-Son magically reunited with her years later. To choose to believe this tale was lunacy. Where was her evidence? But she was so earnest that even rational thought seemed unkind. Why had he come? To satisfy his curiosity about Son-Son?

The old woman drew closer and the smell of Bay Rum rubbing alcohol, powder and Vicks Vaporub suffocated Apollo. His eyes watered. He drew deep drags of air. He had to get out of the room. He had to escape these people. Every word Dinah said hit him squarely in the chest.

His face tightened. A vein in his neck throbbed. He needed to tell her he didn't believe her story. 'Look, Dinah—'

'Mummy,' she corrected him. 'But yuh can call mi Dinah for now 'til yuh get used to mi.'

He knew she had spent over half her life knowing she'd lost her son. And she had so much less than him. Taking this away from her now, would be callous.

'Sorry, Dinah, I gotta go.' He got up so quickly the chair nearly toppled.

'But yuh just come! Why?'

'I can't stay. My parents are expecting me back.'

He saw her body stiffen and flinch at the word 'parents', as if he'd struck her. Sadness marked her face. He was sorry to hurt her. He picked at his fingernails, not sure what to do with his hands.

She suddenly gripped his wrists. 'Yuh will soon come back?'

'Yeah. As soon as I can get away again.'

He felt guilty about making a promise he didn't intend to keep. His chest felt sore, like his heart had been slammed against his rib cage. He thrust all the US dollars he had on him into her palms.

The old woman in the back room was mumbling something he couldn't hear. 'Hush up Mama!' Dinah replied gruffly; she whispered: 'Nuh mind Mama. Har head nuh good. It go and come.'

Apollo heard the *toot-toot* of Eddie's horn at the gate and was thankful for the honking. It seemed like Eddie leaned his whole arm on the horn; it blared, splintering the air. The sun was setting, casting a golden glow over the yard. Stray dogs were barking and Apollo felt giddy, almost light with relief. Damian and Regina were nowhere in sight.

Eddie said, 'Sorry mi was late,' and sped away as soon as Apollo got into the taxi. Apollo looked out of the back window. Dinah was standing in the doorway, arms lifted, eyes skyward. He could hear her singing but couldn't identify the song or the words. A sinking feeling filled his stomach. No, he wouldn't come back. He had to avoid the disappointment in her eyes. Gently and slowly, he slipped the baby necklace off his wrist and tucked it into his pocket.

Inside the house Mama repeated what she'd said to Dinah. 'Mek him gwaan. Is not Son-Son.'

Mama

Mi want to sing yuh a song. Mi used to have a good voice when mi did young. Yuh did know I was pretty? Pretty like money. The song go suh:

Come mek wi reason
Come mek wi chat
Siddung here and don't look back.
Mi have a story yuh need to hear
Help me find it
It gone somewhere!

Ayie-ayi-ayi! Mi can't remember the rest.

Yuh know 'bout Pocomania? Poco-people see, and Poco-people know. Dinah don't know that mi know what going on. Mi see clear-clear. Except when the fog fall pon top of mi, which is more and more nowadays, and mi finding miself in places that mi never take miself to, like Kingston Harbour, or the garment factory mi used to work that get burn down, or in somebody yard wid dem bad dog barking, or in the middle of a busy road in Half Way Tree. Is the fog that want to kill mi off sometimes. Like it know that mi don't want to live suh no more.

Is not like when mi spirit used to travel when we was dancing Poco. That different. Then mi spirit used to fly over the sea and tek mi back to Africa or sometimes mi in the hills of Jamaica.

Still, is one thing mi know and see clear. That boy . . . that boy mi daughter bring 'round here saying is mi grandpickney . . . mi touch him and mi don't feel nothing moving in mi flesh. Him is not of me!

But sometimes mi don't feel anything. So I really don't know if I feel dah way deh 'cause of the fog. The fog move like a cloud, then it pull mi and throw mi like a hurricane and if sometime mi don't even know miself, how mi going know nobody else?

But one thing mi certain of. Yuh can't see it yet but mi know a end is coming.

Selah!

Dinah

The day Son-Son come look for mi, Mama ask mi after if mi really sure is the Steeles. What kinda question that? Mi tell her mi work for the Steeles fi *years*. Of course mi know dem!

Mi know how Mrs Steele eye look. Her ears. Body build. Yuh notice dem things. Mi have to admit that Mrs Steele change, doh. She darker now than before, her hair different and the shape of her nose not quite the same. But don't people feature change as dem age? And is almost twenty years after all! Mi don't look the same either.

Mi don't want to start question miself any more, so when Mama keep pressing mi, mi go outside to chop the jelly coconuts for her coconut water.

Mi start think on it. Is like this coconut. Before mi bring down the blade of the machete on it, mi already know what inside. The white flesh and water. Whether is one mi cut or a hundred. Same so, mi know what inside mi son, and that him belong to me.

Damian

Mi was six when I first see a man get shot right in front of mi. The first time mi ever hear a gunshot, it sound just like fire-clappas, except a gun shot have a echo. It have a special way it ring in yuh ears.

Mi think 'bout this that night in Jack's Hill. We neva expect it. The shot flash like a camera.

The man fall backward, like him get a heavy thump in him chest. Him head dip sideways and I wonder if him dead. Streggo ease down the gun.

'Mek wi leave!' We run through the back door. Di wife screaming out her lungs.

◆

Mi did tell Streggo about de farin yute who say him is Dinah son and live in Jack's Hill. Streggo and de boy dem a play domino at Nicey's Bar and the ole timers 'round di back drinking white rum and ah cuss 'bout cricket. Some other man dem playing drafts and Ludo.

'Where in Jack's Hill him live?' Streggo ears perk up like dog that smell food.

Den mi realise Streggo a form plan and mi have more

chance fi get a US visa than to change him mind. 'How mi fi know dat, boss? Mi just meet him the other day.'

Streggo lift up a bushy eyebrow and narrow him two yeye and mi know fi lock mi mout' and look down. Streggo give a man six-love and bang him dominos hard on the table. 'Take dat!' him seh and strike the chair.

Same time, we see the taximan who did drop off the yute drive by and stop at the gate down the lane. The driver by himself inna de Lada but a pretty browning come out the house to the car. By the time wi reach dem we hear the woman say: 'Uncle Eddie, thanks fi dropping off the thing fi Mama—' then the rest of the sentence dead in har mouth when she see Streggo and mi.

'Eddie,' Streggo say. 'Mi and yuh have to talk.'

Eddie know better than to say him have somewhere else to go.

When him get the information from Eddie about how Apollo live wid him rich white father and the address, Streggo say him going talk to British. And that mi must come.

British

The house belonging to the Area Don, British, was the only one in the Lazarus Gardens community with air-conditioning. It had not one, but six AC units, one in each of the five bedrooms and another in the living room. They blasted all day and night, even the nights when there was a chill in the air after rain. The Don had enjoyed the bitter British winters before being deported back to Jamaica for killing a rival drug dealer. He loved the numbing feeling of coldness. How you could see your own breath leaving your body on the wind. How you had to look down on your fingers and rub them together to feel that they were still there. How the cold air moved through to your bones. And like everybody else living in Lazarus Gardens, British didn't pay any electricity or water bills. Utility companies dared not send their staff inside Lazarus Gardens to disconnect anything.

Policemen did not go into Lazarus Gardens either. They also knew better. The single police station on the outskirts of the community was manned by three cops, who hid inside the grey and blue building all day. The station had been there from before Independence in 1962, a calming presence for the neighbouring upper-middle-class communities. These upscale communities had now declined, transformed into run-down dwellings with untended hedges, rusty, slouching gates and grimy, slowly crumbling walls.

So the police station remained, and Assistant Police Commissioner Davis, who was responsible for the area, didn't have to suffer the indignity of going on national TV and telling the public and the reporters shoving microphones in his face that Jamaica's Constabulary Force had closed a whole police station due to 'criminal elements'. The three policemen clocked in every morning, spent the day playing cards and left before dark. An easy enough assignment.

British and Assistant Commissioner Davis had reached a truce – an unspoken, but well-understood agreement – that no blood would be shed, as long as each kept to their own area. It was British who maintained the law inside Lazarus Gardens. Murder, rape, theft and assault in the community were at an all-time low because 'Brit', as his closest associates sometimes called him, 'nuh play dat'.

British was judge, jury and executioner. Retribution was as sure as it was swift. No one even wanted to be accused; no corroborating evidence or testimony was needed if British believed the accuser. Bodies were dumped into gullies, taken out to sea during the next rainfall or eaten by stray dogs or a hungry crocodile in the nearby gully. There was once a man said to have raped a disabled old woman, and another man accused of murdering a toddler. British kept the men's bones after they were burnt, crushed them down to a grainy powder and kept them in the flowerpots at the back of his yard.

How British looked at it was: God made people and then he, British, turned people into duppies. From spirit to body to spirit again.

He considered the residents of Lazarus Gardens his people. He was their leader. He didn't like the newspapers using 'Area Don' to describe him. It was an insulting term. Demeaning.

He wasn't elected but he was the people's Prime Minister. No, he was their King. They were always coming to him. Always needing him. To pay school fees, buy schoolbooks and uniforms or for money to go to the doctor or corner shop. With British, a man didn't have to look into the open, empty mouths of his children, like they were baby birds ready for a feeding. He didn't have to feel the pang of having no food to give.

British liked to gaze out in the distance at what looked like a beautiful yellow curtain – a sail unfurling in the breeze. It was that time of year when Kingston was blanketed in millions of tiny yellow butterflies. The bloom of purplish-blue buds in lignum vitae trees heralded their coming. Butterflies coated the bushes a pale yellow, danced in the air, floated above traffic lights and across windowpanes. Swarming and pulsing. Almost magical, the way they opened and closed their wings in the sunshine like splintering beams of light. Magnificent hordes of them, some landing on your face and chest and in your hair, yellow mist dusting your earlobes before dying on the road, like intricate leaves falling to earth, amidst engine oil, grease and squealing tyres. Squashed underfoot. Like candles blown out by God.

British was admiring the butterflies the day Streggo and Damian came to him with their plan. He had listened patiently but he didn't care much about robberies. The take from home robberies accounted only for a small portion of his enterprise's revenues. But he viewed the robbery operations as a type of training school – an opportunity for men with an entrepreneurial streak to run their own small businesses, to assemble and lead a team of their own. To plan and execute their own jobs. For those who demonstrated exemplary performance, home invasions were a stepping-stone to senior leadership in his organisation.

British knew that for Streggo, this wasn't about robbing some valuables from a rich man. Streggo wanted to show British he could plan and run key parts of his operations, that he could be promoted, given more responsibility and men of his own to lead. The stakes were high. If Streggo failed, he would suffer the consequences.

Streggo knew British left no room for mistakes.

Damian

So after we leave Eddie the taxi driver, Streggo and me reach the Boss house. Everybody who come there have to check in wid Chucky first. The first person we buck up on after we talk to Chucky is Clevon. We see him as we turn the corner. Clevon act like him is the boss already. Him even dress like British: pure name-brand clothes and ting. But him just look like a likkle boy trying on him fadda clothes. Clevon long and mawga like a clothesline.

'What yuh want to see mi fada for?' Him not looking at we 'cause him using a toothpick to dig out something from under him fingernail.

I tell him that we tell Chucky already and Chucky tell we to go inside.

'Fine, but now tell *me*,' Clevon say and puff out him chest like pigeon. Him want everybody to know him is British son and we must respect him. Streggo face screw up but him explain the plan.

Clevon say: 'Him expecting yuh?'

Streggo exhale loud-loud. 'No, but as mi say, we have a job—'

Clevon hold up him hand to shut him up.

'I going see if him can see yuh. Wait here.' Him go

strutting in front of we and push open the door. Him close it, leaving we standing in the hall. Him come out 'bout ten seconds later and say we must come.

'Daddy, dem men here to see yuh.' Clevon pull a chair and sit beside the Boss. 'Go ahead, Streggo,' him seh, like is him we come to.

'British,' Streggo say, 'we going catch a big fish. Richer than the rest of the Jack's Hill people.'

British just nod.

'Boss, a white man who just come from farin. With no security guard. It aggo tek time to plan but it going mek all the other small job dem look like joke.'

British rub him earlobe, like how him do when him thinking hard, stroking the diamond earring in him left ear. The stud look like a block of ice and shining like him bald head.

Streggo just stan' up there, him jaw slack, barely breathing, while we wait to hear British decision.

'What you think, Damian?' British ask.

All mi coulda do is stammer, 'I-I ...' Streggo shoot mi a wicked look. Him did tell mi already, just as we reach di Boss gate, how now is mi chance to show me is a man. And mi find miself thinking 'bout what it would be like to pull this off. To impress the Boss. The man who have a TV with VCR in every room and a satellite dish. Mi hear him have a toilet mek a pure gold. Money in plastic bags stack up like flour in him kitchen cupboard and a submachine gun inna di oven. Impress a man who drive a pretty, white BMW and have a silver Mercedes-Benz too – all with cassette player. Who have cellphone that fat like brick. Who all the girls love and who have nuff pickney and babymother. Mi suddenly find mi voice and say: 'Yes, British. Easy. Going be a good job. Wi already know the area.'

British nod again. We get the permission.

'Yuh need any men?' Clevon ask.

Streggo say: 'No, mi have that part cover. Is four a we. Mi going take mi usual crew and a new boy mi training.'

This make mi wonder. Mi know me and Streggo need String to pick the lock dem, but is who this new boy Streggo talking 'bout?

Mi thinking 'bout this when mi hear Streggo say to British: 'Wi going need a gun.'

Apollo

'Is it true what that lady said?' I ask my Moms at dinner the same Sunday night I get back from seeing Dinah. Moms looks confused, or pretends to be.

'What lady?' She slices through her salmon.

'The maid at the Browns.'

She's looking at me like I'm growing two heads.

'I mean, is she my real mother?' I shove a head of broccoli into my mouth. Moms drops the spoon she was serving rice with and it makes a loud bang on the plate.

'Apollo—' Pops says. And, for the first time ever, I say to him: 'No, you don't get to say anything now. I'm talking to my mom.' I mean, Pops is a good man and all, but sometimes he needs to shut the hell up.

Pops looks like he wants to say something but doesn't know where to start.

'It's fine, Ray.' Moms gives him her 'I'll handle this' look. She turns and stares at me the way she did when I was a kid that time we went to a picnic at one of Pops' friends' house, and I was playing by myself 'cause none of the other kids wanted to play with me. She'd asked me the same slow, deliberate question she was asking me now, with so much love and concern in it that it could break your heart: 'Son, are you OK?'

Still chewing, I say: 'I'm good. Just trying to figure out if I was kidnapped.'

Pops knocks over his glass and wine runs across the table-cloth to the vase at the centre of the table with the purple and white orchids. Moms drops her knife and fork like they've burnt her. I'm surprised the plate doesn't break. Pops dabs the corners of his mouth with his napkin. His hands are shaking. I see he is trying to contain his anger. His mouth is opening and closing like he's about to swallow the napkin.

Maybe it's the weed, maybe it's 'cause I'm sorry for Crazy Dinah, but I'm in a fighting mood.

'How come you don't have any pictures of you pregnant?' I look at Moms like I'm a cop and she's in interrogation.

'Are you serious right now, Apollo?' Moms says. Then for a long time, she doesn't say another word.

'Answer me.' It's when my palm hurts that I realise I'm pressing down hard on the mahogany table.

'Young man, remember your manners!' Pops says.

I raise an eyebrow and say nothing.

Moms exhales deeply. 'Look, Apollo, I told you about the fire at my parents' place. I was living with them and I lost all my pictures.'

'That's convenient.'

'Apollo, don't talk to your mother that way!' Pops snaps.

'But is she my mother though? You guys have lied to me before.'

I've gone too far. I know that I'm wounding her.

'This is ridiculous! Celeste, let me—'

'No, Raymond, let *me*.' She stares me down. 'Boy, I am your *Mama*. You are my son. That's it. End of story. Now you better get yourself together, child.'

I ignore her warning. 'Is Son-Son my real name?'

Moms' face is a chunk of ice now. I can't read it. It's like it belongs to someone I've never seen before. There's no soft-ness, no recognition there. No light in her eyes. I watch the lines in her face, creases that must have been there before but that I never saw. Her black hair has flecks of salt at the temples.

'That's it, go to your room!' Pops orders me.

'I ain't a little kid no more. I'm a grown-ass man. You can't ground me!'

'Then stop acting like a spoilt brat!' His face is the same colour as his wine.

'When did you leave Jamaica the first time, Raymond?' I shoot questions at him like accusations. 'Did you ever work for the CIA? What happened to your first wife, Raymond? The one you said died of breast cancer? Was she a skinny redhead? Did she teach literature? Did you guys ever live in Africa?'

Pops is gulping like a fish trying to swallow air. He sput-ters. 'Why are we even talking about this? Some ... some lunatic attacks you and now you think she's your *mother*?'

I leave the table. I'm not going to get the truth here.

I can hear Pops asking Moms: 'Celeste, what are we going to do?'

Up in my room, maybe it's the weed wearing off, but I don't feel so mellow any more. Everything hits me then and I'm freaking out. I'm replaying my time with Dinah and everything she said.

Mi did want yuh ... mi always did want yuh.

I dunno why but there's something about Dinah. Some connection I feel to this crying woman. Maybe her voice. Maybe something else. Maybe I just wanna help her find what she's lost. Her Son-Son. Maybe I just want to feel something.

That night I don't dream about the woman singing in the dark room.

Celeste

The maid I hired told me she has four kids already and she's only twenty-five. I marvelled at her.

'So how do you take care of them?'

We were sitting on the porch as I interviewed her.

'They stay with mi mother and mi work to provide fi dem,' she told me. 'That's why mi need this job. Please Miss, I beg yuh to give me the job. Mi can start right now.'

The other candidate is sixty-two, but looks eighty, and didn't seem to have the energy to handle a broom, much less clean a whole house on her own. I gave that one the job to relieve this new maid on her weekends off.

So far, the new maid, Jocelyn, is working well. She doesn't have the selective deafness of some staff, who pretend not to hear you calling, and she's willing to do whatever task I assign her. I decide that I'll add some extra money to her pay each week. Wages here are so low. I would never find a maid for this money in the States.

Jocelyn started the day after that disastrous dinner with Apollo. She didn't complain about handwashing the linen tablecloth with the giant wine stain. She's in the kitchen right now whipping up Jamaican food: curried chicken, yellow yam and white rice. She tells me it will put some flesh on my bones. I tell her I'm happy with my slender size at my age. Sometimes I catch Ray checking out my ass with a hungry look on his face. I must remind her not to get overly familiar. I'm not classist but people must know their place. As a maid, she has no business commenting on my weight.

At every opportunity, Jocelyn proudly shows me pictures of her sitting with the four young children: two are toddlers, straining to jump from her lap, and two are babies, held by their daddy. They're all in a single group shot. She says her boyfriend is a photographer's apprentice in downtown Kingston. The children all look like her. They have her dimples and strong chin. The same wide-set eyes. She's lucky.

I bet none of them will ever ask her who their real Mama is.

How do you convince your child that he's yours?

I think it's like trying to persuade somebody that you're not insane. The more forcefully you plead your case or argue the evidence, the more doubt you create in the hearer's mind. You're either sane or you're not. There's no half-way. Just like you can't be half-pregnant.

What makes a child yours, I mean *really* yours, anyway? Is it just his genes? Motherhood is more than a biological urge or instinct. It's more than carrying a baby for nine months. It's more than delivery, breastfeeding, nappy changing, first words, first step, tears, laughter and the peace you feel watching them sleep. It's more than being in constant awe of this little human who God has entrusted into your care.

Motherhood is a secret thing inside you: a quiet room that gets unlocked; a room that you didn't know existed in your heart before then.

Jocelyn calls from the kitchen door, instead of ringing the little bell I gave her. She says, 'Hurry up and come, I finish cook di dinner.'

I'm the only one who hears her shrill voice echoing

65

through the house, bouncing off the walls. Raymond is working in his study with the door closed and Apollo is off, God-knows-where.

I sit alone at the dining table, eating and not tasting a thing.

Apollo

The next time Apollo comes to Lazarus Gardens, almost a week after his first visit, the sun licks his cheek lazily; sweat scratches a path down his back, and drains from his armpits. The humidity has the stray dogs on their sides, too sunstruck to wag their tails. Their tongues hang from their mouths, blinking as they watch Apollo walk by. They don't bark this time, as if they know his connection to Dinah.

It's Friday. Apollo's eyes sting from burning rotten garbage and the strong smell of bleach coming from inside Dinah's house. A pink and black hog rummages in a pile of orange rinds in the gutter nearby. He pauses in the yard. He's changed out of the long-sleeved shirt and tie he'd worn at the firm that day and into T-shirt and jeans. Still, he is struggling with the heat.

Dinah pulls back the blue and yellow curtains, looks out the window and is shocked to see Apollo standing there, like an errant child placed outside on punishment, shifting tiny stones under the soles of his Nike sneakers. She rushes out to him. 'Hey,' he says, as if they have just picked up from talking yesterday. She wants to ask him where he's been for a whole week but doesn't. This is his home, she thinks – the place Son-Son would have grown up had he stayed with her – and she wants him to feel he can come at any time.

'Mi son!' she says.

He doesn't know what to call her so he simply says 'hello'. She has a mop in her hand.

'Mama just vomit so I have to clean it up. Come in. Come in. I wasn't expecting yuh today at all but I was waiting for yuh every day.'

He sits at the chair in the kitchen as she bangs the pots, filling one with water. She rifles through a cabinet for three green bananas and cuts off the ends to slit them down the middle to remove their skins.

'Now, the key to boiling green bananas is to put a likkle lime juice and salt in the water. Otherwise, they get black,' she tells him, as if he would ever one day decide to boil green bananas. 'Yuh eat tinned mackerel?'

He doesn't bother to say he's never had it before, and just nods his head. While the green bananas are cooking, she pulls her chair next to him.

'Son-Son, of late, I not feeling too well.'

He thinks about the prescription he brought her.

'Not in body, yuh see, but otherwise.' She quickly changes the subject. 'That's why yuh come back in good time. The right time. Mi want to get to know yuh. So, talk.'

'About what?'

'Talk to mi about yuh life. Mi nuh see yuh fi eighteen years. What it was like living with dem people? Yuh did happy?'

'I guess.'

'Why yuh have to guess? Yuh not sure?' She wrinkles her brow.

He thinks about how he can explain, looking around the kitchen to avoid the ferocity of her stare. The shelves are stacked neatly with old crockery. 'You know how in some people's houses they always got that one plate that don't really match the set? For me, growing up with Pops' family was like

68

that. Everyone around me was white flour and I was whole-wheat; you know what I mean? Some of them treated me like I had a skin disease, like I was some kinda rash they were scared of getting. When I'd go jogging in the neighbourhood in the mornings wearing my hoodie, a few times I'd see the neighbours jump when I'd run past them. Old white ladies crossing the street be holding on to their bags, like they think I'm gonna rob them or something. I mean, *come on*. My Air Jordans cost more than their bag.'

Apollo knows he's rambling but he can't stop talking. Something about Dinah's silence makes him want to fill the air. He notices that she measures her words carefully, like testing their weight on her tongue first.

Dinah stands up and puts on the kettle for tea, as Apollo continues: 'Growing up, I didn't know my real dad. My biological one . . . the one my Moms – I mean Celeste – told me about. A Black man named John King. It kinda sounds royal, doesn't it? A strong name. Moms said he was an only child. Orphaned when he was seventeen. He and Moms got married young and quick, so she didn't know much about his extended family.'

'So what about the rest of her family? I don't recall she ever mention dem one time.'

'Moms doesn't spend time with her own family in Georgia. They're pissed she married Ray instead of the guy they had picked for her: some guy who inherited a fortune from his parents' Black haircare company. White men like Ray once owned them, they said. But Moms said, those white men were a part of their ancestry too. That's why her family were so light skinned. They stopped talking to her and I never felt like bonding with them.

'So if you wanna know how I grew up, I didn't come up in the Projects. I'm not from "the hood". Other Black dudes say I ain't really a nigga, no matter how I talk like them. I'm all white on the inside. It's like I'm always in-between and I can't be comfortable anywhere.'

Dinah looks at him as she takes the whistling kettle off the gas ring, confusion on her face. Does she know, Apollo thinks, what America is really like?

'My Pops and his family got dough. Plenty. And money makes a difference. I got a BMW for my birthday when I turned sixteen and I ain't gonna lie: I wouldn't change that. I'm not gonna say I feel bad that I'm rich. The rappers and wanna-be gangsters on TV wanna be rich like white folks.'

'So yuh think "happy" and "money" are the same thing?'

'Nah. I could be happy in a place that's maybe not as rich but where Black people were the majority, running the place. That's why I wanted to come here. Plus Bob Marley is like my idol. Dude was conscious. His jams were sick. He was a *prophet*. Like he put into words what some of us can't say. There gotta be something magical in this place. And you see the women? Boy!'

'So is women yuh come here for then?' She places a chipped cup of mint tea in front of him and adds three heaping spoons of sugar. The sound of the spoon clanging against the sides of the cup is the only noise in the room.

'No, ma'am,' Apollo replies. He knows when it's best he shut up.

Outside, two brown-feathered chickens in the yard are fighting over something too small for him to see. Their writhing bodies and wings create a small dust cloud. A mangy grey cat chases them away.

Dinah studies his face and he feels uncomfortable. The scrutiny is so intense he glances away. He drinks his tea too fast.

'How yuh would describe the kinda fada yuh had?'

'Pops is strong. Tough. He gotta be in control of everything.'

'Everything, including yuh?'

'My folks don't really let me be free to be a man and figure out stuff on my own.'

'Being a man isn't about toughness, control, power or money. Dem never teach yuh that?'

Apollo doesn't answer.

Dinah gets up and jabs at the bananas with a fork. She looks up from the pot and smiles at him. 'Good. Dem ready.'

Regina

Apollo have pretty teeth. You know, like rich people teeth. No cavities. Not a one yellow, brown or black. None chipped or missing, neither. The teeth of somebody who have a dentist who use braces to straighten dem teeth. Not one gold tooth, not like every other wanna-be badman at Lazarus Gardens.

Is late Saturday afternoon and we here at Hellshire beach and he eating a piece of bammy. I going haffi show him how to hold it.

'Yuh don't eat fried bammy with knife and fork,' I tell him.

'It's hard to cut.' Him put down the knife and fork him was struggling with and mi watch him pretty teeth sink into the bammy. I tell him if him want it soft, him must order the steamed one next time.

I know this is not like the beach him was expecting. For one thing, is plenty likkle wooden shacks dotting the shore that selling all sorta fish, lobster and crab. The paint on the shacks in all kinda colour – red, green, black, yellow and some peeling from where the sun hit dem day after day and the nails holding the wood together rusty from the salty air. Yuh pick yuh fish from a white igloo packed with slabs of ice. I make sure Apollo don't pick any fish that eyes look cloudy, that's how yuh know dem catch it long time. They cook the food over charcoal and wood fire.

People selling watches from China, weed, wallets and all kinda Jamaican souvenirs, women walking up and down selling peppered shrimp, girls selling cologne, hair gel, matches, lighters, toothpicks, rags and towels. Boys leading horses asking if you want to pay for a horseback ride. Woman braiding white women hair into canerows and putting beads on the ends. Boom box playing dancehall music loud-loud and men selling bootleg cassettes. Is all business here. The locals in the water swimming and jumping up and down waiting on di fish dem order to fry.

'Man, I was expecting it to be more—'

'Quiet?' I finish him sentence. 'If is quiet yuh want, go Mobay. Not Kingston.'

Him ask mi if we can go into the water after we eat. I tell him yes, but it's not too clean. The grooms that work at Caymanas Racetrack take the horses from there and bathe dem in the water every morning, and the horses doo-doo on the sand and in the water too. Then yuh have the seaweed to contend with. People dump all sorta things into the water, I tell him. One time I even find a floating condom that mi did think was a jellyfish.

'Maybe another time,' him say. 'The food's good, though.' Him nibble on him parrot fish.

When him finish him other piece of bammy, Apollo ask mi how long mi know Damian.

I sip mi Sprite. It ice-cold, like I like it. Refreshing. 'About three years now, since I move to that yard.'

I don't tell him Damian is my dealer and when I don't have money, I trade myself.

'So what kinda dude is he?' Apollo asks.

What to say? Dreamer. Crafty. Hard-head. I take mostly

73

crack and weed; mi can't afford cocaine or heroin. Damian sell me cheap or sometimes just give mi for free. That's why when I short of money and Damian tell me to give a likkle hand-job to one of him bredrin, mi do it.

Him don't like when I use it though, which don't make no sense since him is a dealer. Him monitor how much mi take. Him keep mi on a strict supply. Damian get the drugs from Streggo and him crew who work for British.

I tell Damian I can stop anytime I want. Anytime. I not stopping now 'cause I don't have a reason. It make mi feel good and what so wrong with that? Feeling good is a nice thing. Nice like how Apollo looking at mi now as him sit beside mi at the table. Eyes shining. Him draw him chair closer.

Him have long eyelash, like a woman. Soft-looking lips. Him fingers tearing apart the next piece of bammy look clean and neat. No callouses or dirt under him nail. Apollo have a softness, not like Damian hard-edge. Mi think Damian's toughness is 'sake of him mother, Kathleen, and what she do to him but is not for me to tell Apollo the man business, especially since it's something Damian don't like to talk about.

I just tell Apollo that Damian sure him going be a big deejay some day.

'So what's the deal with Dinah?'

I know Dinah is a good lady. Better than mi mother, Bubbles, fi sure. Dinah look after people.

'She OK.' I break off the head of my fried snapper. I love to suck the eyeballs. Dem remind mi of likkle black beads. Apollo screw up him face. I tell him the head is the best part of the fish.

Him offer mi fi him own. 'Here,' him say. 'I can't eat it.'

I tell him I help Dinah by looking out fi her mother when Dinah gone on the road.

'Oh you mean that crazy old lady?'

I tell him 'yeah'. What I don't say is that I kinda 'fraid of Mama sometimes. Whenever she in her right mind, she say some things weh make her sound like a prophet. She see things that most people can't see. I rub mi eye as the wind whip up a likkle sand and blow it across the table.

Then Apollo come out and tell mi straight: 'So you know, Dinah thinks I'm her son?'

How mi must know? I tell him, truth be told, mi never hear Dinah mention a pickney before and I always wonder why a woman her age never breed. I never ask her though. Dinah not the talkative type. People like that always full of secrets they don't even want to tell dem own self. But a mother must know her own child.

Mi watch a likkle girl throw a red and white ball to a boy a likkle taller than her. The boy miss it and the wind blow it into the sea. The girl start bawl and the boy try to hug her and then him dive in the water after it. But the ball look like it land on a current that carry it far-far out, too far for the likkle boy to reach. A woman, probably the girl's mother, on the shore shouting after the boy, who bobbing like a likkle dot in the water.

'If it's true and I'm her son, it'd be too crazy, right?'

Apollo don't realise that crazy things happen in this life. Trust mi, I know. Like me and a man like him, sitting here eating fish.

I did see Apollo when him come back to the tenement yard yesterday to see Dinah. I catch him as him was leaving, walking down the steps. I was just coming from the corner shop. All I had in the bag was a likkle saltfish and flour fi make fritters.

'Hey,' I say, real casual, like I don't care if him answer or not, but I make sure to stand close to him, in my tight blouse and jeans miniskirt, so close that mi know him could smell mi nice perfume Mr Mack just buy fi me. 'The Scent of Roses' or something so, it name. I was so glad Mr Mack was at work.

Apollo look a likkle frighten and I see him don't know what to say. Him was staring at a spot on the ground.

I say what I know him thinking: 'Yuh want to see mi again?'

'Yeah, I wanna go out with you,' him say. Mi know right there-so, mi have him, and him didn't even know it yet.

As I move past him, mi say: 'Pick mi up tomorrow.'

◆

Is why Black people from farin think that dem know anything about the life of Black people in Jamaica? 'Cause we have the same skin and we ancestor get tief from the same place? I know Black people over there get plenty bad treatment from the police and some white people, fi sure. But dem don't know a thing about the life of a sufferer in Jamaica trying to put food on the table.

Apollo say dem have poor Black people in America. People who live from paycheque to paycheque and can't pay dem rent and have to sleep in dem car under a bridge, or have to go to supermarket and buy food in grocery stores using government food stamps. Is then I realise that Jamaica-poor and America-poor is two different kinda poor. Which poor person in Jamaica have car or can buy a trolley-full of food in the supermarket like regular people? In school, we had to satisfy with the taste-bad Nutri-bun and bag-milk the government used to send to the school for dem who couldn't find breakfast or lunch. Sometimes is that alone I eat for the day.

So I hardly listening when Apollo talking about how Emperor Haile Selassie of Ethiopia came to Jamaica in 1966, how Marcus Garvey woulda been proud that Jamaica get its independence from England so Black people can rule dem-selves, that is the fight for equality weh land Nelson Mandela in jail in South Africa and how I must read a book by some-man name Rodney called *How Europe Underdeveloped Africa*.

'Garvey said that without confidence in self our people are twice-defeated in the race of life.' Him swallow down him Red Stripe beer.

I don't know much about Garvey, Mandela, Rodney and all of dem. Equality and confidence is all well and good. All I know is that Black people also need money in dem pocket. What's the use of dem highfaluting ideals if yuh belly empty? If yuh can't take yuh woman out to eat some fish and bammy at Hellshire?

Apollo can say whatever him want to say, 'cause him have money. Is money set him lips flapping in the breeze on this fine day in Kingston.

When him done talking, I just nod, order a Red Stripe and ask him, 'Why a guy like yuh take a risk and come to a place like Lazarus Gardens?'

Apollo eye widen and I see him taking this as him chance to impress mi. 'I wasn't scared. I guess I'm kinda reckless.'

I raise mi eyebrow. 'So yuh is a trouble maker?'

'You saying you like bad boys?'

I tell him yes, 'cause bad boys like Damian excite mi. Mi bat mi eyelid dem and ask: 'So *yuh* bad?'

'Sometimes.' Him smile, and mi can't help but catch it and smile back when him flash dem teeth. 'Like when I was fifteen and borrowed the car. First off, it's not my fault they left the keys in the ignition. Unattended. What kinda parents do that with a kid in the house?'

'What kinda car it was?'

'My Pops' new convertible. I was in the garage, looking for

something in one of the boxes, minding my own business. I saw the window down and the keys practically begging me like: "Come on, Apollo, you know you wanna." Next thing I know, I'm doing a hundred on the freeway.'

'Kiss mi neck!'

Apollo stare at mi a minute. I make sure to smile.

'Is just a saying. Yuh really go so fast?'

'Top down. Pressing gas. Tyres eating up the road. Wind on my face, the radio going so loud, I'm not hearing myself think, which is exactly what I wanted. The rush. The speed. The excitement. When the cops brought me home after the car ended up in a ditch, upside down, Moms was like: "Apollo, Ray and I were worried sick! You could have died! What were you thinking?" But I didn't have a scratch on me. I was mad 'cause the white cop who found me in the ditch after the accident saw a young Black dude and thought I musta stolen the car. It had to have been jacked. I told him it belonged to my Pops and said Raymond's name. He didn't believe me. I kept my cool, though. Moms taught me that. Always remain calm when dealing with the police. When I got outta the wrecked car, I kept both hands visible. Didn't run or resist.'

'So what happen next?'

'I convinced him to take me home to see I was telling the truth. The wrecker took away the car. And when we pulled up into our driveway, I saw the cop's eyes widen when he saw the mansion. Ray came out and, all of a sudden, there was lots of "I'm sorry sir, didn't realise he was your boy, sir". Helmet in hand. It made me sick. My stomach was churning. I had gotten into the liquor cabinet before I liberated the car. I threw up on Ray's white shoes!'

Mi couldn't believe it. Mi laugh, but inside mi thinking if Bubbles was him mother, she woulda did kill him. And

I wondering what the mansion look like. At fifteen mi was already living with Mr Mack.

'So the police really never lock yuh up?'

'Nah,' him say. 'Pops made it go away. He said my criminal record would remain spotless but I was grounded for like five months.'

Then him tell mi that something about Jamaica make him feel the same rush. The excitement. That something under the surface waiting to get yuh. The energy of the people. Reminding him that him alive. That's why it don't really matter to him when him mother say: 'Don't go out alone in Jamaica. It's not safe. You don't know this place. Always have someone with you.' Or when him fadda say: 'Remember, curiosity killed the cat.'

'Like I care!' him say.

So that is why him seek out Dinah in the first place. 'Cause him mother did warn him 'you need to stay away from that woman'.

'And I knew then, I had to go,' Apollo say.

It look like him not so boring after all. Maybe him seeing the shock on mi face I trying to hide.

Him lean forward and run him hands on the plastic table-cloth. 'I know we only just met, and I only have five months in Jamaica but ... I gotta say, Regina, I like you. I think you're cool. Would you be my girl?'

Mi let him sweat a likkle in the pause before mi answer. I lean back in the chair and look at the clouds, like I have to give it serious thought.

'Yeah,' mi finally say and give him a smile. Him look as happy as mi expect him to be.

'Damn, girl! I love your beautiful smile,' him say. 'I wanna see more of it.'

When I get back home, Damian watching mi funny. I

don't tell him where I went, although is no secret the Yankee boy interested in mi.

When food don't get eat, it serve another master, as my mother used to say.

Apollo & Dinah

Lazarus Gardens, Dinah thinks, *is a place of bones.*

Families lucky enough to afford chicken-back for dinner grind the bones to mush, working their jawbones hard. Mangled chicken bones – sucked dry of juices and crushed between eager gums – litter lanes full of grey frothy water lapped up by thirsty dogs. The dogs' ribs are sharp and painful to see. Even the pregnant dogs with their distended bellies look like walking bones under skin.

Men and women who can barely afford chicken-back got their own bones creaking under back-breaking work: road-building, gathering and moving big stones for bridges, skinny-armed nannies hoisting squealing, chubby children up in the air, kicking fat legs, while their parents ignore them. Helpers like Dinah carrying their burdens in their chest, bones under tight skin, stress encased in tendons binding muscle to bone in faces where smiles don't reach the eyes.

Bones, bones, bones and more bones, Dinah thinks, sucking her teeth. She lights the gas stove with a match and flicks her right wrist where she feels some stiffness.

That Saturday, she sees Damian and Apollo talking and laughing. Apollo coughs between laughs. String arrives.

Dinah purses her lips as she watches Damian and String talk then go through the gate, leaving Apollo behind.

From the kitchen, she says: 'I hear yuh just sneezing and coughing out there, I going mix up a cocktail of local herbs that good to battle a cough – boiled dandelion, black sage, and chaney root.'

Apollo is on a seat near the front step of the tenement yard. Inside is hot in a way he has never experienced heat. Sitting in the shade of the mango tree gives some relief, though the stench of rotten fruit is stifling. The fruits get eaten by worms before they hit the ground.

Dinah comes back from the kitchen with the tea, a bitter brew that Apollo tastes, making a face into the black liquid. He spits on the ground.

'Yuck! That's horrible! No thanks. I'll stick with the coughing.'

'But suppose is the flu?'

'I'll live. I'll do anything but drink *that*.'

Dinah takes back the cup and sniffs it. In truth, it smells bitter in a way she has never noticed before.

'Probably just my allergies acting up. Nothing an Advil can't cure. It must be the change in weather,' Apollo says. 'Geez! Is it always so hot here?'

When Dinah nods, Apollo cracks his fingers absentmindedly. Dinah listens to the cracking sound of bones. She gets him some cool water and wonders how to say what she has to say.

'Son-Son, what yuh want to do with yuh life?' She takes a seat on the ground next to him.

'I'm gonna be a lawyer one day. I just started an internship at a law firm a couple weeks ago. It's been good. Mainly lots of paperwork though.'

'Why law?'

'I wanna help people.'

She chooses her words carefully. 'Mi know that a lawyer can't mix up inna badness ... I notice yuh and Damian together ...'

'Yeah, we've been hanging out whenever I come to see you or Gina.'

'Him ever ask yuh to do anything?'

'Anything like what?'

'Everybody around here know Damian sell drugs, Son-Son.'

'I don't use drugs, Dinah, I mean – apart from a little weed ...'

'Smoking that is the least of what mi worried 'bout. I don't want yuh to mash up yuh future. Damian involved with some bad people.'

She kicks at a rotten mango with her toe and feels a sharp pain in her bone; her kneecap. The mango juice leaves a wet trail in the dust, like a moving snail. 'Yuh know how yuh tell the difference between a mango tree, a orange tree and a breadfruit tree?'

'I dunno. The leaves look different, I suppose.'

Dinah watches him shrug and shift in his seat. A small wind stirs up some dust at her feet and the smell of dirt clogs her nostrils.

'Yuh tell the trees apart by the fruit. Judge people by their actions. What they produce ... yuh can trust mi. I'm yuh modda. I know yuh was going come back to mi in Jamaica 'cause yuh navel string bury in this island. As yuh modda, I giving yuh this warning: stay away from Damian. Is for yuh own good.'

'Dinah, you know, 'cause of how I was raised, I don't have a lotta Black friends. You wouldn't know what that's like.'

'Son-Son, that don't mean yuh need a friend like Damian ...'

'You know I went to school with loads of rich white kids? I was rich too but I still never really fit in. My only friend was this skinny Jewish kid, Michael. We did everything together. Then one day, when we were about sixteen, he gets invited to a party by this popular kid, and in the locker room I overhear the guy say Michael can come but I can't. "People got to stick to their own." I thought Michael would stand up for me. I thought he'd choose me. But he didn't. He let me down. He went to the party and lied about it. That's when I knew race meant everything to some people. And Damian – he's the first friend I can talk to about all this stuff . . . and about music. He's a cool guy. He's my friend.'

Dinah simply said: 'Let mi get yuh something to eat. Is food yuh need in yuh body.'

He nodded, although he knew food could not fix the unease inside him.

The aroma of onions frying in coconut oil on the battered old gas stove tickled his nose. The stove was a dull green. She chopped up scotch bonnet pepper, sweet peppers and threw in some thyme. She opened a can of corned beef, then added black pepper.

Apollo read the empty corned beef can. 'You know how much sodium is in this? You Jamaicans sure love your salt!'

'Son-Son, salt preserved slave food on the sugar cane plantations. They never had no fridges then, so the salt cured the meat in barrels. Corned pork. Saltfish, which is cod that come on ships and get send all the way from Canada . . .'

'And that's why y'all have so much high blood pressure right now. The slave diet is killing you. You're not on the plantation any more! Garvey was trying to get you guys to see that.'

'We develop a taste for it. Yuh don't break out of it just like that. We're slaves to the choices we make. Plus dem kinda food is the cheapest. Why yuh think we still eat it? Is what we can afford and we still on the plantation in some kinda way. Slaves never had two cents to rub together and people out here still living from hand to mouth ... Son-Son, the Book of Proverbs say that "the poor man and the oppressor have this in common: The Lord gives light to the eyes of both" and God have eyes too. Look, yuh see what I doing in the pot? Yuh take the fork and mash out the corned beef like this when yuh cooking it.'

'You trying to teach me how to cook?' What he didn't say was: his people had housekeepers and cooks to do that.

'What I know about teaching yuh man things?' Dinah replied. 'I can only teach yuh what I know. We starting in the kitchen. We going cover the basics. When frying fish, season with salt and pepper only and don't put flour on the fish until yuh ready to fry it. And never ever fry callaloo with oil in a frying pan. Callaloo suppose to steam with butter in a pot. Don't overboil ackee until it too soft, and yuh have to soak saltfish overnight before cooking it, and boil it two time to remove the salt. Yuh flake it and remove the bones and fry it up in the frying pan in oil before you add the ackee—'

'No offence Dinah, but why I gotta know all that stuff?'

'To do big things, Son-Son, yuh have to start by doing the likkle things well.'

Celeste

So this morning Raymond grabs a bagel with smoked salmon and cream cheese, gives me a quick kiss on the cheek and speeds off in the Benz. He tells me he's late for a meeting but Ray is hardly ever late. I know he doesn't want to deal with what's happening with Apollo. He needs breathing space and I get that. I want it too. Raymond tells me not to worry, it's just teenage rebellion. He says it's going to be fine. But I don't know that I believe him. I don't know if he believes it, either. The question bouncing around in my head is: *What if it's not a phase?* What happened to my little sweet boy?

I'm thinking about how I'm going to spend my day. I realise I am bored. Maybe I'll go for a quick jog. I'm meeting Cindy Brown later for tennis. She says she has a great instructor. Maybe I can check into volunteering some time at a local school. I don't like having too much idle time on my hands. I was happy to quit my job to raise Apollo as a stay-at-home mom but when he's off to college, will the days yawn into each other like an unending tunnel?

Jocelyn tidies up the kitchen in a flash and I tell her to iron the linen tablecloth as well as the linen placemats. 'The curtains too?' she asks and I tell her to go ahead. I hate creases.

I go sit on the porch and count the cars passing by on the

street. Jamaicans don't seem to like American cars. I haven't seen a single Cadillac here.

My Papa loved Cadillacs. He told me he loved their power and beauty. A Cadillac took up space and whenever you'd go driving in that big, beautiful car, what people would do is stop and stare and say: 'Man! Would you look at that car? Whoo-wee, ain't she sweet?'

And my Papa would puff out his chest just a little bit more. My Papa wasn't generally a showy man but when it came to his Cadillacs, Papa was proud.

My childhood gave me the feeling like I was a Cadillac. Not so much the beauty and power part but feeling possessed. That I was a thing to be shown off. I was a good girl. Smart. Did the right things. Mama and Papa told their friends and business associates how well I did at everything. How great my grades were. And people would say: 'Ooh! Would you look at that report card! You got a bright one here and so well-mannered too!'

Mama used to tell me all the time: 'Celeste, don't you slouch, sit up straight!' Then she sent me to ballet.

Mama said I was clumsy, always dropping her precious things, so she made me do piano lessons to learn how to control and synchronise my fingers.

'Ladies don't run, Celeste! I ain't raising no floozy! You better slow down in this house.' Then she told our maid, Harriet, to keep an eye on me.

Mama hardly ever spanked me, but she'd get so angry and yell and send me to my room. And sometimes I wished she'd just hit me because at least then she'd touch me. Papa was gone a lot of the time. He was always at work or out at some business meeting.

Harriet, my nanny, was calm and kind. She wore a dark grey uniform with a starched white collar and she always made me laugh. At work, she was proper enough not to set Mama off.

Off duty, in her room, Harriet played cards, smoked cigars and had a way of singing blues songs I knew Mama wouldn't have liked me to sing. When she giggled she threw her head back, showing all her teeth, like she was opening herself to the sky. She made me feel like she was interested in everything I had to say. When I was seven, a girl pushed me off a swing at the school playground, breaking my ankle, and Harriet would lay in the bed with me and read me Enid Blyton books. She knew my favourite one was *The Adventures of Mr Pink-Whistle*. When my leg was better, she showed me how to dance the jitterbug.

When I found a stray kitten, she helped me hide it in my room for weeks, 'cause Mama had a 'no pets in the house' rule. And when Mama heard meowing and got rid of it, Harriet was the one who held me when I bawled.

Mama sent her away when I was eight. I think it was because Harriet and I were getting too close.

Mama never told me I was special or that she loved me. I always felt something was at war within my Mama. Mama's great-grandfather was white and owned plantations and her grandmother had a child for a white man, a girl who became Mama's mother. Mama had a grand-uncle who was lynched by the KKK, had seen crosses burning in her cousins' yards, grew up with signs that said NO NEGROES ALLOWED. She wasn't free to go to school, eat, sit, ride the bus or train, use the bathroom or drink from a water fountain unless it was designated for 'coloreds'. Mama's folks owned shares in Marcus Garvey's Black Star Line before it went belly-up in the 1920s. Treasured their UNIA cards.

Mama taught me about Jim Crow laws along with my ABCs. I grew up knowing all about 'separate but equal'.

Marches. Sit-ins. Bus boycotts. Mama gave money to the causes of Martin Luther King Junior and Malcolm X, though she thought Malcolm a bit too radical. I was ten when Emmett Till was killed for flirting with a white woman in Mississippi and Rosa Parks got arrested in Montgomery.

And it was as if Mama was always uncomfortable with both parts of herself. We possessed and we were possessed. We were slaver and enslaved. The hand squeezing the throat, and the throat itself too. Mama felt too conflicted to be happy.

Her ancestors, she told me, had been freed Blacks during the time of slavery. Ones who had paid for or were gifted the freedom they should have been born with. But they enjoyed their freedom, these mulattoes, while other Blacks toiled in cotton fields. Some passed for white. 'We are survivors, Celeste,' Mama told me. 'Never forget that. Know who you are.'

James Baldwin said, 'To be African American is to be African without any memory and American without any privilege.' I understood, in some ways, what he meant.

I disappointed my parents by the men I loved. Because I had forgotten who I was: a rich Black girl. *Their* rich Black girl.

Eloping with John was a dent on the veneer of the perfect life my parents had fashioned for me. Marrying Ray meant I'd crashed the whole damn car.

◆

A month before we came to Jamaica, Mama's sister, Auntie Rose, called.

I wondered how she got our number. She told me my Mama had died from a heart attack. And she was letting me know 'as a courtesy', that was exactly how she said it, and then she made it clear they didn't want me at the funeral. I didn't know why it wasn't Papa who was calling to tell me the news. The man who, when I was a little girl, would set me on his lap and make me pretend to drive his precious Cadillac. He'd say 'put on your turn signal, baby girl. Hold the steering wheel like this.'

The click on the other end of the phone line came before I could even ask.

Mama

Mi de yah under the lime tree watching a pigeon peck at a piece of old bread and wondering: if somebody sew yuh throat-hole shut, yuh still have a voice? When yuh shout, dem can hear?

When mi did small, mi modda give mi a magic pot that she pour words into. She just drop dem in. A whole heap of dem. Yuh shoulda see dem tumbling down.

I going boil a pot for Dinah. She need the right words for what she have to face.

Dinah pot of trouble bubbling up.

Apollo & Dinah

Dinah and Apollo sat at a small table in Dinah's section of the tenement yard. It was a Saturday morning and the sun's brightness streamed in across the table. In the air was the faint, smoky, sour smell from the Riverton City landfill.

Earlier that morning, Apollo had called Eddie to pick him up since Raymond was using the car. 'How's it going, man?' Apollo asked once he'd slid into the passenger seat.

'Sometimes coffee, sometimes tea,' Eddie replied, which meant business was up and down. 'Mi have plenty moves to make today.'

From inside Eddie's taxi, Apollo had noticed egrets following a tractor in the dump, greedily eyeing the upturned garbage in its wake. Men with handkerchiefs around their noses were sorting through the waste, securing metal and discarded valuables for their families. Dogs and pigs sifted through the trash for food.

Eddie overtook overstuffed buses with people standing on the bus step, hanging from windows as it blared music to deafen the ears of everyone on the street. Eddie's Lada careened around sharp corners, nearly crashing into a crimson Vauxhall Viva and a baby blue Morris Oxford Farina. Apollo gripped the plastic seat until his fingers felt numb.

Eddie honked through a pedestrian crossing with a man standing on the side of the road.

'That man was trying to cross,' Apollo chided him.

'Cho! Him is not a pickney or old woman. Him can always run 'cross.'

Apollo watched a Rastaman selling thatch brooms on his bicycle shouting 'Broom-man!' and 'Broomieeeee!' A woman in a yellow VW Bug pulled over to buy one. Eddie nearly crashed into her car.

Apollo was thankful to have made it safely to Lazarus Gardens. His stomach had finally settled from the nausea of the drive.

Dinah made him a typical Jamaican breakfast: tinned mackerel, callaloo, boiled yam and banana and cornmeal porridge with buttered hard dough bread. There was chocolate tea in an enamel cup to wash it down and a side plate full of star-shaped slices of jimbilin fruit. Happiness filled her chest. Today, her son would have a proper breakfast.

The last time he had come to visit her, she'd asked him what kind of porridge he liked having at breakfast. Did he prefer cornmeal, hominy corn, plantain, banana, oats, peanut or rice porridge?

'Nah, I don't really do porridge. I like bacon, eggs, pancakes, waffles, things like that.'

She'd looked at him like he was an alien. *Who don't drink porridge fi breakfast?* she wondered. What kind of animals had raised her child, Americanising him to the point he didn't know what a real good Jamaican breakfast tasted like? How yuh could start your day without that solidness cemented in yuh belly? When she was pregnant, she ate lots of cornmeal porridge to build up her strength, so she decided that would be the first porridge she made for him.

The porridge was just one point of difference between

them. There were others, like the fact that he preferred Horlicks to the Milo she loved. She made him a cup of both and after sipping, he nodded gravely like a judge deciding a case and pronounced Horlicks the better beverage. The last time he came she had tried teaching him to dance tambu. Mama had learnt it in Congo Town. Dinah explained to Apollo that this was how the ancestors had danced in the old days, when slavery had muzzled their mouths but the drum's tongue spoke for them. She stood behind him and held his hips with her hands. But the boy couldn't gyrate his waistline! She tried to show him the different tambu movements: the mabumba – that shaky motion resembling a violent sea and the shay shay – call and response. But it was like his head was stone! She tried to tell him history was important or people would vanish. Just like the bammy she cooked for him: a cassava cake that was one of the only things left behind of the Taino people, the original Jamaicans.

But Apollo's long fingers couldn't beat a drum. He couldn't feel the music in his soul, as an extension of himself. He shuffled away at the end of the awkward dance lesson. She gave him an abeng owned by her great-grandfather who was a Maroon and he looked at the cow horn blankly. 'Yuh blow it,' she'd said. 'This used to be yuh ancestor dem tongue! Dem use it to carry news of rebellion.'

Now they sat around the table both looking at the steaming pool of yellow cornmeal in his bowl. Time for another part of his Jamaican education. Dinah liberally sprinkled brown sugar over the top and made a series of concentric white circles with the Betty condensed milk. He watched her chubby wrist as she held the tin in the air, circling like a helicopter.

'Drink up, son,' she smiled.

Apollo didn't know what to say. How could he tell her that what he really wanted was an omelette?

Gingerly, he took up the spoon she'd placed on his plastic blue and white placemat. His mother was a germophobe who always told him never to eat from strangers. Though the cupboard was half-eaten by termites, Dinah's kitchen was tidy. The cutlery was old but clean. The kitchen counter was spotless, the plates piled neatly, glistening utensils stacked in order, salt and pepper shakers like generals overlooking a parading army.

He scooped up some of the porridge and plopped it into his mouth. He hadn't blown on it and it burnt his tongue. 'Hush,' she cooed to soothe him and offered him some cow's milk. After he recovered, Dinah blew on his spoon this time.

It was good! He savoured the taste of vanilla, almond, cinnamon and nutmeg floating on his tongue. 'Man, this porridge is dope!' He blew on each scooped spoon the way Dinah had shown him.

'Yuh know yuh talk funny?'

'I'm sorry?'

'Like yuh not really being yuhself. Like yuh never sure of the right words. Like yuh performing, depending on where yuh is.'

'I don't get you.'

'Yuh do. Yuh understand. For boys 'round here that role playing is bad-man or gunman. For the girls, is a sketel, having plenty man and pickney all over the place.' She put a hand over his. 'Yuh don't need to pretend with me, Son-Son. Yuh can be who yuh want. Not say what yuh think people want to hear or how dem want yuh to say it.'

There was an awkward silence as he drank. Dinah was saying nothing, just staring at him as if seeing him for the first time.

The faded yellow curtain shifted gently in the slight breeze blowing in from the dusty yard. A fly tried to dunk itself into the remnants of Dinah's now cold chocolate tea. Another flitted across the plastic tablecloth. There was only the sound of Apollo blowing and swallowing.

'Dinah, I've been meaning to talk to you about something.'

'Mi listening, son.'

'My parents, um, Celeste and Raymond, say you're not really my mother ... I told you before that our surname isn't Steele.'

'Nuh matter. Remember mi tell yuh that people say Mr Steele was a secret agent wid the CIA so Steele probably wasn't dem real name.'

'OK, but the thing is, you got anything like an old picture or paper with their handwriting on it or something?'

Dinah's eyes lit up.

'Yes! Mi have a book. Dem did give mi before dem go back to America!'

She disappeared from the room and returned with a yellowed, dog-eared book of the collected poems of John Keats.

Dinah blew off the dust and wiped it on her skirt before handing it to Apollo, eyes dancing. She was bouncing from leg to leg. 'Yuh going see is truth mi talking! Mrs Steele give mi this. Long time mi don't read it.'

Apollo turned to the title page. Instead of the long elegant swirls of Celeste's handwriting, there was a single word in block letters 'ENJOY!' above the initials 'CS'. The first few pages had some scribbles, but it was hard to make out any of the words.

Apollo flipped through the pages. There was no other handwriting, just marks underlining lines from several poems.

'Dinah ... just 'cause it's my mom's – I mean, Celeste's – initials, doesn't mean—'

The door flew open. Damian walked in, whistling a tune.

'Mawnin', Miss Dinah,' he said, grinning broadly. 'Wah gwaan?' Dinah uttered a faint 'good morning' in response.

'Yo,' Apollo mumbled.

'Weh yuh a say, my yute?' He addressed Apollo. 'Wah happen, blood?'

Apollo replied: 'Yes, King' and they knocked fists.

Damian pulled up a chair next to him. 'How's my American brother doing?' Damian said, adopting an American twang.

Apollo didn't return Damian's smile.

'Hear wha', mi just done write two new song for mi album. Going soon get some money to book studio time.'

'That's great, Damian, but—'

'Yuh want something to eat?' Dinah asked. Damian nodded. Dinah turned to the stove to pour another bowl of cornmeal porridge and Damian followed her with his eyes. His gaze rested on her round rump.

'Yow, yuh modda is a good-looking woman,' Damian whispered. He was tapping his feet to a beat only he could hear. 'Yuh know she look more betta than nuff of dem young girls? She make dem look like dem nah try.'

Something rose up in Apollo's throat. Damian was all arms and limbs, sprawled out like he owned the place. Belonged there. Looking at Dinah like that. The skin on Apollo's arms started to itch.

'Apollo, I going see yuh at the dance on Friday, right? Mi aggo perform a song from mi debut album.'

'Damian, we were having a private conversation, man,' Apollo said. He instantly regretted how mean it sounded. But Damian just smiled wider.

'Is alright, man. We is all family in this yard.' He beat out a rhythm on the table and tapped his feet.

'*Mummy*,' Apollo said, emphasising the word and ignoring Damian, 'this book isn't—'

'Hold on, son,' Dinah interrupted, her back still turned. When she was done filling the bowl, she put it down on the table in front of Damian with force.

'Thanks, Miss Dinah.'

'I been wanting to talk to yuh, Damian, so mi glad yuh come.' She came closer to him and placed a hand on his right shoulder.

'Mi always used to see yuh as a mannersable young man.' Her eyes locked with his. 'But I want to know what yuh doing wid mi son!'

Before Damian could stammer out an answer, she continued, her voice getting louder with each word: 'I don't want him wid bad company. Yuh think I don't notice yuh spending time with that no-good Streggo? Is what kind of life him leading yuh to, boy? I know unnu mix up with British!'

Damian was silent, his lips pressed together in a thin dark line.

'Mi say mi don't want mi son turning nuh criminal!' Dinah came closer to Damian's face, her spittle a fine mist on his left cheek. She pointed a finger at him. 'Answer mi!'

'Dinah, chill out!' Apollo got up and put his arms around her.

Damian stood up and pushed away the porridge. His chair fell over to its side. 'Miss Dinah, mi respect yuh, ennuh, and mi grateful fi what yuh did fi mi when mi modda leave but don't yuh ever talk to mi that way again!' He wiped his cheek with a red handkerchief. 'Mi not some likkle bwoy and if yuh know what good fi yuh—'

'What?' Dinah hissed. 'Tell mi, *if* yuh name man! Mi nuh 'fraid of yuh!'

Damian stood wordlessly, his jaw clenching. He took a step towards her.

'Damian,' Apollo said evenly. 'You gotta go.'

'Mi nuh need dis foolishness.'

'Just go, Damian!' Apollo said firmly. Dinah began to cry, out of frustration. She hugged Apollo tightly, her tears soaking his shirt.

Regina

Lately, Regina has been wondering: *Is so farin man frighten fi pum-pum? Dem behave funny after a likkle sex. Like dem nuh used to it.* Apollo acting so clingy and foolish, like a likkle puppy.

Her first time, she was thirteen and British had given her an ice-cold Pepsi to drink. She had never had Pepsi before, just syrup or sugar with water or bag juice. The bottle felt huge in her hands. It was so cold she felt her palms sticking to it. It tasted bitter. He took the bottle from her hand, tracing the rim with a wet tongue.

She had never seen a man's penis before and it peeped out from the opening at the front of his boxers like a turtle's head. Just the week before, she'd seen two dogs get stuck while mating and she and the neighbourhood boys had stoned the whining creatures. Regina was living with Bumper's sister and British sent one of his men to the house to tell her the way it was for all the girls in Lazarus Gardens when they turned thirteen.

British put her on her back and she remembered pounding on his chest with her fists but it was like trying to bore holes into a zinc fence. He put both her wrists together with his one right hand and held them above her head. He punched her and she stopped struggling. His eyes were molasses-thick, obscene, slick like a dog's tongue, moving across her chest, chilling her skin as her own gaze unspooled.

She remembers the pains and after, the blood. He had used the tip of the empty bottle inside her.

He taught her something valuable: what all men desperately wanted could be found inside her vagina. That was her power and she was going to trade that thing they craved for everything she wanted to get. Sometimes, when she was in a good mood, she wanted money for hairdos or clothes for a dance, new shoes. Other times, it was drugs to dull the pain. She felt pity for the grown men trying to find themselves in the space between her legs. Pity, even for the freaky ones who wanted to stick their tongues where her doo-doo came out. Some of the men were so rough, squeezing her neck so tight she had to wonder: *Dem want to screw mi or kill mi? Dem either strangle yuh or box off yuh head.*

It had only been a couple weeks but already she could see that Apollo was not like the other men. She still asked for and got money from him, but he did things differently. He wrote her poetry. Bad poetry that compared her breasts to clay mounds rising up like the Blue Mountains and her kiss to coconut water and that he thought about her all the time and wanted to spend all his waking moments with her. He bought her a yellow and green bikini and said it would be for when they could go to a nice beach in Montego Bay and lie on a hammock.

'Mi can't swim,' she said.

'But you live on an island! How come?' He was stunned.

'Mi just never learn. I stand in the water up to my chest.'

Apollo used a phrase Damian had taught him. 'Nuh worry, man. Everything irie. I'll teach you.'

Apollo took her on the roller coaster, tilt-a-whirl, scrambler and bumper cars at Coconut Park and when she threw up after the last ride, he held her hair back. They went to Carib theatre in Cross Roads to see movies. He bought her popcorn and nachos. They lay on their backs on the lawns of Devon House and Hope Gardens letting the greenness get into their pores. They went to the Bob Marley Museum – it was her first time – and he told her how Bob Marley reminded him of the things a Black man had to take a stand for.

Apollo bought her *flowers*. Six long-stemmed red roses. The first time he brought them she'd said: 'Wah dat?'

'Can't you see they're roses? You've never got flowers before?'

'No. Wah mi fi do wid dat?'

'Put them in some water. In a vase.' He searched the communal kitchen and found none.

'Mi nuh used to dem something deh,' she said, crossing her arms and watching him, feeling defensive and foolish.

Apollo found an empty Pepsi bottle, filled it up at the standpipe and placed the flowers inside. He put them on the table in the small kitchen. The flowers rested there, like an accusation.

'Dem cyaan stay here,' she said flatly, like he'd brought in unwelcome guests and asked her to house them.

'Look, just keep them here to ... to *beautify* the place. Every time you see them, think about me.'

When he'd left, she threw the roses in the overflowing garbage skip outside and restored the dusty yellow and pink plastic flowers in the Milo tin to their former position on the table.

Apollo brought her expensive chocolates and red and white teddy bears, which she gave away to the children next door. He brought her a kitten next, a long-haired white Persian he called Maximillian.

'Wah mi fi do wid puss? Yuh nuh see how much stray one outside inna the yard?'

'Don't you want something to keep your company?' he'd asked, exasperated.

'Is just a extra mouth to feed.'

'That doesn't matter. I'll give you money to buy the food.'

'Dem animals can't survive in the ghetto. Dem too soft.'

'Don't be ridiculous!'

'Mi fadda don't like animals,' was what she was finally able to persuade him with.

Apollo took Maximillian back to the uptown pet store in Liguanea.

She had told Apollo that Mr McKenzie was her father and he was extremely strict. She told him she wasn't allowed to have boyfriends, so their relationship had to be a secret and he couldn't come to see her at home in the evenings.

Her whole sexual history was sanitised. Whitewashed like the tree trunks in the yard at Christmas time. Yes, she confessed, she'd had lovers in the past but it was just 'cause she was rebelling against a controlling father. All of that was behind her now, she told Apollo, 'since mi meet yuh'. To be fair, the misunderstanding had started when Damian had referred to her as Mr Mack's 'dawta' when they first met. Apollo didn't know that was local lingo for 'his woman'.

Apollo came to the tenement yard during his lunch break, carrying fancy Chinese food from Oriental Court Kitchen. Things like mallah chicken, shrimp and black beans and chop suey. When he'd given her sautéed shrimp to try for the first time, he'd eagerly asked her what she thought.

'It OK.'

'Just OK?'

'Yeah. It alright. What yuh want mi to say?'

He was incredulous. 'It's not awesome? Excellent? Good?'

Regina couldn't figure out why Apollo didn't understand that 'OK and alright' was as much excitement as ghetto people like her could muster. She didn't know how to explain that they didn't deal in exaggeration, not because they didn't appreciate good things but because life had proved you shouldn't express too much excitement, in case the goodness got taken away. Saying words like 'Awesome' was only looking for trouble.

While they ate lunch, Apollo would tell her about office politics. There was Christopher Brown, the senior partner who nobody liked – Apollo said he wouldn't be surprised if Brown was siphoning off cash – a rumour whispered to him by the accounting assistant, a shapely browning he suspected had a crush on him.

He wanted to find out all about Regina. Obscure things like her favourite parts of a chicken (leg, thigh and wing; the breast was too fleshy); how she felt about hugs (they made her uncomfortable and she was always the first to pull away); that she could only fall asleep on the right side of the bed; how she hated the smell of garlic; and that her eyes changed from light brown to a brownish-green, depending on her mood. In deep reflection she put her tongue between her teeth and used one hand to play with the hair under her armpit. He asked about her favourite colour (blue), the foods she liked (everything nice), the places she wanted to travel to (America and England), her biggest fear (drowning) and all her hopes and dreams.

He didn't laugh when she said she wanted to open her own clothing store one day. She was a lover of all things fashion. She didn't want to be a mere higgler, flying to Panama to bring back overstuffed suitcases and barrels of cheap clothes sold on the street from a bed of cardboard or a wooden hand-cart or barrels on the sidewalk in downtown Kingston. No.

She wanted a store with her *name* on it. In uptown Kingston. With a large beautiful window. Where clothes hung on classy mannequins that looked like real people. With changing rooms with heavy doors and ornate doorknobs.

It would be called Gina's Boutique & House of Fashion and she would host fashion shows and the local newspapers would send photographers to take pictures. She would mix with a class of people she'd never dreamed of mixing with before, people who would have otherwise looked down on her but would come to see her as one of them. When she dressed them, these rich housewives and socialites would confide their insecurities and their secrets. She would become the keeper of their inner lives: what they *really* thought and felt beneath their plastered smiles. At Gina's Boutique, she could earn her own money and not depend on a man.

She was surprised she had told him. No one else knew.

'That's a cool dream, Gina,' Apollo said, and he was so serious she knew he meant it. 'I know you can do it!' He read her the little strip of paper that came from inside her fortune cookie: *Success is yours. You will go far. Travel looks favourable.* She didn't believe in horoscopes but listened to them on the radio every day. This morning hers (Taurus) had said: *Careful what you believe.*

She laughed at his encouraging words, despite herself. At his almost child-like certainty. Though they were both eighteen, he wasn't grown enough yet to understand that dreams didn't work like that. Where would she even begin to find the money to open a store? The money she hustled from her lovers was only enough for food and cheap jewellery, maybe pay for an outfit to a dance, not nearly enough to put down three months' deposit on the rental for a store. No bank would give her a loan without a source of income. She had no collateral. Her dream was a fantasy. No more real than the things she saw when she was high. More likely, she would go work at a sensuous massage parlour or as an exotic dancer like her cousin Cynthia in Montego Bay.

The only other person she might have told her dream was her grandfather, Maas Leford, a banana farmer in St Mary, who she'd loved before he died from diabetic complications. Though she was only a toddler, she remembered him taking her to the field on his shoulders. Sometimes he'd let her stand on his muddy waterboots, which he always wore with his khaki pants. She'd play in empty boxes while he reaped his bananas. He made a swing for her from an old wooden plank and rope thicker than her wrists, and tied it to an ackee tree and when he pushed her high, looking at her wiggling feet made her feel like she was walking on the sky.

After Leford died, his daughter Bubbles had a bitter quarrel with Regina's grandmother and then Bubbles and Regina moved to Kingston to live with Bubbles' newest boyfriend, Bumper. Regina didn't see the old lady again until years later when her grandmother finally took the country bus to Kingston to make amends with her estranged daughter and see her grandchild. Regina was ten. When she left, her grandmother's parting words summed up her entire opinion on her prospective son-in-law:

'Eh-eh! Outta de whole car, why yuh choose de bumpa?'

Shortly after that, Bubbles packed up her bags and left. She left Regina with Bumper, who soon got tired of plaiting a girl-child's hair and seeing to it that she was bathed and fed, and he sent her to stay with his sister in Lazarus Gardens. The sister was too busy trying to care for her own kids, much less to pay much attention to an unwanted child.

When she was fifteen, Regina met Mr Mack, when he came to the house to fix Bumper's sister's boyfriend's bike. Bumper's sister had long recognised men taking to Regina like flies at the meat shop; she said that Regina was a grown woman now and should go 'look man'.

Regina moved in with Mr Mack the next day.

Regina didn't want Apollo filling her head with ideas that she could be somebody. He would be gone back to America soon anyway and forget all about her. Yes, there would be Western Union remittances for the first few months, then it would trickle to nothing. He would go on to marry an American woman, probably white, and have a comfortable life. And then when he was old, like in his sixties or seventies, somebody would say they'd just been on a vacation to Jamaica and he would lean back in his leather armchair in his study and fan away cigar smoke and say: 'Yeah, I've been there once', and maybe think of her for a moment, and the rapid blinking and wet, red eyes wouldn't be from memories of her but the smoky haze in the room.

No. She would continue to keep back a part of herself. She would suck him dry like a bag-juice. Just like all the others. Sex was her drug and she intoxicated them with it. Made the bastards drunk, high and foolish. They couldn't fill her emptiness. The loneliness. *Dick*, she thought, *is a soft thing. Cocky only hard sometime. Then it deflate like balloon or flat tyre. And what it good for? Like a plug in a drain, it just stop-up things for a time.*

Only *she* knew how to touch herself so she could feel something. She didn't have to fake an orgasm or lie about it because the men she had sex with, who stank of crotch-sweat, didn't care. She watched them shake and shatter in wet bursts. Not Apollo, though. She taught *him* what to do and how; guided his fingers because he'd asked. He'd wanted to know, was it good for her? The first time he'd asked, she threw back her head and laughed. 'Yeah baby,' she lied that first time and the second but by the fifth time he asked she was sick of lying to his earnest face. So she showed him and he learnt. He covered the little 'Os' of pleasure made by her perfectly puckered mouth with his own lips, so nearly no sound escaped.

◆

Regina thought all of this now, sitting in a hotel restaurant in New Kingston with Apollo. It was Saturday night and Apollo had her out on what he called a Dinner Date. He said people did this when they were boyfriend and girlfriend. There were clean white tablecloths on every table and lavish centrepieces of orchids. Regina looked down at her knife and fork with trepidation. Apollo had tried to teach her how to use them to eat fried rice last week. 'Don't worry, Gina, I got you, baby,' he said. 'Do what I do. It's easy.' She'd copied him like a trained monkey, but eventually, she'd put the knife and fork down and used a spoon, like at home.

The waiter wore a starched white shirt and neat black pants and tie. He had a weathered face, salt and pepper hair and his nametag read 'Jeffery'.

Apollo was looking at the menu which was bound in black leather. He frowned as he tried to decide between the leg of lamb or steak. He picked up the wine list. The good thing about Jamaica was that you didn't have to be twenty-one to drink. But his parents had always exposed him to good wine. He remembered the wines from his trip to France the year before.

'OK, we gotta have some wine. What wine you gonna have? Chardonnay? Sauvignon blanc? Riesling?'

Rahtid! Dis man speaking Chinese, she thought.

Seeing her confusion, he asked: 'Alright, a fruit juice then? A Pepsi? Coke?'

She sat, dry-tongued, as Jeffery looked down at her. She was sweating so she used her cloth napkin to wipe her face.

The likes of you don't belong here. She saw it in his face. A few minutes earlier, she'd nearly drunk the warm lemon water from the finger bowl Jeffery had brought to the table.

She pulled down the hem of her too-tight black dress. She had bought it for an aunt's funeral last year and it was the only thing she owned that seemed fancy enough to wear uptown. Looking down at it now, in the restaurant's bright lighting, it seemed cheap. She'd considered wearing gold and black lamé pants and a red tube top but had decided a dress was better.

'Umm, OK Jeff my man, give us a couple of minutes,' Apollo said.

Jeffery walked away, head bowed. There was a queasy feeling in Regina's stomach.

'Listen, Gina, don't worry – I've got this. Whatever you want!'

Him look like a pickney, she thought.

'Mi just want lemonade.'

'Baby, you don't gotta be shy for *anything* you want.' He shot her a meaningful look.

Yes, see it deh, she thought, her heart hardening. *Back to sex. Always back to that. Man love follow where dem woody lead. Dem buddy is dem weakness.*

'Yuh know wah?' she tipped back the sparkling water in big gulps. 'Mek dem give mi some white rum. Straight.'

'Yeah! That's more like it.'

She looked at him and thought: *I don't like how yuh act like yuh know it all and yuh better than mi.*

But she just returned his smile and picked a piece of lint off her dress.

◆

The next morning, stretching back on the clean, thick cotton sheets of the hotel room, the offending dress lying on the

109

high-polished floor, she let the AC cool her. *Why him intro-ducing mi to dis kinda life for?* she thought. Better to not know what it was like, than to know it and have it taken away. Mr McKenzie was in Manchester spending time with his sickly mother. Apollo said they could stay at the hotel the whole weekend. He'd booked them a couple's massage at the spa, and a manicure, pedicure and facial for her.

Apollo stirred in his sleep and threw an arm around her. She could feel the heat radiating from him. The muskiness of his smell filled her nostrils. The nausea in her stomach had grown and she wished she'd brought some weed with her. She thought she had some in her bag then remembered she'd smoked it to settle her nerves before Apollo picked her up for the Dinner Date.

Instead she pressed her nose to the fresh, cotton sheets; feel-ing their cool softness on her skin. She looked around at the bright white walls and the high ceilings with their ornate fans and artwork and realised, for the first time, the true ugliness of the tiny room she shared with Mr Mack, a room tacked on to the side of the tenement yard, like an afterthought. Here in the hotel room, there was no sunlight peeping through holes in the roof nor poking through irregular pieces of wood held together by nails that seemed to have been pounded in a frenzy of hammering. Here, there was no smell of dampness and mould from where water had seeped in from the last rainfall and soaked the old clothes and newspapers on the floor placed there to sop it up. The air freshener in this room smelt of oranges. Neat and clean, all of it. *And is rooms like this I born to be in*, Regina thought.

She looked at Apollo's neck and compared it to the loose, withering skin on Mr Mack's. She'd always felt he had a musty old man smell. That and blackened fingernails, grease on his skin and he reeked of sweat. Apollo smelt like cologne and his unsoiled, trimmed fingernails showed pink flesh underneath.

Regina inhaled her own skin, the shower soap smelt like strawberries. She raised herself off the pillow cushioning her head and looked through the glass windows at the sunlight breaking through the clouds, which seemed to her to be fluffier and whiter than she had ever seen. A plane was approaching the Norman Manley airport; the sun glinted off it so it looked like a silver bullet moving in slow motion. And though she knew there was traffic outside, the room's panel of thick, streak-free glass kept out the noise.

When she got up to use the bathroom, the grey and blue carpet felt like a young lamb's wool under her toes. She sat on the high white porcelain toilet and held the toilet paper in her hands. *Is good toilet paper dem have.* Its thickness and texture reminded her of a high-quality cotton T-shirt. *Is a shame to have to wipe mi batty wid this.* She carefully rolled the toilet paper over in her hands. She only rolled it twice. She could afford to use much less than the near-transparent, paper-thin toilet paper at home.

She flushed the toilet and looked down at the glittery bracelet on her wrist. A gift from Apollo, with its interlocking yellow and blue gemstones and gold setting. She was still looking at it as she flicked off the bathroom light. *It so pretty*, she thought.

She lifted the covers and settled back into bed. It came to her then: the solution had been in her face the whole time. Apollo would be the one to change her life.

In a couple months she would tell him she was pregnant.

A child would tie him to her. They would marry and he would file for her to go to the States, where she could start her new life, open Gina's Boutique & House of Fashion and have the life she always wanted. For a healthy baby, she would have to give up the drugs; for a time, anyway. Starting tomorrow.

Up until now, she'd never thought of having a child. She'd done everything to prevent it. Tried and true methods like standing up after sex or drinking a hot Pepsi right after. She mostly insisted on the pull-out method of contraception.

'Gina, baby.' Apollo was whispering now, his eyes still closed. He rubbed the small of her back. Propping herself on her elbows, she regarded him. His body had the measured, firm hardness of a man, sinews firm, but as he slept in the dim light his face held the softness of a child. She stroked him.

'Mi right here, honey,' she cooed and kissed him long and slow. 'Mi not going nowhere.'

Celeste

The gardener, Melrose, didn't show up today. Again. Some Jamaicans are so unreliable.

That's why I'm here in the garden on my hands and knees, pulling up weeds, dying for a sip of Jocelyn's lemonade. Pruning is therapeutic. I sit on my butt in the grass to re-pot an aloe vera plant. I like this plant. It's hardy. It doesn't need much water and can survive in deserts. It's tough.

I confronted Ray this morning at breakfast. He was seated at the dining table, happily munching on crispy bacon and scrambled eggs and reading the newspaper.

'Good morning, honey.' He puckered his lips for the kiss he thought was coming. 'Would you like me to ask Jocelyn to make you an omelette?'

'So we're really not going to talk about this?'

He lowered his eyes. 'About what, honey?'

He had the nerve to ask!

'Don't play with me, Ray. And don't "honey" me right now, please. Are we not going to talk about the fact that it's Sunday and our son didn't come home last night and we don't know where he is?'

His smile vanished. He folded the newspaper and put it on the table, next to his plate. 'I'm sure Apollo is fine. He told us he was going to be out with a friend and spending the weekend at a hotel, remember?'

'Which friend?'

Ray shrugged, giving me a wink that said, boys will be boys.

'I bet it has to do with that Dinah woman. Ray, this woman's trying to take our son. I know it. That cabdriver Eddie tells me he's been going down there regularly.'

'It's going to be OK.' Ray crossed his legs, then uncrossed them. That's one of Ray's tells. He does that when he lies or is hiding something which is why I always beat him at poker.

'Oh, really?' I told him I had a feeling we shouldn't have come here.

'Why are you attacking me? We can't turn on each other now.' He spread both palms on his chest, like I was stabbing him and he was applying pressure to try to stop the bleeding. Why don't people actually answer what you ask?

'I'm telling you it's going to be OK, Celeste. Trust me.' Raymond took up his coffee mug and sipped. He likes it black, no sugar. He picked up the newspaper again. Perhaps he was trying to convince himself more than me, because I saw his hands tremble, just a little. My husband's hands are usually steady. He always gets things handled.

'How can you be so *sure*?' I asked him, although I knew he wasn't sure at all.

'Apollo loves us.'

I waited. Down went the newspaper again. He exhaled, long and deep. 'Look, honey.' His tone softened. '*We're* his parents. He knows that. OK?'

'Do you know how much time he's spending in that place? In that *ghetto*?'

Raymond shrugged. 'Celeste, I don't think we should stop him. He's got a good head on his shoulders. He's my kid, after all.' Then he chuckled, but it sounded hollow.

114

I shot him a look and fixed myself some peppermint tea, with plenty of brown sugar. He should know better. Apollo is a teenager and teens are not rational human beings. For God's sake, when I was eighteen I eloped with John King! I haven't felt this distant from Apollo since he was ten and we told him Ray wasn't his real dad. And distracting myself until he snaps out of it is *not* working.

Ray hid behind this newspaper and mumbled, 'Let's trust Apollo to do the right thing. What else can we do?'

I'm mad at myself that I didn't tell him what I wanted to say. That I backed down. Apollo needs Ray to be there for him. A boy needs his father to show him how to be a man.

In many ways, his love for Apollo has always been part of the glue helping to keep us together.

I'm patting down the soil around the aloe vera plant and wondering: why do kids love parents? Because they give them care, protection, shelter, food and nice things? I wonder if they love us at first because they have to, when they're too little to understand, let alone to live on their own, in the world – and then because they've been doing it for so long. Love is survival instinct and habit.

Dinah

I here on my back on the bed looking up at this ugly lizard. Something in mi spirit don't feel right. Is nearly two months now my Son-Son come back to mi, but I hardly see him these days. Him doing that internship, him say, at Mr Brown law firm, Monday to Friday. So him visit mi Saturdays and Sundays. I find another job but is not full-time. I mostly do washing and cooking on Tuesdays and then ironing and cleaning on Thursdays. Is for a Chiney family: a old lady and her middle-aged son who live with her. She insist mi must use Rexo red floor polish and shine the floor on mi hands and knees with a coconut brush. All of di Chiney family other relative dem migrate to Miami in the '70s when Michael Manley say dem must go. But the old lady say dem not leaving Jamaica, no matter who in power and no matter the crime 'cause dem born here and dem as Jamaican as Black people like mi.

I not happy. I notice Son-Son and Damian keep hanging out together wid that loose-tail Regina. Why the three of dem have to fren-up so? Damian who these days always have weed rubbing out in him hand-middle and claim that him a deejay?

Mi feel like mi don't know Son-Son. Him is not a baby no

more. Is a man. What kind of man him is? Mi miss so many of him firsts. First tooth. First word. Him first step. And things from him growing up, when him did break him leg or start look 'pon the girl dem.

Mi want Son-Son to know where him come from. Mi want tell him all the stories Mama used to tell mi, teach him her songs and how to drum, how to read things that don't have words, to fill him up with the remembrances from her time in the country. Mi feel she slipping away more and more, when even she right next to mi.

What Damian can teach Son-Son but fi smoke and sell weed and sit down on street corner? Mi don't want mi son to turn out like dem boy in the area who just working for British. Dem don't know him have him very boot pressing down on dem neck. Dem can't even go from one corner to the next without him saying yes. Can't leave the community or come into it without him saying is alright. Down to dem very life need him permission!

As soon as I open the window today, mi see dem. Damian and Streggo by the zinc fence near to the mango tree talking. Well, Streggo talking and Damian mainly listening. What Streggo doing in my yard? Damian look like him want get away from him. Mi move to the corner of the house closest to the tree so mi could hear but mi couldn't pick up the pieces of conversation flying on the wind.

Of late, I see Streggo have the boy Ratta behind him, like how chicklet follow hen. Him is the only one who pay Ratta any mind, which is a shame since that boy need direction. Is not Ratta fault that him deform and British don't accept him. Everybody in Lazarus Gardens know that whatever Streggo doing, British mix up in it, like how smoke signals fire. All the badness that happen in Kingston, British behind it, and him use people like Streggo who don't use half the good sense

God give dem. This is what I didn't want for Damian. This path only going lead him to the grave. Watch and see. And him too stubborn to listen to mi any more.

If Damian and Streggo working together and Son-Son and Damian linking up, is just a matter of time before Son-Son get entangle with British. Like Damian fren String who fix mi fan last month, who hanging round with Streggo too. As The Good Book say: 'What fellowship can light have with darkness?' I try to warn Son-Son but him not listening.

One thing Mama always say: to kill a tree, you have to dig up the root.

Dinah

Dinah hated earthquakes which, thankfully, in Jamaica, although frequent, were mostly small in magnitude. She didn't like the feeling of the thing she most relied on moving under her feet.

She hadn't learnt about constantly moving magma and tectonic plates, didn't understand that the ground wasn't really steady at all. And even though she liked the idea of travelling to other places, she knew she would never go on an airplane. It was too high up; the ground too far below. Ships were just as bad. She couldn't swim. Water was fickle and could not be trusted. She needed to feel the firmness of earth, cement, road, tile, grass . . . anything her legs could use to hold her up.

She did know from Mrs Steele's books that when seen from space, the planet was a milky blue orb. A cataract-clouded eye pried loose, plucked from its socket and placed neatly on a sparkly blanket dusted with glitter. A child's forgotten marble from a long-abandoned game, spinning, spinning in a move that didn't end, with the vast universe around it. She couldn't contemplate that *terra firma* didn't actually rest on anything at all. There was no comfort in that. No firmness or security.

When she had heard the Americans had put a man on the moon, she was baffled. *How him breathe up there?* Mrs Steele said they had spacesuits and showed her a picture of a man floating in a fat padded suit with something like an umbilical cord coming out of it. Dinah didn't like thinking about the fact that way, way below the earth's surface, there was nothing except a substance thin as air, something in which you could float, hovering forever, like an insect specimen preserved in an alcohol-filled jar. That everybody was on a kind of giant spaceship floating through the cosmos.

Instead, she chose to imagine the world how she had seen it the very first time, as a child, on a poster in Sunday school: egg-shaped and gently resting in the middle of two open palms, presenting it like a jewel. Cupped lovingly. The Sunday school teachers said the disembodied hands belonged to God. Yes, God was holding everything up. Even her. So there was no fear of falling.

This morning, as she watches the light-brown lizard on the ceiling looking down at her, she isn't thinking about earthquakes, milky blue orbs floating in thin air or jewelled eggs. She is thinking about how you can have your feet on something solid but everything is still upside down. The lizard's head looks oversized for its small body, pivoting from side to side, swinging as if to see her better. She wonders if she can touch the lizard but knows it will run if she tries.

Dinah isn't afraid of lizards. Not even the large croaking kind. Small fears, like the fear of insects, were for people who had nothing bigger to be scared of. Like losing your child. Like knowing you gave away your child, because you were scared and not sure if you were more scared for yourself than for what would become of your baby. You were only a child yourself. Like putting down your schoolbag on the floor after school, you simply shrugged off parental responsibility.

Fears like the shame that you couldn't provide for your child. Your only child.

Shame, thinking he could be ashamed of you. Of the life you lived, scraping just to get by. This shame was the worst of all.

Dinah used to be fearful about the kind of mother she could have been. Frustrated, beating her child to sickness or letting him run out into the busy street? Holding his hand over fire to let him know to avoid a burn? There used to be a little boy in the tenement yard known as his mother's 'beating-stick'. She beat him with a board, burnt him with cigarettes, tied him to a pole in an ants' nest, then kicked the dirt to disturb the ants. One day his mother felt something in his side, like a hard ball under his skin. The lump was a stage four Wilms tumour. A type of kidney cancer. He died after that and Dinah felt relief that he would no longer suffer.

Dinah was familiar with shame. She had felt it at the public hospital where she gave birth to Son-Son. The ward was overcrowded, so she had to share a bed with another pregnant woman. She'd been crying, remembering how Leroy said the child wasn't his, how it was a jacket he wasn't prepared to wear. She felt the sting of shame between her legs, running down her thigh, as the doctor and nurse peered down there. The woman beside her was writhing in labour and the nurse told them both to be quiet. The woman had messed herself and the warm filth and sticky liquid glued the bedsheet to Dinah's body. Later, she found out the other woman's baby had been born dead.

The bed next door starts to creak, and Dinah can hear Regina's noisy sex with Mr McKenzie coming from the wall behind her head. No doubt welcoming him back from his months away looking after his sick mother in the country. Dinah had not allowed a man to touch her in over eighteen years. But she had not ached for that soothing touch. Loneliness was something you could get used to. It hugged her like a lover. Of course, a woman had needs but she had buried hers so deep, she couldn't unearth them if she wanted to. A month ago, after Wednesday night prayer and fasting service, Deacon Paul had 'put argument' to her, saying she looked as ripe and juicy as an East Indian mango.

'Oh!' Dinah had said. 'So is so it go? Mi want yuh do something fi mi.'

'Anything, Dinah. Name it.'

'Nuh pick mi. Mi ah beg yuh to leave mi pon the tree to over-ripe and drop!'

It was apparent to everyone, except the newly arrived deacon, that she was a woman who made no time for love, because the love of a man had wounded her.

She wonders now if the lizard had been in the next room first and come over here for some peace and quiet. Something she didn't have. Even now. Sleep does not come easy these days. She thinks now about how a thing like regret could linger in the air, like the smell of a garbage truck long after it had passed.

Dinah drowns out the sound of Regina's animal cries with her own thoughts. She is worried because she has started to see things that are not there. Last week, it was a woman standing on the roadside wearing a white bathrobe and standing beside an empty bucket. She did a double-take but the woman had vanished. Evaporated like water from a sidewalk.

Sanity is a fragile thing. It's a plate that drops into the sink during washing. You think it will break but it doesn't. You can only make out a tiny crack across the middle. But the next time you wash it, the plate comes apart neatly in two halves that you can hold in each hand.

Dinah looks down at her body now: at her breasts and thinks about how she never suckled her baby. She remembers how her breasts were swollen and painful. Full of stockpiled

122

milk. She knows that years from now, her breasts will remind her of Mama's; like withering mangoes. She sees her varicose veins, resembling spider legs. When she was a little girl, she was afraid of spiders. When she was seven, she had laid on a mat, paralysed with fear as a spider darted on to her arm.

'Is just a spider, gal!' Mama swatted it hard, crushing the spider's body into her skin, so Dinah couldn't tell the difference between the spider's body and the hairs on her arm. The slap that killed the spider had hurt her too. It gave her a deep-purplish bruise shaped like her mother's fingers. But the incident taught her four things: to never be afraid of anything you could kill; to associate fear with pain; that pain had a shape which was different for everybody. That you carried yours around with you, like a tattoo.

Mama is in the yard with the gate securely locked, tying, undoing and retying a scarf around her head. Mama is sitting under a tree trying to figure out the exact way she wants it tied to cover her thick plaits. On a stone next to her feet is an enamel cup full of peppermint tea made by Dinah which Mama hasn't touched. She is so focused on the tie-head, she doesn't feel the ants crawling over her feet. Her brain and her hands are at war.

Dinah knows what she has to do. She wishes she could hear Mama's voice now. She wishes Mama could kill the thing growing inside her head. She wants Mama to quiet the earthquake inside.

Dinah

Dinah's thick-heeled black pumps made screeching noises on the white tiles. The floor had just been mopped by a lady wearing a dirty, cream-coloured apron and jeans shorts. She had close-cropped, patchy red hair the colour of Kool-Aid.

The cleaning lady rolled her eyes at Dinah, and leaned on her mop. The smell of bleach hung in the air. Dinah was surprised at how sterile everything was. She'd been half-expecting British's house to be filthy – full of naked girls, beer bottles, food wrappers, weapons, drugs and drug paraphernalia strewn everywhere, held together by a stink of body odour and the funky smell of sex – but this place had the cleanliness of a doctor's office.

She had been greeted at the heavy iron gate by a gruff man who wanted to know 'What yuh want?' He held back two growling Doberman Pinschers. Dinah kept her eyes lowered and said: 'Mi need to see British. Mi need him help mi wid something.' She bent her back and held her stomach, pretending to be sick. The man softened a bit. People came to British all the time asking for money to go to the doctor, or to pay for surgery at the hospital, or a blood test or just to fill prescriptions at the pharmacy.

'OK lady, but mi haffi pat yuh down first.'

She endured the mandatory pat down, the man lingering over her breasts. She was tempted to box his hand away. She had just come from church, so she was wearing her feathered black and white hat and her best purple dress.

The church had been sweltering. The choir sang the chorus: 'Born, born, born again, thank God I'm born again; born of the water, the spirit and the blood, thank God I'm born again.'

When Dinah had gotten to the pulpit, she began her testimony: 'Brethren and sistren, as yuh all know, praise the Lord, my son came back. God is good.'

The church chorused back: '—all the time and all the time, God is good.'

'But church, mi heart heavy. I need yuh prayers. The Devil out to get my son.'

Outraged hisses reverberated through the small church. 'We rebuke him in Jesus' name!' the congregation responded before starting up with the next song. Deacons and deaconess laid hands on Dinah, on her head, back and stomach; their warm hands soothed her.

The woman in the white robe that Dinah had seen before was sitting at the back of the church and smiling.

Now she sat on a bench outside a door marked OFFICE in black letters on a small white plaque. The cleaner moved on to another room. A man with thick-speckled glasses wearing a vest, long sleeved shirt and a tie opened the door and introduced himself as British's personal assistant.

'My name is Chucky.' He added pomp to the name with a fake British accent, and offered her a clipboard with a sheet of paper for her to write down her name.

'Mr Chucky, sir, I come to see British.'

'Evidently.'

'What?'

'Look lady, British is very busy, which is why him have people like me to sift out who is who.'

'Who is who?'

'Yes. So let's begin. Which party yuh vote for in the last election?'

She knew this must be a trick question. Lazarus Gardens was garrison to a particular party; to say the other one was frankly dangerous. She didn't come here to commit suicide. She was here to save her son. She told Chucky the right answer.

'OK, good. So would yuh say yuh are a loyal Party supporter? A true follower?'

'Of course.' For good measure, she added that her family had always voted for the Party. She told the story of how the founder of the Party had eaten stewed peas from the same pot as her grandfather. Chucky wrote down Dinah's answers in a neat little black book. His handwriting was fat and sloppy. The pages were stained with food and ink smudges.

Chucky smiled, peeling back thick lips to show small teeth and large gums.

'Come in, my sister.' He opened the door to another room. 'British will be with yuh soon.' He gestured for her to sit on the chair opposite a massive mahogany desk.

Dinah sat for two hours thinking she had been forgotten. She picked at her fingernails. This was sheer folly, a voice in her head was telling her now. What had brought her here? Why had she abandoned all good sense?

Earlier that morning, on the way to service at church, she had seen the woman again. It seemed the woman was mocking her. She was peeping out from behind a light post and playing a game of peekaboo with Dinah. Instead of the white bathrobe, the woman was dressed in a *shuka*, a brilliant red cloth with purple stripes, wrapped around her like a

Maasai warrior and white markings painted on her face like a maze. Brightly coloured beads and feathers quivered on her head. Dinah had seen a picture of Maasai people in one of Mr Brown's *National Geographic* magazines. The woman peeping at her was a desert flower in full bloom. Rainwater in an arid place. Dinah could smell the dust from her cow-hide sandals.

'Who yuh is? Show yuhself, yuh wretch!' she called out when the woman disappeared.

The church sister walking beside her had looked at her quizzically.

'Mi think mi did see somebody mi know,' Dinah muttered sheepishly.

The other woman shrugged and made a mental note to tell Pastor to do a special prayer for Dinah. The strain of not having a steady job must be causing her to crack. Like Mother Ellis at church, who was convinced demons were cutting up her panties at night and the fallen angels were eating out her salt and sugar, cutting the hose at the back of her fridge and leaving footprints on her pillowcases.

In church, the pastor had preached about Daniel in the lions' den. How this man of God had been thrown into a pit of hungry lions and God had shut their mouths so they couldn't devour him. It was in that moment Dinah decided she was going to go see British, immediately after church.

◆

Dinah reflected on that moment, as she sat straight-backed in the hard, wooden chair, feeling some of her courage leave her. She stared up at the paintings on the wall. They depicted scenes she'd never seen before: a snowy winter captioned 'Christmas at a thatch-roofed manor house in Sheepwash, Devon'; pictures of black and white spotted cows dotting green fields; the Tower of London; Big Ben; London Bridge and Buckingham Palace. She was in an alien place.

'Dear God, abide with me,' she mumbled now. She took her giant Bible out of her handbag and gripped it. She took some of the olive oil Pastor had blessed and dabbed on her forehead, making the shape of the cross. Like the Persian King in the Old Testament, one wasn't supposed to seek an audience with royalty without being summoned. You could approach British if you had good reasons: sickness, school fees to pay, uniforms and groceries to buy, but what she was doing was deception.

She thought about running out, past chunky Chucky, past the sour-faced lady with the mop, and the handsy guard at the gate with his sweaty palms. But no. Son-Son needed her to be the mother who wouldn't give up or let him down. Not again.

She felt as if she was fusing with the chair. Her spine merged with wood until they were one. She couldn't have moved, even if she wanted to.

She had chosen the righteous path. She would not be going downtown to see a 'science man' to buy a powder of Kill Your Enemy or a powder of Turn Them Back. No Set Me Free or Leave Me Alone oil. No lemon water to surreptitiously sprinkle around her yard on evenings and mornings to cut and clear the evil of British. No obeah to ward off the saltiness of bad luck.

She knew British represented real terror. This was no rolling calf, black-heart man and three-wheel coffin story you told children to frighten them from going out alone at night. No Anansi and Bredda Rabbit story. British was darkness. But she was one of God's chosen and no weapon formed against her would prosper.

Like Queen Esther in the Bible before she went to see the

Persian King, Dinah spoke aloud to the pictures on the walls: 'If I perish, I perish.'

Just then, British walked in through the door.

Although the AC was on full blast and she was shivering, British wore nothing more than a pair of shorts and a mesh merino. He moved closer and pumped her right hand vigorously, like a politician.

'Sorry to keep you waiting. I had some business to attend to.' He sat down and poured himself some vodka. He had a clipped, English accent. 'How can I help you?' He eased back in his chair, crossing his legs and putting his hands behind his head.

'Well, British, sir, me name Dinah.'

'I know who you are.'

This caught her off-guard. They had never spoken before. The air in her lungs solidified.

He leaned forward: 'You live on the Third Lane. In the tenement yard with Damian, Mr McKenzie, Regina, Mrs Sinclair and her sons. And your mother, of course. How she doing these days?'

Dinah's mouth felt numb.

'Dinah, there is *nothing* in Lazarus Gardens I don't know about.' British was staring directly at her but because of his cross-eyes, she couldn't tell where he was looking. He seemed to be glaring at a space beyond her head. A spot on the wall behind her.

'Nothing happens here I don't authorise.' He narrowed his eyes. 'Remember that.'

'Then yuh already know why mi come.' She grasped her Bible tightly. You needed a weapon of faith when confronting the Devil. He had a M-16 but she had the Sword of the Spirit.

'This matter is serious.' She straightened her back. 'I'm here to talk about salvation.'

He glanced at her Bible. 'Ma'am, are you a Jehovah Witness?' He dropped the accent, laughing: 'Is evangelise you come to evangelise to me?'

'Mi mean, salvation of mi son, Apollo.'

'You mean the Yankee youth hanging around Damian?'

'That's my child. British, sir, I'm asking yuh kindly if yuh would give the order for Streggo, Damian and all of yuh . . . yuh *associates* to stay away from my son.'

'From what I hear, it's your son who love deh 'round the people in the community. Regina especially. Look, I going to level with you. I never meet your son. I just allow him to come and go until I get some time to figure out how to make use of him.'

'Mr Brit—' she began.

'Just British.'

'*British*, mi son just come back into mi life, him can't dead already. Him is just eighteen and nuh live life yet.'

British rubbed his chin. When he'd turned eighteen, he'd begun working for a major drug-running operation. An internship was what he considered it, until he moved up the ranks and began his own business. His mother had seen his potential early. Had sought to toughen him up when he was a little boy by tying him to a chair and beating him until he peed. As he got a little older, she beat him until he stopped crying. That made him a man. His only regret was that she had died suddenly, when he was a teenager. So she hadn't seen him take over from Pedro Garcia. Hadn't seen the fruit of her efforts flower.

Some mothers, like Dinah, didn't realise their children's talent and what they could become.

'Tell me more about your son.'

'Him studying to be a lawyer,' she said proudly. 'Him full of brains and going to be a big Queen's Counsel like Norman Manley.'

British thought about Beason, the criminal lawyer who defended his men whenever they got arrested; he was getting too greedy, taking bribes meant for the cops, Customs and port authority officials for himself. The man didn't know his days were numbered. He needed somebody fresh, untainted. Somebody he could mould. In time and with training, British could groom Apollo into a good replacement. He needed somebody smart, who could provide advice to British's eldest son and heir, Clevon, when he took over. The boy would feel no loyalty to him now, of course, but that would come in time. British hadn't thought of it before but it all made sense.

'I'm glad you came here today. It sounds like your son can be beneficial to me.'

Dinah stood up. The Holy Spirit had emboldened her. She swore she could hear a lion growling.

'British or whatever yuh name is, mi *warning* yuh – leave mi son alone!'

British wasn't sure what he was hearing. This woman in her old-fashioned purple frock that came down to her ankles and her tattered hat, trying to tell *him* what to do. He sputtered. Vodka dampened the papers on his desk.

'Mi can see yuh for who yuh is! A weak, hateful wretch.'

'Lady, you lose you mind?' He was genuinely concerned. Maybe her mother's madness had seeped into her.

'Mi never been more sane. Yuh and yuh devil business haffi keep away from my son! I serve the true and living *God* and if yuh mess wid mi, yuh Kingdom will fall!'

That word 'kingdom' pierced his chest. Who was this woman to threaten all he had built? People were sleeping with worms for lesser offences. She was rocking back and forth now, like a fat mouse in front of a ghetto puss.

'You lucky you too old fi me or I woulda show you exactly—!'

'Get thee behind me Satan! Fire and brimstone!' Dinah

closed her eyes; could see herself as the weeping prophet Jeremiah, breathing news of Jerusalem's coming destruction. Tidings of doom. She pulled out her bottle of anointed olive oil and splashed it around the room, shouting her lungs raw. 'Is *hell* and powder house in here today! All evilous men will burn!' She began speaking in tongues: 'Rabbabaa–shenen–abbbbbaaaaa!'

What the back-side this mad woman doing though, Lord? British thought.

Chucky and two muscled men burst in and grabbed both Dinah's arms, holding her still. Chucky's eyes bulged as he waited for further instructions.

British waved them away with his right hand, like he was swatting at a fly.

'It's OK, boys, this lady is no threat. Just a stark raving mad woman. Leave us.'

The three men tried to manoeuvre Dinah back into the chair but she had stiffened out like a dead lizard. She slid to the floor.

British finished his vodka in the silence that followed. He walked over to Dinah. Dinah thought about how last night she had killed a forty-leg. Had looked around in time to see the insect slither under the mat and flattened it with her slipper. British could take her life with even less effort. *Mi neva tell nobody mi was coming here. After him kill mi, Mama not going realise that mi missing. When dem don't see mi fi days, who going come look fi mi? Lawd! Who going tell Son-Son?*

British had learnt enough about human behaviour to know what type of punishment would hurt his enemy the most. Some things were more effective than a killing. Seeing a loved one suffer. Burning their house down with a Molotov cocktail – with their family still inside – and making them not just watch, but clap too.

He needed Dinah to see her son work for *him*. Become one of his allies and trusted advisors. That would be the cruellest fate of all. Because this one loved her son more than her life. She was too blind to see the noose tightening around her neck, even now.

'Dinah, don't forget who I am,' he whispered. His breath smelt like ash. '*I run things.*' He considered himself a fair man; it was just, even now, to warn her against her folly. So he told her something his mother, Miss Ivy, had told him: 'When your hand in lion mouth, you have to take time draw it out.'

British

There was a small part of British that admired what Dinah was trying to do. She was a mother looking out for her son. Like his mother had. For British, born and named Desmond McIntyre, Ivy Coleman had been and still was the epitome of motherly love. Neighbours and friends thought her vicious towards her only son. Desmond's father was never in the picture. He'd exited before the camera flashed and the fully developed photograph of a baby boy came out, one of the twelve he made with twelve different women before he disappeared one night never to be seen again. All he gave any of them was his last name.

Ivy was all Desmond McIntyre had and he knew her harshness meant love. It meant that she cared enough to mould him into a better man than his father could ever think to be. That meant licks – yes, plenty beatings, beatings rained on his head, shoulders, torso, legs. Ivy was trying to beat the wickedness out of him.

When he was small, he'd tie pieces of cloth to the tails of cats and dogs and set them on fire and watch the animal try to outrun flames he knew would eventually consume them. Desmond stole little girls' panties off clotheslines and tried to look up their skirts. He would often slice at the other children with a small knife he had stolen from the kitchen and sharpened. One deaf-mute little boy was British's favourite object of torture.

Ivy knew there was cruelty in him but believed the good in her that must be in him somewhere was enough to overcome it. So she would strap him to the chair, pour on the olive oil she had consecrated with babbling incantations and beat the demon inside him. Only she knew what she was doing — trying to save her only child.

At her urging, teachers, school principals, guidance counsellors, pastors and even a policeman had tried talking to him. The policeman was young, tall and handsome in a sharp uniform with a shiny belt buckle and brilliant red pants seams. The boy was defiant in the face of authority. The policeman's words didn't penetrate his skull — the man's warnings about where he could end up (prison or the grave) were stones that plugged his ears. On the way out of the house, the policeman had paused in the doorway, shaking his head: 'Mother, I never meet nobody like this boy yet.' Ivy had known then that no one could help Desmond.

He was fifteen the last time they spoke of that matter. She was going to her job as a cleaner of rich people's houses. British played the conversation over and over in his head through the years. He had been mopping the verandah. Not because she'd asked him to — she never had to. He found cleanliness soothing and scrubbing their little house was a pleasant part of his daily ritual.

'Yuh don't feel feelings like other people do.' His mother looked at him intensely, her bad left eye cloudy and unseeing. Her face was a wizened raisin, the wine of her youth long squeezed out. Although she never went beyond primary school, she was intelligent and sharp. She was the only woman who ever really saw him. The only one he had no desire to physically hurt. But she, like everyone else, would never understand how intoxicating it felt to hold that power.

'Mi know.' He had acknowledged the truth of her words.

'Feelings is something I always try to teach yuh to copy, like a actor in a picture-show.' She imagined the theatre, now torn down, that his father had once taken her to, before she got pregnant: bright-bulb marquee lights and Cary Grant on the silver screen.

'Yes ma'am.'

'But things don't really reach yuh heart.'

'Yes ma'am.'

'Desmond, yuh can be a good man if yuh try. Emotions is a weakness sometimes . . . things like guilt, pain and shame. Strong feelings can make yuh weak and make people use yuh.' She didn't add, 'like with me and yuh fada' but they both knew this without her saying it. The unsaid words hung heavy between them.

'Build up the emotions that make yuh strong. Yuh must promise mi something.'

'Yes, anything, ma'am.'

'That yuh going grow up to be a great man. Make something of yuhself. Make yuh life mean something. Make people respect yuh. Look up to yuh. Even if dem don't like yuh. Even if yuh seem strange to dem and dem don't understand yuh.'

He had promised. Even mimicked a smile, like she taught him, to show he was being genuine.

Her eyes watered. 'Yes, son, that would make me happy.' She touched his shoulder and squeezed it gently. 'And remember to sweep the yard.'

That was the closest she would ever come to hugging him and saying: 'I love you.' He said, 'Don't slide on the wet floor' and resumed his mopping.

A week later, a bus hit her down on her way to work.

Pedro Garcia had paid for her funeral and British joined his gang. Pedro said he could use British's brain and his talent for torture. That he was British's father now and he would always have a home.

British's mother had been wrong. He did feel one emotion: pure love for the woman who hadn't discarded him like garbage in a gully and loved him despite knowing he was a shell, a coconut husk. A woman who had never expressed her love in words, but didn't need to.

If only she could see him now. He spoke with her often. Saw her image in the mirror and in every reflective surface. Even in the freshly mopped, tiled floors or the watery surface of his drinks. He didn't own a picture of her. In his memory her face was like a photograph: flat, her stare glassy-eyed. Their conversations were one-sided, obviously, yet he often heard her speaking to him: 'Yes, son, I am proud of yuh.'

But the voice she used was always his own.

Mama

Mrs Sinclair, how yuh boys Donnie and Lennie? Dem in primary school, right? What! Dem leave high school already? Long time, yuh sey? Where dem is now? Gone visit dem puppa?

Yuh know that a blind man was Dinah grandfada? And I tell yuh the truth, she just like mi daddy. Him never born blind. It come on him suddenly as a big man. Because of pride, no matter how much time people beg him, him refuse to use a cane. Him would bounce into likkle pickney on dem way to school, women coming home from market, man on dem way to work or di farm. Nuff time him drop on him face or him batty.

Yuh shoulda see him walking up and down in the village in him dark glasses. Before him make each step, him used to put out that foot in front of him, raise him knee high and then, slow slow, him bring down the big toe to tap the ground before him, like him testing river-water before him dive in. It take him forever to go anywhere. And half the time him don't know where him going. Or where him is. But him make up him mind that this was how him was going to walk. Argument done. Him don't business 'bout common sense. When mi did pregnant wid Dinah a bauxite truck run him over and kill him dead.

But it in Dinah blood. The stubbornness.

Where dis road going tek har?

Dem sey when plantain want to die, it shoot – bring forth fruit.

Apollo

The music at the dance was so loud you could hardly hear people talking. A woman next to Apollo was yelling 'get yuh patty an' coco-bread an' box juice!' They were in an open playing field in Lazarus Gardens. In the day, the open lot was a dust bowl where shirtless boys in shorts or cut-off pants fought over a battered football. At night, it was transformed. Lights were strung up on poles, wooden stalls erected and giant speakers set up for the disc jockey.

Though the sun was gone, Apollo was still warm: from the lights and the bodies of people around him moving, dancing, yelling, laughing. Vendors were hawking bullas, jack-ass corn and other biscuits, bootlegged cassettes, Craven A and Matterhorn cigarettes, paradise plums and Fanta. Apollo smelt peanuts roasting in a coal-filled metal box at the front of a three-wheeled bicycle, being ridden by a man in a neon green T-shirt, weaving his way around another man brandishing fudge, popsicles and Nutty Buddy ice cream from a cooler brimming with ice.

'Yuh want one, my yute?' the man selling sky juice and sno-cone asked, but Apollo shook his head.

The man gave a purple and yellow sno-cone to an old woman wearing pink tights that matched the colour of her wig. A young man with one arm was selling curried crab; though the smell of the spices threatened to grab Apollo's ankles and pull him towards the bubbling pot, he didn't want to risk indigestion or worse, diarrhoea. None of the people selling food looked sanitary. No hairnets, gloves or anything, They talked, laughed and spat next to the food they cooked. The men peed in the bushes nearby without washing their hands, the same hands that rolled the dough for the dumplings being fried in a sizzling frying pan. The same dumpling Regina was tearing apart now and urging him to try. The potbellied man selling jerk chicken from a coal-filled metal drum coughed as he used a fork to move the pieces on the grill. Regina looked at him. 'Heat kills the germs, man. Dem say "scornful dog nyam dutty puddin''. What don't kill, fatten.'

DJ Electric was playing an oldie on the Killa Soundz sound system. The singer's voice poured over the dancers like warm honey. Lovers clutched each other, wrapped up in the slow melody caressing them. A man shouldered through the crowd, selling dried peppered shrimp in see-through plastic bags, competing to be heard above a lady selling mannish water, duckoonoo or blue drawers made with cornmeal, coconut, cocoa and yam boiled in a banana leaf.

Apollo felt underdressed watching Regina. She looked out of this world, resplendent in a green wig, batty-rider shorts, pink mesh tights and black and white checkered sneakers, swigging Heineken and smoking a Matterhorn. Apollo wore a tie-dye T-shirt with Bob Marley's face and grey acid wash jeans. There was a definite mismatch.

As Apollo handed Regina the sky juice she'd asked him to buy, he could barely make out her words. 'Yuh couldn't dress up more than dis? How yuh fi come inna de dance in a ganzee?' She wiped the grease from the dumpling on the back of his shirt.

'A what?'

'Ganzee mean T-shirt!' She fingered the flimsy material as she swayed. 'And crep too!'

'What's that?' It sounded like French pancakes.

'A puss-boot! Sneakers!' She pointed at his shoes. 'Dem is new-brand?'

'Huh? You mean brand-new?'

Sometimes he felt they spoke different languages. He'd heard people say patois was just broken English but he often had no clue what Jamaicans were saying. Even when they pronounced English words, like sausage (*sat-chiz*), certificate (*surf-fi-ticket*), film (*flim*) and violence (*voy-lenz*). It was like Jamaicans had a hot pebble on the tongue when they said words: *wata* (water), *pi-tata* (potato), *prum-guh-naught* (pomegranate) and *horse-spittle* (hospital). He had even heard callers to radio talk shows bemoaning that ordinary Jamaicans were being held *ostrich* (hostage) to crime and expressing concern about a rise in the cases of child *a-bruise* (abuse). Their combinations of English words were funny too: *hand-middle* (palm) and *head-side*. He had quickly learnt not to take people literally when they expressed shock or dismay by exclaiming: 'Kiss mi neck! Is what dis on mi back-side?' or 'Bird cage! Puss back-foot!' or 'Yuh see mi dying trial? Don't torment mi soul-case!'

He had more in common with his rich white American friends than Black Jamaicans; which he found perplexing. For these Jamaicans, suffering, and the overcoming of that suffering through struggle was as effortless as their heart pumping. Just outside the entrance to the dance, he saw a man stoop down and wash his hands and arms in a stream of greyish water running in the lane. Apollo was baffled at how natural and rigorous the man's movements were and the steadiness of the smile on his face.

Regina was talking: 'Is 'cause di shoes new why yuh stepping like puss 'pon hot brick?' She laughed, exposing her teeth.

He could tell from her slurred words that she was drunk, and had been before they turned up at the dance. Her breath was heavy with alcohol. He'd also seen Damian slip her something in a small bag which she pocketed before he could see what it was. He was tired of telling her to cut down on her drinking. It brought out her ugly side.

He told himself she wasn't trying to be mean. Looking at her gave him a blast of heat in his chest. Regina was sexy, she was daring and she wanted all of him. She excited him. Their relationship had happened whiplash fast. He told her that the first time they had sex was nothing like he'd experienced with his high school girlfriend, a bony blonde, in the back of his dad's Audi. Regina was a woman who filled herself up with him; grinding him with fervour, yes, but also the cold and precise efficiency of an industrial engineer. He was bucking and exploding inside her before he realised, ashamed of how quickly it all ended. As he wilted, melting away before her, Regina spat, wiped herself with a rag she pulled from her pocket and adjusted her shorts.

Regina wasn't very educated and didn't come from a 'good stable family'. She was not the type of girl his parents would approve of. His mother especially. How could he ever tell them how they met? Not that he tried to think about that hand-job – especially how long it hadn't lasted. His friend Kevin back home would have called her a ho. If he were in the States, he'd have to think about what his friends would say about him being with a girl like her, but none of those people were here, so who cared? But Regina was *his* choice, not anybody else's. And his feelings for her were an act of defiance that almost made him giddy. He wanted her boldness to rub off on him, her bravado and attitude.

The DJ switched to an upbeat dancehall tune and the place erupted. Regina eyed a gyrating woman who was wearing a black and yellow checkered buttoned-down top, black leather pants, door-knocker earrings and high-top sneakers. Other women wore lycra fitted dresses, white sweat suits, tube dresses with ruffles, wide-legged pants suits with fringes and gold buttons.

She'd given up trying to teach him any dance moves. All he was comfortable doing was the Moonwalk that he'd seen Michael Jackson do on TV but that would have announced him as a foreigner. He felt as if eyes were on him already.

Regina interrupted his thoughts. 'So tell mi something, Apollo. Is deh Dinah really did deh wid the white man, yuh fadda?'

'Deh?' he said, sipping his Red Stripe.

'Mi mean if dem screw. Yuh is half-white, don't it?'

Regina thought: *If Dinah get the chance to screw a white man, why she never have the good sense to make sure him carry her back to America?*

'No. Dinah says my dad is some dude from Jamaica, an old boyfriend named Leroy. He ran off to Canada.'

'So all dem years yuh never know yuh was adopted?'

'Nope. I mean, I'm still not sure. Moms' family is light skinned, like Dinah's mother. Moms said that my dad, John King, was Black. It's my stepdad who's white. Although I used to think Ray was my real dad until I was about ten when they told me the truth.'

'So you look like John King?'

'Dunno. He died in a car crash when Moms was pregnant.'

'Kiss mi neck! Yuh have a picture of him?'

'Nah. And I don't know his family either. Moms married Pops when I was less than a year old.'

'Backside! No, star. Is things like dis yuh see 'pon TV in dem American soap opera.' Regina turned to face the turntables and resumed her dancing.

He could tell she'd stopped listening. What he didn't know was what she was thinking: *I wonder what a white woody feel like?* She had always heard they were smaller than Black men but she had seen enough Black ones to know not all were created equal. She supposed when she went to the States she might find out.

Apollo wanted to respond with a snarky comment that he was glad his life provided her with entertainment. But he knew better than to say a word. It was too soon to joke with her. Less than an hour ago, he'd complained about Raymond giving him a hard time about borrowing the car. All he'd said was that life was hard and things were rough. Enraged, Regina had immediately turned on him.

'What yuh know 'bout hard? Yuh know how to manage hard life? To take sun and rain?'

'What do you mean?'

'Yuh know what it is to only have water pass yuh mouth on a hot day? To go to bed with your belly button feel like it sticking to yuh spine 'cause yuh so hungry? And when heavy rain fall, rich people like yuh in yuh nice *bed*. Cool and comfortable. Yuh look out the fancy window at the view from the hill and turn over, pulling up the comforter 'round yuh neck. Yuh don't think nothing more 'bout it.' She poked him in the chest as her eyes blazed.

'Middle-class people might have a leak or two: one behind dem fridge in the kitchen or in dem bedroom over the queen size bed. Maybe sliding down the wall in the living

145

room behind the TV. Dem set pan to catch the water and next day dem call a man to fix dem roof. But poor people now, is dem *feel* it. Dem house wash away from offa gully and riverbank. Landslide mek wall collapse 'pon dem board house. That happen to one of mi friend, and we have to use pickaxe, shovel, bucket, pot, pan and we hands to dig her out. We use what we could find 'cause we never have no tractor to call for. And is *me* find her ankle under a piece of wood and as mi touch her mi know she dead! So don't talk 'bout what yuh don't know, and what yuh can't understand. 'Bout rough time.'

◆

The large black speaker boxes were pumping. The selector was telling the crowd to throw their hands in the air 'if dem a bad man' and 'dem a women wid good body'.

Over the heads of wildly gyrating dancers, Apollo spotted Damian in animated discussion with a slightly older guy, Damian gesticulating wildly. He could tell they were arguing, but the crowd was too noisy for him to hear what they were fussing about.

The other man caught Apollo's eye as he watched. He was wearing a brown tweed cap, red-framed sunglasses, and a red handkerchief tied around his neck. Smirking, he pulled down his sunglasses to stare at Apollo.

Apollo looked away and found himself staring right at a couple who looked like they were having sex in the corner, even though they were fully clothed. It brought him the feeling you get watching a dog lick itself: completely natural but at the same time unsettling. He could not drop his gaze.

'Easy nuh, Apollo,' Damian appeared by his side, slapping his back. 'Chill. Enjoy yuhself.' Damian was wearing a Kangol hat, a thin gold chain, a pinstripe yellow blazer with thick shoulder pads and camouflage-print pants. 'Kakafart! In yahso jam up til it ram!' He looked around at the crowd.

'Him mean in here have plenty people,' Regina translated.

'Yow dread, mi need to talk to yuh.' Urgency pierced Damian's voice.

Regina went to get another Red Stripe. She dropped a balled up foil paper and a plastic fork on to the ground. Apollo wondered if Damian wanted to talk about the confrontation with Dinah from the other day. They hadn't spoken since.

He decided to go first.

'Listen, Damian, you don't gotta tell me you're sorry. But stay away from Dinah for a while.'

The confusion on Damian's face told him that that wasn't it at all.

'What? Dinah is the least of my problems. Look, yuh know how yuh always coming here—'

'Yeah.'

'Yuh is an outsider.'

'Nah, man. I'm Dinah's son. We're brothers, right?' Apollo brought his hand up for a fist bump but Damian left him hanging.

'Listen to what mi telling yuh. Me and Streggo was just talking. We do some business together.' Damian turned and beckoned the tweed cap-wearing man over.

'Streggo say as an outsider, yuh must pay tax.'

'Tax?' Apollo asked, as Streggo joined them.

'Yeah, zeen? Tax to come and tax to go and tax to love we women.' Streggo joined in as if he had been part of the conversation all along. It was clear to Apollo that Damian was parroting his words. Streggo looked in the direction of Regina. She had her palms on the floor, butt in the air, feet braced on the speaker box. 'It's nothing personal. Just business.'

'That's ridiculous!' Apollo retorted. The thought of paying to go out with Regina made him sick. How could Damian just stand there while this thug extorted him?

Damian's features darkened. 'Is just a likkle tax. Small money to a rich boy like yuh. Just a few US dollars a week.'

'No way! Look, bro, I ain't giving you no money. That's extortion!'

'Ex-o-what? Is a normal thing, man. British get protection money from taximan, vendors downtown and the Chineyman that have wholesale.'

'Damian, I'm not paying you or Streggo anything. And I'm gonna come and go as I please!'

'Look, farin boy, yuh sure yuh want to behave so?' Damian asked. Streggo had fallen silent. Damian felt a sharp sense of embarrassment jar his spine. He could read disgust on Streggo's face. *Control yuh fren*, that's what Streggo's expression said.

'What you gonna do about it, huh?' Apollo stepped closer to Damian, jutting out his chin. He wasn't sure where this sudden courage came from. He was positive Damian could more than kick his ass. He pictured the scene: him face down in the dirt, spitting pebbles out of his mouth, his face bloodied, Damian with his heel in his back, Regina looking on, embarrassed that her man couldn't fight. And how could he stand up for her if he couldn't stand up for himself?

The deejay turned off the music. Apollo thought for a second that it was so everyone could hear him cry out from Damian's punches and kicks. A hush fell over the crowd. People stopped talking. Breathing. The air pulsed.

The deejay said: 'People, dis is the moment we deh yah for.'

So everybody was coming to see a fight! Apollo thought. Sweat ran down the back of his neck.

'People, unnu ready for this?'

The crowd replied in unison: 'Yeahhhhh!'

Damian's face had a hardness Apollo had never seen before. He was sure people would take bets.

'Unnu sure unnu ready?'

The crowd responded with howls. Damian took a step towards him.

The deejay continued: 'Alright, all of unnu big up the big man, the boss, the Don, wi leader. *Mek we hail up Britiiiiiiiiish!*'

Women began to squeal. The place erupted. People parted like the Red Sea before Moses.

British wore a tilted felt fedora on his head and a black double-breasted suit. Clarks shoes, and a thick gold chain. Two large men were with him, in black leather jackets.

Men came up and patted British's shoulders. British stuffed crisp bills into the hands of a pregnant woman and an old man with one leg.

Apollo turned back. Damian was gone. His shoulders sagged in relief.

Now the sound clash could start. The deejay introduced his challengers, Twin Sounds: a man called Bigga or Biggs, and his twin brother nicknamed Fatta or Fatty.

'Is a sound *claaaaash!*' the MC bellowed. 'Is mi nephew dem with dem new sound!'

The Twins said they were turning the dance retro and began playing lovers rock music.

'Dis is fi the ladies dem!' Fatta yelled. 'Lift up unnu hand if unnu have yuh own man! Yuh nah share him wid no likkle gyal!' In response, scores of hands and cigarette lighters went up in the air.

DJ Electric answered with a tune that evoked high-pitched screams from the women. Changing tack, the Twins responded with a conscious tune lamenting the fate of Marcus Garvey. The rest of the song was swallowed by bursts of gun-fire as male patrons fired into the air. Bigga called out: 'Time fi music fi de man dem!'

For the next hour the clashing sound systems played hit after hit. Regina grabbed Apollo close and slow-wined on him as he moved stiffly. She whispered in his ear: 'The thing 'bout ghetto people is this. Don't cross we, yuh hear? Yuh think 'cause of Dinah, yuh have access, but watch yuh step.'

After DJ Electric ended with the slow dance section, the MC declared a musical tie and promised a rematch. Amid boos from the crowd, Apollo saw Damian talking to the DJ. He handed the man something in a brown paper bag.

'Hol' up, hol' up! We have a new talent in here tonight,' said DJ Electric. 'A young singer/deejay name *Congo King*! Him just start in the business. Lazarus Gardens, welcome one of unnu own.'

There were yells from the women and the men flashed their cigarette lighters. Damian grabbed the microphone and began to sing:

> Lazarus Gardens, a nuh easy life we lead,
> Lazarusssssss, poor people have to eat,
> And if the gun don't kill we,
> Police nuh shoot we,
> People nuh badmind we,
> we have to come through fi wi yute dem.

He owned the stage; a fire in his eyes ignited the crowd. Heads bobbing, the crowd floated with him on the melody. He was their guide as it dipped and rose. It seemed to Apollo that there was radiance in his face. He was glowing. When

Damian finished, there were howls of appreciation, which he took in with a broad grin. One of British's bodyguards did a gun salute.

Regina was smiling in a way Apollo had never seen her smile for him. There was pride there, and affection too.

'Him sound good, don't it?' Regina drew close to make herself heard amidst the noise, breathing warmth on Apollo's cheek. She squeezed his hand.

'Yeah,' Apollo said, pulling away. He was. But he couldn't tell Damian so himself. Not now.

Regina pushed away through the crowd to find Damian, leaving Apollo standing on the sole patch of grass, amongst a growing pool of paper plates, popsicle sticks, empty beer bottles and cigarette stubs littering the ground.

Before leaving the dance with a woman on each arm, British sent one of his leather-jacketed men to deliver a message. The man came over and shook Apollo's hand, like he knew him and gave him a business card that read 'British, Entrepreneur' with a phone number.

'Lawyer yute, come check the Boss. Call him, man. British have a job fi yuh.'

Apollo looked over at the man they all called British. He was far on the other side of the dance and talking to another man; nevertheless, Apollo thought there was little that missed British's attention.

In that moment, British turned around and looked straight at him. British raised his chin.

The sound of the music and people screaming fell away, replaced in Apollo's ears by the echo of ceaseless waves crashing against the shore. There was something chilling about the man. You could feel the danger under his skin: a tightly coiled spring about to snap.

The hand that pushed the card into his wallet didn't feel like his own.

◆

Damian exited the stage to hands clapping him on his back, patting him on the shoulder, men offering him drinks, young women giving him their phone numbers scribbled on pieces of paper thrust into his pants, lingering at his back pocket.

He looked around for Regina and Apollo. Regina rushed up to him, plastering a kiss on his cheek, but he couldn't make out Apollo in the mass of people.

Streggo pulled him away from the adoring crowd.

'Is two months now yuh telling mi yuh going do the job in Jack's Hill. What yuh waiting so long for? Avoiding mi, talking 'bout yuh "been busy". Yuh see what mi was telling yuh earlier, Damian? The Yankee yute don't respect yuh. People like him too high and mighty. Him feel him better than yuh. Than all of we. Yuh see it fi yuhself tonight.'

'Him supposed to be mi friend, so how him couldn't let off a likkle something? How him mean "no"? What him mean by "no"?'

Streggo pulled a spliff from behind his ear. 'If yuh nuh ready to collect likkle protection money, yuh nuh ready to rob him fada.' Flicking his lighter, he watched the end burn, then took a deep draw. 'How yuh going show the Boss that yuh ready? And how yuh going get yuh album?'

And it was that last part that had gotten to Damian.

One of the things he admired about British was that among his many businesses – the car rental, the restaurants, the wholesales and bars – was a record studio. British had produced hits from young men just like him who wanted to rise from the ghetto.

Streggo's eyes met his through the smoke. 'Yuh need

money to book studio time and produce yuh record.' He handed the spliff to Damian. 'Yuh *albums* dem.' That was it. That was all it took. If stealing from Apollo's people was how he would achieve his dream, he was prepared to do it.

Yes, for his dream, he could do anything.

Mama

Dinah is sitting next to Mama on the bed, combing her hair with a yellow plastic comb. First she sections the hair into squares in Mama's scalp, then rubs it with black castor oil, before twining it into thick plaits.

'What we going eat tonight, Mama? What yuh want fi dinner?' Dinah asks, not because she thinks Mama understands and will answer but because she wants to fill the air with sound apart from Mama's ragged breathing.

As she takes each strand and gently tugs it, over and under, over and under, Mama thinks of a recipe:

Take:
One stubborn woman who deny all good sense
Half a man who don't realise him is still a boy
One bad man
Two bad-man-in-training
Two alleged baby tief
One careless, wild gal
and a mad old woman.

Stir up. Blend. Drink it up!

Apollo

Before developing an interest in law, Apollo had thought about becoming an anthropologist or international journalist. He felt that the keen powers of observation needed to really examine people came naturally to him. He had always felt like an outsider, looking into his own life. What he didn't expect was this feeling intensifying in Jamaica.

To blend his fascination with people and law, he decided he'd become a human rights lawyer or a criminal defence lawyer. He had visions of himself as a crusader, saving the small man – delivering justice for people who looked like him through the eloquence of his tongue. With his parents' money he didn't have to think about charging for his services. He could spend his life on righteous causes.

Working at a firm that mainly did corporate law didn't really align with his lofty goals, but Mr Brown said the firm sometimes did pro bono criminal defence work for inner city youth. Apollo had shadowed some lawyers on those cases but it was mainly marijuana possession, illegal gun possession or wounding charges, and he'd quickly discovered most of the accused were tangentially connected to someone at the firm: the office cleaner's grandson or the nephew of a gardener to one of the lawyers. There was no trumped-up murder conviction that he could help overturn. No mother bawling her eyes out at the prospect of her only child facing the death penalty, which in Jamaica meant the gallows.

'You actually hang people? Don't you think capital punishment is barbaric?' he'd asked Mr Brown, whose only reply was 'string up the brutes once they're found guilty'.

'And what about poor people?' Apollo exploded. 'the ones locked up for years who can't make bail?'

'Look, son, Jesus himself said the poor would always be with us. Now how about we grab some lunch?'

Weekdays during his lunch break he'd spend time in the tenement yard, talking to Regina. He knew better than to venture on his own through the entire community and his visits were always during the daytime, when Mr McKenzie was at work at the garage. If Regina wasn't there, he'd listen to his Walkman and watch people come and go. Living their lives, the crunch of the gravelly sidewalk under their feet. At first, people accosted him, demanding to know who he was, asking what he was there for. Some thought he was an Opposition party spy out to make mischief. But that soon changed. His presence was largely unnoticed now. Unbeknownst to Apollo, British had since sent word to leave the Yankee alone.

Apollo considered them his people, even though they didn't claim him.

On this Tuesday, he'd arrived at around one in the afternoon. He'd been able to get the Benz today and he was hoping to see Regina so he could take her out to lunch. As usual, the front door to the house was open. It baffled Apollo that people in the ghetto never secured their possessions as if they were too poor to rob or trusted their neighbours so much. Dinah was at work. Heavy snoring from the back room told him the old lady was asleep. It wouldn't have mattered if she was awake, she was mostly incoherent anyway. Damian wasn't around, which he was grateful for. Things had been tense between them since the dance last week.

Since Regina wasn't at home either, Apollo decided to wait for her on the front steps. It was a hot day and he felt drunk with the sun. Sluggish. He went inside the kitchen and poured himself some Kool-Aid from the fridge, then went back out to the step.

He had a surprise for Regina. A new Polaroid instant camera. She said she had no photos of herself as a kid, and he wanted to give her a picture of them both to keep in her room. Something to make her think of him. He turned the camera over in his hands, heavy, slick, expensive – incongruous on this dusty road. He put his eye to the viewfinder. Across the street a man lay on a wall four feet high, only half as wide as a child's exercise book, pressing his spine along the narrow bricks. Apollo clicked. Not far from him was another man, squatting shirtless, eating rotten seeds from the ground at the base of a tree, leering at a woman wearing a bright baby-blue hat and a pink blouse under a sleeveless, striped dress. He clicked again. He could see somebody patching the inner tube of a bicycle. Apollo snapped them all.

Apollo wished his parents could see Lazarus Gardens as he saw it. The people's lives seemed to fill something in him. *This* was Jamaica. Not the postcards. It was here in the pictures he took. The woman in a black crop top (Regina called it a 'belly-skin blouse'), giggling; the middle-aged man with matted hair, in plaid black and white three-quarter pants, a kerchief wrapped around his neck, holding wires looking like a TV antenna; and the woman in a straw bonnet and fuzzy brown slippers, singing.

For his next series of shots he pointed his camera at a man in a pink knitted tam, riding a bicycle; a girl in jeans shorts watching a man pushing a trolley of clothes and fruit; and a little boy in royal blue shorts kicking a can down the street.

None of them wore the colour of the Opposition party. 'Down to yuh underwear,' Regina had said to him once, pulling down her skirt to reveal the colour of her panties. 'Don't bring none of fi *dem* drawers in here.'

Along with the pictures, he made notes on a yellow legal pad.

The little boy in the royal blue shorts came up, eyeing the camera. 'What yuh writing? Is census yuh taking?'

'Nah, just writing down what I see in my book and taking pictures. Here, little man, look.' Apollo showed the boy the place in the book where a description of him had been entered. For a second, the boy seemed impressed. Apollo handed the boy the photo he'd taken of him. The boy gazed at himself, fascinated.

'Mi can keep it?'

Apollo nodded. The boy quickly thrust the picture in his pocket, before Apollo could change his mind.

'So why yuh doing this?'

''Cause it's interesting.'

'"Inter-esting"?' He pronounced the word like trying out something new in his mouth.

'Yeah, it's fun.'

'Fun to write 'bout people in yuh book and take picture?' The boy looked perplexed. 'What fun can inna dat?' He sucked his teeth.

'Shouldn't you be in school?'

'End-a-term.'

'Where are your parents?'

'Don't know,' the boy shrugged.

The little boy soon got bored and went off to play marbles with two other boys. It brought to mind an awkward conversation he'd had with Regina a few weeks ago. Apollo had remarked: 'Everybody, down to kids, keep begging me for money, always asking me to "let off a likkle ting, nuh?" And I get things are bad. I see dudes on the corner not working. But I don't understand how folks in Lazarus Gardens can have so many kids so young. It's just irresponsible.'

'Apollo, shut up!' Regina snapped. 'Don't pass judgement on we life until yuh live it. Yuh not one of we. Look at yuh.' She poked his chest. 'Yuh nuh know nothing 'bout life as a sufferer. Yuh come down here and think yuh know we?'

'I guess I don't.'

'Yuh get plenty privilege, so letting off a likkle thing is nothing to yuh. And we have family for the same reason other people have dem: love, protection. Survival too, and the fact some of we don't know better.'

He had to admit that Gina was right. He had no right to judge their way of life; not when he couldn't understand it. He knew something else too.

These Lazarus Gardens people could flip on him at any time and he knew it. It came down to what Regina said at the dance on Friday: he had to watch his step.

◆

A homeless vagrant (a category of people all Jamaicans dubbed 'madman' regardless of mental state) paused in his heaping of stones and threw a box of something across the street that narrowly missed a woman. People were burning garbage, throwing old tyres, bathtubs and dead animals into gullies. A bare-chested teen collected water in buckets and loaded them on a wooden handcart. Two toddlers wearing diapers played in a large green bucket.

Apollo paused and watched the customers at the corner shop, Big Mike's Variety Store. The shop wasn't anything more than a lean-to, perched at the side of a dilapidated concrete building which had only half a roof left. Perched on the remnant of the roof was the lower half of a broken office chair with three black wheels. The shop sprang from this husk of a building and you'd think it was abandoned too, if you didn't see people coming and going and shouting 'Serve!' to get Mike's attention before placing their order.

A small glass case at the front showed rows of banana chips, round buns and biscuits and a slot to take the money and pass the goods. Despite the professed variety of the store's name, Big Mike sold mainly snacks. He sold a few other things too, like half a loaf of bread, one matchstick, three eggs, two slices of cheese and half a stick of butter. Mike made sure his customers knew his philosophy in the signs he painted on the wall: 'We Trust In God, not people. Trust mash up business.' This was next to a sign that read: 'I love my enemies 'cause God loves me.'

A skinny little girl in gold slippers came up and shouted: 'Serve!' into the dark bowels of the lean-to. After getting no answer she bellowed again, making her own echo: 'Serve hereeeee! Servvvvvveeeeeee!'

'Mi coming,' Mike said irritably from his stool, awoken from his midday snooze.

She adjusted a plait and the pink bandeau around her head. She was wearing a white T-shirt, a black and white poufy shirt and pink socks.

'Yuh have tea biscuit?' She said it in a tone Apollo knew his mother would have called 'feisty', and Regina would have called 'facety' meaning 'rude' or 'force-ripe', a phrase she told him was reserved for 'outta order' children.

'Yes.'

'Sell mi a pack.' Apollo imagined Regina had been like that as a child. He smiled, watching the girl's fierce expression bloom into being on the Polaroid.

Apollo watched a homeless man, clad only in a pair of briefs, cooling himself at a fire hydrant gushing water and thought again how different this was to the tourism ads. More real. More gritty and full of meaning. The homeless man wore a single slipper, but his bearing was stately. There was dignity there.

The people dressed well, in the brand name clothes sent in barrels from family working hard in the North American cold. They knew how to make do. Regina had told him how one pound of chicken-back could be curried with white rice to feed nine people. He didn't know what it was like for hunger to die inside you. To be so hungry you were no longer conscious of its gnaw. He had seen her eat chicken feet, which looked like the skeletal remains of someone's hand, like the mummies you saw on TV when archaeologists pried open ancient Egyptian tombs. She'd introduced him to the delicacy of condensed milk spread on thick slices of hard dough bread and to saltfish and white rice. Food that was filling and cheap enough for everybody to afford.

It seemed to Apollo that the people of Lazarus Gardens grabbed joy wherever they could find it. Like when Regina had asked him who had thrown water and flour on him for his birthday, some Jamaican birthday custom he'd never heard of. When he said nobody, she'd run into the kitchen of the tenement yard and returned with a bag of white flour that she dumped on his head. 'Now is yuh birthday!' she said, giggling hysterically.

He thought now: *These people have so little, but maybe they have more than I can know.* And he got the same feeling like at the dance that night: that he didn't belong. He was afraid he would never fit anywhere. Would never feel the ease of being among people who were like him.

His last photo was of a woman getting out of a red

car, which resembled Eddie's. She wore a lilac top, white pleated pants and gold heels. He knew that body, that walk and – when she turned – that face. His hand holding the camera froze.

It was Celeste.

'What are you doing here?' Apollo blinked rapidly, nearly dropping the camera.

'I should be asking you that.' She adjusted the tan leather bag on her shoulder, fidgeting with the orange silk scarf tied to its strap. Diamond ring on her finger, gold necklace around her neck. A group of young boys popped firecrackers and she looked shellshocked as if she'd been dropped off in the middle of an active war zone.

'How'd you get here?' Apollo had a sour taste in his mouth.

'How do you think? Eddie.' She waved her hand in the direction of where Eddie was standing beside his car parked out front and adjusted her sunglasses. Dirt had already caked her shoes. 'So *this* is where you've been sneaking off to.' She looked around, the sudden action flipping her braids.

'You gotta go. It's not safe.' He ushered her off the main road and into the tenement yard.

'Then how come it's safe for you? Huh, Apollo?'

'You don't understand. And you can't come in here with that orange scarf on your handbag. That's the colour of the other party. Gimme that.' Apollo untied it and put it into his pocket.

'Apollo, what are you doing here? *These* are *not* your people.'

'We'll talk about this at home.' Apollo took her elbow gently but firmly and tried to take her back through the gate.

'I'm not going anywhere.' She wrenched her hand away and deposited herself on a rickety wooden chair in the yard. 'I'm here to talk to that Dinah woman and I'm not leaving. I told Eddie to wait for me. I'll bring the police if I have to.'

'Why you gotta call the cops?' Apollo gritted his teeth. His palms were sweating. He rubbed them on his jeans.

'I'm sure felonies are committed in places like these every day that the police need to know about.' Celeste batted at the flies attacking an overripe, burst mango on the ground. Her nostrils narrowed at the smell of nearby sewage. She frowned. The odour from the overflowing gullies often intensified with the heat of the sun.

'Does Pops know you're here?' Apollo sucked in the air. His palms were leaving wet spots on his shirt.

'No, and I don't plan on telling him. Neither will you. Your father doesn't need to know about this.'

'You can't stay here. Dinah's not home.' He knew this wouldn't go well. And that knowledge was winding around the back of his neck. He had to get Celeste out of here. What if people saw her here? How to explain her when people thought Dinah was his mother? Dressed like that, Celeste was a target to be robbed, or worse.

'That's fine. I'll wait.' She checked her pearl-band watch, pulled a *Vogue* magazine from her handbag and began to thumb through it slowly and pointedly. She looked up at him. 'I'm your mother and I'm *not* going to allow you to destroy your future.'

'Keep your voice down.' Apollo cautioned her.

That was when Regina and Damian strolled through the gate arm-in-arm, laughing at a shared joke. Their expressions faltered and they stepped apart as soon as they saw him.

Dinah

Just as mi about to pull the gate, I feel a electric charge. At first mi think is the blasted woman in the white bathrobe come to lick mi down. One time, Mama said a duppy box her and it feel like a sharp heat across her face, like somebody lick yuh with a hot frying pan. The first thing that come to mind to ward her off is to stop and chant Psalm 91:

'He that dwelleth in the secret place of the most High shall abide under the shadow of the Almighty. He is my refuge and my fortress. He shall cover thee with his feathers, and under his wings shalt thou trust.'

By the time mi reach the last verse is who I see but Son-Son running through the gate to meet mi? Mi son come to look fi mi! It make mi heart feel glad. Mi so glad I never see di woman stand up beside him or that the woman is Mrs Steele. Hell-george! Fallitaach! What this woman doing in mi yard?

Mama always teach mi that mi mustn't be ungrateful, especially in times when yuh feel yuh have nuttin to be grateful for. I want to find it in my heart somewhere to tell Mrs Steele thanks for seeing that mi boy get a good education and the things him need that mi couldn't give him. Mi did play over and over what mi would say when I see her again. Mi did want say: 'Yuh give him a good life, but him did need mi. Why yuh never write like yuh promise?'

Instead, mi say, 'What yuh doing at mi house?' She is the last face mi want to see. Especially now that mi just coming from work and tired, hot and dirty with mi clothes looking crush up. She standing there in a white pants and purple blouse like she just step off a magazine cover. Me is a crumpled-up bag and she is a clean sheet of paper.

Hear what the bright, facety and outta order woman say: 'What do you want with my son?'

Her son? Like is *she* push him out of her vagina in that dirty, piss-up hospital bed?

'Come outta mi yard!' mi bawl after her. A small crowd gathering but mi nuh business.

'Let me tell you something lady,' she say. 'This is *my* child. And you need to stay away from him.'

Apollo standing in the middle of two of we, hands up like him refereeing a football game.

'I've never seen you in my life, until that day at the Browns. So where the hell do *you* get off, talking about how I stole your baby? Are you mentally ill or something?'

'Save mi, O Lawd, from lying lips and *deceitful* tongues.' Mi repeat the word: 'Tief! Tief! Tief!' like a chorus, clapping mi hands. 'Great pretender, yuh is a actress? Is him yuh performing for?'

'Is it a US visa that you want? You think Apollo can get you to the States?'

I tell her she rude and disrespectful but she don't stop.

'I know that is what people like you chase after! This is the last time I'm going to tell you to leave my son alone.'

She grab Son-Son hand to lead him through the gate, but mi block dem. I hold on to Son-Son hand. She ask

165

mi what mi think mi doing. Then she touch mi. The woman put her hand on my left shoulder and push mi outta the way.

Mi don't know what come over mi, maybe is the woman in the white robe jumping in my bones, but I feel fire rising in mi chest and I push away mi son and I grab her nice pretty shirt and it rip when she pull away from mi.

'You bitch!' she say and then she jump 'pon mi and two of we wrestling in the dirt and I don't know where mi slippers and handbag gone 'cause I fling weh everything and we on the ground rolling and my hair in her fists and my hand grabbing her earrings and I don't know whose body is whose body any more, 'cause we moving sideways back and forth like two barrels that turn over. I kick. She kick.

The people circle around we shouting: 'Fight! Fight! Fight! Done har, Dinah!' and through the dust in mi eyes I see the pickney dem from the yard cheering mi on but I don't see Son-Son.

I feel hands raising mi up. Mi see Son-Son hands, Regina hands and Damian hands. I can't read him face. Mi see a broken camera on the ground.

'Miss Dinah, yuh is a big ooman, ennuh,' Damian shaking him head. 'Dis fighting thing is not fi yuh.'

Regina pull down mi skirt hem that was around mi thighs. 'Come, mek we go inside,' she say, as if is a likkle pickney she talking to. 'I going get yuh some wata.' She wipe mi face with a rag.

Mrs Steele on the ground, holding her right jaw and groaning. Her white pants turn brown like her legs. Mi don't even remember when mi punch her but I can see likkle drops of blood on her purple blouse.

Son-Son staring at mi.

'Come, son,' I say but the words that come out don't sound

166

like that at all. I realise mi mouth full of blood. I spit and a tooth come out. Right there on the ground.

Mi want Son-Son to see that mi will fight fi him. That mi not going lose him again. That mi would flip the world upside down to find him.

'No, Dinah.' Him helping Mrs Steele to her feet. He put her arm across his shoulder and she limp away towards the gate.

'I'm gonna be back later. I'm taking Moms home.'

No 'yuh alright?' No 'she hurt yuh?' No telling her it serve her backside right for coming to pick fight with mi. In my own yard. And him a call her 'Moms'.

In that moment, mi son choose her.

Although mi know she must pain up, she turn har head to look at mi and smile.

Ghetto News Network

There's an informal messaging service which receives and transmits news across every Jamaican community, pioneered long ago by the village gossip, the fabled mout-a-massy Liza. Lazarus Gardens was no different. Here, Ghetto News Network (GNN) correspondents whisper above zinc fences and through gaps in plywood and in the cracks in cardboard window shutters. Nightly anchors sum up the day's news in front of the Big Mike's Variety Store or Nicey's Bar. Reporters submit their stories at all hours of the day in an unending news cycle.

GNN performs an important social function. One needs to know if Maas Seymour is on a rampage from drinking too much rum – so you can stay out of his way, or if he has just beaten his wife you can get her help – or which family is rumoured to be supporting the other political party, so you can make sure to stay away from them, so your house doesn't get firebombed too.

Almost paradoxically, the GNN knows how to keep secrets too. Nobody tells Mr McKenzie that his girlfriend Regina is giving him bun. First, because Regina has always cheated and always will. If the old fool can't see it himself, he doesn't deserve to be told. Second, and most importantly, everybody knows her relationship with Apollo is her only chance to rise up from the slum and 'go 'Merica', a dream so deeply cherished by people in Lazarus Gardens – people of all ages and genders – that no one has the heart deny her.

Today's edition of GNN's evening news sounds like this:

'This just in: fight bruk inna Dinah tenement yard. Farin woman get dust out.'

'And in other news: it look like Damian a fool 'round di Yankee boy ooman. What a prekeh!'

Raymond

Raymond was a pragmatic man; seeing things as they were; not how he wished them to be. This outlook brought him success in business. He could count on suppliers to cut corners, predict that staff would take shortcuts, depend on clients to cry down the price even though they knew it was fair. He'd built multi-million-dollar organisations based on this knowledge. He'd found that people were true to their nature: the good, bad and ugly. Even when they reached for a higher ideal, at the core there was still selfishness; the need to feel good, to be respected, to be well-regarded or remembered or to feel like they mattered. He saw it in himself. He saw this in Apollo.

Being pragmatic also brought sadness because you learnt to question every seemingly kind gesture, everything of beauty, even love. He was sure of his love for his family. Yet he knew he only loved them as much as he could manage, without sacrificing everything or losing himself completely. Investing beyond a point you could bear to lose was folly. To Raymond, this didn't make him a bad person. Just normal. Not inherently more evil or good.

He knew he was good because he chose to be. Because he could just as easily make another choice. Understanding that he could live with making decisions that caused others pain did not unsettle him at all. He could lay off a thousand people as effortlessly as he could tie his shoelaces. Yet he could swiftly reshuffle an entire department just to preserve the livelihoods of a few people. And neither scenario made a difference to how he felt or how he saw himself. This was power and he used his to solve whatever he considered a problem.

So when Raymond saw Celeste exit the taxi that afternoon, all bloodied and bruised, he immediately saw another problem to solve. Another situation needing a practical resolution. He would get Christopher's friend, the Assistant Commissioner of Police, that Davis guy, to locate and lock up whoever was brazen enough to attack his wife, a defenceless woman, in broad daylight.

'Celeste, what the hell happened to you?' He watched Apollo help his limping mother into the house. 'And what did *you* do about it?' he asked his son. 'Did you just stand there while your mother got the crap kicked out of her?'

'Pops, just cool it.'

'It's nothing Ray,' Celeste said. 'Just bring me some ice for my face. Please.' She gingerly deposited herself on the sofa. Lying back into the cushions, she closed her eyes.

'I had a situation to handle.'

'Looks like it handled you. What's going on, Celeste? Who did this to you? I'm going to make sure they do jail-time!'

Celeste and Apollo exchanged glances he couldn't read.

'OK, *OK*. I got robbed. And I've never seen the guys before. I didn't recognise them.'

'Robbed? Isn't that your handbag?'

'They took the cash and threw back the bag.'

'Bullsh—'

'Ray!'

'Stop blowing smoke up my ass! If you gave it up so

willingly, why did they rough you up? Why are you lying to me?'

Celeste winced at him shouting. 'I don't want to talk about it.'

'Oh, we're going to talk about it, alright, and I'm calling the cops right now.'

'You're doing no such thing! It's fine, Ray!'

'The hell it is!'

Apollo stepped in: 'Come on, Pops, Moms is traumatised. Let her get some rest. You guys can talk about it later.' Apollo lifted Celeste up the stairs.

What's going on? Raymond thought. *Just what the hell is happening to my family?* As far as he was concerned, the sooner they all left Jamaica, the better. He had to ensure he concluded his business deals soon.

He picked up the telephone and called Brown.

'Christopher, I need you to have someone keep an eye on my wife.'

'Rahtid! Celeste has another man?' Christopher couldn't picture her as the cheating type but you could never entirely trust a woman.

'No, nothing like that. She's just acting ... weird. Not herself. She claims she was mugged but I'm not sure.'

'Is she OK?'

'Yes. Do you have someone who can help?'

'I used an investigator at the firm last year to keep track of my wife. I didn't trust her and that damn tennis instructor. I'll give my guy a call. You want him to follow her all the time?'

'No. Only on the days I tell him.'

'No problem, Ray. Leave it to me. I'll call you back with the details.'

'And Christopher?'

'Yes?'

'I need another favour. We have to be discreet.' Raymond cradled the phone to his ear and lowered his voice. 'I believe in protecting what's mine.'

'Of course. Absolutely.' Christopher paused, unsure where his friend was going. But waited patiently.

'I need a gun.'

◆

Apollo sat in his cubicle at Chandler, Beck and Brown, his phone on his desk, next to the typewriter they had assigned to him. It was a Thursday morning, several days after the Dinah–Celeste fight, and the air conditioners were on full blast. One of the young secretaries had just brought him coffee. She'd lingered too long at his cubicle as if she wanted to ask him something else, like his phone number. Her desire was there, in the way she reached over and adjusted the position of his stapler on the desk, how she drew close to him, how her hands grazed his when she handed over the cup. She'd even casually placed a paper napkin in his lap. But he wasn't interested in any other woman but Regina. And there had been a lot on his mind, ever since he saw Damian and Regina together, gawking at him.

Yesterday, he'd confronted her. They were in his father's Benz driving to watch *Back to the Future* at Carib movie theatre in Cross Roads, and he wished he had a time machine to go back to that moment in the tenement yard and confront them together.

'What's going on, Gina?'

'What yuh mean?' Regina asked. The midday Kingston heat was shimmering from the road, entering the car in waves.

'What's going on between you and Damian?' Apollo kept his eyes fixed on the road. He didn't want Regina to see the hurt clouding them.

173

'Nothing nah gwaan. Him is mi fren. That's all.' Regina turned her body away from him, stretching her legs and reclining the seat. She rolled up the window. 'Yuh can turn on the AC?' She adjusted the Gucci sunglasses he'd bought her.

Apollo noticed she'd changed the subject but he let it go. He turned the knob and said nothing. Regina ran her hand along his inner thigh, but he took one hand off the wheel and placed her hand back on her lap, where her thighs were bare below the hem of a blue mini-dress. She turned in her seat so her back was against the door and lifted her toes into his crotch, wiggling them.

'Gina, just stop. Please. I'm not in the mood.'

She shrugged and moved her foot, playing with the silver anklet he'd bought her. Then she turned on the radio, popping in the Anita Baker cassette she'd brought in her handbag. The first track started. Regina cleared her throat to join in the singing. Apollo reached across and turned it off.

'Why yuh do that fah?' Regina asked but Apollo didn't answer.

A burst of rain started, pounding the roof like hailstones, and soon there were pools of water flowing in gutters, pedestrians hopping in vain over ever-expanding puddles even as car tyres splashed them. It was an explosion of water and thunder that petered out into a light drizzle within moments.

Apollo turned into a lane and was confronted by traffic. They were at a standstill. The only sound in the car was the sound of the wipers moving on the glass. The windscreen began to fog.

The traffic light in the distance changed from red to green to red again without the car moving an inch. Fifteen minutes passed and they'd only moved a few metres.

Regina broke the silence between them. 'Yuh and Damian should talk.'

'I don't got a thing to say to him, Gina.'

'Him never mean no harm.'

'How could you know what he meant, huh? You realise he was saying I had to pay to see you, right?'

'Yuh don't realise the pressure Damian under.'

'I'm not gonna talk about this.'

'Doh talk, then. Just listen. Yuh need to know Streggo and British is no joke. Believe mi when I tell yuh that.' She was biting her lip; she slowly trailed a red-painted fingernail along the glass. He watched her following the path of a rain droplet as it meandered down the window. As the lights stayed stuck on red, he saw one drop join with others to get fatter and fatter; changing path with each new merging droplet. He tried predicting which droplet would find which. Tried to find something beyond the randomness but soon concluded there was no pattern at all.

Regina turned but he couldn't meet her eyes. 'We going miss the show,' she said.

Apollo shrugged.

He hadn't called British. He'd put the business card into his wallet since he knew British was watching him at the dance, but when he got home he'd torn it up. He had enough sense to know this British guy was bad news. British seemed to be the one Streggo was working for and Streggo definitely meant him no good. He hadn't had a chance to ask Dinah for her advice before the fight with Celeste, and he hadn't seen her since.

Apollo turned back to the legal opinion Mr Brown had asked him to consider, trying to decide if Lord Denning's dictum in a UK House of Lords case was relevant to the argument they wanted to make for their client. The office was quiet except for the occasional hum of the fax machine.

The phone ringing broke his concentration.

175

'Yeah?' He picked up the phone absentmindedly, then remembered where he was. He recited the phone message that the senior associate had provided to all interns.

'Good afternoon, you've reached the offices of Chandler, Beck and Brown. Thank you for your call. Apollo speaking. How may I help you?'

'This is British,' the voice on the line said. It was a voice that was rich and ragged, like Velcro being ripped open. A voice that was sure of itself. One that didn't need to shout to be heard or taken seriously.

Apollo froze. Despite himself, he straightened up in his chair. How did British even know he was there?

In response to his unspoken question, British replied: 'I hear from Damian that you working there. You never called me so I decide to call you.' British's manner was polished and formal but his voice was steely. He was obviously not used to being ignored and wanted Apollo to know it.

'Ummm . . . how can I help you, Mr British?'

'Nah man, call me British.' His tone was casual and friendly.

'British, I'm kinda busy at work.'

'This won't take long. I going to be quick. I understand business. Time is money . . . by the way, your mother came to see me the other day.'

Apollo wondered how Celeste would have known British and why she hadn't said anything to him. He felt fear shoot through him at the thought of her alone with him.

'Dinah is – well, she's something else. She tell you we spent a little time together?'

Dinah? 'No.'

In the silence that followed, Apollo could hear the ticking of the clock above his head. Though the air conditioning was on, the room felt stuffy and his forehead was clammy. *What the hell was Dinah doing with this criminal?*

'Anyway, I have a job offer for you. Do me a favour and take it.'

'A job? What kinda job?'

'For now, as my legal advisor. You can understudy my current lawyer. And then when you graduate, there's a permanent place for you in my organisation.'

Apollo ignored his better judgement. 'And what kinda organisation is that?'

British didn't even hesitate. 'I run several successful businesses: import/export, restaurant, bars, clubs, a car dealership, a record label, real estate and, from time to time, I experience certain – let's call them "operational and logistical challenges" like problems at Customs. These challenges require legal services. I need a reliable, intelligent man. Money is no object. Name your fee.'

Apollo's breathing grew shallow. Something was rising in his throat. He spoke before the nausea could overwhelm him. 'Thanks for the offer ... British. I'm gonna think about it. But I really gotta go.'

'Take time to think, yes, but not too long. And I hope you like the present.'

British hung up.

Apollo sat and stared at the receiver in its cradle. He had an uneasy feeling that he couldn't explain. The whirring of the nearby fax machine sounded like a scream.

He jumped when the phone rang again.

It was Kim, the receptionist, calling from the downstairs lobby. 'Apollo, a package was just delivered for you.'

'What is it?'

'Don't know. It's in a sealed cardboard box marked "private and confidential".'

The ride downstairs in the elevator felt like forever. When he returned to his cubicle, he opened the box with shaking hands. He sliced through the tape across the top with the sharp blade of the silver letter opener. The flaps opened on a glossy brown sheen.

He picked it up. It was a leather briefcase monogrammed with his name. The small card inside read: 'From your future boss.'

Celeste

I can't believe that hovel in Lazarus Gardens is where my son has been spending all his time. I slip Eddie money, and he tells me all I need to know about what goes on in that dump. He told me Apollo had been going to see Dinah.

At first, it felt like a betrayal. Like I gave my whole life to this boy for him to reject me. Like I was a coat he was slipping out of. I wanted to scream at him, then I thought: *No, don't you do that, Celeste.* One thing my parents taught me was this: be smart, bide your time. They didn't get their wealth from being rash. Papa would buy properties in rundown areas, hold them for years and sell when the area got gentrified. Crack houses became coffee shops and loft apartments. When he was teaching me about business as a young girl, he'd say, 'Consolidate your holdings. Study. Get information and wait for the right moment to strike. It's all a game of strategy, baby.'

So that is what I did. I waited. Until the day I told Eddie he needed to take me there.

I confess: I lost my cool with Dinah. My passion got the better of me in that moment, but I thought she needed a little ass whooping. Papa used to box in college so he taught me how to land a mean right hook. I could have used that to send Dinah flat on her back if I'd wanted to play it differently. I got to give it to Dinah, though. She kicked my butt real good. She's tougher than I thought.

I lost the battle but I won the war and that was my intention. Apollo's been more attentive to me. Bringing me breakfast. Spending more time with me at home. So it was worth it, to lose that fight. He was the one who dressed my wounds. He'd gotten out the cotton balls and Band-Aids and did what I used to do when he'd fallen and injured himself on the playground. There was one time he fell off the swings, right on to his head. He got a nasty gash on his forehead and I talked him through each step of fixing it.

We went into the upstairs master bathroom and I sat on the toilet. He put the first aid kit on the sink.

'First, let's get this cleaned up. It's gonna hurt,' he said, applying an alcohol-soaked cotton ball to the cut on my forehead. When I flinched he told me to hold still. It didn't hurt as much as what he said next.

'You know I'm not gonna stop seeing Dinah, right?'

I couldn't bear to talk about her. Instead I asked, 'Remember that time you and Michael got into a fight?'

He just sighed and carried on dabbing at my forehead.

'You boys were nine or ten and he borrowed some action figure of yours and didn't bring it back so you weren't speaking to him for like three days, which is like a year in little boy time. Then out of the blue, he called to invite you to a sleepover at his house and you begged me to let you go? He still hadn't returned your action figure. And when I asked you about it, you remember what you told me? You told me Michael was still your best friend and sometimes when you cared about somebody, your love for them had to be bigger than the mistakes they made.'

'Moms, I remember the action figure and sleepover but don't remember saying that at all.'

'You did. You used to be a wise kid.'

We both laughed. We laughed because we knew Apollo never said that. It was me. I forced him to go to the sleepover. I'd spoken with Michael's mother and set the whole thing up.

'And I used that same line when we told you Ray wasn't your biological father; when I asked you to forgive us for not telling you sooner. As your parents, we do everything we can to protect you. Remember that. I know you want to feel you belong and maybe Ray and I should have done a better job at that when you were growing up, but you belong with us. You always will.'

Apollo didn't say anything. When he was done putting on the Band-Aid, he went into his room.

That was a week ago. This morning, he came into the kitchen and kissed me on the cheek.

'You OK, Moms?' He plopped himself on a stool next to the kitchen island and put down his Walkman.

I told him yes, but he knows me. He knew I was not OK. Still, I could see he wasn't sure what to say next. He must have known he was about to enter dangerous territory.

'So where you headed today?' I asked, ending the silence between us. I tried to sound casual. He was nervous. I knew because he was bouncing his knees up and down.

'I dunno. Around.'

Like your father, you are a bad liar, I thought.

'You're going to that Lazarus Gardens place, aren't you?' The words came out harder than I intended. But they were brittle in my ears. I sounded weak.

'Come on, Moms, give it a rest. Look, I'm gonna see my new friends. Why you gotta be that way?'

'Apollo, you and these people have nothing in common. I'm concerned for you.'

He looked away.

'Listen to me. I am only looking out for you.' I poured him some lemonade, with plenty of ice, how he likes it. He gulped it like a starving man then made to get up from the chair but I was on him fast.

'Look at me, Apollo,' I said. 'Tell me what you see.' I was facing him, with both hands on his shoulders.

'Do I have to?' He fidgeted.

'Answer me, young man.' I tried to pin him with my gaze.

'I dunno. I see my Moms, I guess.' He squirmed.

'Is there any doubt in your mind that I love you, son?'

'Moms, what is this?'

'You better answer me, boy.'

'No,' he muttered. 'I know you do.'

'Good,' I said and released him.

When I saw him rub his shoulders, I realised how tight my grip had been. I was sure that under his shirt my fingernail impressions were embedded in his skin. Like a brand.

Regina

Apollo going have to start seeing me as him future wife soon. Is not 'bout how good mi cook and clean or what mi can do in the bedroom. Is not just 'cause mi pretty and mi body look good. Is not even 'cause mi exciting and have style. Is 'cause mi smart and have plenty ambition. Apollo have good education and rich. Him going go far in life. So mi is exactly the type of wife a man like him – who going be a success – need beside him. A woman who keep her eye on the prize and who don't stop 'til she get what she want.

Mi wonder if Damian going miss mi when I gone to America?

This morning, when mi going through the door, Damian meet mi on the bottom step. Him coming from the standpipe without him shirt. Him muscles wet and glistening in the morning sun. Why him have to look so good?

Him stop mi. Him come close and hold mi hand. 'Is Apollo yuh going see?'

Mi don't have to tell him 'yeah' 'cause the two of we already know. Apollo send Eddie to pick mi up at the gate.

Earlier that morning, I make Mr Mack him lunch to carry to work – a bully beef sandwich. I do it exactly how him like it: plenty onion and black pepper, with butter on thick slices

183

of bread. I make him two sandwich, so that him don't have to come back home fi lunch. When I putting it in the brown paper bag, I tell him is 'cause I know him have plenty work doing at the garage. Him kiss mi and say him love how mi take care of him. I feel bad. Not bad enough, though, to want him coming home at lunchtime to find that I not staying there the whole day, like I tell him I been doing.

'How come yuh not asking mi fi the stuff again?' Damian say.

I tell him I trying to stay clean. No drugs or drinking. I need Apollo to realise I can behave better widout di drugs. Mi know that him never like how mi was carrying on at the dance the other day. Mi sure him wouldn't want him wife to act like that when we go out. And though stopping mean mi did throw up, have headache and feel all mi limb dem a shake, it worth it. When mi is Apollo wife mi can buy anything mi want. Including better drugs.

I tell Damian I have somewhere fi go.

Him hold mi waist and say mi look nice. Mi know him see mi in this same outfit already. Is a black leatherette miniskirt and a red and white striped tube top. I throw on a blue jeans jacket over it, with rhinestones and fringes.

'Yuh sexy,' him say, smiling with all him teeth.

Him tell every woman in Lazarus Gardens the same thing. Damian love flirt too much and mi tell him so. But he better remember how good I look when I in America.

'Yuh know yuh is the only girl mi write a song fah? Yuh want hear it?'

Mi don't have no time right now fi song and fantasies. Not when I working on mi plan fi Apollo fall in love with mi and take mi to America.

'No, man. Eddie soon reach.' But as mi step past him, him belt out a tune:

184

'Regiiiinnaaaaa … Regiiiinnaaaaa … Regiiiinnaaaaa
Inna my life,
mi need yahhhhh.
Let me tell yuh 'bout a girl name Regina
Have har pon mi mind,
Can't leave har.
Plenty man try come take har
Giving har gold chain and bangle
But is one man alone she can handle
She want Congo King blow out har candle –'

Mi spin 'round to laugh in him face. I tell him don't go no further since the first verse not making no sense. Why mi would ever want any man fi blow out mi candle? Mi light shining and I not letting nobody dim it.

Him say mi not understanding him. 'Regina, yuh body is the candle and mi lovemaking going … going *ex-extinguish* it.' Di way him glancing at mi is like him trying to melt mi skin.

I ask him to go look up the meaning of 'extinguish' in the old *Oxford Dictionary* Dinah keep inside. All di times mi did give him a chance with mi body, the only thing that get extinguish was him. 'Congo King,' I say, 'yuh have to have a fire before yuh have something to blow out.'

'Stop the foolishness,' him say. 'Yuh know mi is the only man that can manage yuh. And I going still be here when this puppy love thing wid yuh and Apollo dry up. Remember that.'

Mi don't know what kinda feelings Damian have fi mi, 'cause mi and him both know that sex is not love. And mi not going to give him no more; no, now that mi clean, I going focus on Apollo and making him mi husband.

Before I could answer him proper, Dinah come out and tell we to stop the noise 'cause we making her bad headache

185

worse and stopping Mama from sleeping. Damian draw back a likkle. I know him don't want another argument with Dinah.

Mi ask her when she going need mi to look after Mama again.

'You sure you have time fi that? With all the going out you doing? I notice you and mi son going here, there and everywhere.'

'How yuh mean, Dinah? I always going make time to help yuh.'

She looking at mi clothes. 'Is that the way you go out with mi son?'

How come what mi wear wasn't a problem before? She acting like she don't know that this is how mi dress. When I tell her so, she say:

'That's mi point. Why you don't ask Mrs Sinclair to sew a nice dress for you?'

'Yuh mean like the long frock dem yuh wear to church?' mi answer. 'Only yuh ankle show.'

'Regina, why you have to dress like one of the prostitutes outta street?'

'Come now, Miss Dinah, stop—' Damian jump in to defend mi.

'Is alright Damian,' mi say. 'Dinah, what yuh *really* saying?' I dare her. 'Say it. That yuh don't think mi good enough fi yuh precious Son-Son. What yuh think mi is? Trash?'

'Is not me say so, but that is how you dress. And another thing. Stop fooling 'round with so much man. Have some standards and stop carrying yuhself so cheap. I don't mind if you and Son-Son is fren but—'

I let her know we more than friends and we relationship serious. She ask mi what about Mr Mack and say that she going tell her son mi already have a man.

'Him know 'bout Mr Mack.' Which is true in a kinda way, even though him don't know Mr Mack is mi boyfriend. 'And him don't care. What that tell yuh? Yuh Son-Son want mi. Yes, *me*. The same Regina in the skimpy clothes. Yuh better get used to mi as yuh daughter-in-law.' And something else mi had to tell her. 'And yuh have bigger things to worry about with Apollo than me. Apollo tell mi British offer him a job. Him never want yuh fi know.'

Mi see the shock on her face.

'Nuh worry, mi warn him already.' When mi done say that, mi walk right through the gate and straight into Mr Mack chest. Him in a blue overalls full of grease stain that mi couldn't get out last time mi wash it.

We ask each other 'Where yuh going?' same time.

I tell him mi wasn't expecting him back home this time of day. Him say him eat the first bully beef sandwich fi breakfast and then him start feel sick. Diarrhoea wouldn't leave him, so him come home, so mi could be him nurse.

'Where yuh going?' him ask again, looking mi up and down. I wearing the red heels him did buy mi fi mi last birthday. To tell yuh the truth, if Mr Mack find out where mi really been going whenever I leave the yard, mi wouldn't be surprised if one day him chop mi up or wait to strangle mi in mi sleep.

Mr Mack not a bad man though. Him did provide fi mi when mi did need somebody. Is just time fi another man take over the role. One who can do more fi mi and help mi set up miself in life. Apollo say in order to start Gina's Boutique & House of Fashion I going need what dem call a business plan and him going help mi write. I know that when mi over there, mi going go rich people parties, maybe meet celebrities like Eddie Murphy and Michael Jackson.

I ask miself: *Yuh feel bad fi fooling Mr Mack?* A likkle; but not enough to stop. So mi tell him sorry mi hope him feel better soon, but I have to go 'cause I have an appointment with a fren.

By the time him ask 'What "appointment"? Which fren? Mi know this fren?' Damian beside mi a talk:

'Just cool, Mr Mack. Is a young people thing. Take it easy, man. Is my good fren that Regina going be wid. In fact, that fren is like family. She in good hands, 'cause she have me looking out fi har. Trust mi. Yuh nuh have to worry 'bout a t'ing.'

Mi stand up there fi what feel like hours, with Mr Mack eyes raking over mi and Damian. Him gaze moving up and down; and from one of we to the other, like him looking to spot a crack. What happen to Eddie and him damn taxi? Mi looking at the likkle stones at my foot and tracing dem shape with my right big toe.

'Alright,' Mr Mack say after a while. 'Enjoy yuhself. Nuh stay out too long.'

Thank God Eddie out there in the Lada blowing him horn. I run as fast as mi could in the heels, leaving the two of dem behind.

I not letting none of dem keep mi from mi future.

Dinah

Mi not in the mood for play-play, fun and games this morning.

Since the fight with Mrs Steele, everybody calling mi wrestler and Hulk Hogan. When mi walking to the bus stop this morning, a woman pinning up her clothes on the line, take the clothespin out of her mouth, put har hand akimbo and say to mi, 'What a piece of bangarang! What a way yuh give the ooman some karate chop! Is you name Bruce Lee!'

Another woman who was taking her dried clothes off the same line, pipe up: 'God know, is a bitch-lick di woman get!'

Then a woman on the step plaiting up her hair take the comb outta har head and start punch the air. A lady sitting on a big rock-stone with a wash tub of clothes between har legs, wipe the suds off her hands on her skirt and start jump back and forth like a boxer a do him dance. 'Is Mike McCallum dat!'

The woman that was plaiting her hair chime in: 'Cho! McCallum is boy to Dinah!'

A old woman sitting under the mango tree kiss her teeth and say, 'Unnu gwey! Unnu too young to 'member Bunny Grant. On August 4, 1962, just two day before we get we Independence from England, mi watch Bunny Grant win the Commonwealth lightweight title at the National Stadium.

189

Mi see him thump down a Englishman name Dave Charnley. Bunny had a swift left jab, yuh see! Is fi him technique influence Michael McCallum and Richard 'Shrimpy' Clarke! And mek mi tell yuh something – Dinah badder than that!' And she throw back her head and laugh, showing off her black gums and all her three teeth.

Mi never laugh.

After the fight, mi nuh see Apollo come back around and mi heart heavy. Mi was almost feeling better this morning. When mi did bend down to pick up Mama's chimmy from next to the bed to dump it outside, she look at mi for the first time in a long time and smile. Not a full smile but she raise one corner of her mouth and in that curl-up lip-corner mi see a sign that everything going be alright. And I think she going talk but she don't say nothing but pinch har nose wid har finger and I laugh 'cause she telling mi the pee-pee in the chimmy renk.

Mi nuh see the lady in the white robe from morning.

Now mi sitting here in this fool-fool man office feeling fool-fool. Mr Simms is wi MP. I here looking at the gold plaque with the words 'Wendell W. Simms Esq, Member of Parliament' that him have on him desk like him need it, so him don't forget him name. I feel like turn over the desk.

Simms look half-Syrian and is the colour of butter that get burn up in the pot. Him rocking back and forth on the big leather chair that squeaking hard while I try to find the right words to say next. Him looking out one of him large glass window at the trees outside, like mi wasn't talking to him fi the last fifteen minutes.

We conversation did go like this:

'Good morning, Mr MP, sah. Thanks for meeting with mi.'

'I always make time for my constituents.'

'Mr Simms, I owe yuh a long overdue thanks.'

'For?'

'When yuh come visit the Lazarus Gardens constituency a few years ago, I tell yuh I never have no job and yuh get me a helper work with Christopher Brown and him wife.'

'That's the kind of thing every good MP should do. Remember that at the next election. So how's the job going? Brown is a good man. He helped me out of a scrape many years ago.'

'Dem fire mi.'

'Oh. I'm sorry to hear that. Do you need me to talk with him? Brown's a reasonable fellow. I'm sure we could reach some understanding. Tell me what the problem was.'

'Is a long story, sir. And mi do day's work for a different family now. Mi not looking to get back mi old job, but mi glad for it 'cause that is how mi find mi son.'

'Come again?'

'Is at Mr Brown house mi son come find mi. If mi wasn't working there mi wouldn't get him back.'

MP Simms was looking at mi like mi mad, so mi say: 'Is a long story, and I here on urgent business. It concern mi son, Son-Son, and British. Mi have a problem mi need yuh help with.'

Then mi give him the story of how mi feel British and Damian going try mix up mi son inna badness. And how British offer mi son a job. When mi done talk, this man watching mi like mi is Wrigley's gum stuck underneath him shoe.

'British outta control. So yuh see, Missa MP, sah, you *have* to do something.'

Squeak-squeak-squeak. Him kneading him hands and fingers like him rolling johnny cake dough. 'Arthritis,' him say to mi and smile, but is like a crocodile smile and mi nuh trust it. *Squeak-squeak-squeak* goes the chair again. Him start fanning with a stack of papers. 'Busted AC,' him say, and I see the pool of sweat under him armpit and dampness under him collar. Him pick up the phone and say to him secretary, 'Dammit Christine, tell those jokers if they don't come here this morning and fix it, no more government contracts. They can forget about making a bid on the one to put AC in the new Ministry building.'

This morning when mi walk by har, mi notice that Christine dress so tight it look like it going split the next time she breathe out. When him done talk to her, him look up at mi like him forget I was there.

'Oh,' him say. 'Dinah.' And him say mi name like him revealing deep knowledge to mi.

Mi come to him as mi last hope. Everybody know that the MP is who run things. Lazarus Gardens was just one of the communities that the MP was responsible for. If British is a big Doberman, then the MP is who hold the leash. Him own all of the doghouse dem. Him provide the food.

'Things nah run right.' Mi talk again. 'British too vicious. Been vicious for a long time. Him hijacking the future of the young people in Lazarus Gardens. Enrolling boys into badness.'

'Look, Dinah, I appreciate you coming here today. Every good MP has to make sure their people know their concerns are being heard. Let me assure you of that.'

Him clear him throat and continue like him giving big speech in Parliament: 'But Mr Desmond McIntyre, who you call "British", is a community leader and organiser who is much valued by the Party. He is a major supporter. He works with us. He's an upstanding citizen whom I call a personal friend. Like my great-great-grandfather who came to this country and started his printing business downtown, Mr McIntyre provides gainful employment to the young people.

Offering people work isn't a crime. He is a solid businessman who does a lot for the community.'

'Like what? Train the boy dem to turn gunman and tief?'

Him shake him head violently. 'Baseless, unsubstantiated claims by bad-minded people! You mustn't repeat those inflammatory and slanderous statements. True, Mr McIntyre has had a bit of trouble in the past but he's completely reformed since returning to Jamaica. He's had no trouble at all with the law. Not even a traffic ticket or single criminal charge. I'm sorry but I don't know what you want from me.'

'Mi say, call off yuh dog! Is either that or yuh dog going get chop up or poison! As a matter of fact, put him down. Get rid of him.'

Him throw him head back and laugh. Him start fan himself again with the bunch of papers. A cool wind blow in from the open windows. 'Dinah, the Party doesn't get rid of people. What you think this is? The Italian mafia? We don't carry out hits. Lord Jesus!' Him untie him tie. When him done laugh, him get serious: 'As long as Mr McIntyre continues to play his part as a good corporate citizen, the Party won't have any issues with his continued community leadership. I have a call I need to make. Thanks for coming to see me today.' Just like that, him dismiss mi. Just so.

Mi nuh know what to say. *Squeak-squeak-squeak.* The chair say, 'Lady, yuh corner dark. It well dark.'

And just like that, the desk start to shake and the MP looking at mi like nothing going on and mi foot start move and rattle without mi moving it. Earthquake! How him don't look like him feel it? Is a wave moving under the ground like a snake under the carpet. And a woman's voice that sound like mine start laugh.

When I dive under him desk, mi hear the MP say, 'Christine! Call Security!'

Wendell W. Simms Esq., MP

Much later, after everything had unfolded, MP Simms will recall this conversation with Dinah. At the time, he had thought that the woman was too naïve. The wheels of progress had to keep turning. Some people were bugs on its windshield. She didn't understand that sacrifices had to be made for the greater good. British maintained order in Lazarus Gardens and ensured it remained a Party seat. And, he knew that anything that helped put, and keep, the Party in power was good for the Jamaican people and the future of the nation. It was as simple as that. The logic was unassailable. So what if British was a bit . . . exuberant?

When he heard she had lost her steady job, MP Simms had considered giving her work cleaning the Party office but decided against it. There should be no reward for trying to upset the apple cart. That behaviour could not be encouraged. Dinah was at best, naïve or at worst, unpatriotic.

Simms had been a politician for many years. He considered himself a veteran. He studied international politics. He understood the compexities of the Cold War, knew about the South African apartheid that led Nelson Mandela into prison. Jamaican politics was different from American or British politics. Here, as a MP, you couldn't drive through your constituency, just waving 'hello' and leaving it to the government to provide the social infrastructure. No, sir. The government had no money to spare and in Jamaica, it was understood that a man was giving you his vote to be his MP in exchange for something. And if you wanted it again at the next election you had to make sure you had provided what you promised. So you had to get out of your car and stand in the heat and dust and listen to what he wanted.

It wasn't just about the curried goat and rum you had to give out at election time. Or the work to build roads or clear sewers and cut grass along gullies.

What was the real price of a vote?

Each thing was specific to that man. But it involved the same things: food, education, security, the health of his family, the welfare of the children and the environment in which they lived. Each man cared about what mattered to him. Some men would tell you they can't eat education, give them food. Some men wanted education so they could get food forever.

Simms once had a man, a man who called himself 'a diehard Party supporter' living in one of the hotly contested marginal constituencies tell him the night before an election that he needed the road to his yard paved. 'But, election is tomorrow!' Simms had sputtered. The man had calmly let him know he would not get his vote without a road. So Simms bought the cement and sent some men to start paving the road that night.

How Simms saw it was that a man without light in his house can't watch TV. If you don't send a drum of water to his house, the man can't make himself a little tea. If you don't buy marl for his street, he has no road. If he doesn't live anywhere, the man is relying on you for a decent house. You have to send his children to school. That means uniform, school fee, bus fare and lunch money. You have to give him money for his mother's diabetes medication.

If a man loses his foot in an accident, you as MP have to give him back a foot . . . artificial, of course.

As MP, you are part of the domestic affairs in his yard and you have to take care of all of those affairs. So to get the people's votes you promise them something that is directly affecting them. And if they don't get it, there will be no vote at the next election, and you will have to hide from them.

And no MP's salary could cover these unending needs. That's why MPs had to hustle and engage in what Simms thought of as 'extra income-earning activities'. Taking a little bribe here and there. Dipping into money from foreign governments for grants and aid. Redirecting funds from one source to another. Falsifying the budget. Getting a secret refund on part of government contracts that had been awarded. All because Jamaican people depended on their MP for daily sustenance.

And to a great extent, in respect of the Lazarus Gardens community, Simms had given over this role to British. He thought of it as delegation. British was ensuring everyone in Lazarus Gardens had their needs met so they could vote for the Party.

So what was a little bloodshed to keep the wheels of progress lubricated and turning? What was a little lawlessness to keep the overall social order?

That was Simms' thinking as he reflected on his meeting with Dinah. He would later regret he had not listened to her.

PART TWO

Lazarus Gardens

Damian

It only take 'bout two weeks after the dance, fi Streggo to get everything together for the Jack's Hill job. For days, is like Streggo brain set on a spring, him keep going over the plan with mi and String morning, noon and night, like we is amateurs who don't know what to do. When mi start get vex, is String who crack a joke to calm mi down. Streggo don't like when people quarrel with him.

On the Friday night, we reach there in Streggo old van. First thing, mi think it going wake up the whole damn neighbourhood. Rich people that live in Jack's Hill used to quiet. Dem BMW engine purr just like puss. Dem don't even talk loud. Mr Mack shoulda fix the van but Streggo never want to pay him to do the job. Mr Mack tell him him have a woman to support. Then Streggo say Mr Mack woman is a ghetto bicycle who everybody ride and who love to feel the agony when things get rough. Dem start fight but Mr Mack old and Streggo strong and by time mi drag off Streggo the old man in a bundle on the ground, moaning, him arms and legs spilling out like garbage.

So we in this noisy van with the muffler coughing out black smoke and everything creaking but I glad 'cause now Streggo and the boys can't hear mi heart pounding. This job different. We not doing a daytime robbery when we know the people gone to the country or farin. Or dem at work and the helper gone to market or to gossip with the other helper next door. Every house have a rhythm. You just have to get to know it. I tapping out a beat wid mi foot. To calm miself.

Is Apollo cause this. To think, I just ask him for a likkle tax money and him get vex and behave so. The first time mi spot him at the dance, Streggo was calling mi chicken, saying mi must be backing outta the Jack's Hill job 'cause Apollo is mi fren. But how him is mi fren and have all that money and can't let off some?

Is evening and mi hoping Apollo parents not inside. Apollo say Friday nights dem come home late from some dinner party him father go and always drag him mother. I know Apollo gone out wid Regina 'cause she tell mi. Boasting about how at least him can afford to carry her out to places that she can only see on TV or read 'bout in magazine or newspaper. And mi feel like box har then but I never hit a woman yet and I not going start with Regina, especially since mi think mi love her. I tell her I soon get money and things going change. I going stop pimping her out to men who have money in dem pocket but she must know the things in dem pocket not as big as what in mi heart. 'Or in yuh pants, Damian,' she say, pulling the waist of mi shorts wid her finger. I know dem say she freaky. She rude, that girl, but mi like that. I going take her wid mi when I touring the world, singing my songs, releasing albums. Maybe she can dance on stage.

The van grind to a stop before the house. No car park in the driveway. Lights in the house off. Pure darkness. Nobody home. Good. Mi glad the house don't have no guard dogs 'cause me and String don't like it when Streggo poison dem. String usually make up a mixture that just make dem sleep.

'Congo King! Yuh ready?' Streggo ask mi now, and I feel

a heat go down mi back and mi shiver but mi nod. We did smoke some ganja before, but mi nerves still don't settle.

Ready. Yes, mi ready. Mi tie the kerchief 'round my face.

◆

String carry a light in a bottle that him make from kerosene oil, wire and old cloth. Streggo ask him: 'We come to rob de place or burn it down? How dat thing look like firebomb so?'

String don't answer. Him can make anything from anything, even a wire clothes hanger or even from a piece of string. That's why we call him String. Him is a apprentice to him uncle who can fix blender, fan, radio, iron and sewing machine. String and me was in high school together. One time, him open couple of him big books and show mi different diagrams and all kind of what him call equations. Him say is chemistry and physics but that is farin knowledge to mi. What I know is music and how to hold a gun. I never had to fire one at nobody yet though. Mi learn that yuh only fire your gun when yuh intend to kill; when it come down to your life or theirs. Mi don't believe in warning shot.

The gun we get from British in the back of the waist of mi pants and it feeling heavy. Mi only used to carrying mi knife back there.

Ratta breeze past in the darkness. At seventeen, him is already over six feet tall. String brain move quick, but Ratta brain flow like condensed milk. Him call himself Ratta after the *rat-a-tat-tat* sound a machine gun make. But everybody say the name fit him 'cause him two front teeth buck like a rat.

Streggo hiss after him: 'Hold on, yute.' Ratta too eager. Is him first time on a job. I don't know why Streggo bring him.

The house quiet. We go through the back. Burglar bar is no problem. String pick the lock on it easy. We don't need to cut it. We in through the back door and Ratta start to sneeze. Streggo look like he want to kill him. But why him bring the yute for?

The kitchen bigger than anything mi ever see. Nice floor and high ceilings. Big stove, wide counters. Like you see on TV.

A woman standing up by the fridge. In a pink satin nightie. What de rass dem doing home? Mi realise that Apollo must did borrow the car to take out Regina. That's why we never see it.

She scream when she see we and run to the living room. Mi glad that she couldn't recognise mi 'cause of the mask I was wearing. I adjust the kerchief on my face.

'Raymond!' she bawl out. 'Call the police!'

A big white man come running down the stairs. When him see us, him turn to go running back like him forget something.

'Christ! The gun!' him bark, but Ratta on him heels before him take another step. He throw himself on the man and two of dem roll down the stairs, Ratta trying to strangle the man who bucking like ole bull. String hit the man on the head with a vase. The red flowers in it scatter on the floor. On to dem gold and white rug.

'Who else deh home?' Streggo shout at the woman, while Ratta tie up the man. Streggo forehead look bulgy underneath the stocking-foot over him face that squeeze down him nose to almost flat. Him pin the woman arm behind her back. She make a sound in her throat like a kitten in pain but stop struggling.

'No-nobody,' she say, her voice trembling.

'Good. Now unnu shut unnu mouth. We not looking fi trouble.'

The woman nod. Her lips trembling now.

'Unnu have plenty of nice things and we just borrowing some.'

'Take whatever you want,' the man say, 'but please don't harm my wife.'

Mi don't like the way Ratta looking at the woman. 'Look,' I say, 'mek we get the things.'

String tie up the woman with rope. When him done, him do a fancy knot. 'Clove hitch knot,' him say to mi. The only part of him face I can see through him mask is him eyes and dem look sad.

We leave Ratta wid the gun to watch dem and go upstairs, finding jewellery and cash on the dresser in the bedrooms. Streggo, String and me load up the van with TVs, VCRs, stereos, anything we see and like, even a leather sofa. We know no neighbours seeing we, 'cause the Jack's Hill houses far apart and separated by plenty bush.

Streggo find a safe in the wall upstairs behind a painting of a man riding a horse. Streggo take the gun from Ratta and bring it to the white man face and him wife beg fi mercy. Streggo hold the gun so close to the man eyeball the man finally give String the combination fi the lock. The safe open up to US dolla bills! String count 10,000 a dem! When the three of we see the money crisp-crisp and in likkle blocks on top of each other is like white people Christmas!

The few times we going in and out from the house to the van with the rest of the things, I see Ratta slapping the man's face. It red. Blood trickling from him forehead. I can tell Ratta was butting him with the gun.

'Do something nuh, white man!' Ratta taunting him. The man keep silent. Just getting redder.

Streggo even take a turn boxing him. String and me look away. 'Now the two of yuh do it!' Streggo say and so we slap him, but not hard.

The van sitting low on its tyres now. We full. Time to leave. Streggo get behind the wheel and String get in too.

Now to get Ratta. I put the last things in — Apollo mother jewellery box — and then I hear her scream. We run back inside and see Ratta on top of her wid him pants halfway down. Him brief down too. Ratta hand on her breast and trailing down the front of her nightie. Him trying to wedge open her leg dem wid him knees. Him sweating 'cause she fighting him hard. Ratta grunting like hog.

Her husband straining against the ropes and cursing. 'You sons-of-bitches, I'll kill you. I'll kill you all!' And Ratta just laughing.

String eye wide. Streggo saying: 'Bumboclaat!' I pull Ratta off her and say: 'We not rapists! We nuh come here fi dat!' Mi kerchief loosen and mi pull it up fast so Apollo mother don't recognise mi.

We so focus on Ratta and the woman, we don't realise the man burst through him ropes. Him throw him body on to Ratta and dem wrestling on the ground for the gun.

Next thing, we hear the shot.

We neva expect it. The shot flash like camera in the darkness.

The white man stand up. Then him fall backward, like him get a heavy thump in him chest. Is then mi realise is Ratta who fire.

The man head dip sideways and I wondering if him dead.

Ratta look like him about to fire again, but Streggo ease down the gun.

'Mek wi leave!'

We run through the back door. Di wife screaming out her lungs. Mi heart going *bodoom-doom.*

You, a Jack's Hill Neighbour

You are walking the dog. Your *wife's* dog.

Every month, your wife has a barrel full of Purina Dog Chow shipped down from Miami that cost more than what many of the men who work in your furniture factory downtown earn each month. (It's actually your father-in-law's factory, as he never lets you forget.)

'It's not a child,' you tell her. Why couldn't it eat the turned cornmeal that the helper used to make for your dogs when you were young?

'*She's* family,' your wife said, the dog licking her face. You didn't grow up like that. As a boy, your mother always insisted that your dogs, huge German Shepherds, stay outside and run about in the yard in Havendale. Your mother was a good woman. She disliked your wife for marrying you and taking away the affections of her one son.

The dog is a poodle your wife named Fluffy and it looks like an oversized cotton ball. Fluffy is as pretentious as your wife, but not nearly half as loveable. Christ! The things men do for love, or . . . sex twice a week. It was either buy Fluffy or have a third child, and you'd picked the dog. You're regretting your choice daily.

Fluffy is getting fat. It moves slowly and its belly sags.

Your wife and kids never walk the dog. So you do. And you do it at night, after work, so people don't see you with this useless ball of fur. Now, your wife says Fluffy may be depressed or under stress and you need to take her to the vet tomorrow. Imagine that! If anybody should be depressed, it's *you*.

All Fluffy does is lie around, eat and mess up the place and you're tired of cleaning up dog poop throughout your house, on the sofas, in your shoes, in the closet, in the hallway and even on the bed. So today you are glad for the fresh air. The air feels soft against the stubble on your chin.

A bit further up the hill, you make out a beaten-up white van parked in front of a house. You don't think it belongs here. It's the kind of van that the landscaping or pool cleaning company uses, or a delivery man would drive, but none of them would be there this late at night. The van is covered with more rust than paint and a tingle in your gut is telling you something is wrong. But before you can register anything else, a shot bursts out in the night.

You hit the ground. You flatten yourself on your belly on the cold earth. You are a caterpillar inching towards the safety of shrubbery.

Four men run out of the house – masks on their faces. One of the men stops and calls out, 'Bloodclaat, Ratta! Weh yuh do?'

Another pushes him in the van, yelling, 'Damian, Streggo! Mek we gwaan!'

They don't see you. The van doors slam and the van takes off. Surprisingly fast. Belching out smoke.

You can only make out part of the licence plate. You'll tell this and the names you heard to the police when you call them. For now, you focus on getting to the house. To help the people inside. You must help, even though jolts of fear become cramps moving through your legs. You move carefully and quickly in case they decide to come back.

And the blasted dog never even bark! Not one time. The goddamn animal didn't even tug at the leash or strain against it to attack.

You're beginning to think that a third child isn't such a bad idea.

Apollo

Driving home, my head's buzzing. I'm pounding a beat on the steering wheel on my way back from the restaurant. I can't get what Regina just told me out of my head. It's windy and I turn the lever to roll up my window, wishing I could block out my thoughts the same way. One of my favourite Peter Tosh songs is playing on the cassette player. I was planning on giving the cassette to Damian when I leave Jamaica. Not now though. Not after he tried to jam me up for money. The first time I played Coltrane for Damian, I asked him 'what do you hear? Listen to that sax, man,' and Damian's eyes danced. Like I had taken him to a special place of sound that was blowing his mind. But I can't trust Damian any more. Even thinking about the fact he gave drugs to Gina for the hand-job in the first place – suddenly it hits me – how many times had she done that before? I don't know how many guys she'd slept with. And don't want to know. But I decided I was gonna be smart and wear condoms, because I'm no fool either. How could this happen?

I pull the Benz into the driveway. The front door's wide open and I see this dude I don't know on his knees and a white poodle beside him with red paws. I'm thinking: that's blood. *Whose* blood? The dude doesn't look like he's bleeding.

The guy shifts and I see Pops is on his back in the living room and his T-shirt's completely red. I should be running to him, but all I can think about is that marlin we hauled into the bottom of our boat when we went fishing off the coast last year. How it thrashed, cobalt-blue and silver against white. Moms is screaming her head off that Pops' been shot. The guy with the dog is pressing his palms on top of my Pops' chest to keep blood from gushing out.

Suddenly there's an ambulance, cops and people everywhere. More cop cars pulling up. I don't remember getting out of the car but I'm grabbing Pops' hand and he's squeezing it. His eyes are closed and he's groaning. Something twists in my stomach. I tell him: 'I'm here, Pops. I'm not going anywhere.' And my voice sounds like a higher pitch and shallow. Like it's not mine.

I put an arm around Moms. She's frozen on the spot and not saying anything any more. Her nightgown's torn and she's trembling. The people around us fall away, I don't see anything else but the two of them.

◆

Later, Pops is in the hospital, hooked up to all these beeping machines. Doctors and nurses are in and out of his room, like white doves. Moms is in a daze, not leaving his side. Not even to wash her face or comb her hair.

A doctor comes and says he's sorry but 'it's touch and go' and since the bullet grazed the spinal cord on exit, if there's lasting damage, he may never walk again. Moms bends over like a broken-off flower.

The police come to the hospital, asking us: can we think of anyone who came to the house recently who may be responsible for the robbery? A helper's relative? The robbery happened on Jocelyn's weekend off. She'd left early that

Friday afternoon, but Moms insisted to the cops that Jocelyn had nothing to do with it. The investigating officer asked: 'What about the gardener?' He pressed us: is there anyone who could have observed our routines? Anybody who knew our movements? The cops tell us: 'It's usually someone you have had contact with.'

Moms and I can't think of anybody. Who would do this to us?

Even as I thought it, an uneasy feeling was moving up my arm, creeping its fingers around my throat.

Regina

So mi lean forward and ask Apollo: 'Why yuh like mi?'

Is Friday night and we in the same restaurant we went to on our first date. Mi don't see Jeffery. It must be him day off. The new waiter, a fat man with a double chin who look like him alone eat everything outta the kitchen, look at mi like mi is a roach him just done stamp the bottom of him shoe on. Like him know who mi is, but is only me and him who can see it. That is clear Apollo don't see it . . . yet. Which is the only reason a man like him could be sitting here with the likes of me.

I know the baby in mi belly these past few weeks and mi didn't need the nurse at the public health clinic to tell mi what mi already know. Mi period was plenty weeks late, before the nurse even do her test.

Mi did want to know how Apollo feel about mi. Get him in a good mood before I tell him what mi haffi say. Mi want him buttered up like this bread here in mi plate. Nice and warm.

Apollo lower him head and kinda cock it to the side, giving mi that smile like a likkle schoolboy and that likkle laugh I starting to like the more I hear it. Mi notice how him eyelashes long and pretty. Neat. Elegant, like him long fingers.

Mi want to touch him soft locks. Maybe is the hormones di pregnancy causing making mi want to be so close to Apollo.

Him finally say: 'Gina baby, I like you 'cause you're free and bold. Girl, you live your life like you do what you want and don't need a thing.'

Mi smile freeze up.

Is not true. Mi need a whole-heap a something. Plenty things. But above everything else, mi need people not to make mi feel like I not worth anything. Despite how it start out, I feel like this baby not just a means to a end. That maybe my life going change for the better not just 'cause it mean I going to America but 'cause this baby going grow up and see something better in mi. 'Cause mi is dem mother. This baby going to look up to mi.

Mi realise Apollo still talking. And mi wasn't listening to what him was saying. Mi just hear him say: 'I like that you don't take crap from nobody. And when I'm with you, it's like there's a fire inside me. It's exciting.'

That's when mi decide to tell him the news.

'Say what?' Apollo ask mi. Him acting like the words mi tell him don't make no sense. Like mi string dem together in a language him don't know.

Mi say it again: 'Mi pregnant.' And is like mi words exploding inside the restaurant. Mi never realise mi was talking so loud. People spin 'round. Apollo edge him chair closer to mi and lower him voice.

'How?' Him words sound like dem coming from far away.

'Well, that can happen when people fuc—'

'B–but we always used condoms.' Him gulp down him water. It choke him.

'Yeah, but condom don't work all the time. Dem can break. Look, baby, mi know is earlier than we planned but now we can get married and start life together.'

The silence was like a pain sticking mi in mi side. Apollo rubbing him neck, like a headache climbing up it. Him twist him mouth like di wine taste bitter and rancid. 'What am I gonna do? How do I tell my folks? What the hell do I tell them?' Is like him talking to himself, mumbling real low, so him shock when mi answer.

'Tell dem they going be grandparents.'

'Look, you don't get how serious this is.'

'Baby, we going start a new life in America!' I put a hand over him right hand. In the dim light of the candle on the table, the gold flecks in mi nail polish and the green gems pasted on dem shining.

'We?' Him pull away him hand.

'The three of we. We a family now. Where you go, me go. *We* go. So when yuh going back? When we going get married?'

Apollo look like him collar tightening around him neck. 'I-I gotta think. I need time to think. Come on, I'm taking you home.' Him pushing away him chair and scooping up him car keys from the table. The keys drop on the floor. Him go under the table to pick dem up. When him get up, him take a couple deep breaths. But him look clumsy, him legs unsteady, like a drunken man.

We never even make it past the appetiser. It never matter anyway; mi wasn't hungry no more. The spinach leaves in mi salad wilted. I rubbing mi ear, tugging the giant loop earring as mi watch the people sitting in the tables around we. I wondering how dem can go on with dem lives – cutting, chewing, swallowing, talking, laughing – while my life just crumbling. Something drop inside mi. After feeling nothing so long, mi did begin to feel something again. A life inside mi. If mi have a boy mi did decide to name him Leford, after mi grandfather.

213

Mi could feel the sweat on mi top lip. Mi couldn't meet Apollo eyes. Not just 'cause mi feel embarrass 'bout how him behaving, but 'cause of a bigger shame that mi never want mi eyes fi show. A thing I only going admit to miself.

Damian never wear condoms. Him say him don't like how dem feel. Him love to ride raw.

Even though this is not the reaction from Apollo mi did imagine, mi can understand it. Him never plan fi dis. But him going have to get used to it.

Mi future depend on it.

Streggo

The edges of a story are not smooth. If you asked Mama, she would tell you: 'Story don't walk straight.' So it was with Streggo's story.

It may not have been clear to Damian why Streggo took Ratta along to the robbery that night, but Streggo was pleased about how the robbery turned out. All in all, it had been a success. Streggo considered himself a ghetto ranger. Like a cowboy. No life of working inna a wholesale, or helping auntie wid har stall or likkle construction work or production worker at di factory making shoes or a vendor walking with a cardboard box selling tissue, tiger balm and razor blade . . .

Everybody in Lazarus Gardens knew about Streggo's history. It was transmitted through the Ghetto News Network, in bits and pieces, while hanging clothes on the line, or queueing at the betting shop, standing at the bus stop downtown or waiting to get hair braided or shaved by one of the hairdressers and barbers on sidewalks in Lazarus Gardens.

The GNN report on Streggo said he'd faced challenges. At age seven he had a stammer that got him teased by other children. Adults considered him retarded. His father had scared him out of it by coming home one day and yelling:

'How yuh start and stop yuh word dem so? Yuh is a man. Talk yuh thing!' Streggo never stuttered again.

His first robbery, when he was twelve, was botched. Breaking into the home of a senior citizen in Red Hills, the old man (who he later heard on the news had retired from years of serving in the US military) caught him coming through the window and wrestled him, causing Streggo to drop the homemade gun his older brother had fashioned. Streggo fled, leaving the gun behind.

He'd eventually got another one (a real one he stole from his father) and started robbing the corner store of ice-cream cake. Stuffing his bag with the loot, he told the Indian owner to start buying more of the rum and raisin ice-cream he liked. He hid the gun under a pile of rubbish but forgot about it when his mother asked him to sweep the yard. The next day she asked him to burn the rubbish since garbage trucks seldom came. It wasn't until he heard the shots going off that he realised the fire had caused the gunpowder in the bullets to explode. Shots punctured fences, gates and front doors of his neighbours' homes.

His brother had called him a rassclaat eediat and Streggo promised to give up guns.

Then, at fourteen, he killed his uncle. It was a fight over, of all things, a hose. Streggo had borrowed it to bathe and forgot to return it. His uncle swung at his head and shoulders with a machete, making bloody nicks, and so he hit the older man over the head with a large stone. He collapsed and died. Streggo was locked up in a juvenile correctional facility and released the day he turned eighteen. His father cut him off for killing his only brother.

Streggo's first robbery after his release was of a man downtown, walking on Duke Street. Streggo held the man at knifepoint, but when he emptied his pockets realised the man had only a few coins. Nothing worth robbing. Streggo got so angry he slapped the man across the back of the head and jeered at him.

So Streggo's past was a catalogue of bad starts and failures. Subsequently, Streggo's philosophy was: if you're going to embark on a successful life of crime, get proper training early. That's why he took along Ratta, one of British's younger sons who was desperate to prove himself. Ratta was the runt of the litter; never acknowledged by his father. Big in body but slightly deformed, one leg was bent at an odd angle and longer than the other, so when he walked it dragged behind him. British had no tolerance for imperfection.

Ratta was eager to display the badness deep in his genes. The hatred inside him had blossomed. What drove Ratta most was envy for his half-brother, British's eldest son and heir apparent, Clevon. Streggo knew he could channel that hate to his own ends. Showing his power to British by making this boy into what British couldn't. Streggo could make Ratta useful.

The boy was hungry to learn, even if he was a little too trigger-happy. With mentoring, that could be fixed. He just needed somebody to believe in him – something Streggo never had. Streggo could see his potential clearly, even as the shot went off that night in Jack's Hill, and Streggo watched a crimson rose flower on the man's chest, spreading over his white cotton T-shirt, mushrooming like a beautiful, angry cloud.

Dinah

Sadness welling up inside mi from somewhere deep deep. It pooling in mi chest and most days is all mi can do, not to let mi eyes drown the whole world.

It have to do with Apollo, yes, but also the woman in the white robe. At first, mi think she was mi Granny, Mama mother, watching over mi. She dead when mi young, so mi don't have a clear memory of her face. Mi remember she used to wrap her head and dress in white and a more gentle woman you couldn't find. She did smell of nutmeg and peppermint. Blue Mountain coffee and wet earth. She was always gathering, drying and brewing herbs. She used to rub mi up with herbs and olive oil.

But when mi ponder it, mi say to miself that no, it couldn't be she. The woman in white younger than Granny and something 'bout how she hold her head and walk feel like a different somebody.

She coming to mi more and more. It get so mi fighting to stay awake the whole night 'cause I sure she going take mi away in mi sleep. That I wouldn't live to see the morning.

'Pops is in the hospital,' Son-Son telling mi now. Is two days after it happen. Round him eyes red. Early that Sunday morning we in the kitchen of the tenement yard sitting at the table.

'Mi sorry to hear.' Despite everything, him never deserve that.

'There's something else,' Son-Son say. 'It's about Regina.' Him looking everywhere except mi face.

Mi realise is time fi the talk we shoulda have long time ago. Mi get up, put mi hand on him shoulder and say: 'Before yuh say anything else, Son-Son, I need to talk to yuh 'bout the company yuh keeping. Yuh don't know the proverb: "Hand at bowl, knife at throat" but Mama teach mi dat. Not everybody who offer yuh something is genuine. Dem give yuh a bowl of food wid one hand and draw knife at yuh neck wid the other. Damian is not yuh friend.'

'Dinah—' him interrupt mi, but mi continue: 'Cut the friendship. You have to cut it now.'

Him say: 'I was trying to tell you about Regina—'

'As fi Regina,' I tell him, 'Mama would say: "Yuh fattening chicken fi mongoose come nyam it."'

'I'm trying to tell you that—'

'She have belly.' Mi finish the sentence.

'She's pregnant,' him say.

'Mi know. She walking around the yard and can't stop spitting and few weeks ago a lizard jump on har. Is not yours. Is a jacket she want to give you.'

'How do you know?'

'Son-Son, let mi tell you: read the smoke.'

From the look on him face mi see Son-Son nuh understand.

'Before me and Mama move to Kingston, we used to live on a hill in St Ann. Mi was a likkle girl. And mi school was at the bottom of the hill. Mama used to cook outside on wood fire. We never even have coal. Before mi go school, mi had to go into the bush to look for wood. Mi gather bundles of wood: from tree that get chop down to clear the fields fi planting or from old tree that dead. Anyway, every day when school over and mi a walk home, I had to look up the hill. If the smoke going up and black, that mean is a fresh fire: dinner just start cook. If the smoke white and high high, dinner soon ready. If the smoke coming back down it mean dinner done cook. But if there wasn't no smoke at-all, at-all, don't go home. That mean: go bush first and look guinep or custard apple, starapple, sweetsop or tangerine to eat 'cause no dinner nuh deh-deh.'

'Nice story Dinah, but what does it got to do with anything?'

'Son-Son, what every man need to learn to do is read the smoke. Mi don't like you *galavanting* wid that girl.'

'Gal-what?'

'Floricksing, going up and down outta road,' mi say. 'Set yuh sights on a girl better suited to yuh. One in yuh class.'

'My class?' Son-Son hold mi hand. 'Don't you want me to be with a strong woman like you?'

'Strong yes, but not one that act like cane-trash.'

He pull away him hand. 'Gina's not trash. She's having a baby. *My* baby.'

'All she do is take money from man.'

'Doesn't she look after your mother for you? Keep an eye out for you?' Apollo ask.

'And let mi tell you, Mr Mack—'

'I'm done talking about this. I gotta head back to the hospital to see Pops.'

Him get up. He don't look mi in mi eye but what I see is a likkle boy, scared. Him not ready to hear sense yet. I hold out mi hand before him can walk out the gate. Mi have to try another way. Mi apologise and tell him mi was just trying to help. I tell him mi know him going through plenty stress and when things confuse mi, I go to church. Mi invite him to come with mi.

'I'm not exactly religious, Dinah.'

I tell him it don't matter. While we there, we can pray for him father.

'I don't see how that's gonna help.'

'Well, it not going hurt. Just try. What you have to lose?'

Dinah

As a girl, Dinah used to love to wear socks. The fabric around her toes, heels and calves soothed her. There was comfort in the feel of cotton. But she only had a few good pairs, so holes quickly developed around the toes and heels. She'd stitch the holes up herself, since her mother had taught her to sew as soon as she could hold a needle. But the holes would just re-open again after a few weeks of washing and wearing.

As a grown woman, Dinah wore nylon stockings. When she wore them to church, they encased her feet like sausages. Stockings made her feel overheated on sticky days but even that feeling was a comfort now. They were part of her Sunday uniform. After she donned her stockings and her hat with the mesh that covered the top half of her face, zipped or buttoned up one of her five dresses (all outdated but clean), she would walk up the lane to join the line of women already forming, their hats secured by hat pins, all making an ant-like trail directly to the church. Dinah felt the comfort of the large leather-bound Bible she gripped, felt the sweat pouring down her back, heard the faint crunch of gravel under her too-tight shoes. This was her ritual: this passageway of women so similar in their piety. Marching to their salvation.

Today, as she got ready, Apollo had waited to accompany

her. Before leaving the yard she asked Mrs Sinclair to watch Mama. Apollo could see how Dinah's chest swelled with pride to walk with him by her side. Dinah had borrowed him a tie from one of Mrs Sinclair's sons, straightened his shirt, smoothed the fabric down with her palms. Then she held his arm.

He wished he could believe as she did. He found the service long, hot and boring; he felt himself melting on the hard-wooden benches inside the small church. The only two fans faced the pulpit, where the pastor and choir sat. The rest of the congregation was left to roast. There was no breeze coming through the open wooden louvres of the low-ceiled building. It was like a cake tin.

The preacher droned on and on. Apollo had looked at the giant clock mounted on the wall inside the church when it said 9:40am. An hour or so later the clock still said 9:40: he was convinced the supernatural had happened. The man's preaching had broken the clock!

The sermon was something about forgiveness. Dinah was near rapture during the hymns. Apollo watched her 'get into the spirit', something she said was like being slain. 'Is when yuh forget yuhself, like yuh flesh and its desires; failings and weakness get killed, so all that's alive is the goodness of God in you. All that left behind is di purity.'

And so he pictured the Holy Spirit, the invisible ghost she worshipped, jabbing her in the stomach – piercing her with an ancient, unseen sword. For it was like something had been cut away or cut out of her when she had lain there on the floor, motioning with her hands as if her own blood was washing over her body. Church deacons submerged people in a makeshift pool – a tank of water in the centre of the church. There were shouts of 'Hallelujah' every time the dunked person resurfaced unscathed.

223

Midway through the service, a shabbily dressed, fine-boned Rastaman came in and took a seat in the front pew. He waved a giant Haile Selassie flag. People ignored him. When Apollo asked Dinah about it later, she said: 'Oh! That is Ras. We don't pay him no mind. Him is a madman but him don't trouble nobody. Him come here some Sundays. Him just want to be part of the service too.'

Presently, the Rasta stood and said, in a voice like a gong, his tone official: 'Bredrin and sistren, it is a good and pleasant thing, like precious oil poured on the head, running down on Aaron's beard, down on the collar of his robe, it is joyful and salutary, always and everywhere to give Jah thanks and praise! Jah! Ever-living, Ever-blessed, Ever-faithful and Ever-sure! Jah! Rastafari!' Then he sat back down.

The whole proceedings embarrassed Apollo. He was used to the organised piety of his parents' Catholic church, where the priest, during baptism, daintily sprinkled babies' foreheads with water. Services ended sharply on the hour and they read from specific pages of prayer books.

'Who can talk to God like that?' Dinah asked in disbelief when he described the Catholic service to her. 'What if unnu lost the book? And God don't want to hear what on page fifty-three or ninety-six that everybody talk all the time.'

Apollo couldn't reconcile the idea that this Pentecostal church and his parents' Catholic congregation served the same God. Unless that God was schizophrenic. How could He appreciate the Catholic crispness and dignity as well as this wanton display of surrender after some kind of open warfare? And who were the people here warring against? The Devil? Or a God who had bruised them?

Apollo wasn't sure he believed. He told Dinah as much when she returned to her place on the bench next to him.

'Just pray and ask Him to help yuh unbelief.'

This advice seemed circular to him. How could he ask for more faith if he had no faith to pray in the first place?

He didn't tell her that, at best, he was agnostic.

'Just have faith,' Dinah said. 'It will work out. Yuh love use yuh head too much. Yuh nuh tired to think sometime?'

'But God made my brain,' he countered, feeling smug.

She pointed an index finger to his chest: 'And Him make yuh heart too.'

Now the choir was singing:

Fire fire fire
Fall fall on me
On the day of Pentecost
Fire fall on me.

He didn't understand. Were they now asking to be burnt alive? Dinah explained that in addition to carrying a sword, the Holy Spirit was also fire. When he told her the Holy Spirit shouldn't go around stabbing people, she rebuked him and warned him not to 'vexate the Spirit'.

'I won't. I don't wanna get stabbed.' She elbowed him hard in the ribs. 'Jesus Christ!' he exclaimed. She told him not to take the Lord's name in vain.

He tried another tack. 'Dinah, why does Jesus say, "Suffer the little children to come unto me"? Tell me. Why do they have to suffer?'

He thought he had stumped her, but no: 'Son, that "suffer" is old time English talk. That mean "permit, allow". Jesus just saying: "Make dem come. Don't stop dem." And we are all children, son.'

'Come on, Dinah. You can't believe in a book written thousands of years ago that was used to enslave Black people!'

'Mi mind free, son and I know what mi feel and experience of God.'

Not accepting defeat, he launched his final attack. 'OK, so how come God allowed your baby to be taken away?'

She paused so long he thought she hadn't heard him. He hoped not. Now the words were out he regretted their callousness.

Finally, she said: 'Don't forget Him is a parent. And Him did lose him son too.'

He kept quiet after that. He thought about what Dinah said. He'd occasionally look over at her, her face a picture of peace, and wished again he could believe. Like a raft on a river, the congregation's faith had supported her. During the section in the service where the Minister asked the congregation if they had prayer requests, Dinah stood up and asked for prayer for his father. She placed her hands on Apollo's shoulders as the pastor prayed. His voice boomed to the ceiling and shook with emotion. The whole church said 'Amen' when he was done.

After service, groups of women came up to them. 'Good to see you, my dear, see yuh next Sunday, sister Dinah,' they greeted her, one after the other, each giving her a hug. These people must have been the ones to help her through the loss of her baby and those hard years that followed. He wanted somewhere he could feel that settled; sometimes he just wanted to run away.

Walking back to Dinah's yard, she stopped midstride, looked back and asked Apollo: 'Yuh see har?'

'Who?'

'The woman following wi.'

'I don't see anybody, Dinah.'

'Oh. Mi did think somebody was behind we.'

'You OK?'

'Yes, son. Mi fine. So what yuh think of church?'

Taking her hand, he replied: 'Fulfilling.'

ACP Davis

'You alright, sir?' Beckford, a uniformed police officer asked the man seated in the back of the blue Rover he was driving.

'Yes, Beckford.'

Beckford kept his eyes on the road; both hands firmly on the wheel in the ten to two o'clock position. That's how his passenger liked it. He knew the man missed nothing.

At a red traffic light, Beckford cupped his hand, smelt his breath and wished he had a Wrigley's spearmint gum to chew on but the passenger would frown on gum chewing. He was a man of discipline and order.

The engine of the Rover was quiet, the way it was every morning. It was Monday. Seven-thirty. People were on their way to work: men dressed in suits armed with briefcases, others in uniforms carrying toolboxes, women in skirtsuits wearing pantyhose, carrying handbags, other women in plain simple dresses or housekeeper attire. Schoolchildren in white socks and shiny black shoes played at the bus stop while waiting for the buses.

Vendors – fearlessly treading the white line in the middle of the road like tightrope walkers – balanced plastic bags of pineapple and peeled oranges on one arm, bananas in the other; arms outstretched to commuters racing to work, oblivious to the danger of one misplaced step. The strong scent of overripe fruit filled the air. Fruit flies wafted like dust on the wind.

Stacked on the roadside were cardboard boxes of unpeeled, uncut fruit waiting to fill more bags. Beckford looked over at the American apples in a crate. A man with yellowed fingernails, perched on a stool beside the crate, picked up an apple and cut it into six equal wedges with a rusting knife. His left thumb was missing. Beckford didn't bother to beckon the seller over; he knew his passenger didn't want anyone eating in his car. He liked to keep the interior pristine.

Beckford adjusted the AC. He looked through the rearview mirror into the pensive eyes of Assistant Commissioner of Police Linford Davis and asked: 'Is the temperature OK, sir?'

ACP Davis nodded a reply and took out his reading glasses. He leafed through weekend editions of the *Gleaner* on his lap. The headlines screeched:

BRUTAL WEEKEND SHOOTING IN JACK'S HILL

BOTCHED ROBBERY RESULTS IN BLOOD

ATTEMPTED MURDER OF FOREIGNER:
US OFFICIALS CONCERNED

The Editorial column asked the question: 'Is no one safe?' Beckford turned the knob to switch on the radio as the commentator launched into a diatribe: 'Yes, listeners, the government and the police need to account for what happened in Jack's Hill on Friday night. Can you imagine a visitor coming here and expecting safety, only to be attacked in his home? And the police not doing a thing. When will these criminals be called to answer for their—'

'Turn that off,' ACP Davis instructed his driver.

On the middle of the front section of one paper, on page four under the fold, he read: *Bloody Weekend: Six Killed Downtown; Another Five Missing.*

Blasted journalists! ACP Davis thought. Acting like one foreigner's life was more important than eleven Jamaicans. *A life is a life*, he thought. It was a good thing the American man hadn't died, otherwise, the newspapers probably would have demanded ACP Davis' own life in return. '*The police not doing a thing*': that's what the man on the radio had said. When here he was, already knowing who was behind it and what had to be done; rehearsing in his head the phone call he was dreading.

◆

British hadn't always been this powerful. His rise started when he came back to Jamaica. British was seen sitting in a big car with someone who looked suspiciously like the leader of the then Opposition party, which was peculiar, because the existing Area Don, Pedro Garcia, had refused to get involved with politicians. A week later, British went to the wharf to collect guns from America (crates full of Uzi sub-machine guns and M-16 assault rifles hidden in bags marked FLOUR and RICE). British was introduced to drug dealers in South America. All in exchange for ensuring everyone in Lazarus Gardens voted for the Party at the next national election, and a promise that he would fight the gunmen of the party in power.

That election year, every eligible and ineligible voter voted for the Party – in many cases they voted more than once. The victory was a landslide and it was then that British *knew*. He was unfettered. No politician could *really* be *his* boss, no matter how much the Party Leader might think so. *He* was the real Big Man.

What happened next became a kind of legend in Kingston. ACP Davis had first heard it from an older Senior Superintendent and even among the police there was an admiring tone when older officers told young recruits where British came from. Details were embellished but only British knew how that night went down.

He knew it was time to dethrone the ruling Don, Pedro, a man whose mother had come to Jamaica from Cuba with her young son. Pedro had a barrel-shaped body the colour of dark brown sugar and a narrow face like a mongoose. He had remarkably kind eyes and a hearty laugh.

That evening, standing on the balcony of Pedro's mansion, British had looked up at the moon. It looked like half a white man's face: the good side he showed you whenever he smiled like you were friends. Not revealing his true self. British didn't consider this deceit but strategy, one he understood and respected. 'Black people need to learn to hide their emotions,' he often told people. 'Let your enemy think he is safe before you strike. Make him blind to the fatal blow, the squeeze of the trigger, the fingers tightening around his neck.'

That night, he went into Pedro's room, let in by one of the trusted men in Pedro's personal guard. Pedro was surprised to see him at the door. British apologised for the unanticipated visit and told Pedro he had to get something important off his chest. A lifelong diabetic, Pedro had been about to take his nightly insulin injection. He was holding the syringe in his right hand.

For a moment, Pedro paused in the doorway. His right hand shook. Something passed between the men, as Pedro stepped aside so British could enter. Pedro knew that he wouldn't need the injection. So he put away the syringe.

British closed the door gently behind him. Although his touch was soft, the heaviness of the sound echoed throughout the house. British felt his body heavy as he sank into one of Pedro's leather chairs.

For a few minutes, neither man said anything, feeling the weight of what was before them. They listened to the crickets, the sound of two of Pedro's men outside talking and laughing and a car horn in the distance.

Finally, Pedro offered British some white rum. The two men had a drink. Pedro drank his too quickly; large gulps dribbled on to his bearded chin. Pedro looked intensely at the man he had known as a young boy, running up and down the Lane to go to the corner shop for his mother. British had inherited a dreaded trifecta that had made him the object of vicious teasing: a lazy eye, knock-knees and vitiligo. But to see him now, lean but muscled from the hardship of prison, was to see much more than a ridiculed boy. Pedro had trusted British to help expand his UK operations; throughout his stint in prison he'd never talked to the authorities about Pedro. Not once. Pedro knew British had been loyal, until now.

'Hombre, I'm proud of you.' Pedro spoke through the silence. 'You've come a far way.'

'Yes, and more to go.'

Pedro's eyes watered a little as he waited for what was to come. British stood up and hugged him, deeply inhaling the older man's Old Spice aftershave. He unsheathed the knife and slit Pedro's throat with cold precision, the way he'd seen his grandmother in the country kill a hog, covering the entire room, carpet to ceiling, with a foamy red film. Pedro braced himself against a gooey wall made slippery with his blood. He fell to his knees. There was wonder in his eyes as he clutched the wide, thin smile that had been his throat. Shock at the sight of his own blood, dyeing his white merino red. He mouthed words British couldn't recognise.

Pedro looked up at him. British saw that Pedro understood.

231

It was time. The crown was being taken from him. His men's loyalty had shifted without him knowing, and his ignorance had proved fatal. It made no sense crying out. His security team would not be coming in.

'Don't fight it,' British told the scared man softly. He was going to make sure Pedro died well and with honour.

Pedro had been the closest thing British had to a father. He considered this respectful, doing the killing himself; a kindness, making the death quick and painless. He wanted the older man to see and to know that he, British, was ready.

'I not going let you down,' he told him, after Pedro's heart had finally stopped. He held Pedro's face between his hands, feeling warmth under his fingertips. Pedro's face was slack-jawed and ugly, his eyes wet, yet to British he had never looked more handsome. British kissed his forehead.

After Pedro Garcia's death, British used his street smarts to build himself. To expand his business, to make connections, to grow the profits of his corporation and increase its market share. He brought size, structure and organisation to the gang. Bribes to government officials and kickbacks were part of the cost of doing business. But he wasn't a selfish man. Some profit went back to his people. They were, after all, the shareholders and employees.

And this is what Davis had to go up against. A criminal who didn't think he was a criminal but the saviour of his people.

◆

Beckford knew ACP Davis had a lot on his mind, so he left his boss to his thoughts, undisturbed. It was the same route he'd taken the past five years and everyone knew the distinctive blue car belonged to the ACP. Beckford was accustomed to motorists pulling aside to let the car pass, honking their horns in appreciation, pedestrians pausing to salute or wave. Davis had a reputation as a tough crimefighter; no wonder he was in line to succeed the Commissioner when he retired next year.

Davis' supporters often touted his journey from a bright-eyed boy from the country, his steady rise through the ranks. He'd done it through hard work and yes, a few favours here and there, looking the other way sometimes. Not all cops were corrupt, but neither were all criminals. Davis didn't see life in black or white. He had recently been diagnosed as colour-blind and joked that he'd always seen things in shades of grey. He considered himself a realist. A realist, who knew that what every Jamaican wanted in life was a 'bly'. The bly culture demanded that people be exonerated for breaking the law. The rich paid for getting the break. The poor felt entitled to lenience because they had a hard life. Chaos was the result.

ACP Davis remembered the 1980 election and the bloody year leading up to it: people setting fire to roads, killing their neighbours from other lanes because of where the borders of each party's garrison fell, open firefights across the school yard. They shot men holding babies, old women, children. Guns were buried in the yard like bodies, a sheet of zinc over the grave, where women spread wet clothes to dry to fool the police. Unearthed guns were propped up against fences while little boys kept a look out for cops atop mango trees. He remembered bands of young boys practising like a shadow army at night, marching and going through their drills with their weapons.

Things were not as bad now. There was more order in the communities. He had to grudgingly admit that men like British had helped to keep the chaos at bay. These days the ones being killed were enemies of the Area Dons who were criminals themselves.

Today, instead of jubilant acknowledgement of Davis' car, he was greeted with solemnity befitting a funeral procession. He might as well have been part of a motorcade for a fallen officer killed in the line of duty. There was no car horn; no shouts.

Beckford fiddled with the AC again, finding the silence in the car unnerving. He turned his head to take a sip from his coffee. And that was enough. That instant, a child playing with her schoolmates dashed into the street to escape the reach of her squealing friend. The friend's fingers caught and loosened her brown ribbon as she took off, bolting into the road.

In that awful moment ACP Davis saw everything unfold in slow motion ... Beckford's hand slamming on the horn, the twist of the steering wheel, the lurch of the car. Davis instinctively called out to the girl, even though she couldn't hear him through the glass.

The man with the crate had knocked it over in the excitement. Apples rolled into the road. Apples hit against tyres, turned to white and red pulp as they were run over by speeding motorists. Apples raced by, and on to, the feet of pedestrians.

Davis felt the car swerving into the next lane, thankfully empty of traffic. Beckford applied the brakes and the jerk of the sudden stop forced Davis forward in his seat. His forehead collided with the rear of the driver's seat.

'Beckford!'

'Mi never see her, sir.'

'Exactly! Don't I always tell you, keep your eyes on the road?'

The girl raced back to the bus stop, pigtails bouncing. ACP Davis expelled a long breath.

*

When he got to the office, ACP Davis looked out the window of his office at the cars swirling below, like currents in a river. He reflected on the little girl and thought about how easy a life could be lost, without you having an idea what was coming. Some people were like that: careening towards danger without knowing or caring. They needed people like Davis to scream, to shout, to warn them what would happen if they didn't change course. Tell them about the danger up ahead. Other people were the danger itself.

Davis didn't want to make the call, but he had to. Their contract had been breached. Petty robberies of the local middle class were one thing but now a foreigner had been hurt. And not just any foreigner: a wealthy, high-profile white man. A connected man. It had only been three days, but the media was still applying pressure. So was the US Embassy. The Prime Minister. And now both the Commissioner and the Member of Parliament had told him to get the criminals behind bars before the next weekend. Everybody wanted the investigation closed almost as soon as it began.

British would know who did it. Nothing happened with people from Lazarus Gardens that he didn't know. And word on the street was that Lazarus Gardens thugs were behind the recent robberies in Jack's Hills. He would ask British to deliver the culprits. Anybody would do, whether or not they were guilty didn't matter. British could send him men who had fallen out of favour with him. Davis didn't care. They would certainly be guilty of other crimes. They were going to prison for a long time. Justice would be done.

A witness, a Jack's Hill neighbour who had been on the street that night, had given the police a partial licence plate but the police hadn't been able to track down the van. It was probably already burnt or in some scrap heap. The witness heard the names 'Damian' and 'Streggo', but those could belong to any man in Lazarus Gardens. Everybody there had an alias. People had pet names that didn't appear on their birth certificates. There was no description of their faces since it was dark and they'd worn masks.

Davis lifted the handset from its cradle and with each number he turned in the rotary dial it was like the telephone cord was tightening around his neck.

'What you calling me for?' British demanded, instead of greeting him.

'You know why,' Davis said.

'Why you think I know about some white man getting shot last Friday night?'

Davis laughed, despite himself. 'How you know I calling about that?'

'I watch the news, *Inspector*.' British mocked him. 'Like any law-abiding citizen.' That last part wasn't untrue; British stuck to the laws he himself had created.

'That's Assistant Commissioner to you, Desmond.'

Even down the line he could hear British's hackles rising.

Davis continued: 'And we both know you know. Bring me the parties responsible. This one's not going away. The US Embassy pressuring the Prime Minister, who's pressuring the MP, who's pressuring me. I'm in this too long and too close to the top to mash things up with this foolishness. This whole thing doesn't look good.'

'A black eye on the image of Jamaica and on the police force!' were the exact words MP Wendell Simms had hollered at him.

'OK,' said British. 'I going handle this. But you owe me.'

Davis' back stiffened. Shame flushed his skin. Humiliation crawled up his arms and legs. Imagine, a man like him having to kowtow to a no-class deportee with no breeding. An old nayga and buttu. Not a cultured man like him who had done

236

courses through the London School of Economics! To calm himself, he shuffled a stack of paper on his desk but a sharp edge cut him, drawing blood from his index finger.

On the other end of the line, British heard Davis' sharp intake of breath. 'Don't worry, *officer*. Everything cool,' he said.

Davis winced.

'Let we assume I know who was involved in the shooting. You don't think I already dealing with this man for how him mess up the robbery?'

Davis didn't respond. He sucked the blood from his finger.

'You know what the best way is to make sure your enemy sees you?' British paused before answering his own question: 'Dig out his eyes. After that, all he will see is you.'

Davis listened to the whine of the dial tone. British had hung up on him. He sighed. He was looking forward to retirement in seven years. When all of this would be over.

His secretary came in bearing a silver tray with a medley of sliced fruit. She placed the tray on his desk. 'It's from Beckford, sir. He says sorry.'

Streggo

On Tuesday, the day after Davis' phone call to British, they found Streggo in the street.

His eyes were still open. He'd been left in front of the police station located just outside of Lazarus Gardens. The police hadn't even realised he had been out there for hours. The three officers in the station were inside playing a game of dominoes. One man with a bladder full of Heineken beer had gone to the side of the building to relieve himself – the police station bathroom hadn't worked for years for lack of water. Zipping down his fly, the officer noticed what looked like a pile of clothes in the middle of the street. Moving closer, he could make out it was a man! He nearly peed himself.

'Hey bwoy! Weh yuh ah do inna de road?'

No response.

Imagine! A drunken man lying right in the middle of the road! He would fix his business! 'You out deh so!' the officer yelled, 'yuh want mi tek the police vehicle and drive over yuh?'

The man didn't answer. The officer looked around at the street. It was empty. Odd. Nobody at all was walking on the road in the daytime. That's when he realised something was wrong. He felt a tension in his chest. This could be a trap.

He ran back inside and the men radioed for backup. Five police cars swooped down on the station like metallic John crows descending on a carcass.

Streggo did not blink. The last thing he'd seen was the man killing him. A man who had let him know he didn't appreciate heat being brought down on his operations. Because Streggo had been messy. He couldn't plan or execute a heist. A simple robbery had gotten the better of him. A white man had been shot. That meant all hell would break loose unless there was a blood sacrifice.

Streggo was the offered lamb.

There was a note on his chest. It read:

This is Streggo. Tell Officer Davis not to call big man again.

Streggo's eyes were wide open. His eyeballs were missing.

Mama

Mr Mack! Mr Mack! I looking fi mi comb. I just put it down somewhere and come back and can't find it. Yuh see it? Yes, mi check mi dresser already. Ask Regina if she see it. How yuh mean you don't know where Regina is?

One time, yuh had this woman, yuh see, who had a pearl. And the woman never expect that she would get something like this pearl. She find it sudden one day. She was minding har business, walking down the road, then it was sticking outta the ground. It was a big pearl too, so she buck har toe on it and fall down.

She never see a pearl like this yet. And to know that this a fi har make har feel glad. Plenty time, she go bed hungry even though she coulda sell the pearl anytime fi bread. All because she never want to lose it.

But then hard times start take the woman so she ask a friend who sorry fi har fi hold it.

Just hold it.

In exchange, the friend give har some money. So the friend holding the pearl until the woman can repay har. Til she can get back on har two foot again.

And would yuh believe that, the same friend that the woman trust go weh wid the pearl and don't come back?

And that fi years, the woman don't know where the pearl gone?

I going tell yuh five things about this woman.

One, she nuh have no sense. Everybody know if yuh give somebody a pearl, dem not going give it back.

Two, she looking everywhere fi di pearl now. All stone 'pon ground, di tablets doctor prescribe, pieces of animal bone in dirt, one button . . . anything that small enough and white, she think is the same pearl.

Three, the woman had a modda, who box out everything out of har hand that the woman try take up and claim is the pearl. To protect har. To end the search the modda know not going give the woman weh she want.

Four, the modda did love har but maybe never make the woman feel like a pearl harself. 'Cause one time the modda lose something too and never know how to tell the woman. And so now, that's why the woman looking so damn hard fi this blasted pearl.

Five, when the woman lose that pearl she lose something else in harself she can't find back even now.

Dinah

The University hospital in Mona, St Andrew, was a cluster of buildings – a constellation of bleached structures set back from the main road to August Town. The public hospital was completely ringed by a one-way road. Its private wing, with its separate entrance bordered by neatly trimmed green hedges, was reserved for the rich.

Here, in the private wing, the equipment was more up to date, there were more nurses to attend to each patient, and doctors spent more time at bedsides. Patients had their own rooms closed off with drywall, unlike patients in the public wards who shared a large hall with grimy green curtains separating a dozen beds. Patients here had a call button to push whenever they were seized by pain, a device which immediately summoned a nurse. Unlike those in the public section of the hospital, they didn't have to yell down a long passageway and hope the pitch of their voice had risen high enough – that their cry stood out in the orchestra of suffering – the chorus, like antiseptic, enveloping the hot stifling room in which overworked nurses filled out mountains of paperwork to drown out their groans.

When she entered the private wing that Wednesday, the smells of bleach and disinfectant assaulted Dinah's nose. The nurse at the desk was in a gleaming white uniform. She had dark green eyeshadow over bulbous eyes and a tongue that seemed to be falling from her mouth. The manner and looks of a frog.

'Hello, Nurse,' Dinah said, politely filling her voice with the respect the nurse's position demanded.

The nurse responded courteously, 'Call me Nurse Frederick. How can I help?'

'I'm here to see a patient ... Raymond ... him get shot last Friday.'

'Oh,' Nurse Frederick said. She looked up and down on Dinah's tattered but clean blue dress and scuffed black shoes. 'Are you a friend or relative?'

'No, ma'am, but—'

'You're early. Visiting hours don't start for another hour.'

'Yes, Nurse, but yuh see ...' Dinah thought about what she could say. She didn't like lying. She always felt God was listening.

Nurse Frederick paused and studied Dinah with those large, blinking eyes. She flicked her tongue across her large front teeth.

'I'm a helper,' Dinah said. 'Mi bring him some soup.' She unzipped her bag and held up the plastic container she had brought.

'Well, I'm not supposed to let anyone see him. His wife gave strict instructions and he is supposed to get some rest.'

'Him wife know mi coming.' Dinah asked God to forgive her for the outright lie. 'And is chicken foot.' She smiled, showing all her white teeth, and removed the lid from the soup container. The aroma of chicken seasoned with herbs and scotch bonnet pepper swimming in noodles filled the room. 'Is him favourite.' At least, she told herself, that last part was true. She remembered Mr Steele loving her soup.

Nurse Frederick softened. 'Alright then. I suppose it's OK.'

When she rounded the corner at the end of the hall and found his room, Dinah was surprised at what she saw. The figure in the bed wasn't the towering man she remembered. His face was ashen. His eyes were sunken. It looked like the bed was swallowing him slowly. She went into the room, watched his chest rise and fall to ten beats. Dinah closed the door behind her softly, and then knocked on the door from the inside to wake him up.

He jolted, startled. His eyes darted around the room.

'You!' He hoisted himself up on his elbows, settling his stare on her. 'What are you doing here?' He was looking at the small tables on either side of him in search of the call button.

'Yuh looking for this?' she said, holding up the button. She placed it out of his reach.

'How did you get in here? You get outta here right now!' His wheelchair was on the other side of the room. He wouldn't be able to get himself out of bed quickly if she attacked him.

'I don't come to harm you, sir, but mi need to talk to yuh.' Dinah sat on the chair next to the bed, folding her arms in her lap.

Perceiving no immediate threat, Raymond lowered his voice and spoke calmly: 'Stay away from my family. Lady, I don't know who you think I am, but I've never met you before.'

'Yuh right. Yuh don't know mi. Mi is a stronger woman than yuh left mi. Mi did come to say mi forgive yuh but mi can't say it. Unnu hurt mi too bad. What kind of people take people pickney under false pretence?'

'Apollo said you gave up your son.'

'Unnu shoulda write to mi,' was all she said. 'Mi did deserve to know him and him did deserve to know mi.'

Ray said nothing. Outside a gardener in khaki overalls and water boots was watering the lawn with a hose. They both watched the man, unable to meet each other's gaze.

'Mi know unnu love him,' Dinah said finally. 'Mi glad fi that.'

Nurse Frederick knocked on the door, pushing in a small cart with smaller trays of medication. 'Time for your meds, Raymond.' She placed her clipboard on top of the cart.

She must have read the simmering anger on their faces or felt the tense air in the room because she said to Dinah: 'I think the patient needs his rest now.'

Dinah got up, leaving the cooling soup on the table.

Apollo

'Yuh didn't tell mi yuh was coming!' was how Regina greeted Apollo when she saw him exiting the tenement yard that Thursday afternoon. She was with Damian, who kept looking around him, questioning every shadow and movement. He barely looked up, just muttered 'yow' at Apollo.

'Um ... actually Gina, I was visiting Dinah. And I gotta go.'

'So quick? I been using the payphone up the road to call the number yuh give mi at the firm and not getting no answer. I not hearing from yuh. Yuh couldn't tell mi yuhself you Daddy get shot? Is Dinah tell mi.'

'I've been busy.'

She thought: *Yuh never was busy before. Before mi tell yuh mi pregnant*, but she said nothing.

'Sorry, Gina, with Pops getting shot, I've been spending more time at the hospital and I took some time off work.'

'Yuh want mi come to the hospital wid yuh? Mi can come now.'

'I don't think that's a good idea.'

Regina didn't know what to say. She watched a roach hide under a dried leaf next to her slippered foot. Her ankles had started to swell so her shoes barely fit any more. Her toes were coated in dust that was disturbed by the wind.

'Sorry 'bout yuh fadda,' Damian said, avoiding Apollo's eyes. He hoisted his backpack and turned to survey the road. Nobody was around except two boys in cut-off shorts kicking around a box stuffed with old newspapers and mango tree leaves. It was an overcast day. The clouds were dark and grey, rimmed by a sky with faint tinges of pink.

Regina eyed Damian; she knew why he was being so quiet. He gave Apollo a final nod then moved to go inside the house but Regina held his wrist. He could easily have pulled away but he let her hold him back.

'Apollo baby, let we all go somewhere go eat some food and talk,' she patted her belly. 'I could do with something nice to eat. Yuh nuh hungry?'

'No, Gina,' Apollo said, at the same time Damian said, 'Nah man. Mi cool.'

'Both of unnu going. Mi know a good place in Port Royal.' She gave them a no-nonsense look; clearly she wouldn't be taking 'no' for an answer. Damian squirmed and she cut her eyes at him.

◆

Port Royal was once the playground of pirates. A place full of swashbuckling men and enterprising women who profited from debauchery until half of it sunk under the sea in the 1692 earthquake, and the other half was battered by the resulting tsunami. Centuries later, after several earthquakes, fires and scourges like yellow fever and British dominance, Port Royal was transformed into a sleepy coastal village of peeling shacks and abandoned buildings at the end of the Palisadoes peninsula. The peninsula nearly framed the Kingston Harbour. As they drove in, they passed vultures, known in Jamaica as John crows, fighting over what looked like the carcass of a dead dog.

They sat around a wobbly table outside the restaurant while waiting for their steamed fish, bammy and crackers. Regina was the buffer between the two men. She felt Apollo and Damian needed to get past the bitterness that had hardened between them.

The drive from Lazarus Gardens had been a silent one and now Apollo was looking into the horizon at gulls dive-bombing the sea, emerging with fighting fish, writhing against air. He had thought they could swim here but Regina said the water near the shore was polluted – littered with trash thrown into the sea or refuse washed down from the clogged gullies and sewage from the factories nearby. Regina directed him to stop at the Giddy House, a red-brick building that was an old Royal Artillery Store, tilted by the 1907 earthquake.

Damian appeared jittery in his plastic chair and for the first time since Apollo had met him, Damian wasn't singing, humming or beating a tune on the table with his hands. Just before they'd left Lazarus Gardens, as soon as Apollo had unlocked the car doors, Damian had quickly slipped into the car, slumping down into the backseat. He'd rolled the tinted windows up, hissing 'Drive!'

Apollo could feel Regina's eyes on the back of his head. He knew what she was thinking. *Talk to him*, she had urged in a whisper.

'So, Damian, you finish that album yet?'

'Working on it. Needed a likkle more money for studio time. But something worked out.'

A waiter came out with a huge tray bearing two brown-stewed snapper fish and a steamed parrot fish for Regina. Regina widened her eyes and smacked her lips. Since the pregnancy, she had been craving seafood. Her appetite had generally ballooned. The baby bump was hidden under the black jacket covering her tight blue and white tube top and denim miniskirt.

Damian finally spoke: 'Apollo, 'bout yuh fadda ... mi never want something like that to happen to yuh family.'

'Thanks, man. Pops is a fighter though. He's gonna pull through.'

Regina was licking the gravy from her fish off her fork when Damian said: 'Look, man, mi sorry mi ask yuh fi money. Is Streggo idea and mi never think it was a big deal.'

'That's alright, man. I know you didn't mean any harm. It's that Streggo guy. But, I heard you sing at the dance. You're good. People are gonna buy your albums one day.'

Damian nodded and looked away. It wasn't the reaction Apollo had expected. He wished things could go back to how they were. Aside from Dinah, he had nobody to talk to about things with Regina and the baby.

'You know Streggo dead?' Damian said.

'Whoa,' Apollo said. He didn't like the guy but still ... *dead*? 'How?'

'Mix up with bad company,' Regina said, matter-of-factly, looking at Damian.

'What happened?'

'Somebody murder him,' Regina said, sipping her drink.

'Do they know who killed him?'

'No,' Damian replied, quickly stuffing a piece of fried festival in his mouth after using the bread to sop up some gravy from the fish.

'Maybe I could ask Christopher's friend, the cop, to look into it.'

'No!' Regina and Damian both said, looking up from their plates. Damian added: 'Listen, Apollo, mi could be ... going away fi a while.'

249

'Where?' Apollo asked. It seemed like this was news to Regina too; she stiffened in her chair, mid-chew and put down her sorrel drink.

'Mi don't know yet, rasta, but mi will let yuh know.'

Apollo was convinced the reason Damian had been so cagey had something to do with Streggo's murder. He'd never trusted the man. He wondered if Damian had gotten mixed up in some scam or drug deal with Streggo and now owed people money, money they were after him to collect. Why else would Damian be going into hiding?

He was willing to bet that British was somehow mixed up with this. No more gifts had arrived. There were no more phone calls either. But Apollo knew it was just a matter of time before British found him. He felt the man watching him all the time. He'd started having nightmares of British finding him in bed with Regina and gutting him: a neat line from his chin to his waist. When his entrails spilled out Regina hadn't screamed or cried out. Instead, she collected his snake-like bowels into her arms, gently, like cradling a baby.

Regina's belch took him back to the present.

'Look, Damian, you're my brother, man. So if you need anything, lemme know.'

Damian pushed away his plate with his half-eaten fish. An emotion Apollo couldn't read flashed across his face. Regret? Guilt? Sadness? Shame? It didn't make sense that on the cusp of recording his album, fulfilling his dream, Damian didn't seem happy.

'Apollo mi is yuh fren. Remember that. Look, I have something fi yuh from the odda day. I been keeping it safe.'

Damian pulled the Polaroid camera from his backpack.

'Yuh did drop it the day Dinah get into the big fight and mi fren String fix it.'

250

'Wow. Thanks, man.' Apollo didn't know what to say. It was supposed to be a gift for Regina but it didn't feel right going into that now. Apollo asked the waiter to take a photo of the three of them. They drew their chairs close. Regina was in the middle, her arms around them both. The salty breeze whipped her hair around her head.

'Eat up, Congo King!' Apollo said, 'You're gonna need your energy to record.'

Regina got up. 'Make sure yuh put me inna the video!' She gyrated her hips. When Damian grinned, she burped her approval and they all laughed. Something had softened between the three of them.

'Order a next fish to go,' Regina said.

◆

Later, after a few more Red Stripes, Damian and Apollo staggered towards the shore and sat on two large rocks jutting out into the sea. Regina was snoozing in the car. The sun was about to set. Apollo looked into the sky and spoke without glancing at Damian: 'I'm worried about my Pops, man.'

'Him going make it,' Damian said, patting his shoulder. He put the beer to his lips and took a long drink. 'I never knew my old man,' he said. 'Him go away when mi was a baby. Mi did lose mi mother, too, so mi know how it feel ... Dinah was there fi mi.'

All Apollo could think to say was: 'That's rough bro, sorry.'

◆

When Apollo dropped them off, Dinah stood at the window and watched Damian and Regina get out of the car.

It was in the way his shoulders slumped, that she knew. He moved just behind Regina, almost hunched over as if trying to fold into himself. Dinah could see he bore an invisible

251

burden. Instead of standing up under it, he was shrinking. She'd seen it before. When he was a boy.

Regina waved Apollo goodbye and Damian turned and watched the backlights of the Benz disappear, arms stiff at his sides. Regina ran up the stairs, followed by Damian's heavy steps.

Dinah went into the hallway and spoke as gently as she could: 'Damian, what I tell you about you and my son?'

'Easy, Miss Dinah. Mi know. Mi hear yuh. Trust mi, mi never woulda do anything to purposely harm Apollo or you.' Damian looked at Dinah and gave her a feeble smile. Dinah noticed it waver.

◆

As soon as he got into his room, Damian pulled out the second drawer of the battered old dresser and took a stiff, yellowed paper from an envelope marked Airmail that he'd had since age twelve. It was from his mother, Kathleen. He ran his fingers over the pages, coarse and dry like old skin.

Damian used to imagine that one day when the album was done and he stopped in the US for the North American leg of his world tour, Kathleen's would be the face he'd instantly recognise in the crowd: a sturdy Jamaican woman wearing a tie-head, pushing against the screaming, young female fans at the front of the stage. Bouncing away their lithe bodies with her girth. She would come up to him after the concert, burst defiantly through the burly armed bodyguards, and grab him into a hug that was both defiant and triumphant. 'Is my son dis!' she would say, right into their disbelieving faces. And he would just nod, acknowledging her before everyone else shuffled away.

Although he hadn't touched the letter in years, he remembered it. It was delivered a month after she left him.

Dear Damian,

I hope these few lines find you in good health. I know you is a big man. You more grown up than plenty other twelve-year-old boys. So mi know you going understand why mi had was to leave you. You see, son, dry-head mout-a-massy Myrtle spread a rumour that mi vote for the other party in the last election. That is people like me who cause the party to lose. Is not true and why mi would keep that secret for three years then suddenly tell Myrtle? This just come down to badmind. Myrtle think mi was fooling with her man. This was the quickest way to get rid of mi.

Anyhow, is she tell MP Simms and next thing I know I hear that people looking fi mi to kill me. Thank God for mi good fren, Sophia, who is babymother for one of British man 'cause she hear him say dem was going firebomb our house that night. And Sophia tell me. I had was to run away. I couldn't go back to country bush 'cause nothing not there to go back to in mi mother's house. Sophia said she have a way for me to go to America.

That night, mi lay low in Sophia's uncle's house until Sophia sort out mi papers. Her sister did just get through for a US visitor's visa but she take sick and dead sudden, so I just paste my picture over hers in the passport. I never fret so in my life when mi was in the US immigration line. The man must never did notice the sweat on mi face in cold AC but him let mi through.

So mi not up here straight. Sophia cousin, Keith, is a mechanic over here and him say him can arrange a business marriage with one of him American fren. I going to meet the man next week in Florida. If it work out mi will get mi permanent stay and file for you. Keith say him know about a old lady in Florida who need somebody to take care of her. Keith say that him just need me to

253

take a package for him fren for him. I didn't bother put Keith address on this letter 'cause I not going be here after next week.

When mi reach Florida and know where mi staying mi will write. Sophia say she coming here too in another few months and she will take some things back for you from me.

I think about you all the time. I don't have the heart to call you because you going ask me where mi is and when you can come. And I don't have no answer for you. Not now. The best way to tell you about this is to tell you a story. Maybe you will understand.

Mi used to work for a man who did collect stamps. The same ones like what on this letter. Him used to live in England. Him did fight in World War Two and when him get old him return to Jamaica to live. Him say him kill plenty bad people that did name Nazis. Him used to keep the stamps in a big book that look like a photo album. Every Friday him would take out the book and turn every page. Stamps of the Queen and all kinds of birds, flowers and even motor car. One day I notice this stamp of a giant yellow and black butterfly. Mi never know the name but him tell me it called Jamaican Swallowtail Butterfly. Him say is him favourite stamp. Him hold up the book and I stand back and look. Him never allow nobody to touch it. 'Sar,' I say, 'why is you favourite stamp?' Him say: 'Because this stamp can fly.'

'Fly?' I shocked. I wasn't going say anything else 'cause this man was old and start to lose him head.

'It fly,' him say. 'You don't see?' I start to stare at the stamp 'til mi eyes blur.

I never understand it until now, Damian. When you love something you want it to fly. And sometimes you see it fly

*and sometimes you have to trust in your heart it going fly
even when you can't see it.*

*I need you to listen to the adults in the yard. Talk
respectful to Dinah, Mr Mack and Mrs Sinclair. I ask dem
to look out fi you. I couldn't tell you what mi was planning
'cause mi didn't want you in harm's way. This way, you
could honestly say you don't know where you mother is.
But leaving you that last night was the hardest thing mi
had to do.*

*Remember how from you was three you say you going
be a singer? I know you can sing but is not everybody turn
Bob Marley. Grow out of it and learn a trade. You can
become a mechanic like Mr Mack. Keith say that mechanic
earn big money in America 'cause people love dem car,
especially Cadillac.*

Be a good boy now.

With love,

Your mummy, Kathleen

It was the only letter he ever received from her. There was
never a barrel full of notebooks or pencils for school, Ivory
soap, Spam, Uncle Ben's rice, Aunt Jemima pancake mix, and
Tide laundry detergent. No phone call, no package of clothes
sent through Jamaicans returning from Miami.

The night he got that letter was as bad as the night she
went missing. The night she had left the moon was like a
scythe – a hacked off toenail. The last thing she'd done for
him was to peel an ortanique. He couldn't even remember
what his last words to her were. He remembered the smell
of the rind on her nails as she stroked his face. When he had
gotten up in the morning and not seen her in the kitchen, he
knew something was wrong. There was no breakfast of oats
porridge made for him to go to school.

Dinah was the one who told him the news. She had him sit on a chair next to her, held his hand and rested his head on her breast while he pretended not to cry. It was like a piece of his heart had chipped off, like a part of a cliff collapsing into the sea.

Even before Kathleen left, Damian would sometimes hear Dinah sobbing softly through the thin wall. He used to think it was because Dinah had no one except for her mother. There was no man or child to bring her joy. But he knew children were never to ask grown people about such things. By the time he was twelve he understood that emptiness. Kathleen's absence always poked at him like the phantom itch in an amputated limb. His life became 'before' and 'after' her leaving – a split like the parting of a curtain in a room he could not re-enter.

He often wished he could grow big overnight so he could take Dinah into his arms and comfort her like she cuddled him that morning in the kitchen when the realisation that Kathleen was not coming back fell like blows on his head. And when he had his first wet dream, it was Dinah who was in it, stroking him.

Dinah had made sure he was fed and went to school until age fifteen when he decided to stop, to be his own man and follow his music dream. Mr Mack offered him apprenticeship at the garage where he worked, which he turned down.

He became a man the day Kathleen left. Even as he waited for her to come back, refusing to move from the yard so she'd always know how to find him: untethered from boyhood. But that was the day he started looking out for himself. Making his own choices. Choices that had led him here: hiding from British, fearful of being caught by the police, regretful about Streggo, betraying Apollo, guilty about Raymond and a disappointment to Dinah and Regina. He closed his eyes and pictured the sea at Port Royal.

He longed for Kathleen. At Port Royal today he thought about her, imagining she was alive, and thinking of him, in that moment, somewhere on the other end of the sea.

Apollo

'You sure you OK, Pops?' Apollo fluffed the pillows behind Raymond.

They were in the private wing of the hospital. Celeste was feeding Raymond green Jell-O with a teaspoon. It reminded Apollo of when he was a kid and she used to bribe him with Jell-O for dessert if he promised to finish his vegetables.

'Yes, son. With all the sweet stuff they feed me, I may have diabetes by the time I get out of here, but other than that I'm OK.'

Celeste laughed and Raymond laughed too, until he winced with pain. They were trying to be cheerful. One week after the shooting, and Raymond's operation seemed to have been a success. The doctors had just come in to say although Raymond was lucky to be alive, he had a long road to recovery ahead of him. But it was too soon to know if he would be able to walk again.

Apollo had noticed the way Celeste squeezed Ray's fingers when she heard the progress report. She was so measured and controlled and the reassuring squeeze was as much emotion as she let slip in front of Apollo. It was as if she had locked the events of that night inside a box and hidden it in soil. Buried it like the roots of a young tree she was transplanting.

Nurse Frederick appeared at the door. 'You have a visitor,' she said with grave solemnity, as if announcing the arrival of a member of the Royal Family. She almost bowed.

ACP Davis entered, carrying a large basket of fruit. He looked around awkwardly, not knowing where to place it. Celeste took it from him and put it carefully on the table beside Raymond.

'Good afternoon,' Davis said. 'Sorry to intrude on you folks. I regret that I have to see you again under these difficult circumstances, but I wanted to update you on our investigations.'

'Appreciate you coming by in person, Davis. Your boss sent some very nice flowers, too. Do give him my thanks.' This message was clear and Davis caught it. Raymond was connected and any delay in solving the crime would be swiftly escalated up the chain of command.

'Have you caught the guys?' Apollo asked, impatient.

Davis turned between Raymond and Apollo, his smile slipping. 'We've had some positive developments this week, including the discovery of one suspect.'

'How soon will there be a trial?' Apollo asked.

'Well, never.'

There was a moment's pause in the room as the family processed his reply.

'I don't understand. Why?' Celeste asked.

'He was found dead by the police after the robbery. It's common for criminals to turn on each other after commission of a crime. It's not surprising in a case like this that has gained national and international attention.'

Apollo noticed how careful and formal Davis was with his words; so precise they sounded almost rehearsed.

Nurse Frederick re-entered the room and they watched as she handed Raymond a small white paper cup with multi-coloured pills and a glass of water.

As soon as she left, Ray sat up straighter in bed. Apollo saw, despite his pallor, the businessman in him had returned. His father was still the man who knew how to get what he wanted. 'Look, Davis, I've been in touch with the US Embassy—'

'They've called us too,' Davis interrupted.

'And there were four men that night. So what about the other three? You know what they tried to do to my wife?' His voice, already so thin, caught, like a fishing line snapping taut. Celeste's body seemed to echo it, as she moved towards her husband's side. She avoided Apollo's gaze. Until now he had barely allowed himself to think about the way his mother's nightdress was torn, or the bruises still visible on her arm.

Celeste picked up Raymond's water glass and held it to his face. Davis looked politely out of the window as he drank noisily, water dribbling down his hospital pyjamas. But when Raymond looked up again his face was composed. 'We won't be satisfied until all four are brought to justice.'

Davis stuck a finger in his collar and pulled it away from his neck. He tried to match Raymond's tone but his eyes fled to the window again, as if he wished to follow. On top of having to negotiate with a low-life like British, he didn't need a self-important white man telling him how to do a job he'd done for almost thirty years. He cleared his throat and swallowed his resentment before replying: 'Let me assure you: we're working on all leads and doing everything in our power to apprehend the offenders. These active investigations are at a sensitive stage, so unfortunately I can't say more about the other suspects at this time.'

'Can you at least tell us the name of the dead one?' Celeste asked.

'We don't yet know his legal name. He wasn't found with any identification and no next of kin has come forward to identify him.'

'So you're telling me you don't even know who he is? Why do you even think he's the one who shot me?' Raymond's hands gripped the crisp white sheets as if they were Davis' lapels. His face darkened.

'We do know his alias. They call him "Streggo".'

Davis tossed out the name as if were a piece of trash, but it hit Apollo dead-centre like a truck. He rocked back on his feet, disbelief on his face turning to rage. Celeste called out in confusion but he left the room before she'd even finished asking, 'Apollo, where are you going?'

Apollo

So it all made sense. I get why when we met, Damian talked about the nice things in Jack's Hill houses. And why he became my friend. It was all a setup. That shakedown at the dance too. His wanting to get close to me. There's this thing that means a lot to me: loyalty. People being real and sticking with you.

It's like I'm being stabbed. It's Michael and the kid in the locker room all over again. Except worse. This time Michael's Black.

I head straight home from the hospital. The place feels bigger and emptier without our stuff they stole, without my folks. I go up to Pops' study and pull out a drawer in his desk. The one second from the bottom. I knew he sometimes kept condoms, cards or cash there. It was always my first stop before my dates with Regina. Three weeks ago, I went there and saw a huge brown envelope. A gun was inside.

He obviously didn't want Moms to know about it, which must be why he didn't keep it in the safe. Moms hates guns and doesn't want them in the house, but Pops always said guns are harmless, it's the people pulling the trigger you should worry about. He told me how he could shoot as soon as he could walk and his dad would take him out hunting deer and bears in the woods. He always said he'd take me someday. What if Pops can never walk again? Who goes hunting in a wheelchair?

It's a good thing the robbers didn't find the gun, which feels cold in my hand. Heavier than I thought. I never held one before.

I tuck it in my waistband on my way to see Damian.

Damian

'Jah know, star, everything frig up, String!' Damian said.

'Yes ennuh, dawg, sheg up!' String echoed. They were inside String's grand-aunt's house – a tattered, slouching wooden structure, squatting over the lane that bordered Lazarus Gardens and the neighbouring community. British's men had firebombed String's mother's house last night. Luckily, she and the other children had been visiting family in the country and String had been lying low at his uncle's. It was a week after the robbery and it was obvious now they weren't going to stop at Streggo.

'I easing out tonight,' String said. 'Before dem find mi.'

Damian could feel the sweat pooling under his armpits. Immediately after the robbery, Damian had marvelled at the possessions that had summed up a man's life: TVs, sofas, jewellery and cash. It would be enough money for him to record his album. But with British running the music studios, he had no chance.

Now Damian thought: *No man, this don't feel like how I think this was going feel.*

He was trapped.

Before the loot could be divided between them, Streggo said he had to take it to British so the Boss could take his cut and leave the rest for them to share. That was the last time they had seen him. Now he was dead and soon they would be. British had picked off Streggo and deposited him like filth outside the police station to make a point. The entire Lazarus Gardens Ghetto News Network was buzzing with the news: 'Streggo dead! Who next on British list?'

Ratta had gone into hiding. Like a crab in a deep hole. British made no secret that he was upset. And there was one unwritten law in Lazarus Gardens: don't upset British.

String was trembling as he packed clothes into a knapsack. He was trying to stuff school certificates for outstanding academic performance and science competition trophies into the small bag.

'Yow, leave dem things deh,' Damian said. 'Dem can't help you.'

String looked like he was about to cry. His shoulders shook. He had been jumped by British's men the morning before, and only narrowly escaped by scaling the zinc fence. His uncle, afraid for String's life after the bombing, had been trying to get him to his grand-aunt's house in the first light of dawn when two men fired at them.

'Di shot dem a beat after mi!' String said to Damian now, his voice shaky. Afterward, when String retraced his steps to find his uncle, he'd seen the man's body sprawled out on the sidewalk.

'Mi pull him foot and him nuh wake.' String fingered the trophy, picking away at the gilt paint.

Damian remembered the day he'd won it. Only a few years ago, when they were boys at school, but it seemed like a thousand. He was tired. He yawned and rubbed his eyes. He hadn't been able to sleep since the robbery. Every time he closed his eyes, there was the white man's body blossoming red, his mouth opening and closing slowly like a caught fish.

'String,' he said now, placing a hand on the smaller boy's shoulder, 'take care of yuhself.'

String started to blink rapidly. Damian knew he had to lay low too, but he didn't have anywhere else to go. It was just a matter of time before British found him.

As his friend turned to go back into the blinding sun, Damian knew he would never see String again.

◆

Dinah knew death was coming because on Friday morning she had a dream her mouth was closed and couldn't be opened. That and her foot-bottom was scratching her. And a cock had started to come on her rooftop every day at six-thirty early for the last two weeks. All these omens pointed to one thing. Death.

So that morning when she woke up, she wrapped a white scarf around her head and decided to warn. She slipped off her slippers so she could feel the damp earth under her feet. To feel the firmness assuring her. The woman in the white robe was by her side too, watching her but saying nothing.

'Repent!' Dinah bawled out. The sound of her cries pierced Damian's eardrums as he lay in bed, trying to sleep. Sleep was hiding from him again. Each pore on his skin seemed wide open and his head felt like it was floating.

◆

It was Clevon who brought the message from British around noon on Friday. After String fled, Damian saw Clevon's men enter the lane. He climbed a wall and hid in some bushes near a cherry tree. They were looking for him. He shuffled in the bushes, crawling on his hands and knees like a dog. It was from this vantage point he saw Clevon's shiny shoes. Thick leather Clarks, tapping on the pavement, just inches from

Damian's fingers. Clevon had neat cornrows and a tattoo of a cross on his right cheek.

'Yow, stand up,' Clevon said, rolling a toothpick between his teeth. Damian brushed his dirty palms on the legs of his jeans. If he was going to die, he wanted to do it like a man on his two feet.

'I not going kill yuh ... at least, not yet. Yuh lucky yuh not dead, in truth. You, Streggo and String bring down a heat unnu can't manage. And to think, unnu get the idiot bwoy Ratta involved too. The Americans need somebody picture to go in the *Gleaner* showing who shoot the white man. We giving you twenty-four hours to turn yourself in. If you wait too long or run, believe me, I going find you.' Damian's breathing quickened and he rubbed his chest. He met Clevon's gaze and saw nothing there. The man's face began to swim before his eyes. Clevon had inherited his father's cold stare. He broke the toothpick against his teeth and threw it on the ground.

Apollo

I wait for him in his room that very afternoon. It's Friday, so Dinah's at work and Regina's not around. I slip inside and find a spot in the corner. I pull back the hood of my grey hoodie. I want him to see my face.

When he comes in and sees me he freezes. Like he's expecting somebody else. He smiles when he realises it's me.

'Apollo, mi yute,' he says, coming towards me.

'Stop right there.' I lift the gun. There's a queasiness in my stomach.

'Wah dis man? How yuh coming at mi wid gun, my bredda?' Damian holds up his hands and backs away.

'I'm not your brother. Were you there that night? Did you and Streggo rob my house and shoot my Pops? Dude, he may never *walk* again.'

'Is not me shoot him.' But I can tell from his face he's ashamed.

'But you were there.'

'Yeah man. Mi sorry. I was just trying to get money fi mi album.' Damian drops his hands and takes a step to me.

'Your *album*? Your stupid Congo King dream? My dad could have died, man! Is your album worth his life? Is it worth yours?' I come closer.

I brought the gun for protection but now I realise I have to shoot him.

'Nuh shoot.'

'Why not?'

'Nuh do it.'

'Why?'

'Mi is yuh fren.'

I couldn't help laughing.

'Some friend.' I want him to feel the venom of my words. 'Trying to kill my Pops. Robbing my family. Nearly raping my mother! My *mother*, you sick sonofabitch!' My hand on the gun is unsteady.

'Raping yuh mother? I wasn't going let *nobody* rape yuh mother. Mi was there to make sure things was under control, my yute. Nobody was to get hurt.'

'My folks are traumatised.'

'Nobody was supposed to get hurt,' Damian says again, weakly.

'But look what happened.' Anger is making my eyes blurry and my voice deeper. It's hard and stiff like coming from somebody else. People are all the same. They let you down.

'Apollo, yuh is not a killer.'

'How do you know?' I growl. 'How do you know what kinda man I am? I didn't think you were a criminal either.'

'Mi neva intend fi anything to happen.'

'But it did, man. What were you thinking bringing those dudes to my house?'

'Things wasn't supposed to go down like that.'

'I hope it was worth it for you.'

'Mi can fix it.'

Damian's watching me, and I'm watching him and the rest of the room feels like it's falling away. My heartbeats are filling the room, so loud I feel like Damian can probably hear

269

them but he's not saying anything. He isn't quaking and on his knees begging for his life, like I imagined he'd be. He's just standing there, looking at me like he's sad and tired. And I ain't getting the respect I thought holding the gun would give me. It feels cold in my fingers and heavier by the minute. I'm clenching the fist of my other hand so hard my fingernails almost cut my skin.

'Give mi the gun,' he says. 'Is not yuh this. I going fix it. Mi going go to the police, Apollo. I going tell dem everything.'

'You ... you promise?' But my voice sounds weak. The walls are coming closer. Every muscle in my body connects to the muscle in my trigger finger. Suddenly I ain't too sure about what I'm doing here. Damian's right. I'm no killer. I'm not like him. I can't hurt people, even the ones who deserve it.

In handing over the gun, I squeeze the trigger. I didn't mean to. It was an accident. The clicking sound explodes.

I collapse like a ragdoll. Strength leaves my body. No emotions are left. Nothing's left.

I wait for Damian to fall too or clutch his chest. To die. I wait for the blood.

Damian doesn't flinch.

'The safety on,' he says, smiling at my shocked face. He shrugs. 'Killing a man is no joke. But yuh couldn't shoot mi, even if yuh did want to.'

We stand there in silence for a while. He gives me back the gun without another word.

That night, when I put the gun back in the envelope inside the drawer in Pops' study, I handle it like a sleeping snake. Then I go into the bathroom, close the door softly and throw up.

Damian

Nobody from Lazarus Gardens had ever walked through the gate of the police station. So when Damian strode in the next morning, one of the three officers who was taking a break from the checkers game to get another Heineken dropped the bottle on the ground.

'Rassclaaat!' the officer yelled and grabbed at his waist for his gun. He belatedly realised he had left it on the table inside.

'St-stop right deh-so!'

'Officer, I surrender,' Damian said. He held his hands up so the officer could see his palms.

'Mi say stop!'

'Mi know unnu looking fi mi.'

'Who is you?'

'Damian Miller.'

'Who?'

'One of the man weh rob di Jack's Hill white man.'

The officer hollered for his two colleagues. Next thing Damian knew, he was on his knees on the ground, being tackled by three men. Pain surged through his body as they rained down with kicks and yanked his arms into handcuffs behind him.

'Weh de gun deh?' a short officer, his body the round shape of a breadfruit, demanded.

A taller one had his boot on Damian's neck. His vision blurred.

'Mi don't have no gun ... ' Damian inhaled dirt and felt gravel on his tongue. It tasted chalky. He spat blood.

'So yuh is a badman! Gunman without a gun! Unnu nearly kill dat white man! How yuh like it?' they jeered.

After stomping on him some more, they raised him to his feet and carried him inside. They dropped him on the floor of a cell head first and took off his shoes and belt. He heard their zips being undone, he couldn't see as his eyes were swollen shut, but he felt the warm pee running down his face, burning the cuts on his skin. He felt a burning in his crotch and realised the tall one was stomping him again. Officer Breadfruit was smiling, holding a lit cigarette.

'Which eyeball?' Breadfruit said.

The officer who saw him first was saying to Breadfruit: 'Sarge, let's call ACP Davis.'

'Alright, since you can't choose ... the left one.' Officer Breadfruit brought the lit end of the cigarette closer to his face and Damian stiffened but didn't say a word. Life had weighed his worth as a man and found him wanting. He was too weary to be afraid. The feelings inside him had given way to something hard he couldn't name.

He remembered how he had felt when Apollo first confronted him with the gun. He'd wanted in that moment to live. More than he ever had before. He felt every pore, the weight of his own skin, felt his own blood pulse through his brains. The stink of fear nauseated him. He would live. Had to live.

'Pussyclaat, cry nuh! Bawl!' Breadfruit was shouting at him now. The cigarette was dangerously close to his left eye.

Damian wouldn't break.

'Alright.' Breadfruit drew back and put out the cigarette under his right boot. 'Yuh tough. Mi respect that. We going call ACP Davis.'

PART THREE

Iguana

Wendell Simms & British

'Wendell Simms, mi can't believe is you.'

'Been a long time, eh, British?'

Lazarus Gardens' MP Simms stood up from his chair and shook British's hand. Then the two men sat around the table in the restaurant at the Liguanea Club in New Kingston. British didn't fancy himself a tennis club type, but he knew this was Simms' territory. Much had happened in the week following the robbery and that Saturday afternoon Simms had sent British a message to come meet him at the Club.

British adjusted the collar of his shirt. He didn't want to appear uneasy among the laidback wealth of the men born on the correct side of Half Way Tree, the uptown gentlemen who flaunted the entitlement they felt like silk around their necks: the certainty that life always had something good to offer them. These white, mixed Indian and Chinese men who were used to helpers wiping their bottom from the time they were children, always having people bending over backwards for them. You could see it when the waiter, who looked as dark as British, came and filled their water glasses, never meeting Simms' eyes, his back bent.

This was the kind of thing British saw in England too. That you could make a man think, on his own, without you having to keep telling him all the time, that he was always to stay back and know his place.

It angered British that the only thing that people like Simms would have thought a man like British – who had no education to speak of – could do was to probably wash their car, collect their garbage or cut their lawn. But *he* had changed course. British was proud of who he had become. He wasn't going to bow and scrape before any man, including Simms, who was looking at him now as if British owed him something.

'Good of you to come,' Simms said, gently patting the table with his left hand. 'It's been a while. We have a lot to discuss. So what would you like for lunch, British?'

'I eat already.'

'Come on, man. Have a drink. It's on me. They have nice desserts here.'

British ordered an Appleton rum. Simms leaned back in his chair, taking his cup of coffee with him. He held it up to his face and took a sip.

It was the way Simms' fingers were gripping the handle of the cup, with such precision, firmness and control that struck British. Simms had brought him here to display the one thing he knew British would never have, the one thing money could not buy in Jamaica: his class. That was something you were born into.

It confirmed for British why Simms had chosen the Liguanea Club as the venue for their meeting. This place with its squash and tennis courts, swimming pool, gym, guest rooms, meeting rooms, restaurant, bar and well-manicured grounds. Simms' great grandfather Sir Fielding Clarke, then Chief Justice of Jamaica and the first President of the Club, opened the Club in 1910. He'd watched it become the centre of activity for British expatriates living in colonial Jamaica.

Popular among the elite over the years; Simms' father took his son there in the 1960s to see British actor Sean Connery, leading man in the James Bond flick *Dr No* who was staying there as a guest. The Liguanea Club featured in the film's opening shots. After Independence, the club opened up membership to rich locals. Well-connected men like Simms. It was a show of power. To remind British to remember his place.

The Club's terrace restaurant overlooked a lush garden. It was truly an oasis in the heart of the buildings in New Kingston. Proud egrets paraded across the lawns; hummingbirds flitted from flower to flower and red-tailed chicken-hawks perched at the top of the nearby high-rise buildings. There were also ground doves, green parakeets, bananaquits in the daytime and at night, patoo owls.

Tranquil. That was the word to describe this place.

Simms finished his coffee and got a whisky.

'So, Simms. Why you want to see me? My political donations to the Party need to increase? You want more money for campaigning? Community projects need finishing? I going leave here writing a cheque?'

'You know how Liguanea Club got its name, British?' Simms stared into the distance just past British's shoulder. While Simms talked you could see all of his even, white teeth. 'It got its name because the Club sits on the Liguanea Plain, which you know the city of Kingston is built on.'

British grimaced. He knew Simms just wanted to talk before he got to the real reason he wanted to see him. He decided to humour him.

'We call this area Liguanea now because you used to have plenty iguanas up here and so the Spanish call this place 'la iguana', after those giant lizards. But the British couldn't pronounce the name so they corrupt it and say Liguanea.'

Simms paused to take a sip of his whisky.

'Imagine. How is it that a place that the Spanish run for a hundred and fifty years before the British come capture it in 1655, could – just like that – get called a different name by people who couldn't say the original name properly?'

'Simms, it seem to me like that is what the whole of history is about: one conqueror taking something from another conqueror or the other, who did already take it from the conquered. I wonder what the Arawaks used to call this area before the Spanish arrive? The place must did have a Arawak name.'

Simms was stumped at British's observation. Finally he said: 'That's a good question, British. But whatever that name was, it's lost to history, since the Spanish killed them all. And there are no iguanas in this area any more either. In fact, they're believed to be practically extinct. And those lizards used to be the largest native land animal in Jamaica.'

British bit into the lemon poppyseed cake he had ordered, but it was drier than he had expected. He pushed the plate away. He should have asked for the cornmeal pudding he'd wanted.

'Is a history lesson you really carry me up here for, Simms?'

Simms laughed. The kind of laugh where he threw his head back.

'I like your honesty, British. You're a man who like when people tell you things straight. So I'm going tell you why I mention all of that history. I'm making the point that power is something that pass from one group of people to the next, and the next. That flow is natural and it's not something you can stop. Me and you, after we long gone, this thing going keep going on and on. Who knows? If it still here, maybe this place going to get called by a different name by another set of people.'

'Simms, what you want?' British had already emptied his Appleton and had ordered a vodka. He took a sip of it now.

'I hear you're having some problems with Customs at the wharf, with heavy custom duties being levied and goods been held for a long time. Contents from some shipments unaccounted for . . . that kind of thing.'

Beason, that sonofabitch! The rat. Spreading news.

British fixed Simms with a hard stare. 'It look like Beason forget about a thing name attorney-client privilege. Which is funny since that's the one thing me pay him for.'

'Look, British,' Simms leaned forward. 'He and I have a long personal and business history. I could lie to you and say is not Beason come to me but he did, and he did because he's trying to be enterprising. He wanted to come to you with a solution to your problem. To show his value.'

Beason must have sensed he was losing favour and approaching Simms was his last-ditch attempt to avoid the inevitable.

'And, when Beason came to me I saw an opportunity to connect with you myself.'

'Why?'

'To help you. So we can help each other.'

Now it was British's turn to laugh. 'What you want to help me with, Simms?'

'I can make the Customs problem go away.'

'And in return?'

'In return, you give me more suspects involved in the shooting in Jack's Hill.'

'I just deliver a man to Davis on Tuesday. Davis crawl back to me Thursday and say the Americans still pressuring him so I make sure another one turn himself in early this very morning. What more you want?'

'The Americans ramping up the pressure. The man that got

281

shot said there were four people there that night. We need all of them. And I also need you to keep things calm in Lazarus Gardens. Keep us out of the news.'

'Simms, is my job to run Lazarus Gardens and I doing that. I been dealing with it,' British said through gritted teeth.

'The man that got shot is well-connected in DC. You should hear some of the names I've had calling my office this last week. The Americans don't like to hear about a man like that being hurt on this island, where he should be safe. He has a right to feel safe in his own house, without interference from hoodlums. It's getting plenty attention that the Party . . . the government don't need.'

British waited until the waiter took away his empty glass. He declined the offer for a fresh drink with a sweep of his hand.

'British, it was a messy business to begin with. Robbing houses in an area like Jack's Hill. Something was bound to happen. Rich people buying licensed firearms like never before. And they not afraid to defend themselves either. These guys were a bunch of amateurs or what? And how you let that happen under your watch?'

British's lips were pressed into a thin line. 'I still not clear what you asking me to do.'

'That's the thing. I'm not asking.'

Simms motioned to the waiter to get the bill ready. He pulled a wad of crisp bills from his pocket.

'I'm *telling* you. Stay quiet, British. Keep your head down. Don't let any more criminal elements from Lazarus Gardens create any more bad press for us. The Americans are suggesting political corruption could be slowing the efforts of the police. If the heat don't die down soon and things don't stop, then the government going have to take more drastic measures.'

'Like what?'

'Like showing the public and the Americans we are tough on crime, by delivering up a major drug kingpin. To crack down on criminality.'

British laughed so hard the other diners turned their heads and craned their necks to look. It occurred to British then how strange it must look to see this prominent politician sitting with a notorious criminal like him, having what appeared to be a casual afternoon drink. Except nobody here seemed to know who he was. He was just another regular person talking with a politician. Probably begging some favour or brokering some deal.

'Simms, you really looking me in my face talking about criminal elements and criminality, when the biggest criminals are politicians? I going have to remind the Prime Minister about the things I bring down and give out for him to ensure him win the election?'

'I telling you again, British. Keep things quiet.'

British leaned back in his chair and intertwined the fingers of both hands, resting them across his chest. He crossed his ankles and stretched his legs out in front of him.

'You remember when I just come back from England before Pedro Garcia dead?'

'You mean before you kill him.'

'Same difference. You remember what you tell me that day in the Party Leader's car when you give me the green light to get rid of Garcia?'

'No.'

'You said Garcia had outlived his usefulness. Is those exact words you use.'

'And?'

'And at the time it seem strange to me that a man who didn't know all there was to know about another man could say something like that about him. I wonder to myself: *Useful to who?* and I decide that day that the only person I was going to be useful to was myself. You know why?'

'Why don't you tell me?'

'So nobody could look at me and tell me when *my* usefulness was done. Or tell me what to do, or not do, to anybody ever again. And you know what other things you say that day? You say, we can run things, that my life not going ever be the same and power was ours. That last part remind me now about your iguana story.'

'What you mean?'

'You were only partly right. Power is *mine*. And is time you know that.'

Simms' face went red.

'You playing a dangerous game, British.'

'I know. I been playing it a long time.'

'Too long maybe. Is like you forgetting yourself.' Simms sat upright in his chair.

'No, Simms. My problem is not forgetting. The problem for you is that I remember *everything*. All who get kill or get threaten 'cause they were suspected of voting against the Party. People couldn't think for themselves if that thought would go against the Party.'

'Party interest is Jamaica interest. Those people weren't patriotic. They don't love their country.'

'And that is why they had to suffer? I think you believing your own lies now.'

'I'm warning you. You don't want to make an enemy of the Party. You know what? I should have seen it the day that woman come to my office saying you were trying to recruit her son into your gang.'

'Ah yes. I heard she came by your office. I bet she gave quite a performance, eh? Carried on bad, like when she came to me. Look, Simms. What I offer these young men is opportunity. I giving her son a chance to be trained into the position of legal advisor in my organisation.'

'If I had done something then, the white man wouldn't have gotten shot. She was right about you. You needed controlling. That time I thought she was crazy, but now I see is you who is the crazy one.'

'Tell me, who in this whole country sane, Simms? Who?'

British saw the sunlight catching Simms' grey hair at his temples. His hair was thinning. He hadn't noticed before.

British folded his white linen napkin and placed it neatly on the table. 'I manage my affairs. I don't need your help with Customs. And Simms, don't tell me what to do about anything again, or even call me. Not unless you want to end up like the iguana.'

He got up and left, striding past the waiter who was staring at him open-mouthed.

Mama

Dem used to call mi modda a obeah woman. People would come to har fi the cure fi everything. Bad stomach. Bump pon face. Bruk foot. Warts. Lazy eye. Cheating husband. Ulcer. Cancer. She did always know what bush, leaf and bark fi boil up. She tell people exactly what wrong wid dem. But the funny thing is – though she help dem, dem hate har. Hate har 'cause dem expose dem private, shameful, ugliest self to mi modda. Dem show dem shame to har. And, in return, she would look dem inna dem eye, bold-bold, and without blinking, open up har hand and sey: 'Here, take this.' And that root, flower petal or seed would take away whatever pain dem.

And she would bathe dem and sprinkle powder over dem and tell dem what to drink. Sometime, she would make dem open up dem mouth like a young bird and sing wid har.

Dem shame 'cause dem need har and har healing. Dem couldn't take it. On Sunday, dem in church in the pulpit or pew crying down the evildoers and iniquity workers and hollering out how wicked people who practise witchcraft must die. Outside, dem spit when dem sey har name, Mildred, like is a curse. Dem sey at night she take on different skin and fly 'bout de place like bat. Pickney sing song 'bout har. Dem parents used to frighten dem, telling dem that if dem bad, mi modda going put dem on a wood fire and nyam dem.

But people fear har too, so dem don't sey these things where and when she can hear. But nobody come over to we verandah fi drink tea or invite mi modda over to dem house. Dem nuh want nobody to know she did help dem. Shame is like that. It seep inna yuh blood. Mi never understand it 'til mi get Dinah.

◆

Is a button cause the whole thing. A blasted button!

Mi was in mi twenties but in plenty ways still a pickney 'cause of how mi modda shelter mi. Being a obeah woman daughter mean yuh neva keep fren. As soon as dem parents hear that dem chat to yuh at school is pure licks dem get when dem reach home, then dem avoid yuh after that. I stop go school by the time I turn thirteen and I used to help mi modda in har work. Sheltered pickney is like a lamb to the world of wolves. That's why mi try to raise Dinah different. I try toughen har up.

Mi was trying on mi modda dress – a pretty, bright orange one with shiny, gold buttons down the front. Mama neva had plenty nice things but this dress was one. She never used to charge much fi har healing work and what she earn, she would send to har ten brother and sister dem and har parents.

I used to wonder who give har the dress but she never sey, so mi never ask. The dress used to hang up in mi modda closet as long as mi could remember. She never wear it often – just special occasion and she never have many of those. Mi would see the dress on har twice a year – on her birthday or Christmas.

Anyway, I go take up mi fast self to try on mi modda dress. Har most cherished possession, 'cause I think I name woman

287

now. Yuh can guess what happen? Long story short, mi modda was a slim woman and shorter than mi. Mi had more breast. Mi turn to see myself good in di mirror. Mi didn't see the button pop, but mi hear it hit the wooden floor. Mi didn't see where it land. Mi bend over and hear a rip loud like thunderclap. Well, I strip naked right then and there. Lawd! I search and search and couldn't find the button. Mi think sey the button slide through a space in the wood floor and gone under the house. So I crawl on mi hands and knees under the house and all I get is cobweb in mi face, dirt under mi nails and I nearly get sting by scorpion and bite up by mad ants. I find a stinking dead rat. No button.

Would yuh believe that mi find out later that the button end up in the pocket of another dress that did hang up on the same closet? It fly right in deh. So two weeks later when mi modda search in har pocket fi money to give mi to go market, she sey: 'Wah this?' and open up har palm. When mi see de button mi nearly bawl.

Anyhow, if mi had the button at the time, I could sew it on back, 'cause mi modda teach mi. The first thing I think is that mi need fi find a button that look just like that button. It look like a closed-up rosebud. I remember that Mr Spence, the tailor, who we call Missa S, and him wife, the dressmaker, live not far up the road. One of dem must have a button that resemble this.

I have to tell yuh: is not that mi did 'fraid mi modda was going beat mi. Mi was too old fi that and mi modda never lick mi, even when mi was likkle. No, it was not har anger mi was running from. She was a gentle and calm woman. She used to always tell mi that 'humble calf get to suck the most milk'. She tell mi 'Chile, settle yourself – your time will come.' I was 'fraid of the look pon har face when she find out I take har most precious thing and spoil it. To know that is through mi stubbornness, mi wilfulness, I take away de likkle joy from har life.

So after mi put on mi clothes, I run go Missa S house. I never run so fast in mi life yet. When mi reach, mi chest puffing out, I so short of breath.

Missa S sey: 'Girl, the devil chasing yuh? Yuh want some water?'

Him wife wasn't home. I tell him I don't want no water. I tell him 'bout the button. I had the dress wrap up in a bag, so him could see what the other button dem look like. But I realise that I run out the house so fast mi leave the bag on the back step after mi fasten mi shoes. So I sey to Missa S that I soon come back.

Him grab mi wrist and ask where mi going so fast. Then before mi know what happening, him rum-soaked tongue heavy in mi mouth and him pin mi underneath him. I scratching and fighting but Missa S was over two hundred pounds. Him push him thing inna mi and it hurt 'cause mi was a virgin. Then I see a opening and I dig mi fingernails inna him eye. Him fall back wid him pants 'round him ankles and sey: 'Ow-ow-ow!' I run out the door. Him calling after mi that mi is a Jezebel to come seduce him in him own yard when him wife deh on the road and nobody going believe mi, the obeah woman daughter. That mi is a nasty whore.

I run back home and inna mi room. Mi lie down on di bed and bawl. Mi modda find mi there three hours later when she come home. That is after I done bathe in the river and let the water wash over mi.

◆

Yuh ever see where a river start yet? Mi used to do helper work fi a man who work at the Ministry of Agriculture and him tell mi that yuh have this thing dem call a water table

289

that underground and inside mountains and is there-so river come from. 'That's the source,' him sey. Him sey, you have something name aquifer: rocks that soak up water like a sponge. Mi tell him mi never see rock behave like sponge yet and him laugh. Mi also tell him mi never see water sit down 'round table.

'No, not like regular table,' him sey, patting the top of the dining table. Him get a piece of paper and draw two mountain with a valley between dem, then this broken line across the base of the mountain. Him point to the gap between the mountain dem where the broken line touch the valley, and sey: 'The river starts here.'

This never make no sense to mi at all. Mi ask him how the water get there in the first place. Him sey: 'From precipitation – that's rain – there's a whole water cycle. When it rains, the water goes underground to aquifers, forming the water table. Then the water evaporates – dries up – from the surface, and goes back into the air, to fall again, restarting the process.'

'But where it start?' I sey. Which step come first? The drying up from the ground or the downpour? Him look like him don't know what to sey fi a while. Then him ask 'does it matter? It's like that question about "What came first: the chicken or the egg?"' Mi didn't want to talk about chicken unless mi was plucking it, cutting it up and cooking it fi dinner. So mi never sey nothing more. My silence seem to satisfy him. 'So you understand?' him sey, and I nod to end the argument.

Mi saying all of this to sey: life is like that: a circle going 'round and 'round, like the water cycle. And trying to outrun certain things is like trying to outswim the currents when the river come down in flood time.

◆

When the time come fi Dinah to born, it was just me and mi modda. She help mi deliver right there in that same room. Dinah come at night, early on a Wednesday morning. Mi modda boil up some roots and leaves and give mi to drink and rub mi all over. Dinah slip out like she rub inna butter and olive oil. Still, mi couldn't stop bawl.

Missa S sey him is not the fadda and is lie mi telling on him. The constable in the district never believe mi. Missa S wife start the rumour that is want mi did want har husband. Everybody could see Dinah nose and forehead look just like fi him own.

Mi modda never sey a thing.

Missa S dead soon after that. Dem sey a heart attack.

◆

Nobody never ask mi nothing. Is not my business but mi going talk anyway. Poco people not 'fraid to talk things. Yuh can hear plenty things when yuh stop listening wid yuh ears. It funny. Never did mi ever think that a woman like me, who love chat, would have a tongue that swell up sometimes. It fill up mi mouth whenever the fog come over mi. Dem times mi can't talk, or mi talk but nobody understand what mi saying.

Dinah seem doom from she born. I try to help that girl. I try. God see and God know. But is like part of har know from she was a child that the piece of har that belong to har fadda, sometime mi just couldn't stand to be 'round it. Mi couldn't stand to look in har face.

And a softness inside Dinah. A trusting nature mi had to stamp out and harden. Before people take advantage of har. Mi couldn't protect miself when mi had to, so mi had to teach Dinah to protect harself. Mi try mi best. Mi best amount to nothing 'cause she still give weh har pickney. That child was

291

mi chance to try again. Mi never even get fi see him face! Mi never see him born. Mi did home that day wid bad stomach.

Dinah come from the hospital with har two empty hand. When mi ask har: 'Gyal, weh mi grandpickney?' she sey di Steeles take him. 'Tek him weh?' mi ask. 'Home,' was all she sey and start cry. I tell har mi want to know how No-Breast Mrs Steele going find breast milk to give Son-Son to suck.

After that is like a light get turn off inside Dinah head and when mi look inna har eye is like nothing not in there.

Mi try everything fi feel mi grandson spirit. When we used to play the drum and beat the tambourine it was almost like mi could see Son-Son in the room. Mi could smell him. Then after a while, nothing happen. Then Dinah stop want fi dance or sing or do nothing at all.

The boy who dem sey is Son-Son hard to read. Him hanging 'round that loose-tail Regina like how fly follow meat inna butcher-shop. Meanwhile, yuh have careless Damian and him coming and goings with Streggo and String, in-between when him and Regina have dem carryings-on. All mi know is: nothing good going come of it.

Sometimes yuh think yuh running from something, but all yuh doing is running right towards it.

Regina

Me and Apollo in the same restaurant we had we first date. But now is a skinny bwoy with him face full of pimples wearing a badge that read 'Carl' serving we. Him starched white shirt and black pants blowing off him like a kite. I wonder what happen to the other waiter from the first time, the old man named Jeffery. The place look exactly the same like last time: clean white tablecloths on every table and orchid centrepieces. But it feel different now. Like mi never come here before. I call Apollo 'cause I want to talk. Damian in prison and mi don't know what to do.

'Damian locked up,' mi say, like I never say it to Apollo already; but him face set like stone. I trying to read emotions that not there. Why Apollo acting like him don't care? Damian is him fren. Apollo never eat no appetiser. Him order a drink that him don't touch.

'Gina, there's something I gotta tell you about Damian.'
Mi wait.

'He–he's not the kinda guy you think he is . . . he belongs behind bars.' Then him stop talk.

I know they saying that Damian mix up in what happen to Apollo's daddy, but it can't be true. I tell him that is not the Damian mi know. Is true Damian sometimes act like him can't see beyond him two hands stretched out in front of him. Him is a hothead who don't think through him actions, but him is no gunman. Him don't shoot people. And mi didn't need to be in the house that night to know that. I don't care what anybody, including Apollo, say.

When I done speak mi mind, mi suddenly feel hungry, like something in me need to get feed, so I decide to get a conch and pumpkin soup, when Apollo change course and say: 'We gotta talk about the baby.'

'Mi know. I starting to feel him moving. Look. You want to touch mi belly?' The baby rolling around more and more inside like the baby know mi stressed. About Damian. About Apollo. About everything.

'Maybe later. Look, we didn't plan it—' Apollo folding and unfolding his napkin. 'Regina, things with us happened way too fast.'

'Yes, but it happen. Yuh tell yuh parents yet?'

Apollo shake him head.

'So yuh not going tell dem?'

Apollo don't answer.

'Yuh need mi to tell dem for you?'

Apollo tell mi him don't intend to say anything until him figure out what he going to do.

'They gotta focus on Pops getting better.'

Is weeks now since him fadda get shot.

'Look, yuh want to be wid mi or not? When we going to America?' I need to know. I tell him mi did do all the right things. Mi stop doing drugs and drinking. What more him want?

'Gina, it's not that simple.'

I wondering: *How come?*

Mi reach for him hand the moment Carl reappear with the soup. Apollo sigh. 'I wanna be there for you, Gina. I do. Whatever happens. But . . . you sure you wanna keep it?'

294

Mi draw back mi hand and hold mi jaw like him strike mi. Mi feel the end coming. Even so, mi wasn't prepared for when him say: 'Gina baby, I don't think I can do this.'

Do what? mi thinking. *Love me? Love us?* The soup lose flavour. A metallic taste coat mi tongue. Mi inspecting the soup's contents, swirling it 'round and 'round in the bowl with mi spoon.

When Apollo say, 'The last thing I wanna do is hurt you, Gina,' it sound like it coming from far away.

But yuh doing it, mi want to say. *What I going to do now?*

'Look, mi having yuh child and yuh going to have to step up to yuh responsibility.' Mi keep staring at the soup, feeling sick.

Apollo looking like him can't find the right words. Him know anything him say going to anger mi.

'Gina, what are we gonna do?' Him put him head in him hands. 'I mean, we're still kids!'

'We going get through this,' I hear myself say, my tone soft–soft, and mi voice stronger than mi feel. 'Once wi stay together.'

Regina

Mi mother, Bubbles, used to see signs everywhere. She used to have to get her horoscope from the *Jamaica Gleaner* every morning. Bubbles was a Scorpio. That sign look like a scorpion about to sting you. We couldn't afford the *Gleaner*, so every day she would send me to borrow it from Mr Lawrence up the road who have the shop. Him used the *Gleaner* to wrap up saltfish, yellow yam him cut or green banana for him customers. The thing is Bubbles couldn't read too good. So she used to ask me to read it for her. I used to sit on the floor of the one-bedroom shack, crossing mi leg, smoothing out the newspaper and spreading it in front of mi.

Mi would read that: *Today's going to bring you unprecedented luck.* Or, *An adventure suits you.* Or, *Take risks today . . . embrace the unexpected.* Every time, Bubbles would repeat it, her lips trembling, like she praying. After mi read it, she would smile and say: 'Is so mi day going go.'

'Gina girl,' she used to say, 'yuh is a Taurus: headstrong and tough. Your sign is the bull.'

The thing is, Mr Lawrence never used to give mi the paper for that same day. Him always take the *Gleaner* him give mi from an old stack. Every day, mi used to look on the date on top and it was always from last week or last month. Mi did think about telling Bubbles the truth but on one level, mi think it wouldn't make no difference. Bubbles did take every word of the horoscope as the gospel truth. And that smile in the morning is the only time mi used to see Bubbles smile.

What it matter if I was telling her about the day she was supposed to have last week or three months ago?

And when mi wanted Bubbles to listen to mi, mi would make up the horoscope. Mi would say: *Spend time with loved ones. Put your child above everything.* And Bubbles would nod and pay attention to mi that day. Mi even use it to try to get her to get rid of Bumper. Bumper wasn't a bad man but it feel like him float in and out of we lives, even when him standing right there. Mi find out him was keeping other woman wid Bubbles. When Bubbles send mi to Mr Lawrence shop, mi see Bumper on the road with him hand 'round a woman waist.

That day I read: *Watch out for your man.* For the first time, Bubbles ask: 'It say so fi true?' When mi nod, she close her eyes, bite her lip but she leave it right there and say nothing more about it.

The morning she leave, not long after granny come to visit, mi know something was wrong. She never ask mi to read her horoscope that day. She never look mi in the eye when she was packing up her things.

'Yuh is a big girl now,' she say. 'Remember yuh is a Taurus. Nobody can rule yuh. Yuh going be alright.'

'Nuh leave mi.'

'Mi will come back soon. Mi just need a likkle breeze-out. Sometime adults need to clear dem head.'

Mi know is a lie she was telling mi. She sit next to mi on the bed and the last thing she say to mi was: 'Remember yuh are a bull.'

◆

If I could talk to Bubbles now she would say the signs not pointing to something good. Mi feel the baby kicking every minute, like him can feel mi worry. 'Is a hard road I have to walk,' mi tell the baby. Behind mi on that road was Grandpa Leford, the country, Bubbles with her horoscopes and Mr Mack.

Ahead of mi is the life mi can have with Apollo in America: big house on a wide shiny street, big car, money to buy whatever mi want, to never again know what hungry feel like.

These days, Apollo hardly come see mi. We don't talk much. When we talk, him can't meet mi eyes. Like Bubbles before she leave that morning.

Mi can see Gina's Boutique & House of Fashion getting dimmer and fading like a dream.

Then yuh have Damian. Mi don't know how to feel about Damian and him music dream. Is like Damian don't realise is only few ghetto people get to live dem dream. Him remind mi of the moments when Bubbles used to sit down to hear mi read her horoscope. That time of day where things fresh. And anything can happen. The newspaper page in mi hand might as well be blank 'cause it only have the meaning mi give it.

And sometime those mornings, mi feel like close up the page dem, inhale the smell of paper and dry ink that stiff between mi finger dem, and just tear it up. Mi picture miself saying to Bubbles' confused face: 'Yuh make yuh own life!'

The choice in front of mi now is to make mi own life. Mi rub mi belly and say out loud, though mi know Bubbles can't hear: 'Yes, mi is a bull.'

◆

Mi is a girl who make things happen, so when Apollo say him nuh tell him parents about the baby yet, same time mi know that mi was going tell dem miself.

So the next time Eddie come to Lazarus Gardens to check him niece, mi flag down him Lada quick-quick.

'Hi Eddie,' mi say, leaning over, wid mi hand on the car top, so him can see mi chest. When mi tell him what mi want, him screw up him face. It look like it even swell.

'Mi don't think it right for me to do that.'

Mi straighten up. Time to try a different approach. 'Eddie, yuh is a taximan, don't it?'

'Yes. Yuh know that already.'

'And don't a taximan job is to take people from one place to another place?'

'Yeah.'

'Well, mi just want yuh to take mi to a location. Simple. Real simple. I not going make any trouble. Is surprise mi going surprise him.'

Him face soften a likkle but him look like him thinking. What him not saying but mi know him must be wondering is: *How come she don't know where Apollo live when him is her man for four months now?*

Him say: 'Mi don't want to get mix up into Apollo's personal business.'

'Look, nobody going know is yuh tell mi where Apollo live or take mi there. Mi promise.'

Him start smile now. 'How much money yuh have?'

◆

The ride in Eddie Lada up the hill did uncomfortable. The hills steep and the road bumpy. Mi had to tell Eddie to take time since mi nuh ready to deliver the baby yet. Him laugh and say him is not nuh midwife. This child going be huge 'cause mi belly stick out farther than it did last month.

When we reach Jack's Hill, him point out the house and let mi off a likkle further up the road.

Is a cream two-level house wid balcony and whole heap of pretty, white column. The grass so green it look fake. How dem lawn so big? You could put another house there. I move closer to the front so mi could see better. Some plants blocking the view of the verandah. Mi think mi can make out a woman in a white shorts out front. But when mi reach near the gate, a piece of bad feeling take mi, probably 'cause of how Eddie shake mi up, and mi feel like mi going faint. Mi feel miself falling and I grab the closest thing mi could find, the fence. Mi nearly twist mi foot.

Mi hear a woman voice say: 'Are you OK?' Fast-fast, she at mi elbow helping mi up before mi realise what happening. She smell like something fruity and sweet, like jasmine. 'You nearly took a nasty spill. Have a seat on the porch a while.' The woman tall, slim and strong-looking wid a face that look kind. Her eye dem warm. 'It's OK, come on, let's go inside.'

Next thing, is mi that sitting on the verandah wid mi feet up on a chair. Mi straining mi neck to see inside the house and fanning miself wid mi hand dem.

'There. Isn't it better in the shade?'

She call out and a helper in a grey uniform and white apron come out wid a glass of cool lemonade and set it before mi on a silver tray she put on the likkle glass table. She leave the glass jug of lemonade too. The helper also have a rag that wet wid ice-water. The nice lady point to mi head and motion that mi must use it to pat mi forehead.

'We're fresh out of coconut water. Sorry. That would have been best. It's so damn hot here and in your condition' – she point to mi belly – 'It's just not a good idea for a pregnant woman to be out in this heat.'

'Thank you, ma'am,' mi say. Mi lip dem don't feel like my own.

'Have we met before? Your face is familiar.'

Mi don't want to remind her it was me she see with Damian the day she come to the tenement yard and she and Dinah fight. Is a good thing mi never get to introduce meself before Dinah turn up. Me nuh want Apollo's mother to think less of me since me was holding on to another man. Worse, mi watch somebody beat her up and never help. Is not so she supposed to meet her daughter-in-law. What kinda first impression dat?

Mi trying to remember the speech mi did practise. How it go?

Mi come here today to introduce miself to yuh 'cause yuh should know about mi. Mi is carrying yuh grandpickney. Mi want to know what yuh going do to help mi and this child 'cause Apollo look like him not going do anything.

But now mi don't know where to start.

'How far along are you?'

'About four months, ma'am.'

'Your first?'

'Yes, ma'am.'

'Please, cut out the "ma'am" thing. I'm Celeste.'

Mi notice that what mi did think was a statue is really a white man, sitting on a chair wid a blanket 'cross him leg dem.

'That's my husband, Raymond.' Him snoring wid him mouth open and a fly on him nose.

'He's heavily medicated,' she say, like mi did ask her for a explanation. 'I didn't catch your name, dear.'

'Regina.'

Mi wait. The tile dem so pretty and shine like we standing on clear water. Mi wonder if Apollo ever talk 'bout mi before. No. Mi never see no sign flash on her face that mi name mean anything.

'I hope you don't mind me asking, but if you're headed somewhere near here, I can call a taxi or I can ask my son

301

Apollo to give you a ride. He should be home with the car soon.'

'No, that's OK.'

'Is the place you're going close enough to walk to?'

'Yes, ma'am, mi mean, Celeste. I close.'

Mi think on it. *Why mi not talking? Why mi not telling her what mi plan to say? Why mi lose mi courage now when this woman looking right in mi face?* Is not that mi frighten of her but something feel like it blocking up mi throat.

Mi face must did look twist up from all that thinking, 'cause she say: 'Are you in pain?'

Mi shake mi head.

While I trying to find the strength to say what mi have to say, the lady say: 'I remember when I was pregnant with my son, I was sick all the time. Threw up everywhere. I was on bed rest the last two months. When I was in the hospital delivering him, my blood pressure spiked, doctors thought they'd lose us both. But he's my little miracle.'

I trying to make sense of what mi hearing. Apollo already tell mi how Dinah think this woman and her husband tief him from her; and Dinah will tell anybody who half-listening about how her son get take away and come back to her. So I real confuse.

Either this woman for real or she belong on TV. 'Cause she better than dem actress on *The Young and the Restless*. But some people lie real good too. Like when dem say 'I love you.'

'So, Regina, forgive me for saying this but you're so young ...'

I didn't say nothing and she look embarrass 'cause she never finish the sentence. I take a sip of the lemonade. It need some more lime. And sugar.

'Look at me, going on and on, dear. I'm not usually like this. It's just that things have been rough lately. My husband

302

was badly injured and just came out of hospital and, well, my son is missing in action these days. I mean, even when he's here, he's not. I haven't really talked to anyone in a while.'

Now is a good time fi mi to talk.

'Yuh see, Celeste—'

'Are you feeling better? Need a refill?' She adjust her glasses and slide down deeper in the chair next to mi chair. She stretch out her hand dem and foot like a puss relaxing.

'Mi OK but yuh see—'

'Regina, may I ask you: how's the father of the baby taking this big change?'

Mi swallow the lemonade the wrong way.

'I'm sorry. You don't have to say anything. It's really none of my business.'

Mi want to say: *Is more of yuh business than yuh know.* But why this strange feeling coming over mi?

'Him-him not taking it the way mi did hope.' Mi pat mi belly. 'Mi think him about to leave mi wid the responsibility.' Mi lips trembling.

'I'm sorry to hear that. Men can be such jackals. Well, I gotta tell you that a child changes your life completely. You care about nothing more than your kid. A mother will do anything for her child. You'll do everything to keep anybody from hurting them; and to even keep them from hurting themselves.'

She start talk real slow and pull off her shades and look at mi. 'Do you understand what I'm talking about, dear? About a mother doing *anything* to stop *anyone* from ruining her son's life? From destroying all her dreams for him? Dreams that she won't allow him to give up because of mistakes he may make in Jamaica? Even the ones he thinks he can get past her? Sometimes a mother's got to attend to things a son doesn't know she knows about.'

303

Something come 'cross her face now and mi can't breathe. Is my moment now. I telling miself: *Regina, say it. Say. It.* She looking at mi open mouth. I suddenly feel hot-hot and like mi head lifting. What sucking up the air out here? Mi keep hearing her words over and over in mi head: *Anything for her child. Anything . . . Anything . . . Anything.*

Something sour in mi throat. Hard and dry like Excelsior water crackers. It bitter on mi tongue. Mi couldn't help it. Mi stand up fast and knock over the pitcher of lemonade on the table.

The white man didn't even wake up.

Mi expect her to screw up her face or make mi feel shame. But she never even blink. All she say was: 'Don't you worry, Regina. I'll get this cleaned up. You can use the bathroom to freshen up.'

But mi leave. Mi couldn't stay there no more. Mi didn't even tell her thanks for the drink or goodbye. I just run. *Run. Run, Regina. Run.*

Mi nearly get lick down by the black Benz that fly past mi. Mi don't know how I reach the bus stop.

Apollo

That evening, as Apollo exited the law offices of Chandler, Beck and Brown, the sky bore the purplish-pink hue of a healing bruise. It reminded him of the skin of a Jamaican fruit Dinah bought especially to let him taste for the first time: a star apple. The fruit was the size of an orange and looked like a regular apple dipped in purple dye, except for the star-shaped indentations in the white pulp when it was cut in half.

Apollo had worked late to refine a submission for Christopher that was to be filed in the Supreme Court in a week. He'd been absorbed, wondering whether his arguments were cogent enough, whether he'd applied the legal principles from the cases he'd read correctly, had he arrived at the right conclusion? He wanted to make a positive impression. He didn't want the lawyers at the firm to think of him as an entitled, empty-headed brat. He wanted to spend his life doing law.

The firm was located on Duke Street, in downtown Kingston. Bordered in the front by a broad one-way street and at the back by a narrow lane which was also one-way. To the right of the lane was the firm's car park. The security guard, Maitland, would ordinarily escort staff who were leaving late to the car park, where there was no separate security guard. But that evening, Maitland was too busy chatting up Kim, the receptionist, trying to convince her why she should leave her new man. Despite the serious expression on her face, the laughter in her eyes showed she was enjoying the flirtation. Apollo signalled to Maitland that it was fine, he would walk to the car park alone.

'Look from when him was to come pick you up? I tell yuh, yuh boyfriend don't love you,' Apollo could hear Maitland saying. 'Mi will treat a woman like yuh right. Mi nuh have car but mi woulda carry yuh everywhere on mi bicycle.'

Apollo smiled as he pushed open the door leading to the lane. Jamaican men had earned their reputation for having what Dinah would call a 'sweet mouth'. Then he thought of Regina and his heart sank. He had got what he thought he wanted: a nice Jamaican woman. But it had all gone wrong. He was going to be a father. To a kid he didn't want.

A young boy riding a rusted bicycle startled him. There was a tiny stream of water running along the path, probably from a broken pipe. He hopped over it to avoid dirtying his leather shoes. He sniffed the pungent smell of sewage and the scent of roasting corn, which somebody in one of the neighbouring criss-crossing lanes was roasting on a coal fire for dinner. The firm was close to what Christopher Brown referred to as 'depressed communities' – neighbourhoods the firm donated to in annual treats for Easter, Back to School in September and Christmas. It was their civic responsibility. These communities hadn't been depressed when the firm first opened its doors in the 1930s. Years of political violence had caused the middle-class residents to flee, leaving their empty houses to be occupied by poor people from rural Jamaica seeking opportunity in Kingston.

As soon as Apollo entered the car park he saw it. It was the only other vehicle there, aside from his dad's black Mercedes and Beason's grey Volvo. Christopher's green Audi was already gone. The car Apollo saw was a white BMW, sitting low on huge shiny rims, waiting like an animal about to pounce. Engine was running. Windows rolled up. A chill moved through him. He recognised the two burly men standing outside the car. They didn't appear to have any weapons, but they didn't need them. Their size was sinister enough. Even though it was dark, they both were wearing sunglasses – just like that night at the dance in Lazarus Gardens.

He knew their boss was inside the car.

He turned around but Maitland was still inside. What could Maitland have done anyway? He didn't even carry a gun. Only a baton and a whistle. Apollo knew he was alone in this. There was no time to run back into the building.

The back door opened. British spoke, almost in a whisper: 'Yankee boy, come in.'

'I gotta get home.' He tried to say it with a nonchalance he didn't feel, willing himself to remain calm.

'This won't take long. Get in, man. Just need to talk some business with you.'

British motioned for him to enter on the other side. When he closed the door behind him, the driver locked it. The BMW had a moon-roof that let in light from a streetlight near the car park. British was looking at him, smiling. He was wearing sweatpants and a red Gucci shirt, a heavy scent a weed emanating around him.

British brought the spliff to his lips slowly. The smoke burnt Apollo's eyes but he tried not to cough. British offered him the spliff and he shook his head. He didn't want to be here but he could see no way out of this conversation.

'So you liked the gift?' British asked.

'Yeah, thanks.'

'So you accept my offer?'

Apollo had to find a way to stall.

'British, come on. I ain't even started law school yet. How it works in the States is you get a college degree first *then* do your JD. *Then* to practise in Jamaica I gotta do a conversion course at Norman Manley Law School and pass those exams. All of that is gonna take years! I won't be able to work as a lawyer any time soon.'

British wasn't perturbed. His grin was plastered on his face.

'That's no problem. You can get your law degree at university here. That would be quicker, right?'

'Yeah, but it takes time—'

'But nothing. I have you covered, man. You not going have any issue getting through here.'

'Why me, seriously? You literally can get anybody to work for you! How about hiring a lawyer already practising here?'

British thought of all the reasons: *'cause of your mother and how she talk to me that day. 'Cause you think your family status and power make you safe and untouchable. 'Cause people like you walk through life with an expectation life owes you something. 'Cause even with all your power and riches, somebody like me – who come from nothing – can still own you.*

But he doesn't feel Apollo deserves an explanation.

As British stared at him, Apollo didn't know what else to say.

'So is a deal then? Or you saying you not working for me?' British's eyes narrowed. His grin dissipated. 'Listen, Yankee boy, people don't tell me no.'

It felt stifling. He was hot, although the air conditioning was on full blast. He had to escape. But he couldn't think how. British's palms rested on his knees and the gold ring engraved with a giant lion's face seemed to Apollo like it was taunting him. Even British's hands looked to be getting bigger and more menacing.

Apollo heard the click of the doors unlocking. The rear passenger door on British's side swung open. He recognised Beason, one of the senior partners of the firm. Maitland must have stopped flirting long enough to peep outside. Suspected that Apollo was about to be kidnapped and murdered and sounded an alarm. Sent Beason to intervene.

Please, God.

Beason, who was wearing his usual grey pinstriped suit and white shirt, had the body, bearing and whiskers of a sea lion. His flustered face didn't even register Apollo's presence. If he was surprised to see him, he didn't let on. Instead he addressed British. 'Sorry I'm late.'

'Me in the middle of something right now.'

'We have a problem at the wharf.'

'Again?'

It was then it sunk in. British hadn't come for him. He was having a meeting. And Beason was his attorney.

Beason continued: 'I just got a call. The latest shipment of . . . rice you're importing won't be cleared by Customs unless we pay . . . additional duties.'

'The little customs boy them say *what*?' A vein in British's neck throbbed. He knew who was behind it. Bloodclaat Simms! He turned to the driver: 'Take me to the wharf.'

He motioned Apollo out of the car with a flick of his hand. 'We going continue this next time. I need a answer when I see you again. And one more thing, Yankee boy, don't think about leaving Jamaica. I have associates in America that can finish the job that get start on you parents.'

Beason gave Apollo a cross look and leapt in once Apollo tumbled out. The car sped off, tyres squealing, splashing through puddles of water in potholes in the narrow lane.

Apollo searched his pockets for the car keys, then realised they were already in his hand. All he could think was: *Beason works for British*. The partner of his Pops' old college friend. British was already closer than he had thought. The tiny hairs on his hands were standing up. He inhaled long and slow. He bent over, holding his knees.

The air smelt fresh, like he was breathing for the first time. The breath unplugged his ears. He could hear a baby crying in the distance and people quarrelling. Sounds he wasn't aware of before. It was then that he heard heavy footfalls on the pavement. Maitland had rushed out of the building.

'Apollo, wha' happen, man? You alright?'

Apollo

'Come again, Apollo?' Moms asks me.

I'm thinking: *You know you heard me right the first time, Moms.* But I repeat it anyway: 'How soon can you get outta Jamaica?'

I can tell she's confused. She's happy I wanna go but she's wondering where this is coming from. This urge to run away from the country all of a sudden. All I know is: as long as British is here, Jamaica's not safe for my folks any more. The entire drive from work, my hands were unsteady on the steering wheel. I dunno how I got home safe. I wasn't seeing lanes or traffic lights, cars or pedestrians or nothing. Just British's face floating in my windshield.

I found Moms on the porch drinking a glass of wine, with her high heels kicked off. She's rubbing the sole of her left foot with her thumb. Kneading it like bread dough.

She goes back to focusing on her feet. 'There's nothing for you to worry about Apollo, but ... when the doctor came today he said your dad had a complication. He's going back into hospital for some more tests tomorrow. It'll be a few weeks before it's safe for him to travel.'

'You sure you guys can't go back earlier?' I ask.

'You mean leave you here?' Her eyes widen, and she bites her lip. Her pink lipstick's smudged. She's probably thinking

I want to spend more time with Dinah alone, and worrying I won't be coming back to the States at all. Her frown deepens. When she gulps her wine, it dribbles down her chin. A couple of drops spill onto her blouse.

'I just gotta tie up some loose ends here,' I say.

'Loose ends?' she echoes.

I dunno how to tell Moms that having a relationship with Dinah doesn't mean I'm picking Dinah over her, but I can't figure out the words. I'm never gonna choose between them. I know Dinah could understand what's happening with British in a way Moms wouldn't but I can't let Dinah know either. She'd worry. Or do something stupid like confront him again. I don't want to give Dinah any more problems than she already has.

Moms watches me closely and clears her throat. 'I had a visitor today ...' She stops as if I'm somehow supposed to know what she's talking about and fill in the blanks. '... and we had a nice chat.'

I look at her blankly.

'Son, you know there's nothing your mom won't help you through, right?'

'Yeah, of course, Moms.'

'I wish you'd open up to me.' She puts on her shoes. 'Look. We're all going to leave here as soon as Ray's better. *All* of us, you understand me?'

I try again. 'How about you go ahead and leave me here with Pops until he's better?'

'You can't be serious! You? I just can't see you as a nurse. As a kid, you barely took care of your pets!' Moms laughs like she's mocking me. 'I'll stay with your father. But I think it'd be best if you go.'

I wanna scream. *I'm not leaving you guys alone here.* Something is tearing inside my chest.

I grab a seat next to Moms. For a while, we listen to the crickets, and watch the city lights twinkle in the distance, looking like chili-pepper string lights on a giant Christmas tree. Like the ones we always had when I was a kid; sometimes we'd have three or four trees up at once.

We sit there, each of us waiting for the other person to talk first.

'I'm tired, Apollo,' she finally tells me. Her shoulders slump, and I get up and massage them, like how I used to as a kid. The way I've seen Pops do it many times. I'm standing behind her and she tips her head forward, chin into her chest. Relaxing into my hands.

I am buttering her up for what's coming. Once she starts to make that low 'mmmhh' sound, that's almost a groan, I figure it's time. So I bend down and whisper in her ear: 'I really think you guys should go.'

Her back stiffens and she shoots out of her chair. 'Stop this nonsense! We're not leaving you behind. Tell me what's going on, Apollo!' she demands.

'I can't, Moms.' *It's for your own good.*

And when she asks me 'Why?' all I can think is: *'Cause British will kill you.* I hear his words in my head again. See the sneer etched on his face when he called his killers in America associates, like they're lawyers in a law firm. He can't be for real, can he?

British wants me to believe he can find us anywhere. Finish us off any time. I don't know if he's lying.

The cops in Jamaica can't protect us. British's too powerful. If I tell Moms she'd just do something dumb like call them and word would get back to British fast. This is Jamaica, like Christopher Brown always reminds me. Things don't happen the same way they do in America. Cops and crooks are sometimes on the same side.

313

Moms grabs the porch railing, drawing more and more shallow breaths. I know she's mad but I think she doesn't know what to say. Or how to say it. Her face is half-lit in the moonlight spilling on to the porch and she looks so young but so exhausted too. Drained.

She tries one last time. She turns to look at me, holds me by the wrist, then puts my hand in hers and begs: 'Apollo, if you tell me what's going on, I can help you, baby.'

Maybe I should just do what British wants. That'd be easier for everybody. But that's not the kinda life I want, not the future I pictured for myself.

I kiss her on her forehead, and her skin feels warm. Or maybe my lips are cold.

Dinah

So Regina and me in the kitchen, picking out the bones from the saltfish that just boil for the ackee and I waiting for the right time to say my mind. I thinking about how I was picking saltfish not too long before Son-Son come back in mi life and now here I am again. And now this woman claiming my son is the father of the child she carrying.

I was talking to the woman in the white robe yesterday . . . well, I was talking and she was listening. She did come into mi room and sit beside mi on the bed. I tell the woman that I don't know what I going do about this trouble my son is in. Him young and him whole life spread out in front of him like dem pretty highway in farin that you see on TV. Now this careless gyal come to mash up him life with her worthless self. I will not allow it!

Regina wearing a yellow dress with red and green stripes on the neckline and sleeves and grey and black leopard print tights. She walking around the kitchen patting her belly that look like she just eat plenty food. Resembling a swollen bullfrog. The amount of man she sleep with, who knows if is Son-Son's child?

The thought jump out my mouth as soon as I think it. 'How yuh know is not Mr Mack pickney?'

'Mr Mack can't make pickney. That's why him wife did leave him. And 'cause of him diabetes, him can't get it up half the time.' I thinking that's not what it sound like when mi used to hear dem through the walls.

'But you sleep with Damian too. Yuh think I don't know about yuh nastiness? Go blow yuh nose where yuh catch yuh cold! Mi know is not my son pickney.'

'Apollo is mi baby fada.'

Mi decide to take another course. 'What yuh tink? What you going do wid baby? You think is dolly?' Young girls out here spitting out babies. Breathe on dem and they have a child. Not knowing what baby going bring.

I remember when mi was pregnant with Son-Son. How mi was confused, sad and never had nobody.

'How yuh morning sickness?'

'Real bad. Mi vomit most mornings.'

'Yuh must eat some water crackers. And I going show yuh how to make ginger tea like Mama show mi. It going help . . . And if yuh tell the truth about the real father, mi could give yuh some help to take care of the baby.'

'Yuh can barely take care of yuhself and yuh mother.'

Mi ignore the insult. Mi pour off the boiled water from the ackee and use a strainer to catch it from falling into the drain. 'Having a child is serious business, Regina.'

'Mi know.'

'Listen to yuh conscience,' I beg her.

'Who tell yuh mi have one?' Regina ask. 'Dem accept conscience at the cashier in the supermarket? What it can buy?'

I try for a likkle softness in mi voice. 'Despite everything, yuh is not a bad girl. Yuh know the right thing.'

'Living in America is a good thing for mi and mi pickney.'

'Knowing dem real fada is what is good for this pickney.' I put oil in the frying pan.

'Don't talk to mi about mi own flesh and blood.'

I sigh a deep sigh. A fly following the smell of the saltfish and mi swat it away. 'Listen, mi don't want to fight yuh,' I say after a while.

'Mi don't want to fight neither. Yuh been more of a mother to me than mi owna modda.' Regina cutting up the onion and green pepper. She like tomatoes in her ackee and saltfish, so I hand her two small ones to cut up. Regina been asking mi lately to show her how to cook. I think she lonely 'cause Apollo not coming to see her. She cut the onions up into tiny, neat pieces. All even. Just like I teach her. Is things like that she shoulda learn from her mother.

I feeling some kinda shame for the mean things mi say about her to Apollo. Regina is just a victim. Like all young girls in Lazarus Gardens. British turn her into a woman before her time. She just want a better life.

She turn her back to mi and put the seasoning in the hot oil and sautée dem, moving dem around in the frying pan with the big fork.

'Come here,' I say and she sink into mi arms. We belly touch and mi feel something flutter. We eyes meet. The baby kicking!

'Is like when Son-Son used to kick mi,' I tell her and she nearly smile but then her lips tremble.

'Mi know is not Apollo baby,' she say. 'Mi find out when mi go to the free clinic and-and . . . ' All di sobbing make the rest of the sentence disappear from her mouth.

She not looking in mi eye. Mi spirit tell mi she have more to say, but mi know to leave it there. She add the flaked salt-fish and then the ackee to the frying pan and mix everything around. I tell her to sit down 'cause I will finish the cooking. I beat up some ginger with the handle of the knife and plop it in water to boil her a cup of tea.

There is just so much a person can take before dem break.

And though she feel solid in mi arms, Regina remind mi of the figurine on top of Mrs Chin dresser mi break last week. The figurine was standing on tiptoe on top of a pink and white crotchet, with one of her foot in the air. Mi never know it so fragile 'til it fall out of mi hand when mi was dusting it. Her neck break so that the head fly off. I never want Mrs Chin to take money out of mi pay so mi find the glue in the cabinet and glue her back neat. Mrs Chin don't realise the difference but every time I go in the room is like the ballerina looking on me like mi conscience, as if to say: *I know.*

'What yuh going do, Regina?' I say now. 'Yuh don't think with all dem science dem have in America, Apollo not going find out one day? What yuh going do that time? Eh?'

Regina not answering.

'What yuh going do?' I ask again and I feel like the ceiling of the house getting lower and lower to flatten wi on the ground. What mi could tell har? Cotton inna mi throat. And the walls sucking up the quiet.

I don't know how it happen but the saltfish start sticking to the bottom of the frying pan, nearly burning. The water for the tea was boiling so long, half of it evaporate.

The woman in white watching we from the doorway.

◆

I so shame I can't tell Son-Son my secret. This one I have to take to my grave. The only other living person who know is Mama but her brain seal up tight.

I already tell the woman in white 'cause she can't tell anybody either. When I done, she staring, staring like she shock. Imagine! *Me* manage to shock a duppy or whatever she is. The truth is she don't tell mi where she come from. Sometimes she smell like ashes, so I figure she escape from the fire and brimstone of hell. But sometime she smell like

318

honey from the heavens. Sweeter than the roses Mrs Chin keep on her dining table.

'A true?' she ask mi when mi done the story, but her lips don't move.

'Yes,' mi say. 'Life strange, eh?'

She don't condemn mi. I wonder how a spirit can understand flesh and blood matters.

Lawd have mercy! Yuh want the whole story? Here is chapter and verse. The truth is: mi nearly kill Son-Son.

Couple days before the Steeles did throw mi that baby shower. After mi get the news from Leroy that him leaving mi. Mi get home from work that day and stand up in the kitchen and read over the letter. It say:

Dear Dinah:

I'm leaving for Mobay.

It hard to write this. I know you will hate me. And I understand. I never mean to hurt you. I never set out to fall in love with Shelly but it happen.

Dinah, me and you not ready for a child. We don't live life yet. One thing I know is you don't need me. That was one thing about you. You were a giant stone and I was just breeze blowing over you. You are a strong woman and that's how I know if you decide to keep this child you can do it on your own.

—Leroy

Tears was sliding down mi face like the silver trails snails leave on the ground. Leroy was predictable as wind and harder to hold.

It was raining that night. Lightning, with thunder clapping.

Next thing, I rolling on the ground thumping mi belly. Big lick too! Not likkle thump. Thump like what a big man would give. Son-Son in there taking it and couldn't do nothing. Honest to God, in that moment mi wasn't thinking about how him feel because mi did want all parts of Leroy out of mi. So mi didn't care about Son-Son suffering. And this is not something mi ever think mi would do.

I find myself in the room looking for a wire hanger and when I find it, I take the curved part and was pulling down mi panty when Mama catch mi.

'Weh yuh doing?' She grab away the hanger from mi. 'Yuh want to kill yuhself and mi granpickney?'

What she never say but mi hear clear-clear was: 'Gyal, how yuh could so wicked?' and that sting more than the slap she give mi 'cross mi face.

And is like that is when mi senses come back. Before that, mi wasn't thinking about anything but freedom.

I drop to mi knees and bawl fi the evil act mi nearly do. I make up mi mind to love Son-Son with all mi being. And I did fall in love with him as soon as mi see him after him born. Him was so perfect – soft, shiny skin, no blemish. No sign of what mi do to him. That was a miracle. That him born healthy.

And it look like him was smiling as if to say: 'Don't worry, Mummy. I forgive you.'

I was so glad mi heart feel like it bursting open. I promise to spend my life loving that boy. I change mi mind about giving him up. But then mi think about what life I could give him. And worse, what if that madness seize mi again? How could Son-Son be safe? Mi couldn't take that chance. So mi give him to the Steeles. Because mi wanted to save him from everything – including myself.

And that was my cross to carry. The burden like a sore; a scab mi couldn't pick off.

◆

Regina finish the tea. And I thinking: *We are what we tell wiself.*

There are different versions of a story. I play dem all in mi head. In one story, me is a selfless mother giving up my child so he can have a bigger, better life.

In another one, mi a monster.

I understand how Regina feel and the position she in.

Regina say: 'Dinah, I know what mi going do about the baby.'

And as she telling mi that she keeping her child no matter what, I realise she is a better woman than mi.

Apollo & Dinah

'Why you not telling mi what bothering yuh, Son-Son?' Dinah asks Apollo. She takes two cups, stirs in heaping spoons of Milo. Adds warm milk, a little sugar and mixes it. Although it doesn't need it, she adds a sprinkling of nutmeg too. She hands him one and sits beside him on the creaking couch in the Lazarus Gardens tenement yard.

'Why don't you let me take you to all the fancy places in Jamaica I know you've never been to?'

'You think I need better food than what I cook for myself? I know you know mi can cook good.' Dinah laughs.

'Yeah, but don't you want to be pampered? To see new things?'

'I seeing all I need to see. Right here. My son.' She pats his arm and sips her Milo. 'Nuh change the subject.'

Dinah wonders if he's worried about British. She's kept quiet about what she's done to protect him; about going to see British and Simms. She doesn't want to alarm or alienate him, not after the relationship they've built.

'Doctors say Pops is doing much better. A week ago he had to go back into hospital for more tests, but he's going to be OK.'

'That's good.'

'Moms is starting to look like herself again. Pops sits up in bed all day and looks at her fussing over him and he's grinning in spite of everything. A physiotherapist comes to see him every morning and she says he's doing better every day; and he'll eventually be able to walk on his own, without a walker. By the way, Christopher Brown and his spider-limb wife came to visit Pops a couple days ago, talking about how: "Jamaica's going to the goddamn dogs! That's why I tell Cindy I'm glad we have our green cards. This foolishness wouldn't happen in the US!"

'I was gonna tell him that people get shot in the States all the time. Black men especially. Moms musta read my mind 'cause she gave me the "you better be quiet" look. And Christopher wouldn't shut up, saying: "And just the other day, I was driving and the front wheel of the Audi drop into this God almighty pothole! A pothole! Burst my tyre same time! If the government can't fix a hole in the road, how they going keep criminals from shooting innocent people?" I couldn't help myself so I said: "It's a damned shame about your tyre, Christopher. Such a tragedy!" Moms glared at me. But he didn't even pick up on my sarcasm. He was like: "And don't get me started on crocodiles! You see how many coming out at the beaches near the swamps in Portmore? And the do-gooder environmentalists saying don't kill them! Tell me: what crocodile doing for the country?"'

'That sound like Mr Brown, fi true,' Dinah says, cupping the cup with both palms. She likes to inhale the smell of Milo.

'I had to leave the room.'

'So yuh going stop going on and on about Mr Brown and tell mi what yuh really want to say?'

Apollo wants to tell her: 'My folks are making plans to go back to the States.' Instead he sidesteps her question, saying:

323

'This Milo's good, thanks.' Tipping his head back, he drains the dregs from the bottom of the enamel cup.

Dinah takes a deep breath. 'Yuh tell the Steeles about the baby yet?'

'I can't. Not now. Not with everything.'

Dinah turns her cup round and round in her hands. Apollo wonders: *Can I just walk away? Man, I can't imagine a piece of myself out there that I don't know. Did Dinah used to feel like this?*

'Son-Son, I know this hard to hear, but—'

'The fact is, I ain't ready to be a dad. Dinah, I can see my dreams of travelling the world, being free, going up in smoke. It's like when we wanted to go skiing a couple winters ago but I broke my leg roller-skating, so we stayed home. We saw on TV there'd been an avalanche on that same slope. Four people died. A survivor, some guy they dug out from under the snow, described it like a giant waterfall of snow falling straight from the sky. He said there was a boom – a loud crack like thunder, when he went under, like somebody turned off all the lights in the world. He couldn't tell which way was up. That's how I feel.'

Dinah holds his hand tight. As Apollo tries to hold back his tears, she pulls him towards her chest and hugs him, close.

◆

She's soothing him, but he knows he doesn't deserve it. He *must* tell her the truth – about Gina, about Damian, about British. He has to get the words out. Because he believes she'll understand him. She alone will understand the mess he is in. She can help him. Her own life had been flavoured with pain. That pain made her wise. She knew its deep contours and curves like those of an old lover.

How to tell someone like that you'd made a mess? The small, vain parts of him frighten him. And even though he knew Dinah could already see these shameful parts of him, more clearly than Celeste could, he felt assured that Dinah would listen as the words poured out of him and still love him. When the last thought had drained itself from his head, she would embrace him and say: 'Hush, child, it going be alright. Son-Son, it's OK.' And when that moment came he could gratefully take her love for him from her hands – love tinged at its edges with the pain that had given birth to it.

As his tears dry on her faded housedress, Dinah squeezes his shoulders then holds him back, looking him straight in the eye. 'What it mean to be a man, Son-Son?'

Apollo sniffs, wiping his eyes. 'What'd you mean?'

'I'm asking yuh: what make a man a man? Come, let we go outside and feel some fresh breeze.'

Apollo considers her question. What comes to mind is courage; the absence of fear. Being a man means not being plagued with a feeling of smallness, like he wasn't enough and could never do enough. Since his encounter with British and the growing awareness that Regina's pregnancy wasn't going away, and what had nearly happened in Damian's room, he has felt a smallness that shadows him wherever he goes; a feeling he can't put into words to anybody.

Dinah interrupts his thoughts. 'Yuh think is about the money you have? The nice car yuh drive or the big, fancy house yuh live in? Is more than that. Much more. Plenty more things make a man a man. I was hoping yuh would see that for yourself. When last yuh did something for somebody without getting something back?'

'I been doing that since I was a kid.' Apollo looks around the small yard, at the dusty leaves on the ground around the star fruit tree. 'My school, one time, when I was like eleven, had a can drive for food shelters in our state.'

'Can drive?' Dinah shoos a fly buzzing around her head.

More are congregrating around the carcass of a dead rat under the mango tree.

'It's like, collecting cans to donate to, you know, poor people. They get food at these shelters if they're homeless.'

Dinah clasps her hands. 'Oh, yuh mean yuh give away tinned food. We do that at our church every third Saturday of a month. Street people come from all over Kingston. Is a good thing to do.'

'I decided then I was gonna bring the most cans. I knew I could beat my best friend Michael. Couple days later, Michael brought in cans of tuna, sardines, peas, beans, tomato sauce, stuff like that. Eighty-five cans, which he and his dad carried in large shopping bags. He looked triumphant. I just smiled back and didn't say a word. I'd gotten Pops to come with me to Walmart, with his credit card. So later that day, a whole truck, full of cans, backed into the school yard. I'd won our bet.'

The fly comes back. Dinah rolls up a section of old newspaper and swats it.

'I didn't expect what happened next. Everybody started treating me like some sorta hero. Like I'd singlehandedly ended world hunger. The teacher did a whole speech to the entire school about how selfless I was and that she wishes more of the kids were like me. The local newspapers came and interviewed me. I was on local TV. My folks were so proud.'

He looks over, expecting the same look of admiration on Dinah's face as he remembers on Celeste's that day. 'It felt good to be doing something good. To get respect for it.'

Dinah keeps staring at her hands, as if reading the lines on her palms. She doesn't look at him as she speaks: 'But yuh don't realise that all yuh did was use Mr Steele's money to make yuhself feel good? Son-Son, you selfish.'

Apollo is floored. Dinah goes back inside without turning back to look at him and after an uncomfortable few seconds, he follows her into her kitchen, blinded by the return to semi-darkness after the searing sunshine. He enters the house as gingerly as he had the very first time. She goes over to the stove and ties on an apron, pouring coconut milk and cornmeal into a pot. Apollo notices the solidness of her back and the neat little bow where she has tied the white apron, smudged slightly with various seasonings and spices. He watches the firm, expert movements of her wrist, unsure what to say.

'Son-Son, the biggest thing that make a man is to forgive other people and to forgive himself. That last part is the hardest of all.'

She spins suddenly; looks at him full in the face with such force, he feels as if she has slapped him awake. 'Sometimes I 'fraid yuh going turn into yuh fada.'

'My father?' Apollo thinks of Raymond then John King.

Dinah said: 'Not the fada yuh know, or the one dem tell yuh 'bout. The real one yuh never meet. Leroy. Yuh see, Son-Son, Leroy is not a man. Him is a boy that run away from the man him could be. Run straight into the coward him is. But what Leroy didn't know is that him was really running from himself. A man can't outrun himself, Son-Son. No matter how hard he pump his legs.'

Apollo sits there trying to make sense of what he is hearing. He studies the floral gold and green tablecloth under its sticky plastic cover, tracing the pattern underneath with his fingers. He shifts in his chair but doesn't get up, not wanting to break the moment. It seems so soft and fragile that if there is another sound, like wooden chair legs scraping on the tiled floor, she would stop talking. And he needs her to talk.

She is breathing hard, like she's drawing air for both of

them. 'Son-Son, I wanted to set a better example for yuh than that. I so sorry. I need yuh to forgive mi.'

'Forgive you, for what? You're the only good thing that's happened to me since I got to Jamaica!' he blurts out.

He realises his words must have stunned her, because she turns off the stove, sits next to him and holds his hand for a long time. He could tell her eyes were tearing up but she doesn't cry.

'Dinah, what we have is the only honest thing in my life. I can be myself. I don't want to let you down. Ever.'

'There is something mi did do to yuh before yuh even born mi sorry for and I say I would never tell yuh and mi never mean to tell yuh now, but—'

'It's OK. Past is past. Let it go. Weren't you the one just talking about forgiveness?' He tries to laugh to lighten the mood, but it sounds hollow in the hot airless space of the kitchen.

She nods slowly, and gets up to serve him the turned cornmeal and mackerel. He's grateful for the distraction of eating, the mechanical movements of knife and fork on plate, the cutting, the chewing, the swallowing and the repeating of the process. He enjoys the flavours competing on his tongue.

She pours herself juice, tops up his glass and watches him eat. 'Yuh see Damian? I go visit him in jail yesterday. Every few days, mi bring him some food, though him look like him hardly eating. Him wasting away . . . Him is—'

'Look, Dinah, I don't want to talk about him.' He stuffs more food into his mouth.

She continues as if he hasn't said anything: 'Yuh going listen to this, Son-Son, 'cause yuh need to hear. Mi did think him was a old dutty criminal.'

'He is.' Apollo piles more cornmeal on his fork.

'True, him do things that not right, but him take responsibility. Him stand up to it.'

'Yeah, but that doesn't make it right, does it?'

'No. But what yuh don't know is that after him mother Kathleen run away and leave him, Damian became like a son to mi. That's why mi was so vex when him was leading yuh down the wrong path. But Damian is not a bad boy. Him have good in him.'

Dinah points to a vase on the table holding faded pink plastic flowers. 'Once you break a vase, the vase not going be the same, no matter how good you glue it back. Damian can't make it so that they un-shoot Mr Steele but everyone of we in life, we do things like breaking a vase. What Kathleen do to Damian was like breaking a vase. Yuh get what mi mean?'

Apollo shakes his head, not wanting to attempt to understand.

Dinah takes a slow, deliberate breath. She grabs the vase in both hands with a wild look in her eyes and for a moment he thinks she is about to smash it on the floor.

'Giving up yuh baby is breaking a vase. Taking somebody baby and never telling dem where they baby is, is like breaking a vase. Having a baby for a man yuh know don't love yuh 'cause yuh see it as yuh only way outta di ghetto is like breaking a vase. Working for trash like British and putting a man life at risk is breaking a vase. Sometimes the vases are things smaller than that. But yuh don't realise the vase breaking 'til it nearly done break already.'

He carefully takes the vase from her hands and restores it to its original position on the table. Dinah still holds her palms inches apart as if clutching an imaginary object.

'Son-Son, it take a strong-strong person to take responsibility for that breaking, seeing as how dem can't do nothing to fix it, and that a likkle part of dem done break off too. So how yuh to respond when dem do painful things to yuh? Eh?

'Accept it when people say "sorry", and move past it when dem act like dem not wrong, 'cause piece of dem shattering too, even if yuh don't see it. Or dem pretending not to.

'No matter how much she love you, there are things a mother's love don't teach you. Yuh have to learn dem yuh-self. One of dem things is being decent. I don't mean how to talk nice or dress fancy. I mean treating people right. With forgiveness and with love in yuh heart.'

Her words are swirling in his head. Mama is making gurgling noises in the bedroom. She starts singing: 'Lemelemelem-ho ... Lemelemelem-ho ... Lemelemelem-ho ...' Then, the old woman pleads: 'Angel of Death, yuh come for me? Yuh finally come? No! Don't leave. Take me. Not dem.'

Dinah goes to check on her. Apollo can hear her voice soothing Mama and singing a low lullaby. He can't make out the words.

Dinah returns after a few minutes and pulls her chair close to him.

'Yuh think it easy fi mi to see Mama like this? When mi did likkle, that woman was like a giant. Nothing could hurt her. Now she talking to the people on TV like dem in the room, turning on the gas, water and light, thinking she turning dem off. You know she carry pieces of garbage into the house like is treasure she hiding? She turn into a baby. She alone inside di kinda house we can't enter. As a mother, Mama was hard with mi. Always. 'Cause of what, I don't know. I don't know what her pain is. Maybe it have some-thing to do with who mi fada is, who I don't know to this day. But what use it would be to punish her now? All I can do is forgive.'

330

Apollo's head is spinning. His head can't take in another word. Looking into her face, he can tell Dinah has left a lot unsaid. He stands and, over her protests, helps her wash up the dishes before going home.

That night, he has a restless sleep thinking about a vase. He realises the vase is him and he is toppling in slow motion, falling off a giant table.

Regina

Regina is getting married.

She is on a beach. The white sand is soft under her feet and she is wearing jewelled sandals. A pearl and diamond-encrusted headband sits atop her hair.

She recognises that she is at Montego Bay. The hotel behind her is a beautiful green and white building, set back against a lush hill.

All around her is white and she knows this is a dream even as she is having it. The blue of the ocean and the sky is draped around her shoulders. There is an atoll ahead of her.

Her legs feel heavy as she walks to the little pagoda set up near the water's edge. The sand has become quicksand.

She looks down at her swollen belly and feels the baby leaping.

There is a man at the ocean's edge, waiting for her there, but she can't see his face. His back is to her but he is singing her a song.

Apollo & Dinah

Apollo came back to see Dinah a few days after their talk. And she knew she had to tell him the thing she'd left unsaid before.

They were in the kitchen in the tenement yard in Lazarus Gardens while she washed the plates. They'd just eaten oxtail and rice and peas she had cooked. Dinah had saved up her money from her cleaning job so she could buy the costly delicacy, though it was more bones than meat. The sun was setting, bathing everything outside the window in an orange glow.

'I talked with my folks and—'

'Hmmmmph,' she grunted. She knew he had come to tell her goodbye, but he had been dancing around delivering the news all afternoon. 'So what dem have to say?'

'They're leaving Jamaica real soon. Pops is doing good but he needs more treatment back in the States.' He didn't say that his parents had vowed never to come back to Jamaica. 'They want me to go with them.'

'I see,' was all Dinah could muster. There was silence between them. It seeped into her without a sound, like a blow to the stomach.

After a while, Apollo said: 'Listen, Dinah, it's hard for me too.'

'It hard?'

'Yeah. I mean, you know I've come to-to care about you a lot.'

She didn't say anything. The woman in white, who was eavesdropping, was standing in the doorway. The woman was about to say something.

'Shut up!' Dinah snapped at her.

'What?' Apollo asked.

'No, son. Is not yuh mi talking to.'

Apollo spun around. 'But I'm the only one here.'

'Nuh mind.'

'Umm ... I was saying, Dinah, you've been like a mother to me.'

'Like? Boy, me is yuh mother.'

He didn't know what to say.

'This is hard for me,' he repeated. It felt as if he was bruising her with every word. That he was piercing her somewhere deep, in a part of her she kept shielded – the one area of softness she had left. He couldn't help it. He didn't want to. He had come to feel a tenderness for her which was just a shade lighter than love – even with her bizarre outbursts, her tendency to tempers and to thoughts that sometimes seemed to be hovering on the edge of sanity.

'So how come yuh having a pickney with Regina and yuh still leaving?' Dinah asked roughly. Her eyes sparked with fire. 'A man don't run from him responsibility. I thought yuh woulda learn dat by now.'

He bristled at her words. She didn't have to say 'don't be like Leroy' because it hung between them. She wanted him to be a better man. A man worthy of respect.

Apollo hadn't yet worked out what to do about Regina and the baby. He knew he didn't want to marry Regina. She wasn't the woman he saw his life and future with. It pained him because he did care for her in his own way. The pregnancy had ended their relationship, had sobered him up. Showed him he was far from ready for anything serious. He hadn't been man enough to tell her this himself yet, face to face.

'I told you I'm gonna take care of my kid. I'll make sure the baby is provided for. I'm gonna take care of you too.' He came close to where she stood at the sink and held her chin. He took a white envelope from his pocket, fat with money, and held it up.

'Mi don't want yuh money!' Dinah pulled back.

'I don't mean to offend you. I know you're a proud woman. You work hard. But you've got a hard life. I can help.'

'Money is not everything.'

'I never said it was.'

'Family is the most important thing.'

The silence pooled between them. He still kept the shell necklace she had given him on their first meeting. He felt for it now in his pocket.

'I don't hear your mother singing today,' he said, changing the subject.

'She alright.' Mama was sleeping. All she did these days was bargain with the Angel of Death, trying to convince him to take her.

Dinah sat at the kitchen table. 'Anyway, mi talk to Regina.'

Dinah sounded proud. 'She is a strong girl. Stronger than mi did think.'

Shame chewed on him. He hadn't spoken to Regina in a while. Truly talked the way they used to. He had been avoiding her under the guise of attending to his father. His absences had not gone unnoticed though, prompting the community gossips to issue the breaking news bulletin on Ghetto News Network: *Apollo and Regina dolly house mash up!*

He had been half-hoping, half-dreading Regina would be home when he arrived that afternoon. He deserved her anger, her scorn – the reception he had played over and over in his mind. He could feel the slap she had reserved for his face. He knew Regina deserved a better man than him. She'd opened up her dreams and hopes to him. And all he had done was break her further. Apollo had studied her the way a zoologist scrutinises an exotic bird, lovingly cataloguing its features and habits, enjoying her beauty and strength, before releasing it. The seeds of charm he had to feed her had run out.

He'd felt a knot loosening in his belly when Dinah said Regina was out. 'She gone to look for Damian at the lockup.'

Though Damian was where he should be, Apollo still felt pity for the man who had once been his friend. Even after everything.

'Mi know for a while now that yuh don't have no pickney,' Dinah said.

'*What?*'

'Is not your baby,' she said again, matter-of-factly.

Was this for real? He dared not allow himself the hope. 'How do you know?' he asked, feeling simultaneously relieved and nauseous. He was dizzy.

'Is women thing that. Mi know. And she know too.'

'But why would she say it was?'

'Don't be stupid, Son-Son. Yuh don't think people want to go America?'

It wasn't hatred he was feeling. Just the dull ache of anger. He couldn't hate Regina. Even for this. For her trying to find a way out of the ghetto of Lazarus Gardens. But he was hurt.

'So whose baby is it?' he asked softly.

'Damian's.'

Damian's! He had believed Regina's denials. Told himself it was nothing when he saw the two of them together.

Blinded himself to the flirty looks. Apollo didn't know what to feel. Betrayal of course, but some relief too that Damian had somehow saved him.

The kid's not mine. The thought became a refrain in his head. *The baby isn't your responsibility. You are free. Free to start again. Free to live.* He barely heard Dinah speak again: 'There is one thing yuh have to do for mi before yuh leave, Son-Son.'

'Name it.'

'Get Damian out of prison.'

Dinah read the shock on his face. 'Remember what I told you about forgiveness? If not for the sake of the child, do it for me. And make sure yuh talk to Regina.'

Regina

I used to let him call mi Gina-Baby and Gina-Doll, 'cause with him, mi could be somebody else. Not me. Not Regina from Lazarus Gardens, but Gina who going own Gina's Boutique & House of Fashion. Now, Apollo's words just bouncing off mi like stones skipping 'cross the surface of a river.

I just catching pieces of it: 'Talked to Dinah yesterday ... lies ... how'd you do this to me?'

Mi look off in the distance. We at Hellshire Beach sitting on plastic chairs. Is nearly sunset. I double up my chairs 'cause I 'fraid dem would break from mi weight. It was my idea to come back here. To we special place. Where him ask mi to be him woman.

Mi notice something 'bout the sky. How the wisps of cloud crinkle up so the colours of light bouncing off dem; looking burnt orange with a likkle bit of blue, pink that almost red, bursting through brownish-grey clouds. The sky look new and different. Like when yuh take a blue bowl and a big silver spoon and swirl 'round different flavours of ice cream: strawberry, vanilla and chocolate; just like the one named Neapolitan that Apollo used to bring fi mi.

Strange things happen under a sky like this. Like telling a man the truth. A man who say him used to love yuh but yuh know don't love yuh no more. A man can change colour so quick, like the sky.

Some pickney – two girls in matching yellow two-piece swimsuits – playing; dem building castles on the seaside but the sand too lumpy, too wet in places and full of tiny stones. The walls of the castle heavy and keep crumbling. A woman who look like dem mother come and tell dem she packing up now and is time to go.

Mi don't want to talk. But mi can't keep things inside no more. Like the sky colours, truth going peep out.

'... is it true?'

Mi never hear the first part of the question, but mi know him want to know if Damian is really the father of mi baby.

When mi say 'Yeah', mi see di relief on him face. Mi vex 'bout that. Until I see di anger blended up in him eyes too.

'I feel like an idiot! He was my friend! How could you do this to me, Regina?'

No more Gina-Baby or Gina-Doll.

I leave the question right there. No point telling Apollo mi was sleeping with Damian long before him come into the picture.

I rip up something mi can't fix. I past shame and hiding. I just know the pieces on the ground and somebody have to take dem up and that person is me.

'I sorry,' I tell him and I hope that's enough 'cause that's all mi have. 'Mi really sorry.' I never mean to hurt him. But to be honest, mi never think 'bout him much, either. Just miself.

Mi never wanted to end up like mi Uncle Wayne, who the closest him come to farin is working as a janitor at Norman Manley airport. The US Embassy turn him down for a visitor visa every single time. Dem was 'fraid him was going overstay and run off, which is exactly what Uncle Wayne was planning to do. Him know him life would be better over there. Yuh can imagine how him did feel every day, leaning on him broom, looking through the glass, watching the planes take off? Mi never want that fi mi life.

But is time to think 'bout other people. My baby and mi baby father.

Apollo say: 'I was going to give you money for the baby. I wouldn't have let you struggle.'

'What the baby need is to have a fada that outta jail. Yuh going help Damian?'

'Dinah already asked me.'

'So yuh going do it?

'Look, Regina—'

'Please. Fi me. Please. We need yuh.'

Mi want to grab him hands, but mi know Apollo don't want mi to touch him.

Is who betray who? How yuh can drop mi so fast?

The words that hanging between the two of we are: *Did you ever really love me?* That's what we both want to ask.

The mosquitos start to come out. Apollo slapping at him hands and foot dem and scratching where dem bite him. Him arms and legs getting pink spots.

All him finally say is: 'Come on, let's get outta here before dark.'

Apollo

'Rahtid, Apollo! Is what you *really* saying?'

Mr Brown's choice of words catches Apollo off-guard. They are in Christopher Brown's office at Chandler, Beck and Brown, and the word that comes to mind is 'sharp'. Sharp-edged paintings in gold frames hang on Christopher's wall. The sprawling glass-top desk shines in all its sharp-cornered glory, with stacks of paper and files; and it seems to Apollo there is an island between them. Christopher usually sticks to standard English except if, like now, he is in shock. Through the fourth-floor window, Apollo sees a cloudy sky. People are on the street, going about their business, while he is in here, trying to fight for a life.

'I clearly not hearing you right, so start again.' Christopher pulls out a desk drawer, takes out a Cuban cigar and lights it.

'Mr Brown, you know I'm not called to the Bar in Jamaica, so I can't do it myself. I need this firm to act for Damian in his case. To defend him.' Apollo adjusts his collar and straightens up in his chair. He sees his reflection on the gleaming surface of the table.

'You mean the man who shot your father? You crazy or what?'

'Trust me, I wanted to kill Damian myself. But he didn't

shoot Pops. One of the guys he was with did. And he's taking responsibility—'

'And that makes it OK? Young man, you hearing yourself? You want *this* firm to be part of freeing one of the men who shot my good friend, *your* father?'

'It was a mistake.'

'Some blunders you don't recover from. Like mistaking Krazy Glue for your eye drops.' Christopher chuckles at his own joke.

Apollo knows he isn't doing a good job of convincing his boss. 'I just want justice for him, Mr Brown. That's all. He deserves that.'

At this, Christopher laughs. A hearty laugh that fills the quiet of the office. Apollo had barged into his office after lunch, with such seriousness etched across his face, Christopher had asked his secretary to hold all calls. But the boy was a fool.

'"Justice"? Justice? Apollo, you know what that looks like?'

'Yes. A good defence lawyer. A fair trial, or better yet, a deal to bring the real person behind this to justice. His boss, British. He's the bad guy. The one pulling all the strings. He runs all the robbery rings and drug deals and murders happening in the city.'

Christopher blows tiny smoke rings into Apollo's face. 'Apollo, sometimes I don't think you live in the real world. If what you're saying is true, a trial in Jamaica is not going to put a man like British in jail. He's too connected. Which jury and which judge brave enough to do that?'

Christopher tells him he's wasting his time.

Christopher finally says: 'Look, I know British is a client of Beason's, so this firm has a conflict of interest. That means my hands are tied, even if I wanted to represent Damian. And even if fast tracked, that trial isn't happening for years. And I

342

guarantee you, he'd be convicted, even with a good defence lawyer, which he obviously can't afford. He already confessed! So he'd have to convince a judge the police obtained that confession by force. I'm willing to bet that he'll fail to get a judge to throw it out. And because of the heinous and high-profile nature of the crime, a heavy sentence will be imposed; most likely life imprisonment. Anyway, son, law can't help you now. No matter which law firm you go to, you can't solve this case in a courthouse. Save yourself the time and effort.'

What lingers between them then are the words in Apollo's head: *What's Damian going to do now?*

Christopher taps the end of his cigar forcefully against a heavy glass ashtray and buzzes his secretary for his two o'clock call to be transferred to his landline extension. 'We're done here.'

Apollo doesn't move from his seat. 'With all due respect, I'm not going anywhere until you help me.'

Christopher moves from his desk, in his sharp black, pinstripe suit, silver cufflinks in the shape of the Scales of Justice. As he nears Apollo with his hands balled into fists, for an instant Apollo thinks he will forcibly remove him from his office.

'You are going to help me. You *gotta* help me.'

Christopher grips Apollo's right shoulder and lowers his voice. '*There's* the fire that makes a real lawyer. I admire your determination to fight for this boy. Alright, I'll tell you. Do with this information what you will, and don't tell Ray. You need to make a deal.'

'With who?'

'The man with the power. The one with the ability to talk to the Americans. Wendell Simms, the MP. British operates in his constituency.' Christopher pauses, draws on his cigar thoughtfully. 'Let me explain something to you. I own two horses at Caymanas Racetrack. One named Case Dismissed and the other called Hefty Settlement. You see their trainer, Mr Feanny? He's been a trainer at Caymanas for twenty years and you know what he said to me last week? He said, as a trainer, he needs the jockeys to do their job. To give him straight information on how the horse is performing. Same thing with the grooms. To do his job, to inform me properly, Feanny has to rely on other people. You know what he called that?' He gestures with the cigar, drawing an arc of smoke in the air. 'Alignment. You need alignment for any system to work. Same thing with Jamaica. Simms can't do his job without Area Dons, like British, running the city. Dons need politicians like Simms to tell the cops to look the other way. The cops need Dons to keep law and order in the communities cops don't want to go to. You see when you upset that balance? The result is chaos.'

Christopher pauses to scribble on a piece of paper. 'I'm going to give you Simms' number but keep me out of it. You hear me? I don't want anything to do with this . . . and one more point.'

'What?'

'You better make a good deal.'

'How do I do that?'

'So you telling me that you really didn't learn anything in this internship then?' Christopher looks exasperated. 'Apollo, the art of a deal is to give somebody something they can't get on their own. Ask yourself: "What does Simms want? Who is the person causing him embarrassment in front of the Americans? The one who's out of alignment, creating chaos? Who does Simms want to be rid of?"'

◆

Simms greets Apollo at the door of his office like an old friend; that oily way a politician grips your hand in a handshake with two hands, both of his hands encasing yours, pumping it twice and smiling while looking into your eyes, as if talking to you is the most important thing in the world.

'Come in, young man!' He ushers Apollo to his seat with an outstretched arm. Apollo sinks into the plush leather chair.

His secretary, wearing a tight black skirt, brings Apollo a cup of coffee. It's clear Simms knows who Apollo is. 'I was so glad when I heard you wanted to talk with me. How's your father doing?'

'Some days are tougher than others but he's a fighter.'

'All of Jamaica is wishing him a speedy recovery. We want all visitors to our island to feel safe. *Trust* me when I say the government is doing everything to bring all of the perpetrators to justice. Although two men are still on the run, topnotch policing led us to find two of the suspects.'

'Thanks, Mr Simms. That's kinda why I'm here. I heard you have someone, Damian Miller, in custody.'

'Yes and I assure you he's never getting out of prison. I promise you that.'

Apollo watches the smile slide off Simms' face when he tells him what he wants.

But when he says the words: 'In exchange for freeing Damian I can give you British,' the smile creeps back.

◆

After Apollo tells him his idea, Simms says: 'The police going into Lazarus Gardens for British would be a bloody business. A recipe for disaster. It's action I'd rather leave as a last resort. So I can get ACP Davis on board with your plan. But you have to accept that in no scenario does Damian walk away from this scot-free. The best I can offer you is this.

345

The Americans always want kingpins like British for drug smuggling into the States. So I'll give them British for trial. Damian turns state's evidence against British. Serves some years in jail and goes into witness protection over there. The Americans can grant him citizenship after British's trial and all that, maybe even a full pardon.'

'Can that work?'

'It's not without risk. British's tentacles extend very far. There are members of his organisation everywhere. Damian can never contact anybody in Jamaica again.'

Apollo thinks about the baby and Regina. How would they get to see Damian? But Apollo can't say no. This is the only way to get Damian out of jail. To give him a chance for a fresh start. A new life.

Apollo decides then not to tell Damian about this. Not until everything is done and his future secured. He'll explain it then; why this was the best thing. And maybe, after a while, Pops would be willing to help Apollo bring Regina and the baby to the States to join Damian in witness protection.

Apollo says: 'You have a deal.'

Apollo

Apollo waits in the blistering heat of the sun on the lawn near the entrance to Devon House, away from the shadow of a grand arch.

Devon House sprawls languidly around him; a Georgian-style mansion built by Jamaica's first Black millionaire. In the 1880s the wealth from a Venezuelan goldmine was poured into the towering wooden building with its marble steps and graceful arches. Now a crowd of tourists buzz around the entrance to the museum and public park.

Apollo stands alone.

He has picked the meeting place. Here, ACP Davis' men can blend in, pretend to be out with their women for a Sunday stroll in the park and Devon House ice cream. The women are undercover cops too. There are two main access points and Davis' men have them all covered. British will be cornered. Police in unmarked vehicles with CB radios are posted around the perimeter.

Apollo looks at his watch. Ten minutes past three. British is ten minutes late.

Yesterday, Apollo had called him at the number on British's business card and said without preamble: 'You win. I'll take the job.'

'Smart move.'

'I'm gonna need one thing,' Apollo said. 'I want to talk to you, face to face. Man to man.'

'Don't you mean, man to boy?' British laughed.

'Meet me at Devon House tomorrow?' Apollo ignored the jab.

'Why you can't come to me? You 'fraid?'

Apollo had paused on the line, unsure of what to say. He felt transparent, like British could see right through him. 'How am I going to advise you if you don't trust me?'

After what seemed like forever, British said: 'We'll play it your way this time. See you three sharp, Yankee boy, don't keep me waiting.' British was a stickler for time, a habit picked up in England.

He was making himself bait.

He can see ACP Davis in the distance, in a cap and sunglasses, lying on a red picnic blanket, casually playing with the braids of a skinny female officer posing as his wife. Above their heads, in the branches of trees, birds are singing. The birds call to each other, their cries a symphony, as branches sway in the breeze like a conductor directing an orchestra.

Apollo wipes his forehead with a handkerchief. His shirt sticks to his back. The heat seems to be coming from inside him. He knows he may very well be trading his life for Damian's. *What if British shows up just to kill me?*

No. He won't think about that. He reminds himself Davis' men are everywhere and fully armed. There is a squadron of ants making a trail near his right foot, carrying crumbs from a broken ice cream cone. Apollo moves away and the sound of gravel crunching under his sneaker is magnified in a way that startles him.

At half past three, Apollo can tell, even from this distance that Davis is restless. It's in the way he moves his long legs as he pretends to look at a distant tree. At forty past the hour, Davis' fake wife is wiping sweat from his face with a rag. Apollo knows that under her pink blouse, tucked into the waistband of her jeanskirt, is a gun.

Apollo picks up and strokes a dried leaf that has blown on to the bottom of his jeans. He remembers bringing Regina to Devon House, the first month he'd arrived in Jamaica. Just after visiting the Bob Marley Museum up the road. They'd lain down sideways on the grass so they could stare into each other's eyes. He'd told her how impressed he was that a Black man had once owned this whole place. A self-made man who worked hard to make his money through sea trade and mining. It was like what Garvey always said. 'It's all about Black enterprise, Gina-Baby.' He'd swept his arms around, as if he'd taken his own two hands and built the mansion himself.

That was before the baby, before Pops got shot, before Damian's arrest, before meeting British. Before everything.

The wind dies down.

At quarter to five, they know what they still know at five fifteen: British is not coming. Davis signals his officers to pack it up. Davis' fake wife brushes grass off her skirt and goes to buy a grapenut ice cream cone.

Somehow, British knows a trap has been set. Maybe through one of Davis' men, but Davis insists his people are loyal. Maybe some other source. Maybe it was the way Apollo spoke on the phone. Either way, British hasn't come and they know he is never coming.

Apollo leans on a column of the old mansion. His legs feel wobbly. A sickening feeling lacerates his body.

He realises he can't free Damian. He can't give Dinah the one thing she's asked for.

◆

'Are you telling me you won't help him?' Apollo knows he is arguing in vain. It's the day after the failed Devon House operation.

He grips the phone tightly and struggles to keep his voice down, so people within earshot of his cubicle at Chandler, Beck and Brown don't hear. Secretaries at nearby desks have already looked up from clacking at typewriters, cocking their eager ears towards his conversation. A young associate in a black and white pinstripe suit, on his way to the photocopier, gives Apollo a disapproving look.

'You didn't keep your end,' Simms says. 'Simple as that. British didn't show. You knew the deal.'

Simms hangs up.

Apollo makes several more calls to Simms' office that day and in the days that follow. Whenever Simms' secretary, Christine, answers, she says Simms is unavailable.

Apollo realises Simms has refused to see him again. Apollo suspects Simms told his secretary to advise Apollo he was busy every time Apollo tried to set up an appointment.

After hanging up on Apollo that day Simms' next call is to Davis.

'Simms, what you expect to happen when you send a child to do a man's job? Didn't I tell you he was too young and inexperienced for this? You should've seen how he was shaking the whole time at Devon House.'

Simms simply replies: 'Alright. Back to the original plan.'

◆

'You did what?'

Raymond's voice – edged with coldness – booms in a way that Apollo has never heard before.

Apollo had gone straight to Raymond's bedroom as soon as he got home from the firm the day after he was to meet

British. His father props himself up on royal blue silk pillows that Celeste has fluffed. Spittle flies from his mouth in a fine mist. Celeste is perched on the edge of the kingsized bed holding a tray with his medicine and a glass of water. A burst of wind coming uphill whips up the long white curtains, bringing with it the rich view of the bougainvilleas.

The gardener is mowing the lawn and the noise of the machine nearly drowns out Apollo's words: 'Hear me out, Pops. I gotta use your contacts to help Damian. You know anybody who has sway with MP Simms?' His voice is unsteady, as if it is trying to latch on to something in the air.

'Are you out of your mind? You don't seriously think I'm going to help the man who nearly killed me, do you?'

'He's not a bad person. And-and he has a kid on the way. A kid who's gonna grow up without him,' Apollo squeaks.

'What about *my* son? The one who nearly lost *his* dad?'

'Ray—' Celeste tries to intervene, but he moves his hand to silence her.

'No, Celeste. No. It's a no. And frankly Apollo, I'm disappointed you'd even ask me. Are you part of this plan, Celeste?'

'No, Ray, but he called me from work today and told me about Damian. I think we should consider helping him. Our son is trying to do something good—'

'—for a man who nearly raped you in our house? I'm not supporting this. And Apollo, I don't know what this Dinah woman is doing to you but you better snap out of it fast.'

British

This fassyhole take big man for a joke.

That Yankee boy too hard-ears. As Mama Ivy always say, 'Who don't hear, must feel.' So I going have to do something. Set another example that you can't tell British no or set British up like some fool. This one I going do myself. To see him, eye to eye. Him still staying in that house in Jack's Hill.

People like him and Simms think dem better than ghetto boys like me. No matter how much money we have or how good we talk English. I worked hard to build my organisation. I have men and their families who answer to me. In England, white boys were calling me nigger and darkie and spitting in my face. Looking down on me even after calling me 'mate' and saying 'you're a good bloke'. After all that, you think I going allow anybody to disrespect me in my own country? *I run things.* I am the boss. People answer to me. I am bigger than the Prime Minister.

Is clear my original plan to make Apollo work for me not going work. So instead of Dinah seeing her only son work for me, she going have to live the rest of her life knowing three things: (1) him dead, (2) that is me kill him and (3) she can't do nothing 'bout it. I going deposit the body on her doorstep. In a sealed barrel addressed to her.

They could have avoided all of this. Things go right when people just listen to me. Do what I say. Then life easy. But some people love to do things the hard way. Is like them can't help it. Actions have consequences. Mama Ivy taught me that.

As for Yankee boy and him parents, what Streggo and him crew do to them going look like playing dolly house. When I was dealing with Streggo, some of the man vomit and Chucky look like him was going faint. Only Clevon stand up strong beside me. Is a good boy that. That's why me let him go after Damian and String himself. With him own men.

Everybody know the lesson already: nobody can cross me and live. If is a choice between me and you, then it's no choice at all.

Streggo woman come to me afterwards and bawl down the whole place. And because I was feeling merciful that day, I tell her she can continue to live in Lazarus Gardens. I tell her I'm going to make sure her three children can go to school and get food to eat. That she not going miss out on money, now that Streggo gone. I could see that she understand what I was really saying – 'Woman, don't do anything stupid, you have three pickney to live for' – 'cause she get real quiet and go back through the gate. My men know is not that I'm getting soft. I'm a hard man but I'm fair. I keep all the things Streggo steal – that was the cost of cleaning up his mess. To pay back for the problems that him screwing up a simple robbery cost me. Before him dead, Streggo confess him get the worthless Ratta involved, that tough-head boy who him mother say is my son. I give that job to Clevon and him men to handle too.

As for the Yankee boy, him don't even realise how much chances him get. My patience is like a string. Draw it too much and it snap. Imagine! After I give him my business card at the dance, and send him that leather briefcase, the kind I couldn't even dream of when I was his age, him try set me up. Him think me stupid?

This is how I going get rid of Apollo. And people going to re-tell the story.

On a night after the Yankee boy done screw Regina, and gone back to what him think is the safety of him house on the hill, I going be right there. I going be inside already. I done deal with the parents. I will make their end quick. I'm no monster. I tell them it wasn't personal. I tell them that with Apollo I going take my time. But I spare them seeing that.

Apollo going come through the door, throw down the car keys, start take off him shoes and when him bend down to unlace him sneakers and look up, him going see me. Him hand that reaching for the light switch going tremble, like the mouse in my snake cage at feeding time.

Him going go on him knees and beg. Going tell mi him change him mind. Him ready to work for me now. That him sure this was what he really wanted to do from the beginning. But it's just that he needed time to think and to put things in order. Him going hope him smooth tongue will convince me.

'You take me for fool?' I going say, and kick him in the mouth.

Him going ask me what happened to him folks. And when I don't answer and the truth sink inside him, that is when him going cry like a little bitch. Not no pickney-cry. But that bawling where the shoulders go up and down and breathing get shallow.

I going tell him to take it like a man. That a man has to know how to die well. That Pedro Garcia show me that. A man has to learn how to have everything him love get taken away and him still don't crack.

'Are you a man?' I going ask. 'Is skin you have, or eggshell?'

I will tell him it won't be fast or easy. That him going learn how much pain he can take.

'You ready to start?' I will say, as I handcuff him to a chair that I take from around the dining table.

And instead of nodding, him going cry louder and snot going run down him face and soak him T-shirt, since him can't wipe it with the back of him hand.

Then we going do all the things Pedro teach me and I practise in England until I had it perfect. How to break a man's ribs, one by one, how to burn him in the most sensitive parts of him body, how to squeeze him neck until him nearly dead, then release it just in time to bring him back again just so you can start over. How to make him feel like him whole body on fire.

I going tell him is his fault. Is because of him why his folks dead and why I doing this. That is really him force me to do this. I will remind him how easy it would have been if he had taken my offer. He'd have money, women, drugs – anything he could desire. I would have taken care of him. He would have had a future in my organisation. After I'm gone, he would have worked for Clevon.

While I'm taking a break, I'll explain to him I'm trying to build a legacy. I'm going to leave something for my boy, something my father never did. Mama Ivy used to call my father a wutliss bum. He *was* worthless. All I got was his name. Desmond. A little name from a little man. He was as weak as Mama Ivy was strong.

Halfway through, the Yankee boy going beg for some water. Him won't cry 'cause him realise the tears sting when them run into the cuts on him face. Him tongue going be too swell-up for him to swallow anyway, so I going say no. Him eyes going feel like electricity running through them.

Maybe I will ask him what it's like to grow up with a

father. I will ask him if him can imagine not knowing what him father look like. Or picture what it's like to think of a father you don't know when you going to bed hungry. But I will also tell him that growing up like that makes you tough. And as Mama Ivy used to say, only the tough survive.

Then in the last hour, with him eye so swollen him only seeing shadow, him might beg me not to hurt Dinah. And his woman. That plea will come out like a groan.

No, I assure him, them going live. If not, who going re-live your death every day? Who else is going to feel that loss deep in their bone marrow?

In the last few minutes, him going nod at what him know coming. What will happen after that, I can't predict. Some men are brave and some men piss themselves or vomit. Like Streggo.

But if him take it like a man, I going tell him that I will let Dinah and Regina know. That at least him wasn't a little boy at the end.

'Do it!' He might spit blood at me and try to jump out of the chair. Then I will know him ready.

After, I will enjoy the silence of that house, sitting down at that big dining table and feeling the softness of the rug under my toes. Breathing deeply in that stillness and inhaling all the smells in that house.

Then I will dance.

I will leave a trail of bloody footprints leading right out the front door into the quiet, cool night.

Dinah

Son-Son here telling mi him sorry. Him had a way to free Damian but it all fall apart two days ago and him feel so bad him can't even tell Damian. Can't face Damian to say there was hope and before him could grab it, it disappear.

Mi take him hand and lead him outside, so the woman in white don't eavesdrop on wi conversation. Mi did see her go into the room where Mama lying down. And mi think: *Good, that going occupy her for a while.* While she was distracted, mi did take up a plastic wash tub to collect the clothes on the clothesline.

Some pickney barefoot in the yard playing with water from the bucket dem carrying from the standpipe. Dem squealing and two likkle dogs at dem feet barking and wagging dem tail. One of the pickney fall down and a puppy whine, put him paw on the boy chest and lick him face.

The sky been hazy all day. The clothes barely dry. They feel cold to mi touch.

Son-Son take a seat on a big stone and watch mi. 'I tried, Dinah. I really tried. But nothing worked.'

I tell him it's OK. Him do more for Damian than what others woulda do. I putting the clothespins I removing from the line into a pocket of my skirt. 'Plenty time, a man going try and fail. Is so life go. The failing just mean yuh put out effort in something. Mi proud of yuh.'

Him say him don't know what going happen to Damian now.

'It outta we hands. In life, some things bigger than we. The Book of Proverbs say: "Many seek the ruler's favour; but every man's judgement cometh from the Lord." That is how justice going come.'

Outta nowhere, Son–Son say: 'You know, I never seen my father's grave. How messed up is that?'

I ask him what him talking about. 'Moms said the accident that killed John King was so bad, the car caught on fire. In the explosion, his body burnt up, so they cremated him, scattered his ashes on the coast. I don't even have a grave to visit.'

Mi folding the sheet and nodding but I wonder why him telling mi dis foolishness when I already tell him Leroy is him daddy.

'You know what it's like, Dinah, to be just ... I dunno, without something to hold on to? And to have the man you looked up to – who raised you – fool you for the first ten years of your life? I didn't find out John King existed until I was ten, and it's 'cause of the kids at school. They told me I was too dark, that I looked nothing like Pops. They figured out something was wrong before I did. I felt like nothing was ever gonna make sense again. Dinah, except for you, I got nothing to-to *anchor* me.'

Same time, I put down the pan of clothes that smell of lavender fabric softener and hug him. How mi can tell him that if the woman in white have her way, him going lose me too?

'I went to Pops for help with Damian and he just slammed the door in my face and Moms let him do it.'

I stroke his hair. The curve of his ear remind mi of Leroy's.

'No matter how much yuh feel dem do wrong to yuh, forgive dem.'

'Why should I?'

I know is the hurt talking. Mi don't tell him that soon dem going be the only parents him going have, 'cause the more the woman in white talk to mi, the more I forget. Is like she stealing the memories straight from mi head, drawing dem through mi mouth with a invisible hook and line, like a fisherman hauling in him catch. Whenever she come, mi brain start lose sense of place and time. Mi moving on land where mi feet not firm.

'Cause mi can't tell him that, I tell him the other truths instead: "Cause dem love you and that's the right and decent thing to do . . . and doing it going give yuh something money can't buy.'

'What's that?'

I tell him straight: 'Dignity.'

◆

The last time mi see Mrs Steele was when mi was leaving the hospital, after I go see her husband days after the shooting.

We did meet up in the corridor. Mrs Steele was in a pink and white floral dress asking me: 'What are *you* doing here?' and wrinkling her nose like she smell something bad or mi is an insect she want to squash.

I tell her I come to visit her husband.

'Don't make me have to call Security. You've got no business trying to see Ray.'

She have some nerve!

'Yuh should call Security on yuh own damn self. Yuh is a tief.' But I willing miself to calm down. I not going give away mi power again like last time when we fight. I going keep mi strength by keeping cool.

When she tell mi I crazy and mi must stay away from

her family, I respond as quiet as I can manage: 'Yuh steal mi family. *My* boy. But you can't undo it, so I just have to forgive yuh.'

The nurse with the big eyes popping outta her head come up and ask if everything alright, but is Mrs Steele she look at and ask. Not me.

'Thanks, Nurse Frederick, it is. This woman's just leaving.' And she cross her arms.

I nod. 'Yes, I going.'

As I walk away, mi didn't have to look back to know she was still standing there, watching.

I hold mi head high.

◆

When I done fold up and put away the clothes, me and Son-Son make June plum juice in the kitchen. To take him mind off things, I make him wash the June plums, cut up the bright yellow flesh to remove the seed and blend it with a likkle ginger. Some people peel the fruit before dem dice it up, but I always make my juice with the skin on. That way, the colour greener even though the drink more sour.

After we strain it, I add brown sugar and just a likkle lime juice. By the time I take couple sips from my glass, Son-Son nearly finish off the whole thing.

I make sure that I give him something important before him go. I take out the letter I had in my pocket and give him to give Mrs Steele for mi. Him turn over the envelope and I glad I did seal it.

I tell Son-Son him can't open it, though I know him want to know what mi write. I ask him to give it to her after they gone back to America.

The letter say:

Mrs Steele,

What you and your husband did was wicked. I not going get back the time you rob from me. But the thing you must do for me now is take care of my boy. My Son-Son. Your Apollo. He going need you, and always need you. I asking you this, mother to mother. And no matter what kind of woman I may think you are, I know you love him too.

◆

Son-Son go into the room to tell Mama goodbye and him come back and say him don't see her. I ask him what him mean and go check for miself. All I see is the empty bed and sheets. I look under the bed. I go to Mrs Sinclair's room and ask if she see her. Mrs Sinclair say no.

I say aloud what we both thinking: 'Mama missing!'

Dinah

It don't make no sense. Is the woman in white take her? Why she would do that? And how the two of dem slip past wi? It must be the time when Son-Son and me was in the kitchen and mi back was turned fi dem few minutes.

We in Son-Son's car driving from lane to lane and I looking. Searching every shape. Every single body I see that nearly resemble Mama own, I ask Son-Son to drive closer to dem, but when dem turn around, I see is not her. And I vex with dem for not being her. I mad dem wasting mi time. I upset that dem even exist and taking up space on the sidewalk.

I start cussing miself. *How I could be so careless?*

At one point I was going jump outta the car and run but Son-Son grab mi hand and say we can cover more ground in the vehicle than on foot. And him right, but I picturing Mama alone, walking by herself. She probably leave Lazarus Gardens already. Is nearly night and I seeing the yellow light from the street lights, the electric wires on the poles criss-crossing like nets where people tiefing light from the Jamaica Public Service, with kites trapped on it; pieces of plastic and tangled cloth on wires flapping in the breeze and I wish I could be up there to see better. To find Mama from the air.

Son-Son holding mi hand: 'It's gonna be OK, Dinah, we'll find her. I promise you,' even though him in no position to make promises about a future him can't guarantee. 'You told me she's gone missing before. And you always find her, right?'

I praying and asking God to lead me to Mama. All I seeing now is men in the streets smoking and women standing around laughing and chatting with dem fren. Life moving on, like Mama not missing.

Missing. The one constant thing in mi life over all these years. *Gone.* I tell Son-Son we have to find her. Before she do something to harm herself. Or worse, somebody harm her.

A pain plunging deep into mi belly.

◆

We drive outta Lazarus Gardens and reach where downtown Kingston meet the Harbour. No Mama. How a old woman could move so far so fast I don't know. In the distance, mi see wooden fishing boats – a red and yellow one and another green and blue – tied and bobbing up and down in the water, waiting for dem owners to take dem out the next morning.

We see a madman wearing clothes that look like dem get dipped in ash.

'Maybe she circled back?' Son-Son ask, him voice full of hope. Him turn around the car. I can barely see through the tears in mi eyes.

'Wait – what's that?' mi hear Son-Son say.

I look where him pointing. Still no Mama. But right there in the middle of the road: something mi recognise. Mama's yellow and green striped housedress! We get outta the car. We get out so quick, Son-Son leave the doors open and the engine running. If him leave the keys in a fancy car like that, we not going come back and find it. Him remember and turn back to shut it off and lock the doors. Him put the keys in him pocket.

I take a few steps. Next to a old piece of cardboard, mi find Mama brown brassiere; and in the gutter her black and white polka dot panty!

I grab up her clothes and then a blue slipper. I only find the one foot.

The trail leading to the sea.

I feel Son-Son behind mi every step. Then mi see her. Mama sitting at the edge of the pier like she is a mermaid that rise from the sea. As mi get closer, I can see she dry though. Seagulls above her head and Mama looking like she and dem in conversation.

'Mi is a bird,' she say, as soon as she see mi. I glad to hear her voice 'cause these days, sometimes all she do is stare into space without a sound or grunt.

'Who him?' That was how she greet Son-Son.

I tell her we was looking everywhere fi her and she can't be walking all over the place and naked too.

'Mi is a bird,' she say, huffing. 'Yuh nuh see that?'

I tell her yes, mi see, but she is one bird that need to put on clothes.

Mi see some teenage boys in the distance leaping into the sea and clapping each other and I want her to be covered before them turn and look on we. Mi don't want to call attention to weself. She not allowing me to get the dress on, so I just throw it over her top to cover her breasts. She refuse to step into the panty.

Son-Son didn't say nothing but mi know him was relieved we find her. I hear it in the way him say: 'Let's get to the car.'

When we reach the car, mi arm around Mama, mi see a man wearing a grey T-shirt and black shorts come outta nowhere and say: 'Gimme the bumboclaat keys.' The man tall-tall and have a dirty kerchief tie 'round him head. 'Is my Benz dis now.'

Him talking to Son-Son. Him not paying me and Mama nuh mind.

'What the—' is all Son-Son could say before the man run and come grab him up by him shirt-front, right under him neck. Him hold him so tight, mi wonder how Son-Son breathing. The man like him trying to lift him off the ground.

Before mi could do anything, Mama start to cry out.

'Old ooman, shut yuh mout'!' The man let go Son-Son and push Mama down in the road. Quick as anything, mi see Son-Son hand come up and hit the man hard-hard in him face. The man stumble and drop.

'Don't you put your hands on her!' Son-Son say.

Mi just as stunned as the man and Son-Son. *Where Son-Son learn to fight?* But him face is not Son-Son's face no more but a man in a rage. Him have the man on the ground stomping him over and over and mi think Son-Son not stomping the man but the system that couldn't free Damian, him anger at the Steeles, him hurt from Regina and the unfairness of everything that him feel wrong in him life.

'Stop!' I shout and pull him off. The man face bloody, nose broken. A knife fall outta him pocket too.

'Is enough,' I say. Son-Son look up like him surprised him not alone. Like him not expecting to see nobody here. 'Mek wi go!' mi say. Son-Son holding him right hand with him left hand, like it in pain. Mi wipe him knuckles with the scarf mi had 'round mi head. The man limp away, leaving a gold tooth shining on the black tar of the road.

We help Mama into the car and drive off. I check and see that nothing broken and she alright. When we reach Lazarus Gardens she spread out in the back seat. She have her eyes closed but I know she not sleeping.

Mi look over at Son-Son and don't say nothing. Mi don't have no words to rebuke him. Sometimes, a man have to let the anger out. Uncork it before it kill him.

◆

While Son-Son wait in the living room, I settle Mama in bed, kiss her forehead and tell her I glad she back in her nest. Before she close her eyes, she say: 'Tell the boy thanks.'

When I come outta the room Son-Son sitting, cradling him bloody knuckles in my headscarf. Him look mi dead in the eyes.

'Look, Dinah,' him say, drinking the water mi give him. 'I haven't been straight with you about something. There's something I shoulda told you a long time ago.'

British trying to get him. As him mention the name, mi pulse get a likkle fast. Son-Son explain that British did offer him a job that him turn down and in trying to free Damian, him set a trap for British but British was a no-show. Son-Son say mi is a target. 'You don't set up a man like British and walk away. He could go after the people close to me.' Mi ask him why him telling mi this now.

'I never told you earlier 'cause I didn't want to worry you. I want you to be safe. Promise me you'll lay low, and watch your back.'

But I not 'fraid of British. I not letting him or anybody chase mi outta my home. I just glad Son-Son soon leave. Life have bigger monsters to fear.

Then him say: 'Dinah, I'm-I'm so scared.'

I hold my boy. The way I never got to hold him as a child. I don't tell him. But mi 'fraid too.

PART FOUR

Butterflies

British

It was the stillness that told him. The awful quiet. From the upper balcony, British couldn't see street light shining down on anybody – not in the main streets nor any of the myriad little lanes. No game of cards on the corner. No men slamming down dominoes. No laughing from Nicey's Bar or in front of Big Mike's Variety Store. No sound of children at play. No women arguing with their men, or each other, at their gates, fences or front steps. Unusual, even for a Wednesday night.

Maybe the people of Lazarus Gardens could sense it too, in the air. And like birds that could feel danger before it struck, without knowing *exactly* why, the people had retreated into the safety of their nests, jammed together in the narrow lanes, separated only by rusted zinc and thin pieces of plywood and cardboard.

British was alone on the balcony. It was four days after the boy had tried to trap him at Devon House and he was still seething, waiting for his moment to strike. He knew his men were where they always were: stationed throughout his mansion, guarding every floor. The night was broken only by the sound of huge air conditioners blasting cold air. He felt a chill run through him for the first time in a very long

369

time. Looking at the stars, he thought about how a hundred years from now, none of this would exist in the way it did now. His body, the mansion, this community. Would he be remembered?

'Boss.'

He spun around at the voice interrupting the night. One of his lieutenants stood before him, head slightly bowed. He was a boy, really, in a black leather jacket too big for his shoulders, a single gold chain around his neck. A pendant swung, the width of a man's fist, shaped like a machine gun.

'Bossy, everything secure.'

They had completed their rounds, scanning the perimeter of British's compound. It was a routine exercise. Like soldiers who cleaned their weapons and did drills during a time of peace. No one would dare enter Lazarus Gardens and try to unseat its King. Not even the police.

With a nod, he dismissed the boy who left as silently as he'd come.

Yes, he thought, the place was dead, like the dull-eyed stare of a crocodile. Full of menace. Like the pause that stiffens your whole body at dinner when you first feel the bone wedged in your throat – hard like dread – the bone you know is about to choke you. The pause a Rottweiler makes the second before it seizes you. Or in a car accident, that pause just before your head hits the windscreen and the steering wheel explodes into your chest.

Yes, British knew something was coming and he braced for it.

◆

He found himself thinking about something that happened in jail, in England. He had been locked up at Pentonville prison in London. It was around half eight. An inmate next to him had been watching the telly with the rest of them after the evening meal of god-awful bangers and mash, when the man, a bloke named Killian Turner, started to breathe shallow. Turner jumped up, knocking over his chair. At first, British thought the man had gone mad and was about to fight him. The week before, someone had called him a darkie cunt, then broke his nose. This man was twice his size. British felt fear shoot up from beneath his feet like a spear rooting him to the spot.

Instead of attacking, the man flattened out on his back on the grey laminate floor like a dead fish.

'Bloody hell!' Turner wailed over and over. 'I'm gonna die.' He spoke with finality and panic. His eyes bulged out, as he took each breath. The other inmates made a circle around him before three guards rushed in and dragged him to his feet and to the doctor.

When Turner came back, and before they transferred him to another jail, inmates and loose-lipped guards talked about what had happened to him. Not a heart attack or something like that, but a fancy thing none of them had heard about before called anxiety neurosis. They joked that Turner belonged in the mental hospital at Broadmoor prison.

British remembered that moment now as his breathing became sharp.

Did he see or just *imagine* a shape move in the distance? Was the swaying of the tall bushes the wind or a man? Many men? His grip on his gun tightened. He waited for the stillness to shift to reveal what was underneath.

◆

Despite his size, Ratta inched up the back wall with the grace of a cat. He had removed his black and white Nikes and hidden them under a nearby bush. He didn't want them squeaking on the tiles. He was on his hands and knees, moving slowly.

Clevon lived on his father's compound. British had built his son a mini mansion of his own to the west of his. Usually, there were men stationed outside Clevon's house, but all security had been diverted tonight to beef up security for his father. Clevon was alone and this was when Ratta was going to strike. He was not here to win back his father's love, but to destroy the object of it.

Ratta slipped through the back window. He was nimble despite his bad leg. His sense of purpose made him move with a dancer's poise. He knew the layout of the house because his aunt was one of the women British paid to clean it. His footsteps made no sound. The walls were several feet thick.

He felt like he was entering a tomb.

The night air was cool on his skin. He could make out two sleeping forms on the bed. The smaller one stirred when he entered.

He cut off her scream with his hand, but her jerking body woke Clevon. Ratta leapt. As the two men wrestled on the bed, the naked woman ran from the room. Clevon tried to overpower him but Ratta was bigger and younger. Rage had made him strong. He wanted Clevon to see his face. That it was he – the one British and everybody forgot – who would bring Clevon's end. He put him in a headlock. Sounds tumbled from Clevon's gaping lips.

'Yuh dead now,' Ratta said, pulling back the neck until he felt a snap. And just like that, British's legacy was snuffed out.

Ratta carefully laced his black and white Nike sneakers and went out the way he came; into the still night, enjoying the quiet.

He didn't see the policeman until it was too late.

Davis & British

ACP Davis loved to garden, orchids especially. He would pursue this full-time when he retired. Orchids were sensitive. Each type was suited to a specific environment. If you overwatered them, they died. If you put them in the full blast sun, they died. They needed special food, the right soil. It was the same with a clandestine operation. You needed the right team of men: ones who asked no questions. Ones for whom darkness and operating outside of the bounds of legality created a spot they loved to occupy, like an orchid relishing the patio's shade.

For some reason, orchids are on his mind now, as he strides through the hallway of the upper floor of British's mansion. He hasn't seen a single flower in the place. It's odd what you notice in life and death situations. The shooting had died down.

'ACP,' Deacons, a burly man the colour of night was speaking to him. 'We round up the man dem. Shot some of the wanted ones. The rest we going put in the van.'

Davis looked at him and said nothing. Deacons knew that Davis was only interested in the real target.

'British is in a room at the back. One of the men we arrest who say him name Chucky tell us British have five man in there with him as protection. We going there next.' Deacons pointed to the battering ram.

'I coming with you,' Davis replied.

The way to get at British was not to break down the door or to smoke him out with tear gas or rain down a blaze of gunfire. It was a battle of intelligence. Him against British. It was a fight Davis felt he could win. He had to, or he would be dead.

Instead of instructing his men to force their way through the door, Davis walked up to it slowly and calmly, stepping gently, and knocked softly – the way he would at his teenage daughter's bedroom door after she'd thrown a tantrum and locked herself inside.

'British,' he said, 'this is Davis. There's no way out of this. Let's talk. Just the two of us. We can settle this like two intelligent men.'

For a while, he wondered if anyone was inside. The only response was silence. He looked back at Deacons, who nodded that yes, British was in there. They were sure.

Then the door opened a crack and there he was. British in a red-trimmed black bathrobe, oversized grey T-shirt and Versace sweatpants. He beckoned Davis inside: 'Come in. But just you.'

British watched as Davis took off his bulletproof vest and handed the two guns on his waist to Deacons. Davis could tell by the look on Deacons' face he didn't think this was a good idea.

The two men sat down across from each other, like they were playing a game of chess. British's men moved forward, forming a semi-circle around him; they were all armed. A chill ran down Davis' spine. Nevertheless, he made the first move.

'I've come to negotiate the terms of your surrender.'

374

British's gaze seemed to play in the space between them for a minute, then he threw his head back and laughed viciously.

'Surrender? You realise you in here by yourself? That you don't have no back-up?'

Davis glanced at the closed door separating him from his officers.

'By the time them get in here, you dead long time.'

'Then is 'fraid you 'fraid of me, British?' Davis chuckled. 'You can't manage me by yourself?'

British's face darkened. His features seemed to liquefy then harden themselves into a solid knot. He bared perfect white teeth.

Davis gestured to his now-empty gun holster at his waist. Boldness seized him. Pressing his luck further, he said: 'Tell them to leave us. Let's talk like men. My people outside won't trouble them. I promise.'

British's tone was cold. 'Your word mean anything? You said you would never come here.'

'It's time for big man talk. Just me and you.'

British scowled but beckoned the men to leave. One said: 'Boss, yuh sure?'

British shot him a dark look. The man hung his head like a puppy that had been kicked. Davis got up and went to the door, opened it and told his men to step back and put their weapons down so the five men could leave.

'OK, time for business,' he said, after he'd taken his seat again. The padded leather chair was comfy. He allowed himself to sink into it. The softness against his skin was soothing. 'So British, you're not going to offer me a drink?'

British watched him stonily. 'See the gin and whisky behind you there. Help yourself.'

Davis dared not move. He would not turn his back to British. 'The MP has a message for you.'

British moved forward in his chair. 'So why him not man enough to come tell me himself? You is him messenger boy?'

Davis tightened his lips. He wouldn't be goaded into a fight. 'What Simms want now?'

'The MP said you went too far. With that white American getting shot, you brought down too much attention from the Americans. He warned you this was coming.'

'You joking! Wendell Simms is an ungrateful brute. Is *me* keep him in power.'

'No, the people vote, British. That's what happens in a democracy. MP Simms works for the people. People are not happy about your actions.'

'Which people? Not the people in Lazarus Gardens. Those people out there are *my* people. Nobody else care 'bout them. Not you or the politicians. Unnu leave them here to struggle and live hard life while unnu in unnu mansion and big car. You care how them get food or send them pickney to school or get money to go doctor or bury them dead?'

'Brit—'

'All unnu care about is unnu self! I take care of them and that's why them need me and respect me.'

'It's over, British. All of it. These people are no longer your responsibility. They will have to fend for themselves.'

'You think I going let you carry me to prison? Make unnu lock me up in a cage? Mi go England prison already. Mi not going into a box again.'

Davis said nothing. Anger had twisted his face. British felt drawn to the ugliness of it. The outrage there mirrored his own. The nerve of this man to come into *his* house and threaten *him*! This was an insult he couldn't forgive.

'Don't forget I can talk what mi know. And you think when I done talk the Americans not going demand the arrest

376

of the MP, the Party Leader and even you when I done tell them all about what unnu doing? The government going deport all of unnu and unnu going know what American prison is like. Prison life rough.'

British watched Davis stiffen. He licked his lips. 'You think you can survive in American prison? A pretty boy like you will melt like icing 'pon cake. You soft. Them going turn you into them woman. Take you regular.' He lowered his voice, smiled slowly. 'Tell me something Davis: you like it in yuh batty? You know what dick taste like? Suppose I make you find out now?' British stood up and lowered the waist of his pants.

Without a word, Davis smiled and bent over in his chair.

'I always had a feeling about you, Davis. That you like them things.'

Crouching, Davis reached for his ankle. The pistol he had strapped there slipped easily from its case. He saw British's eyes widen a moment. He had miscalculated. He broke his cardinal rule to never trust the police.

'Mother—' was all British was able to say before he fell.

The shot had gone cleanly through his neck.

Davis' men barged in to find him standing over British's corpse.

'Take that, pussyhole,' Davis spoke flatly, gazing at British's body. 'Is that to reach you long time. Chat too much.'

◆

Davis noticed the fat leather-bound journal on British's desk. When he opened it, he realised it was British's writing. It recorded not only the tonnes of cocaine, heroin and marijuana exported, weapons bought and sold, and money earned but also gave a glimpse of the perversions and psychological torment he had waged as well.

377

As Davis flipped through it, a sickening feeling crept into his stomach. His throat tightened and his fingers tingled. He slammed the journal shut. Davis felt weary. He couldn't wait to get home to attend to his orchids. He realised Deacons was next to him.

'Burn it,' Davis said, handing Deacons the book. 'Burn down the whole blasted place.'

You, a Jack's Hill Neighbour

You are watching the evening news in your favourite armchair and wondering if this is actually an action movie showing on your new satellite dish.

You had your usual gin and tonic after dinner. You needed to unwind. To dull the headache creeping in behind your eyes. You kept squeezing the bridge of your nose between your thumb and index finger, but it wouldn't go away. The kids are upstairs asleep. You snapped at them for making noise at dinner for which you now feel sorry.

It had been a rough day at the furniture factory. A worker's hand got caught in a machine and he nearly lost it. The cutting blade sliced through a thumb before the supervisor switched it off and you had a fit, yelling at them both. Luckily, the guy didn't lose a finger but it meant production was stalled for an hour and your father-in-law stormed into your office and blamed you for the back up and reminded you you had orders that were delayed from last week.

You remember the worker's shrieks and pinched face as you tried to pull his hand from the machine. It makes you think about the man you found those weeks ago, shot in his house the night you took Fluffy for her walk. The haunted expression on his face. The rapid opening and closing of his mouth as if he wanted to drink the air. The slowly blinking eyes. You came home with his blood on your shirt, legs and hands. The blood of a man you didn't know. The smell hung on your body. No matter how hard you scrubbed your skin in the shower, you smelt it even in your sweat.

When you came home that night, your wife thought at first that you and Fluffy had been hit by a car, that you had barely survived to stumble home. When she saw you at the doorstep, her first words were: 'Oh my God! Is Fluffy OK?'

'Becky, come listen to this!' You holler for your wife now. She pads into the living room, giant pink curlers in her hair, wearing the red silk kimono you bought her for Christmas last year. When she looks at the television her eyes are wide and unblinking, reflecting your own shock. The news anchor wearing a stiff black wig and loud red lipstick is saying:

'We'll be bringing you live scenes from this evening's raid at the compound of notorious alleged gang leader and reputed Area Don, Desmond McIntyre, otherwise known as "British". Acting on intelligence, members of an elite squad under the command of Assistant Commissioner of Police, Linford Davis, descended on the mansion of Mr McIntyre tonight. A shootout ensued. Although no policemen were injured, there were a number of civilian fatalities, including Mr McIntyre. A fire of indeterminate origin subsequently broke out. One eyewitness said that the massive blaze "raged like hellfire", becoming a devastating inferno within seconds.

Firefighters from the fire station assigned to the Lazarus Gardens community were called to the scene but could not respond due to the absence of a fire truck. When a truck was obtained from another station, it had to be refuelled. On arriving at the scene of the fire, firefighters discovered that the fire hydrant was not working, so their efforts were hampered by lack of water. Efforts to get a comment from the Jamaica Fire Brigade have proved futile.

Before the fire consumed the house, police were able to seize several kilograms of cocaine, heroin and marijuana. They retrieved a number of illegal high-powered weapons, including a hand grenade, several rounds of ammunition, cash and recovered stolen property recently taken from the home of a Jack's Hill resident in a brazen robbery. More details on the extent of the items recovered in this raid later.

Our reporter, Tony Jones, is on the scene. Tony?'

When it cuts to Tony, you can't believe your eyes. In the background is a huge fire that looks like it's burning up the sky. Dead bodies covered in white sheets are being carried into police vans. You can see a leg that slips out from under the sheet. The foot wears a black and white Nike sneaker.

Bloody men, their heads bowed and wearing handcuffs, are being crammed into the back of police cars. A group of women hold their bellies and wail. Their faces and clothes are dirty from ash and smoke.

'Dem was innocent,' the woman on her knees is saying over and over. 'British was wi leader. Is wickedness how dem kill him . . . '

'Murder!' another screams, hands on her head.

The reporter Tony is standing next to ACP Davis, who looks as cool as if he were out for an evening stroll and mayhem wasn't unfolding all around him. ACP Davis is telling Tony: 'Today, we have rid Jamaica of a major player in the drug trade. Mr McIntyre, aka British, was a criminal who managed to elude law enforcement for many years by the clever concealment of his activities. However, our intelligence led us to his mansion today and to a major drug bust.'

'ACP, a source has said that unarmed men – men who

didn't engage the police – were killed. Can you confirm that, sir?'

'We deny that allegation. On arriving at the scene, we were challenged by British's men and returned fire.'

'But how did a fire start, ACP? An eyewitness claimed that the fire was set by your men deliberately. The witness claims to have seen your men bringing in cans of kerosene.'

'Completely untrue. We are not certain of the origin of the fire and there will be a full investigation in due course. However, it's likely one of British's men shot a cooking gas cylinder in the kitchen in the crossfire and the cylinder exploded.'

'But in that case ACP, how come the police were able to take out all the drugs and guns before the whole place went up in smoke?'

'Lord, man. We got them out before!'

'One more question, ACP. I understand that there are wounded men here in need of medical attention.'

'And they'll get it as soon as the hospital can locate and send a functioning ambulance. We understand there is a shortage at the moment.'

'But couldn't your policemen take them to the hospital?'

'Our vehicles are not properly equipped and we are not trained medical personnel. I'm not taking any more questions.'

'Thanks, ACP. Back to you in the studio.'

'Thanks, Tony. Member of Parliament for Lazarus Gardens, Wendell Simms, has just issued the following written statement to the press . . . ' The news anchor paused to clear her throat: 'My fellow Jamaicans, this government applauds the diligent work of its dedicated officers led by ACP Linford Davis. We want to assure the public and our diplomatic partners that we take crime and the eradication of criminal enterprises very seriously.'

You turn off the TV because you can't watch any more. Fluffy jumps into your lap, sniffs your face and licks your hand. Her cold nose feels soothing on your fingers.

Your wife says: 'Let's move to Miami.'

Aftermath

Dinah saw the news the night of the siege. All she could think was how her God was a God of vengeance.

My Deliverer has come through for me.

Then she dropped to her knees and praised.

◆

Apollo heard the news on the radio of the Benz as he took a long drive. He had decided to go back to Port Royal that night. He loved the yellow and red lights sparkling in the hills from the Palisadoes road. He pulled over and shuddered in relief.

◆

Mr and Mrs Christopher Brown caught the news while sitting in their living room.

Turning to his wife, he said: 'Jesus, Cindy! Is Beason client that!'

◆

Celeste and Raymond watched the TV at home in Jack's Hill. They didn't say anything for a while until Celeste shook her head and said: 'I can't wait to get out of this god-forsaken country.'

◆

Regina went directly to the site of the fire at British's mansion. She didn't want to watch it on TV. She wanted to see the fire for herself. She had to hear its sound and feel the heat on her skin.

She watched the reporter Tony interview ACP Davis. She didn't join in the group of women mourning. She saw ACP Davis walk towards her, and then get into his car.

What she wanted to say but could not, was: 'Thank yuh.'

◆

The mother of Clevon McIntyre viewed the news from her mother's house in the country and wept for the son she knew was dead.

◆

Ratta's mother was on the scene. When she saw the black and white Nike slip from under the white sheet covering the dead bodies being carried out by the police, she collapsed.

◆

Dinah's mother heard the news on the TV from where she was inside the bedroom. Mama fought angry tears. She had been cheated. Death had overlooked her again.

◆

Wendell Simms silently watched the news from the comfort of his bed. His TV was on a stand at the other end of the large room. His secretary, Christine, had typed up the press release hours ago so it could be ready to be sent out as soon as the police operation was over. Christine was in bed beside him, playing with the grey hairs on his chest.

Simms got up and turned the giant black knob on the television set, shutting it off.

◆

The Ghetto News Network, GNN, had their own edition, repeated under street lights and across zinc fences and between gaps in walls. Their headlines said: 'When mighty tree fall down, mongrel dog jump over it. The Boss Man Dead. Clevon Dead. Dead like chicken without head. Blood going run.'

ACP Davis

The next day, ACP Linford Davis picked up the handset of the giant black rotary phone on his desk. It looked like an overgrown beetle next to the framed photo of his wife and their teenaged daughter. He had paperwork to complete and his IN tray was piled high with folders and papers needing his review, approval and signature. But he had to make this phone call. He had been putting it off all morning. There was a pile of messages on his desk to say he'd missed several calls from the MP.

The first thing Wendell Simms said when he heard Davis' voice on the line was: 'So you had to kill him? Davis, we talked about his arrest. Charging him with conspiracy to commit murder and attempted murder for that shooting of the white man. What happened to extraditing him to the US on the drug charges? Eh? You understand we need the Americans on our side at the next election? I never said kill him. Jesus! It's a good thing the press statement my office prepared was general enough.'

Davis inhaled deeply and slowly and looked out the window at the people walking by. From this height, they resembled ants. As a child, he used to lie in the garden of his grandparents' house and watch the trail of ants carry pieces of leaves, twigs and food. According to the *World Book Encyclopedia* that Davis' father, a high school headmaster, had bought him from a door-to-door salesman, an ant could lift fifty times its weight. The elder Davis had hoped to fuel his son's fascination with nature and learning. Davis thought now that he should have pursued his childhood dream of becoming a natural scientist. Human nature was too vicious.

'Davis, you there?'

'He was going talk,' Davis said. 'I had to.'

'Had to? So you *had to* burn down the place too?'

Davis pictured Simms opening and closing his giant mouth slowly. Like a reptile sunning itself on a rock.

No, killing British hadn't been part of the plan. But Davis could even now picture British's face and see him taunting him. *You think you can survive in American prison? A pretty boy like you will melt like icing 'pon cake . . . I always had a feeling about you, Davis. That you like them things.'*

He'd killed him because a man like that could look in you, through you, and pull out a part of you that you might not even admit to yourself.

'We have one of the shooters in custody,' he offered weakly. 'He was probably part of British's drug ring too. We can tell the Americans that.' Even as he said it, he knew that wouldn't be good enough.

They both knew what British's death meant. The order he had maintained in Lazarus Gardens had been torpedoed. A new leader would arise from the ghetto. The remnants of British's men and those loyal to British's old rivals would kill off each other in a gun battle until the victor asserted power. This was going to be a bloody year.

'You going to have to tell the Prime Minister yourself how this happened.'

'I know.'

'And Davis, after we meet with him and the Commissioner on Monday, let's talk about you taking early retirement.'

◆

After he hung up the phone, Linford Davis thought about a boy. One with a desperate mother who'd once asked Linford to speak to her son, when he was a young police officer just recently assigned to a high school on the outskirts of Lazarus Gardens. Linford was the community policing liaison officer. Newly arrived from the country; a newly minted cop fresh out of his teens himself. In a new policing initiative that had been blessed by a young, progressive and freshly elected Member of Parliament, Wendell Simms, the Senior Superintendent had urged Linford to engage with whom the programme referred to as the 'troubled youths' of the surrounding communities.

Linford had felt the programme had promise and it was a shame it had been discontinued once the opposing party came to power – part of a systematic dismantling and erasing of the legacy of the previous administration inherent in Jamaican politics.

For the most part, the talks had scared some young boys into leading lives as law-abiding citizens. The men Linford saw years later were working honest jobs: as shopkeepers, bartenders, postmen, factory workers, taxi drivers, electricians, plumbers or mechanics. They all thanked him for intervening in their lives. Except one.

Linford remembers his words to the distressed mother of that young man as he was about to leave the house: 'Mother, I never meet nobody like this boy yet.'

And Desmond had looked up at Linford with a stony face, one of hate, anger and fire. It was the same face Linford saw again last night. It was as if there was a veil of calm spread across its surface, but you could still see the venom seething underneath.

Linford had seen the same face when he had delivered the news to that boy, weeks after their first meeting, that his mother had been killed instantly after being run over by a bus. They'd stood at the little verandah of the dusty yard, after the boy had let him through the rusty gate, broom in hand. The boy looked at his shoes. His face was expressionless, except for his eyes. Linford had expected any emotion: shock, disbelief, grief – any response but the blankness of his features. In the boy's eyes something hateful was smouldering.

The Senior Superintendent had told Linford to cover up the fact that the bus was owned by a private company that had as its single shareholder Mr Wendell Simms.

'Unfortunate accident,' is what his boss had called it.

But an ambitious prosecutor with the office of the Director of Public Prosecutions had brought a criminal charge of vehicular manslaughter against the driver and owner. Simms brought in criminal defence attorneys, Beason Beck and Christopher Brown, and the charges got dropped.

Davis saw now how his life had come full circle. When he closed his eyes, he couldn't escape British's face.

Those eyes.

Wendell Simms

There was a fly on the wall in Wendell Simms' office. It flew to the ceiling then circled and descended like a helicopter, landing on the forest-like debris of paper clips.

Simms was speaking into his speakerphone, using his thumb and index finger to repeatedly pinch the top of his nose, right between the eyes. His head drummed, echoing the whine of the fax machine.

Pinch–release–pinch.

'Davis killed him,' Simms said. His head throbbed.

'I realise that,' the Prime Minister replied. 'All of Jamaica heard it on the news last night.'

'It wasn't the plan.'

'You got that goddamn right. I need to know how this happened, Simms!'

'Mr Prime Minster, I don't know. I wasn't there.'

'You said you were going to control this.'

That's when Simms realised this headache wasn't about the fax machine at all but had started from when he'd heard British was dead. He looked across his desk at his Rubik's cube. He hadn't solved it yet. He also had a 1200-piece jigsaw puzzle of a NASA spacecraft on a small table in one corner of his office. Simms was a lover of jigsaw puzzles. Spent hours putting together something that he knew he would pull apart again. He wasn't one of those people who glued the pieces of the assembled puzzle together and framed it. If you broke it apart, you could make it whole again, as many times as you wanted.

Simms realised he had zoned out the Prime Minister.

'What are we going to do about the DEA?' the PM thundered in his ear.

'Davis had to. British was going to talk.'

The fly settled on a crumb on a saucer, the remnant of the blueberry muffin Simms had eaten with his Earl Grey tea. The fly drank the spilled tea with its proboscis. Through the half-closed window blinds, Simms saw tiny dust mites floating on the beams of light. The fly dive-bombed the remnants in the teacup.

Regina & Damian

When the lockup was built a century ago, the colonial powers hadn't cared about the comfort of men accused of crimes. Post-independence, the politicians used government funds for other purposes, focusing on building roads and schools – doling out building contracts that could be leveraged for kickbacks or employment that secured voter support in the next election. So the lockup intended to house forty-five detainees now held over a hundred. Men awaiting a court date to plead guilty or innocent; to make a case for bail or awaiting trial after bail had been denied.

The clogged criminal court system meant that men sometimes languished in the lockup for years. One man, a labourer named Willie, who prosecutors determined was of unsound mind, had been jailed for stealing his neighbour's mangoes and assault (stoning the tree had resulted in one hitting the owner standing nearby). Due to missing paperwork from Bellevue, the mental asylum, and his inability to afford a defence lawyer (the one assigned by the legal clinic lost his file), Willie had been awaiting trial for ten years.

The lockup rats were, as the prisoners said, 'big like puss'. The rats often bit the men, fighting for scraps of bread. Then the injured men had to be taken to the hospital for treatment for leptospirosis. The squalor and human filth of the lockup often forced false confessions so the accused could be taken away to jail to serve their terms in less discomfort. Prison had fewer rats.

Today, Regina had brought Damian ackee and saltfish, his favourite. The place smelt like rot and urine. She saw roaches, flying ones, as broad as her face, that made her shriek. Flies were everywhere. If anything, it was worse than her last visit and she felt like turning around and running away. She was shocked to see his face – bloodied, bruised and swollen.

'Yuh alright in here?' Regina asked.

Damian shrugged. He looked as casual as if he was in his living room. He was putting up a front for her.

She told him Apollo was leaving. Dinah had told her so, but she didn't have to. Regina knew enough about men to know when their affections had dried up. Her plan had long failed.

She told Damian British was dead and he said nothing, He'd already heard. They both knew someone else would take his place.

'Yuh hear no news 'bout String?' Damian asked.

She shook her head. 'Yuh know Apollo was trying to get yuh outta here?'

'Fi real? What happen?'

Regina told him what Dinah had explained about the failed plan and MP Simms. They were quiet for a while. Damian couldn't believe Apollo would do all that for him. After what he had put Apollo's family through.

'Regina, yuh really care 'bout what happen to me in here?' He took in her loose green dress floating over her growing curves.

'Of course! Yuh is mi friend.'

'Just yuh friend?' He looked disappointed.

'Mi did think yuh was mi good friend, yes, but yuh pimp me out with Apollo,' she replied, her voice hard. 'Apollo wasn't the first time yuh did that to me either. Wah kinda eediat thing dat?'

'Stop act like yuh never want to. Like yuh never want the drugs worse than yuh want anything.'

'Is true.' Her admission stunned him into silence. 'That was true, that time. I want different things now.'

'Mi sorry,' he mumbled. All he'd done was disappoint the people he cared about. He'd thought of her relationship with Apollo as transactional. A short-term deal that became more than he had imagined it would. But he was seeing it all better now: like an eye adjusting to light as it gets dimmer and darkness comes.

'Wid me and yuh, was it just sex?' She searched his startled eyes. Her eyes were hard like marbles.

'Yuh know it wasn't just that.'

'Mi pregnant.'

He drew a sharp intake of breath. His suspicions were true.

'Mi was telling miself is just weight yuh putting on. Is whose?'

'Not Apollo's.'

Apollo was a painful subject for Regina to think about. He hadn't made her heart go *boom-titty-boom* the way Damian did, but she thought they might have had something solid. He had given her hope. Then he had taken it away.

'How yuh know is not Apollo pickney?'

'I did go to the free clinic some weeks ago and when the nurse work it out, mi was pregnant before mi meet Apollo. Mi never know 'cause mi period not regular. Is yours, Damian.'

'How come yuh never convince Apollo is his?'

'Mi try but mi couldn't go through wid it. Is not the right thing to do. I tell Dinah the truth. Mi couldn't do that to the baby. Not when mi know the baby real fada. And mi couldn't do that to yuh.'

The tenderness in his eyes surprised her.

'I going have a yute and lock up in yah so.'

He wanted the core of the earth to open up and swallow him.

She went closer to him so he could touch her belly through the bars, wringing her hands to keep at bay a growing sense of dread. She didn't recoil from the sourness of him, his staleness and the stink around him in the room. Something was settling between them.

'Mr Mack throw mi out.'

'Mi just take a deal to avoid trial for attempted murder. Dem say mi going get thirty years. How we going manage?'

'Dinah say she and Apollo will help. Me and Dinah going to see MP Simms next week about a job. Or mi could move to Montego Bay. Mi cousin Cynthia work as a dancer down there. Mi could get a job in a hotel after the baby born.'

'Regina, how yuh manage to make this happen—' Her sharp look cut off the rest of his sentence.

'Yuh wasn't thinking 'bout that when we was screwing.'

'Alright. Alright. It going be alright.' He could see by her misting eyes that she was in a prison of her own. He'd said the words with an assurance he didn't feel. She needed his strength. She was a thing of beauty that didn't belong in this ugly place.

He held her hands as she cried. Her tears were for both of them.

◆

There was something else she dare not tell him. Something else the nurse had said. When the test results came back she said Regina had something she thought was only reserved for battymen and sadamites. Some new-fangled disease from farin. A sickness called AIDS.

Damian

When mi really ease back and check it out, mi wonder what mi do to end up here, watching this roach climbing up a wall. It going through the top of the wall and through bars that mi can't go through, yuh see mi?

Right here now, the more mi think 'bout it, the more mi thinking this road start from when Kathleen leave me that night wid the smell of orange under har nails, on har fingertips. 'Cause a pickney need a parent, worse when him don't have a father. And Kathleen shoulda know that. She was the adult. She call herself my mother.

And she left me, just like that. Like yuh drop a orange peel on the ground.

So now mi in this jail, locked up and, hear what, mi don't see no way out of it. The other day, mi sit down and try go over some lyrics in mi head and is like it so far away, like is not me write it. Like the lines dem mocking me. Mi say I going try write dem down, but the lyrics don't look like dem have no life. Dem just flat pon the paper.

And things get worse after Regina come and say mi going have a yute born out there widout mi and is like mi study it and say to myself, *Rahtid! Is the same thing mi fada do mi*. Leave me to be raised by mi mother. But this worse, 'cause is not like one day my boy going come home from school in him khaki pants, school bag on him back, and push the gate to find me sitting on a stool chatting wid him mother and drinking lemonade. No. When mi done my time in prison, my son going be a big man, wid pickney of him own and when dem ask him 'bout dem grandfather, what mi boy going say? That dem granddaddy was like a tiger in a cage, like one of dem animals in a zoo, yuh see it?

Jeezam! Is what this mi bring down on miself? Yuh really telling mi say is so it going go?

Same way so.

When I close mi eyes, mi can see the dress Regina have on the day she tell me the news and the smell of har, the smell of baby powder and olive oil, coming back to mi. But in mi brain, it different, is like the dress not loose but paint on har skin and har tummy look like a football, and I thinking that is just the other day mi was a barefoot boy kicking football down the lane in Lazarus Gardens, kicking up dust wid the other barefoot boy dem and it feel like a lifetime away from this moment now in this hot, stinking cell that smell like piss and fart.

Mi never say what mi want to say to Regina. All mi say to har was: 'Sorry baby, that mi treat yuh like mi was yuh pimp.' Mi wanted to say mi was going be that man to take har from Lazarus Gardens to somewhere better. That she didn't need no drug in har veins when she could have a dream that in har heart bursting out. That she is a better woman than she think.

I was thinking to ask Regina to check Apollo for help wid the baby but mi pride wouldn't even make me form the words. Dem dead under mi tongue, bury between mi teeth. After all, Regina was supposed to be *his* girl but is *me* give har a baby.

And after what mi do to Apollo family, why him woulda

want help me? I sorry how him father nearly dead. Really sorry 'cause just like that him never woulda have no father. The last time mi see Apollo him had a gun in mi face and when mi hear the click, mi never flinch 'cause that time mi was thinking maybe it woulda be easier to just dead and done. Either that or run weh. But running is no life at all and somebody have to stand up for what happen to Apollo daddy. Streggo dead and String gone but mi don't know if British did reach him too. Only Ratta did leave and mi hear that police kill him at British house before dem murder British too.

Mi remember Apollo eyes when mi tell him killing a man is no joke. Dem big and round and frighten like a pickney and him mouth was open and closing slow and him jaw trembling and him whole body trembling from the weight of the gun and what him nearly do.

But what mi say is lie though. Killing a man is no joke but it easy. Easy like the light-light sound when yuh open yuh mouth and laugh at something funny. It just take a squeeze of one of yuh finger.

After mi done think on it and think on it, the night after Regina visit me mi beg the guard fi a piece of paper and a pencil and start write down a new song:

> Yuh may think yuh in the majority
> But yuh have to find yuh own key
> Live yuh life the way that's right and good
> No regrets to wonder what yuh could do
> Life is like a big fat orange peel
> It not always sweet, it sour bad
> Yuh have to stick to what yuh know is real
> And give Jah thanks for what yuh had.

Cindy Brown

Mrs Brown cut up the garlic and a bit of scotch bonnet pepper and scallion on the wooden cutting board. Next, she diced the onions and sliced the imported Portobello mushrooms, wincing when the knife nicked her left thumb. She plastered on a Band-Aid. From the kitchen, she could hear her husband talking to Celeste and Ray. She poured extra virgin olive oil into the pan for the beef stew. It was one of the few things she knew how to make.

They'd found a replacement for Dinah, but the new helper had been a disappointment. She'd left Mrs Brown no choice but to fire her when she came home early one afternoon to find Valerie – a bug-eyed, skinny girl from Trelawny – standing inside Mrs Brown's walk-in closet admiring herself in Mrs Brown's slinky new red dress. 'Ah just trying it on,' was all the girl said when she was caught. There was no apology and her tone was almost defensive.

When the girl hauled off the dress, Mrs Brown saw she was wearing her bra and panties too – a chocolate-brown set. Lingerie that Mrs Brown hadn't been able to find for the past several weeks. She thought maybe she had left it at the home of her tennis instructor.

That was the last straw. Valerie couldn't cook (she salted the chicken to the point it became inedible), burnt the rice, was horrible at washing (had bleached Mr Brown's favourite blue shirt). But the final straw was the red dress. Mrs Brown had brought the red dress for herself for her twenty-fifth birthday. And the girl had been eyeing up Christopher too! She had noticed Valerie would wear her tightest and shortest shorts for dusting or cleaning when her husband was nearby and had been surprised at the rush of unfamiliar jealousy. And she felt something in her heart swelling when she realised Mr Brown barely noticed Valerie. When she'd told him she had decided to fire the girl, he glanced up from his newspaper and said: 'Do whatever you want. You run things in this house.'

When Mrs Brown closed the gate after the sniffling girl and watched her, suitcase in hand, walking up the road to the bus stop, she decided then she would make Mr Brown's favourite dish – well, the only dish he liked that she could make.

Mrs Brown certainly missed Dinah's efficiency. Her cleanliness. And obviously Dinah had never had any interest or chance with Christopher.

'You're looking good, Ray,' Christopher was saying now. She could hear the thumping sounds of her husband hitting Ray's back in excitement. Ray's reply of 'Take it easy, Chris,' came out like a groan. She looked out from the kitchen and saw Ray put his cane beside him as he slowly eased himself into the seat.

Mrs Brown sautéed the strips of beef, enjoying the sound of them sizzling in the pan. She added water and beef stock and turned the fire low before stirring in thyme, oregano and parsley. The spices transported her back to her grandmother's kitchen, when she was a girl and it was time for Saturday beef soup. She hadn't been tall enough to see above the counter, so Granny would pick her up and put her to sit on a nearby table while she cooked.

Entering the living room, Mrs Brown stooped next to Celeste on the couch, gently touching her shoulder. 'Can I get you another drink, Celeste?' She took the empty glass from Celeste's fingers. It was still cold, three cubes of ice melting at the bottom.

'No, that's alright,' Celeste said. Her eyes were rimmed by dark circles. She looked like she hadn't slept well in a while.

Mrs Brown took the glass to the kitchen and put it in the sink. She hated washing dishes. She'd get to it tomorrow, unless Christopher got fed up of seeing the dishes in the sink and did it himself. He had promised to buy her a new dish-washing machine.

She added in browning and some soy sauce and Worcestershire sauce, hearing snippets of conversation wafting into the kitchen.

'So we're leaving in a couple weeks,' Celeste was saying.

Her husband added: 'I wish we hadn't come to this country. Sorry, Christopher. No offence.'

'None taken, Ray. I understand.'

'And the worst part is, we can't get through to Apollo. You know he asked me the other day to help the man who nearly killed me? He thought that I'd use my contacts to make a deal with some politician named Simms.'

Mr Brown took a sip of his drink. 'You're not serious. I wonder where he got that dumb idea from?'

'I don't know, Chris, it's like we don't recognise our son any more—'

'And it started with that Dinah woman,' Celeste interjected.

'Can you believe she showed up at the hospital when I was in there?' Ray asked.

Mrs Brown turned the heat up to dry out some of the water in the gravy and returned to the living room carrying her own drink, a rum and Coke.

Celeste asked: 'Christopher, could she become dangerous?'

'No, of course not,' Mrs Brown piped up.

Celeste said: 'Who knows what she'll do next? I don't like the influence she's having on Apollo either. Christopher, can you talk to that police friend of yours, that Davis guy, get him to do something? '

'Yeah, sure I can—' Mr Brown said.

'Do you really think that's necessary?' Mrs Brown said. 'I admit Dinah is a little—'

'Crazy,' Raymond said. 'Bonkers. Certifiably insane.'

'But if you lock her up, what'll happen to that mother she has to take care of?' Mrs Brown asked.

'Based on what Dinah told you, she's mad too!' Mr Brown gave a dry laugh.

'Look—' Mrs Brown began. She felt the blood rushing to her neck.

'No, *you* look, Cindy,' Celeste said, her eyes were fire, voice shaking. 'She attacked me here. In *your* house. Then she shows up at the hospital. She could have done something to Ray. I mean, what's next? We're leaving soon, but suppose she comes to our house? I don't know how desperate she'll be to keep Apollo here. I have no idea what she's capable of. She refuses to leave our son alone. I'm not trying to get her locked up or turn her mother out into the street, I'm not heartless, but she needs a talking to.'

'Listen,' Mrs Brown tried to keep her voice level and soft. 'Dinah worked for us for years. She's not a bad person, and doesn't mean any harm. I think she should be left alone.'

Mr Brown stood beside her, held her shoulder and gently caressed it. She felt the warmth of her husband's body next to hers.

'Ordinarily, I'd side with you, Cindy,' he said into her right ear, his breath heavy with rum. Turning to Celeste and

Raymond, he continued: 'But since it would make Celeste feel better ... If Dinah comes to you guys again, give me a call. I'll give Davis a heads up.'

Ray and Celeste nodded.

Mrs Brown felt something inside her drop. She wasn't sure what she had been hoping for. It was as if he had missed an opportunity to stand with her, to back her, for once, and be the husband she wanted him to be.

But maybe she was overthinking it. She wasn't sure why she was so bothered by Dinah's plight. She and Dinah weren't friends. People were never friends with their helpers. As strange as it was, the intimacy of being a helper meant you knew the household secrets, you cleaned people's clothes, underwear, toilets, bathrooms, beds and floors that were full of their blood, sweat, urine, spit and other bodily fluids, hair, skin cells. You wiped mirrors full of their fingerprints, you cooked the food that fed them, comforted their whiny, crying children, you listened to phone conversations, overheard family meetings and knew all their secret shames and public scandals. Yet you, the one with this intimate knowledge, were never treated like an equal. Many times, the pets got better treatment and food to eat. And it was like you were not even there.

Dinah reminded Mrs Brown of an older, sadder version of her childhood helper, Hortense, who at ten months had taught Mrs Brown her first word. Not 'Mama' or 'Papa', but Hortense's name.

Dinah had served them well, despite how things happened in the end, and it felt like they were being disloyal to her.

The food was done cooking.

She looked at them all and spoke what was on her mind. 'Celeste, I'm sorry to say this but it sounds like you're more jealous of Dinah than truly afraid of her. Excuse me please

405

but I've suddenly lost my appetite. Feel free to serve your own dinner.'

Mrs Brown left the room as the smell reached the living room – a wave of herbs and beef burning.

Celeste

Dinner at the Browns was awkward after what Cindy said. As Ray and I silently drove back home that night I had to admit it. She was right.

I'm jealous of Dinah. How easily Apollo clings to her. The fact that she's eased his troubles where I couldn't. She gives Apollo a sureness Ray and I haven't been able to give him.

And I thought I'd feel different, now that Jamaica is nearly behind us. Apollo starts college in a couple weeks and I never have to see Dinah again. I should be free of her. I should be relieved.

But I feel like we're taking her with us.

Apollo and Ray are talking again, thank God, though I know Ray's refusal to help Damian has wounded him. I see the hurt in Apollo's eyes. It's just one more time we've let him down, despite everything we tried to give him.

This afternoon, I was standing in the living room, trying to figure out where I'd left my sunglasses. I'd just burrowed through the sofa cushions. All I did was find some coins that must have fallen from somebody's pockets.

'Apollo,' I yelled, 'have you seen my sunglasses?' He was on the front porch and barely looked up from his book when he answered sarcastically: 'Yes Moms, I'm wearing them right now.'

I told him not to sass me, but I'm smiling because Apollo has been less brooding, less silent these days.

Ray, wearing his blue bathrobe and grey pyjamas, hobbled out on his wooden cane. By the time he got to the porch, I heard the scraping sound of his foot trying to regain balance on the tiles. The straw mat shifted under his slippers and Raymond's legs buckled.

Before I could get to him, Apollo was there. Apollo's right shoulder was under Ray's left arm, hoisting him, taking Ray's weight. How did my boy get so strong?

As he held and guided Ray, I realised they're the same height. How did I miss that?

Apollo lowered Ray on to the chair. 'I got you, Pops. I always got you.'

And I knew then, my boy was grown.

Dinah & Apollo

The last time Apollo went to see Dinah, they sat down in her kitchen for a long while without speaking.

'Dinah, something's been on my mind. How's Damian gonna look after a child from prison? Regina can't do it alone.'

Her face softened, as if his question pleased her.

'Now yuh asking the right question, Son-Son. Yuh learning. Yuh thinking of somebody other than yuhself. Mi will help dem using the money yuh give me the other day.'

'I'm gonna send more. I'm going to see about getting Damian a good lawyer.'

Apollo had let his body sag in the chair next to hers. He felt like he had been running a marathon. A strange exhilaration mixed with sadness filtered through him. The feeling seemed to stir the curtains, like puffs of breath.

There was nothing else to tie him to Jamaica, except Dinah. She couldn't come to America, of course. He couldn't file for her as he had no proof she was his biological mother. But what would her future here be? He resolved to send her money on a monthly basis. Those remittances should keep her buoyed up against the waves of a rough life.

'I'm gonna come back to see you. You know that right?'

His words hung in the air between them, like an intruder.

Though he may not be able to keep this promise, in the moment he said it he meant it with everything in him.

Dinah knew she would never see him again.

She was happy he would have a better life. Jamaica would hold her boy back. America was a place of wide-open spaces where opportunity sprang up from the highways and radiated from tall buildings.

Plus, there was the woman in white. She kept Dinah company. The woman lived in the house with Dinah now and Dinah knew only she could see her. The woman in white had told her what was coming: that if he returned to Jamaica, Dinah wouldn't know who her own son was.

He broke her reverie. 'I'm glad I met you.'

She didn't need to say anything. He could read the love and pain in her eyes. Whenever he thought back on this moment in the years that followed, he thought of it like an arc. He kept returning in his mind to the point when life swung away, curved to where it was at this moment, but he could never return to her; or her to him.

He handed her a beautiful red box, tied with a gold ribbon. Later she would open it and discover a white silk bathrobe. Just like what the woman in white wore.

◆

Although Dinah knew the date and time of his flight, she didn't go to the waving gallery at Norman Manley International Airport to see him off. But she did walk all the way from the tenement yard in Lazarus Gardens to the Palisadoes road that led to the airport. She passed lignum vitae trees, leaves heavy with butterfly larvae, shuffling in the breeze. Female butterflies depositing eggs so that their young would have a constant food supply when they hatched. The caterpillars would be well fed as they cocooned, transformed.

Dinah stopped near the airport, sat on a large stone jutting out near the sea and watched the American Airlines plane fly away.

Eventually, all children have to fly, she thought.

A passerby saw a woman in a white bathrobe, feeding the seagulls.

Dinah remembered the last thing she had said to him before he left. Apollo had asked: 'How are you gonna manage when I'm gone?'

'Son-Son, yuh know one time mi read in one of Mrs Steele books that glass start out as sand? Look how something so hard, tough and brown turn into something clear that can break. To change sand, yuh have to heat it up high–high to ten thousand degrees.'

He looked puzzled.

'Me is sand,' she said. 'Mi can take plenty pressure.'

A week later, she wrote him a letter, one she knew she would never post. It was a simple letter she knew by heart:

Son,
 Mi glad you come back to me. I pray you grow into
a good man. A strong man. Remember where you come
from. Remember family is everything and your mother will
always love you.

Mama

Now that dem tek mi from mi daughter and carry mi come to dis place full ah old mad people, yuh have to learn to bathe mi properly.

Yuh see when yuh bathing me, I want yuh to warm up some water on the coal fire. Inna the boiling water, put some cerasee, soursop leaves and lemon grass. Wait and watch the water turn greenish brown. Then pour it inna one big pan wid some cold water. Put three drops of coconut oil inna it and some mint and bay leaf. Dip the rag inna the water and test it on yuh skin first.

There is a tonic yuh must boil, to build mi body and purify mi blood, wid these roots: chainey root, man wis, sarsaparilla, hug-mi-tight, blood root, strong back, pine root, shamamaka, red water grass, bamboo root, pine root, coconut root, banana root and penguin root. Add white rum and nutmeg.

Mi want to be clean. To wash off all these worries and crosses.

Rub mi skin wid aloe vera. Then, mi will start to sing.

Acknowledgements

A book is the part of us that lives on after we are gone. Reflective of our humanity, it is the product of collective effort. I have many to thank.

Credit must go to:

My agents, the amazing Hellie Ogden (#HellieHasItHandled), Allison Hunter, Ma'suma Amiri and the team at Janklow & Nesbit.

Virago Press and Little, Brown Group. My brilliant editor, Rose Tomaszewska, for her patience, attention to detail and creativity which significantly improved the manuscript. The diligent desk editor Zoe Gullen. The legendary Leone Ross, who copy-edited the manuscript so beautifully.

Professor Jane Bryce, my mentor, who taught the post-graduate creative writing course at the University of the West Indies, Cave Hill Campus, where this novel had its genesis as a short story. To guest tutors on that course: Philip Nanton, Karen Lord, Ingrid Persaud, Yewande Omotoso and Stewart Brown.

To Commonwealth Writers, who shortlisted the story in the 2018 Commonwealth Short Story Prize. Special thanks to Emma D'Costa.

To the Bocas Lit Fest team, including Marina

Salandy-Brown, Nicholas McLaughlin, Marielle Forbes and former staffer Malene Joseph. To the judges of the Johnson and Amoy Achong Caribbean Writers' Prize (including Professor Funso Aiyejina) and to Dr Kongshiek Achong Low, its generous sponsor. To the writers I met at Bocas Lit Fest in Trinidad in May 2019, especially my workshop tutors.

To the National Cultural Foundation in Barbados and especially its former literary officer, Ayesha Gibson-Gill, and the judges of the National Independence Festival of the Creative Arts.

To the Arvon Foundation, including the team at Totleigh Barton, Devon, and every participant in the Introduction to Novel Writing course who made my stay in the UK in October 2019 memorable. Thank you to the tutors: Rob Doyle, Chibundu Onuzo and Mick Kitson. Special thanks to Arvon's head, the kind Andrew Kidd. To Kerry Young for insightful comments.

To Lorena Goldsmith, Daniel Goldsmith Associates Ltd and the judges of the 2020 First Novel Prize, Eve White and Chris White.

To Dr Michael Bucknor and Christine Marrett and other supporters of the Talking Trees Literary Festival in Treasure Beach, Jamaica. Thanks to the phenomenal writers I met there including Alecia McKenzie and Curdella Forbes.

My teachers: Kei Miller, Jacob Ross, Dr Erna Brodber and Wayne Brown.

Abigail Jackson of Black Girl Writers (BGW) and my BGW mentor Emma Herdman, who invested in me.

Imogen Pelham for time spent reading drafts and giving helpful suggestions.

To editors of journals who published my stories. Judges of competitions who shortlisted or longlisted me.

My teachers from St Andrew High School for Girls, especially my literature teachers, including Miss Bala and Lisa Tomlinson. (Miss Bala: I don't know where in the world you are but the day you read my short story about a Rastafarian man on a crowded bus to my entire second form class and said how good it was, you made me feel for the first time that I had found the thing I could excel at.)

To my Writers' Circle: LaFleur Cockburn, Anderson Lowe, Brian Franklin and Professor Philip Nanton.

My Barbados writing family, particularly Writers Ink, Esther Philips, Theo Williams, Zoanne Evans, Harclyde Walcott, Hazel Simmons-McDonald and Cherie Jones. Nailah Imoja and Arts Etc's Robert Sandiford and Linda M. Deane. Writers' Central group, including Donna Every.

My writer friends including the super-talented and supportive Shakirah Bourne, Richie Maitland, Alexia Tolas, Joanne C. Hillhouse, Rashaun Allen, Kumbi Chitenderu and Lizzie Calkins.

To the writers who generously gave their time to review this book.

To friends who encouraged my writing, including Jean Look Tong, Claire Inniss, Karen Philips, Tricia Smith, Lisa Foster and Esan Peters. My girls from law school: Jamila, Luciana, Kaydian, Camika, Camille, Tracey, Jeromha and Patricia. To my family and friends who endured long periods of non-communication and frequent absences as I worked on the novel, often becoming so engrossed that I missed special occasions. Thank you all for your love and forgiveness!

To everyone who supported me and kept me sane. To everyone I forgot to name.

To every hardworking helper in Jamaica, particularly those who served my family and formed the inspiration for this book, including Veronica and Rose. And especially Hortense, my helper when I was ten months old, who taught me my very first word: her name.

Finally, to my beloved mum Yvonne Christie and brother Sean Taylor, my first readers and tireless cheerleaders. My dad Winston Taylor, my grand-aunt Josephine Walton ('Aunt Rita') and my family, who always believed.

Sharma Taylor is a Jamaican writer and attorney living between Jamaica and Barbados. She holds a PhD from Victoria University of Wellington, New Zealand, obtained on a Commonwealth Scholarship and has completed various writing courses, including at Arvon and postgrad courses at the University of the West Indies. She has been shortlisted three times for the Commonwealth Short Story Prize (in 2018, 2020 and 2021) and has won the 2020 Frank Collymore Literary Endowment Prize and 2019 Johnson and Amoy Achong Caribbean Writers Prize for emerging writers. Her short story 'How You Make Jamaican Coconut Oil' won the 2020 Queen Mary Wasafiri New Writing Prize. An earlier version of this manuscript was awarded Second Prize in the 2020 First Novel Competition (organised by Daniel Goldsmith Associates Ltd, UK). *What a Mother's Love Don't Teach You* is her debut novel.